The Cause

Mandy K O'Brien

MK O'Brien Publishers
London
England
www.mandykobrien.com

Paperback edition 2021

A catalogue for this book is available from the British library.

ISBM 978-1-8384029-0-7

Printed and bound by

CLOC
10 Milmead Business Centre Mill
Mead Industrial centre,
Tottenham
London N17 9QU

Paper type is uncoated 80 GSM

For my Mum and Dad

The Cause

The Easter Rising, Ireland, 1916

The man leaned his head and shoulder against the door frame for support as he looked around the darkened room, the lines on his forehead had deepened and despair was clear on his face. The low turnout to fight was unanticipated. They had been ill-prepared to fortify the building. The desperate situation at the GPO needed to be reported.

The windows had been covered but in the dim light he saw a boy amongst the half dead men laying on the floor, others in the next room already were. The boy's head was bowed with exhaustion but he was awake and uninjured.

"Son I need ye to pass a message." The fatigued boy lifted his head and his eyes fluttered open. His struggle turned to elation seeing his hero. He jumped up, he was tall and thin. He'd be starving like the rest of the city but was eager to impress, "Yes sir Mr Connolly."

The man was revived by the boy's transformation though concerned by his Midlands accent, "Are ye able for this?" The boy exclaimed, "I'm Sir. I'm a Fianna Boy!" The man suppressed a smile. He recognised him from the proclamation. His dedication to the cause was palpable. He passed the folded paper, "to the Green, good luck."

The boy hesitated. The man sighed; his face troubled. "Do ye know the way?" The boy nodded, "Who should I give it to?" The man smiled, "Don't ye worry about that." The boy pocketed the message, not like any he'd delivered before. He put on his cap and buttoned his threadbare jacket. The men were roused, understanding the heroic action the boy was taking which he himself was unaware. Some men nodded, patted his leg as he passed and he heard a whispered "god bless ye son."

The boy felt encouraged as he left the gloom of the dark room. The rear of the GPO didn't show the same damage of the fighting as Sackville Street. He knew these back streets, walking with his uncle selling bits and pieces door to door. He was less likely to be seen crossing the Liffey.

He was young leaving home but his Uncle needed help. After the lockouts this work benefited everyone. His oldest brother had emigrated. Two others were on the docks. Only one stayed to work their bit of land.

In the eerie half-light as he passed his uncle's tenement, people were already going to work. On the bridge, the bangs and shouts had ceased or were excluded by the embrace of the river. He'd returned to a world unaffected by the fighting, he shared the disillusionment of the men and women he'd left behind who feared the British soldiers that were flooding their streets.

The boy kept to the doorways. The smell of breakfasts made his hunger return but he was excited by his task, he drew his mind back to the note he was carrying and he pondered what it could say. He was proud to be helping to take back their land from the English which would stop their starvation. His father had spoken of the famine, he had experienced lack of food at home and it was the same, if not worse, for some people in Dublin after the strikes.

He felt happy that he'd be able to return home after this rebellion. The gun shots in the distance accelerated his pace, he sang about Bold Robert Emmett *"the love of the land I was born in.... land of the free.... I lay down my life for the emerald isle."*

The boy had never taken the route from the Quay to the College of Surgeons but he Couldn't fail Mr Connolly, a revolutionary leader, as the likes of Emmett and Wolf Tone. He was also proud to share his forename with James Connolly and this was why he hadn't joined his brothers at Dublin castle, the symbol of English rule.

He was cold and he felt the rain but he was relieved when he saw the church knowing he was not far from his destination. He hoped for a piece of soda bread when he got there. He recalled Patrick Pearse's proclamation, "the ownership of Ireland.... Provisional government." They'd shouted their desire for freedom. The Irish tricolour was still raised high. A time of great change that they would never forget.

At the Royal College of Surgeons, a man with a rifle stepped forward. He was in a rebel's uniform with ICA on his collar. The boy handed him the letter; he didn't open it. "Who sent you?" The boy brimmed with pride, "I'm from the GPO. It was Mr Connelly himself." The man gave a half smile, the nearest to one in many days. "Sit ye down over there. I will get ye something to eat."

The boy waited for the soldier, who returned with the promised food and he jumped up, nodding his thanks as he took a bite of the soda bread. The boy was hopeful, "anything in reply?" The soldier shook his head. "Go on now. Mind how ye go." The boy was desperate to return and though hungry he didn't stay to eat his food. He could eat it on his journey back or at the GPO. He wanted Mr Connelly to know that he'd fulfilled his quest. Then a loud bang, a gunshot turned his excitement to fear.

The boy was running again and he kept to the doorways. He'd never heard noises or felt a buzz like it. Then he saw British soldiers and he stepped backward so not to be seen, his panting had turned from exertion to fear. The soldiers had halted a group of men and young lads who were just going about their normal business. Most Dubliners had seen marches before and must've viewed this as another training exercise.

The British soldiers were calling them rebels. They denied this, saying that they were going to work. A young lad had run away. Another was following. The boy knew they weren't involved in the fighting. He moved forward to tell the soldiers. He was pulled backwards by his jacket.

He turned surprised to see the old man behind him. Now he smelled the smoke from the pipe, lingering in front of his shrivelled face. The old man hushed him and then a shot was fired. He was drawn back to the scene when he heard the shouts and screams. The noise from the guns was terrible. The lad who'd ran also fell. In the silence, the soldiers kicked the bodies on the ground.

Seeing the boy's outrage, the old man whispered. "It'll be ye next if you carry on." The boy heeded the old man's instruction. The boy was sickened and was shaking his head in shock and disbelief, "They are murderers." The old man nodded, "That's true enough."

The hate that splashed across the boy's face would never leave him.

All changed, changed utterly: A terrible beauty is born.

William Butler Yates - Easter 1916

Part 1

1970's

England

Part 1: Chapter 1 - The Flats

Hugh was standing at his usual spot at the bar but he was not wetting his new born baby's head as he would normally do. The pleasure of his baby girl was being overshadowed by the terrible events in Derry. He and his friends were trying to make sense of it. Why had a peaceful rally ended in the death of so many of their fellow countrymen?

Without more news, they talked again about the Christmas day rally at Long Kesh prison. Hugh's friend Tom, had attended as he had been home for his holidays. He retold the events to McCann, as he hadn't heard the story before. "The ole English bastards were waiting and enjoying every minute of it." McCann asked "Were you hurt? do you know anyone that was hurt?" Tom nodded "Ahh a bit of blood that's all," touching the back of his head as he spoke, "Handy with the batons, those boyos were." The other men shook their heads. Not in shock but in vexation. They had heard it all before.

Hugh shook his head, "when I got the Democrat last Tuesday there was still nothing about these protest's." That being the newspaper that was sent to him from home every week. Tom sneered "And why would there be? Wouldn't they have to give the results of the Hurley. You need to be reading An Phoblacht for proper news!" Hugh replied "Jaysus, Clare wouldn't let me have that newspaper in the house."

Tom took a newspaper from the inside of his jacket pocket, "Have a look at mine. It's for a true Republic, not just a free state." As Hugh read, he started to feel angry. Without any more information, it wasn't worth staying around. He left the pub to go home to his flat. To his family. He knew no one wanted to celebrate today. He Couldn't believe that his daughter was born on such a terrible day in Irish history.

#

I'd slept for a long time and I was woken up by the nurse, "How are you doing there Clare?" I felt shaky and cold. The nurse had brought me my baby to hold. She explained that the baby was fine, a real fighter. I shuddered at that description as it was a word worthy of my father's beliefs.

I listened to her explain about the blood loss and how lucky I'd been to survive. "Your husband Hugh, popped in to see you but left as you were sleeping. I told him what had happened and that you were both fine." Then he would have been sent away as was normal.

I was tired and thankful; I prayed a *Hail Mary* for saving my life. The child another daughter, was now laying in my arms. She was unaffected by what had happened. I hoped that Hugh would not be disappointed that the baby was another girl. It had been a difficult birth. I decided that there would be no more children. I knew Hugh would agree. His mother though was another kettle of fish altogether. I knew that She'd expect me to continue trying until I'd a boy.

My mother-in-law had come to England to mind the children whilst I was in hospital and was to stay for the baptism. Despite my feelings about her, I was grateful for the help, having no mother of my own. The tears came as usual when I thought of my own Mammy and sadness swept over me. I let the tears flow this time. No one was watching. The curtains were drawn and I was totally alone.

My tears were silent as I didn't want my baby to wake. I changed position and a rush of physical pain added to the anguish I was feeling about having no family. I realised that I must have torn my insides badly when I was pushing the baby out. The pain was still bad now but nothing like when they had used the forceps. The actual physical pain was taking over my thoughts now.

The nurse opened the curtains and looked at me. "I'll get you some pain killers Clare." She glanced at the baby to check that she was okay. Then she moved swiftly away closing the curtains behind her. The baby was awakening now but didn't make a sound. She opened her eyes and yawned. She looked confused. I thought it was strange. Then her two fists rose towards my face. I wondered what the hell I was going to call her. I only had boy's names picked out.

It was getting nearer for me to be discharged. I still hadn't thought of a name. I couldn't register her birth until I decided. I was now reconciled to the fact that the baby would be taking her grandmothers name as her baptismal name, Bronagh.

I wanted her first name to be memorable. Though it hadn't done my mother much good. Marguerite. It had always seemed very exotic to me. It sounded like a movie star, which of course it was. The same name as the actress of her mother's favourite film.

Her father had called her Maggie. He had said often, "to stop ye from having ideas above your station." Her mother had been a dreamer. She had wished for a

14

different life and rightly so, the way her short life had ended up. Her own mother died young herself. Not before she had shared her love of literature and the stage to Mammy.

My mother got to see many plays at the Abbey theatre and of course her favourite movie; *How Molly Malone made good* at the Cinema. Yes, that's it, ...Molly! it is a shortened version of my mother's name too. No one could argue with that. This baby will do good, not like her grandmother. I will tell her what my Mammy had told me. Not the stories of war that my Father had taught me. They were away from Ireland now; the anger would not affect them anymore.

Hugh smiled when he heard the name, "I like it, but where in god's earth did you get it from?" His eyes twinkled and he started singing quietly *"In Dublin's fair city, Where the girls are so pretty, I first set my eyes on sweet Molly Malone.* I shushed him and he stopped. They were in a long open ward and the other women needed their rest.

Before I could explain he said "O so it is *Molly Maguire* then. I, she is the symbol of the suffering of Catholics in Ireland. Being that she was thrown out on the street, like she was. That's very fitting for this Irish colleen."

As he tickled the baby's face he continued. "A true republican she will be too." I signed, "will you stop that now, it's not Molly Malone or Molly Maguire. It's a shortened version of my own Mothers name." Hugh was confused "but your mother was Maggie was she not?" I pursed my lips. "Well, that's what my father called her."

Hugh seemed to take the hint that I didn't want to talk about my family. "It doesn't matter to me where you got it from but I don't know what my mother will say." He laughed in anticipation of how She'd react and I gave him a wry smile both of us knowing what to expect.

#

When I got home, I saw my mother in law's suitcase in the hallway of the flat. She was obviously ready to leave. I heard her talking to her son, Hugh's brother Michael. I knew he was taking her to his house for a "rest." She had told me in the hospital that she needed it badly because my children were such hard work.

I went to our room first and laid Molly onto our bed. She remained sleeping. I left her wrapped up tightly as it was a cold winters day and the flat was not much better. My mother-in-law was used to lower temperatures than this harsh winter that we were experiencing this year. She had said she didn't know what I was giving out about.

As I walked into the open plan kitchen, I took a deep breath to ready myself about what was to come. Hugh's Mother had her back to me. I heard her say "Would ye believe it, that name... Molly! whatever is that woman thinking? I thought Jenny and Kitty were bad. There's not an Irish name among them."

I walked past her to the sink and responded "We do live in England you know." I started to make a pot of tea as she replied "Only because you have to," in her normal disapproving manner. She continued the conversation about names. I was annoyed that she always managed to make me feel inadequate.

I steeled myself for her response as I reminded her that Molly was named after my own mother. She was aggrieved, "Even Margaret would be better." I replied facetiously, "Oh after the queen's own sister?" My mother-in-law bristled at the talk of English royalty. She sniffed and ignored my question, "Well at least she has an Irish middle name now." That would be the nearest to thanks that they would get for giving Molly a middle name, Bronagh, that meant sorrow.

Mrs O'Donnell smiled, "Now, Saoirse that's a good Irish name. Strong. Geraldine knows how to name her children." I nodded "well she does live in Ireland." I felt a surge of sympathy for my poor sister-in-law having to deal with her Mother every day. Michael agreed "Sure tis a great name. Saoirse. Freedom!" Mrs O'Donnell and Hugh nodded along with Michael. I just looked down, staring into the teapot. I didn't want to discuss this especially after what had happened in Derry.

She continued as if I'd not spoken, "Ahh now, ye should see her!" She had been addressing most of the conversation to Hugh and Michael but now she turned and looked at me with her eyes flashing. "Yes, ye should see her. How many years is it since ye were home now Clare?" I was feeling frustrated by her always questioning me, "Oh you know, it's very expensive and I don't have any family to speak of."

Mrs O'Donnell wasn't happy with that answer, "What about your own Father? What about Hugh? He would like to see his family and friends you know?" I was getting annoyed now. "Hugh's family are mainly here anyhow," pointing at Michael. "And isn't that just why you have come over here to visit."

She turned away from me and spoke to her sons again. "Well at least there is one Irish woman in England that knows how to name her children. She had the good sense to call her daughter Jacinta." I knew that she was talking about a neighbour from Hugh's homeplace, that was living here now too. I'd thought it was a Spanish name. I remembered that although it was a flower that it actually also meant sorrow. I kept tight lipped about that too. I'm sure She'd say something like, to get freedom you would have a lot of sorrow.

"And Mrs McDermott has had her seventh boy, Sean." She was excited, "'The seventh son of a seventh son.' You know what that means?" Michael nodded "And her with a priest in the family too." I saw him smiling about things that impress people in Ireland.

Thankfully Hugh finally spoke up. He was probably worried as well as I was that She'd say something about us not having any boys. "Sure, she must be a good age now to be having another child. It's a wonder it didn't kill her!" His mother's response was "Strong as a horse, so she is."

She then turned to Hugh. "She is very grateful to you getting the oldest lad digs. I'm sure she will thank you, if she ever sees ye again," she sniffed disapprovingly and shot me a look of distain over her shoulder. It didn't concern me as it was a regular occurrence.

She told Michael "We won't wait for tea. Clare seems to be struggling with it. I don't want to put upon her." On cue Molly started crying. By the time I'd settled her, my mother-in-law and brother-in-law had left. They hadn't even said goodbye. I sighed at the rudeness but was pleased that she had gone.

#

It was my first outing since having Molly. I kept my head down as I walked to the back of the shop. Not just from the cold, I'd seen the group of women from the estate. They had been making my life a misery since the day I moved in. Despite my best efforts, they did see me and the whispering started immediately. It was either about me or Ireland in general, but we were one in the same to them. I could work out some words "shot dead" with smiles.

I knew their point of view would be different to mine but there was no attempt to commiserate with the deaths in Derry. There were so many women and just me. I'd no hope of trying to explain it all to them, but I didn't even understand it myself. I hovered at the back of the shop but I only had a few bits to buy. I'd to go to the till knowing they still hadn't moved.

Some of the women were queuing. Others had already been served. They were waiting for each other. One woman was looking at me but talking to her friend. "Be careful, you never know what their sort will do. Even our embassy is not safe."

One very loud woman called, "You go first girl. You seem like your finding things hard." She was only pretending to care. She whispered to her friend "Best not get on her bad side. She might burn you in your bed." I felt like crying. It was terrible about the bomb in Dublin. I didn't know how to show this to them. I just stammered "Thanks." Anything to get out of there more quickly, though I would normally wait my turn.

I was so intimidated by the group that in my haste to pay I dropped the coins on the floor. I rushed back up to the flat. I got the children settled for their naps. I sat at the kitchen table. I put my head into my hands and cried. Then I shook myself for being so weak. I thought of what my mother had put up with. I dried my eyes. I got up to start the dinner, vowing to myself that I would not let them get to me. It wasn't my fault. I couldn't apologise for what I didn't do or agree with.

#

Later in the week we were sitting at the kitchen table listening for more news on the radio. Hugh kept shaking his head, "This Derry tribunal will be a cover up, mark my words." All I could say was "God help us" for the hundredth time, which was an unanswered seemingly pointless prayer.

Molly, who was in my arms, seemed to agree as she started to cry. I was shaking my head not knowing what to say. When I said "I just don't understand why?" Hugh was horrified. "It's simple Clare, the lads were just protesting in Derry and Dublin. It was the English Government that caused all this, yet again."

I said "We live here now so I can see both sides. I just want it to all end."

Hugh was outraged by my answer. He was very frustrated with me, "How can you be neutral for god's sake, you have to take a side. Think about why you are here." He was shaking his head, running his hands through his dark hair yet again and his already drawn face was more concerned.

I felt his pain but it wasn't the same for me. I'd a completely different reason for being here. If I agreed with Hugh, in my heart it was like I was agreeing with my father, which I could never do. There was no agreement between us so I took Molly and left the room to take her away from the troubles not just in Ireland but in our flat too.

#

Only a week later there was more news to highlight our different opinions. Hugh came out of the bathroom. He had had his 'wash and brush up', as he always said when he was going out. "Surely you are not going out tonight." He looked surprised, "I always go out on Thursday, for darts." I was worried "I know, but after the Aldershot bombing.... There could be trouble especially in the Oak Tree."

Hugh replied "I pay my taxes along with the rest of them so I should be able to go where I like." I was anxious "I'm not talking about you. They have a right to mourn there dead as much as us." Hugh was furious "There you go again taking their side. I won't stop what I'm doing to keep them happy." He whirled round and was out of the flat before I could respond.

When Hugh got to the pub, no one was playing darts. His friends, were in the corner of the bar talking about the barricades that had been put up in Derry for the march. Hugh could feel the tension in the air. He knew Clare was right, it could turn at any time.

Tom knew survivors of the march. "It's not like they say at all. No way would they have had guns, it was peaceful. Did ye read in the newspaper that there was a running battle? The only running there was the boys trying to get the hell out of there." His voice was low as it might crack. "I'd have been there meself, if I was still able to live at home." The men were nodding in agreement trying to pacify him.

Then the other men were telling their own thoughts and experiences. This though seemed to rile Tom even more. He became more justified in his beliefs saying "How dare they take away our right to march? How else are we going to be heard? They think that interment is necessary, its barbaric is what it is.

The ole bastards must have loved it. Any excuse for them soldiers, itching for it they were. They couldn't wait to use their guns. They have wanted this from the day they moved in on us. Three years it's been since they took over. I never thought I'd have to leave and they'd get to stay." He was becoming angry and the level of his voice was rising.

The English men were looking over, they had been listening and not liking what was being said, one man shouted, "Why are you here, crying into your pints? It's right that the IRA are locked up or dead. You all should be too. You're scum, burning our embassy and bombing our barracks, killing our people." Then he bellowed "GET OUT OF MY PUB!" and his brother shouted "You shouldn't even be allowed in our country." He and his brother started towards them. They were definitely looking for a fight.

Tom moved forward. He was too quick for Hugh, so he Couldn't stop him as he passed. He was shouting at the Englishmen "No I won't. If you hadn't taken our country away, we'd still be there now." The barman was walking towards the brothers. He rested his hands on their shoulders, to stop them moving any further forward. Then his shout, "OUT!" as he pointed to the door. "All of you Irish, GET OUT."

Hugh pulled at Tom who was beside him now, and he pushed him towards the pub door. Tom continued to face the brothers despite Hugh's stronger push sideways. Hugh was apologising to the barman, "A lot of hot heads at the moment. We don't want any trouble. We're going now, aren't we lads?"

Hugh had turned and was drawing his friends in front of him. He patted each of the men on their shoulders, to calm them down so there wouldn't be any fighting. He shepherded them towards the door. Hugh didn't show it until he had turned away, but he was really angry too. He was focussing on getting the lads outside.

When they had all left the pub, two of the men walked to the left shaking their heads and muttering to each other, but saluting Hugh goodbye. Tom didn't look like he was going anywhere. Inside the pub the bell was ringing for last orders. Hugh wanted to get him away quickly.

Tom was saying, "For fecks sake, why did you stop me? Did you not hear what he said? "My pub!" he mimicked "who got thrown out, us. I spend just as much in there as he does?" Hugh laughed to reduce the tension "A lot more probably. Forget about him, for God's sake. Let's be going home now. You've got work to go to in the morning. What would happen if you went in with two black eyes?" Tom was confident, "Jesus Hugh, I could have taken that long streak of piss!"

Hugh laughed, "But what about the other ten of them?" The was a pause "Go on now. I'll be seeing ye." He watched as Tom walked down the street to make sure he had left. When Hugh turned, his face was troubled and it looked like he was making a decision.

I was enjoying a rare cup of tea alone and my mind wandered back to when I'd come to London. I remembered my anxiety at being alone but even when the loneliness was at its worst, I didn't miss the Meaney's or Ireland.

Working in a pub meant it had been difficult getting to dances like everyone else. Hugh had come to the pub. He was handsome. Full of the craic. He loved to sing, even though they were mostly rebel songs. It had felt like forever until he had asked me to go to a dance. Hugh hadn't pushed me about my family history. Other men had been confused by me. By unspoken mutual agreement Hugh didn't ask about my family and I didn't complain about *The Cause*.

Lost in my memories, made me late for collecting the girls from school, so I was still flustered on my way back and forgot to go the long way around. I saw a group of women from the estate. They were standing in a huddle. I'd to steel myself for what they might say. I saw them looking at me. It seemed to be taking longer than usual today.

One of the English women sneered, "Your lot were causing trouble again?" I didn't answer. I didn't want any trouble myself. I looked down, keeping my head low, thinking about all the people that had died. I moved more quickly now but as I was passing, "You're IRA scum. You got what you deserved."

I squeaked "No." I'd to stop myself crying. I didn't want them to know how scared I was of them. I didn't want the girls to see how the women were affecting me either.

23

#

When I was preparing dinner, Jenny came to stand by my side. "Don't be upset by those women Mum. They're just not nice people. I saw it on the news. Lots of people are dying. Daddy explained that it's a war." I was angry now. Hugh knew I didn't want talk like that at home. I sighed "That's why those people were upset. They do not consider it to be a war."

Jenny continued "Daddy told me that the Irish Catholics have suffered for hundreds of years. That there are British soldiers on the streets of Ireland now." This talk reminded me of my Father. He had been full of hate and bile but I couldn't lie. History spoke for itself. "There have been some terrible times. When people remember the past, it makes what's going on now even worse. All we can do is pray that the fighting stops."

Jenny was optimistic, "Shall we light a candle at mass on Sunday then?" I nodded in agreement.

When Hugh was eating his dinner, I sat opposite him, "Why in the world would you talk to your daughter about the troubles?" He sighed at the same conversation, "Clare I did no such thing. Jenny asked me about the bomb and I explained." I was angry and frightened "And what did you tell her?" He was matter of fact, "About the English and how they plundered our lands and killed our people."

"Jesus Mary & Joseph, please don't. They are English and must not be brought up hating the country they live in." I was so shocked I couldn't believe his attitude after all we had discussed. Hugh had stopped eating and stared at me. "They are not English. Why are you so against them knowing their history?"

I tried to explain "I hate that people have suffered in Ireland. Now it's here too. It's getting worse not better." Hugh exhaled. "Clare, if the English were not in the North, there would be no fighting. If the government listened instead of ignoring the Irish then they wouldn't set bombs in England."

"But they bombed Euston for god's sake. Who do they think uses that station?" I was imploring. "Well, we don't." I took that as a criticism that we hadn't taken the children to Ireland yet. Hugh relented "Ok, I won't talk about *The Cause* and what the IRA are trying to achieve. But I will not stop telling the girls about their Irish history.

For god's sake, don't they go to a catholic church? Wont they all go to catholic schools. Who do you think their friends will be? They will be Irish no matter what you say. The girls need to see Ireland. So, we will all go home as soon as we have the money."

I knew he was right. I should not stop the children seeing where their parents were born. Just because I didn't feel that it was my 'home'. I didn't have to see my father or seek out the family who had forgotten me. But I would not let them be taught about *The Cause*. I stared at Hugh to make him understand how I felt but I was not sure he wanted too.

#

It just kept happening as expected. On my way back from school I saw the same group of women. With their dark looks and the taunting whispers. In my heart I believed them to be right. I wished and prayed that the troubles would be over. I knew that the girls were starting to be taunted too and I didn't know how to prevent it.

They were laughing now, they seemed very pleased about "Direct Rule" by England in Northern Ireland. I knew it meant more problems. I deliberately didn't tell the children about things that were out of our control. Although I didn't like it, I knew that although the girls were born in England, they would never be English and never be truly Irish either.

As I passed, there was shouting now. I heard "bold as brass." "...Own country." and "How dare she." All things that I'd heard before and would hear again. One of my neighbours passed by me and had seen what had happened. I knew she was Irish herself but I didn't know her well. The English women never bothered her. She stopped exasperated with me, "Ye need to pick a side and stick to it. It's just the way of it." I knew I couldn't. I wanted to see both sides so I said nothing as usual. The look etched on her face was of annoyance and pity as she walked away.

On reading and seeing the news we both declared that we agreed with Harold Wilson. He said that a United Ireland was the only solution or to at least let Derry back to the Republic of Ireland. We didn't agree with the government's version that the people that were protesting were waging a war, and these fighters needed to be stamped upon.

We recognised the anger of our fellow Irishmen. We were really concerned that the English were feeling more distressed, by the bloodshed here than in Ireland. Hugh voiced his anger. "The soldiers are not the victims in this. They didn't even listen when our elected members spoke to him. He won't last long that one. But who the hell will the next prime minister be and what will he do to Ireland?"

I didn't say anything though I felt that there were victims on all sides. I didn't want to voice that opinion to him or to anyone else. I'd enough of that talk in my own home when I was a young child. I didn't want to hear it again, especially around my own children. Jenny was so bright, she understood what was going on around her. I feared that when playing with the friends that she had from the estate, there could be problems. Especially if she said something that their parents wouldn't agree with.

Of course, I knew about the days of the black and tans and the women that were tarred and feathered. I also knew about the beating of young men, burning of homes and the land that was taken away. I'd been brought up on those stories. I'd developed a terror but not only of the English. I could recite a whole history but whether it would match the truth, I didn't know.

#

Other buildings were being destroyed. The people in Ireland, the Irish in England and the people I lived side by side every day were all affected. I could understand that they would resent, even hate me and my countrymen. I would though do as I has always done; listen and say nothing.

I thought about the black flags, the stones and the burning bottles. I saw the ashes of the building on Merrion Square on the TV. My mother had told me that it had once been a cinema. I felt a wave of sadness in my heart for her and the different history she had told me. About poets and plays with love and romance, from the great writers that she had seen when she was young. Words that didn't seem to be heard by the Irish people anymore.

#

We were all watching the TV. The girls would normally be in bed but it was a Friday and they were too excited to sleep. Jenny's holy communion was on Sunday. There was going to be a party for everyone at the catholic club, everyone's family and friends were invited. Even the big hall would be packed.

We would come back to the flat after. I'd been saving some of the money Hugh gave me. We were so lucky that he was getting the overtime. When for so many people there was a three-day week or were unemployed. The cost of food was so high. It was hard to save but I'd upped the potatoes and reduced the meat to pay for the holy communion dress.

It was breaking news, there were four car bombs in Ireland and people were dead and injured. The pictures were shocking, I was listening to the newsreader and forgot that Jenny and Kitty were watching this too. It was Hugh that took them by their hands and walked them to bed. I was shocked by the news. You'd never expect this would happen to Dubliners going about their daily routine. Innocent people. I'd been to Dublin with the Meaney's and seen those places which made it all so real.

I heard Hugh talking to our daughters in a low soothing voice as to not wake Molly. I didn't know what he was saying, I was transfixed by the news. When Hugh came back in to the kitchen, the newsreader said "No one had taken responsibility." Hugh sighed, "Now will you see. We all know its them. The English Government. They will be behind this, so they will. I will tell you that for nothing."

Thank god we had a holy communion to look forward too. Jenny looked lovely in her dress, the veil and new shoes. After Jenny had had the bread and the wine, there were photos outside the church. My sister-in-law had brought her camera for us to use for the occasion.

I looked around at our group, all of Hugh's family were there but none of my own. No one mentioned it but I was sad that I'd no family to speak of. People must assume that I was an only child and that my parents were dead. They would be shocked to hear that I'd six brothers and sisters and that I didn't see or even know where they were. I imagined what they might be doing.

Then I was sad again, thinking of my beautiful mother who died so young and had lived most of her life with a brute of a man. He refused to forget his roots or his anger about how his family had been treated. Her father had always said "I took her on when no else wanted her." I knew the reality. My mother's parents had died and he married her. Moved into her fine house then spent her money to buy land.

He beat her and the rest of our family when the urge took him. Otherwise, he would be indoctrinating us. I believed him to be alive and kicking. I'd not heard otherwise but then I didn't want to find out, in any case. I never wanted to see him ever again and going to Ireland would potentially do that. Someone called my name and I smiled for the photo. When I thought of my father, I felt his anger. I hoped and prayed that the troubles in Ireland would finally end and that everyone's anger would go away. I only wanted to think about the here and now.

We went into the school hall and I watched the girls showing off their lovely dresses and the boys in their suits, not short trousers for this special day. Their shoes were shining and they were proud of themselves. Then they were dancing and singing.

When we left the hall and went to the flat, I'd the food and drink ready. The children were running up and down the communal stairs with the children from Hugh's family and our friends from church. All except Molly who was still a toddler. When I checked on her, she was watching them through the railings and she was giggling along with them.

We were lucky to have such an amazing family and friends and I didn't even mind when the singing changed from country songs to rebel ones. The children were not around and I knew that the O'Donnell's were republicans through and through. The talk of the Dublin and Monaghan bombings had saddened them all. Prayers had been said at Mass. I knew Hugh was affected more than he said.

#

On the news there was another bomb, this time it was a pub, in Birmingham. It was so terrible to see the people that had died. I didn't understand the point of it all. Hugh saw my face and said "It's no different to what's happening in Ireland." My voice was low, always concerned that the girls would hear anything at all. "I know you see it as war but innocent people are being killed, just having a night out."

Hugh continued "The English army do it at home to our innocent people all the time. Its war, a war for a united Ireland! Not for some free state in another man's country. The six counties belong with us. You need to remember the terror and devastation they have caused us." I was conflicted, "I do but we live here now. This is our home." Hugh was agitated "but we don't want to be here. If they hadn't robbed our lands, we would still be there. Not evicting us from one home to the next whenever they felt like it. It killed my father." I'd no argument for that. "I know that your father was a great man. But it's different for me." Hugh shook his head; I knew he would ever understand me.

On the railway bridge the same group of women were there. The jeering had turned to real anger and they surrounded me. The girls had run to the wall, taking the buggy with them, but they watched in horror. One woman spat, "Was the Old Bailey not enough for you, you IRA bitch?" I didn't answer I didn't know what to say. Her spittle hit my face. Jenny ran and hit one of the women on their back. They were shocked so we had a chance to run.

I was crying now, just like they wanted me too. Kitty was running with the buggy. When I took hold of it, her face was full of anger, saying she hated those people. All the while, Molly was crying even though she definitely didn't understand why.

Jenny held my hand until we got home. Only when we got through the front door could I breathe more easily. As I walked into the kitchen Kitty was complaining that I'd not shouted back at the women but Molly had thankfully stopped crying. Jenny followed me into the kitchen with an envelope in her hand. "Mum, I found this by the door." I was already starting to get the tea on when she handed me the letter. I stared at it. I knew it was from the council straight away and swallowed hard. I knew the rent was up to date but I was still worried.

When I opened it, one word stood out "DEMOLISON." I was horrified and it must have shown in my face. "What's wrong?" asked Kitty. They both were either side of me now trying to read the letter. I turned around, my mind was racing and I felt sick. Where would we live? I steadied myself with my hand on the sink. I took a deep breath and read the letter from the start.

Dear Mr & Mrs Hugh O'Donnell

RE: Cudham Close

On 12th November 1974 the council decided that the above block will need to be demolished.

This Demolition will take place as soon as all the residents have moved out with our deadline as 1st January 1975.

Your Housing Officer Mr P John will be visiting you to discuss moving out of your property.

You will be offered up to three other properties that are suitable for you. You may not be able to stay on this estate and could be offered any other areas of the borough.

I'm sorry for the inconvenience this may cause you.

Yours sincerely

District Housing Manager

I was so shocked that I'd to read it again. My hand went limp. Kitty took the letter out of my hand but Jenny was already bent over reading it. She frightened the life out of me when she jumped for joy. She made a whooping noise and then shouted to Kitty "we are leaving!."

Kitty started to twirl around, singing "We're leaving those horrible people" over and over. Then we were all dancing, although there was no music. When Hugh got home, we were still celebrating. He smiled as he read the letter. He looked at me. I knew he understood, how relieved I was to be leaving the people on the estate. He lifted Molly high, "Things are looking up." Molly was looking down into her father's eyes and was laughing.

When Mr Johns came around, he offered us three properties. All were houses but on other estates. I didn't want to seem ungrateful. I knew the houses were all better than the beautiful shell of a home where I'd been brought up, the room at the Meaney's and the attic in the pub.

I dreamed of a street where people took less notice of your comings and goings. I would like somewhere nearer to the girl's school. More importantly to stop seeing the jeering women. I told the man that I was still deciding. He explained that there wasn't much time left. I prayed to god for his intervention.

I saw an ex-neighbour when we were collecting Jenny and Kitty from school. I smiled at her as she wasn't like the other English women on the estate. She had never mocked me for being Irish. She had lived in our block of flats but she had already been moved out. "Have you got somewhere yet?" I shook my head.

"There's an empty one next to me. Come on and have a look." I was surprised. We eagerly followed her down the road. She stopped in front of a house that was empty. "There you go, it's a three bed. What do you think?" It was a house on a road. I smiled "I'm going to the council right now." We all ran up the road. I felt very optimistic for the future. I was confident that we'd have no trouble on a street.

Part 1: Chapter 2 - The Street

It happened so quickly, that it felt like a dream. Mr John from the council had looked into it. He said yes it was available and yes, they could have it. I was so happy. It was a three bedroomed house. It was more than I could have ever have imagined.

It was five minutes' walk from the girl's school and not near the estate at all. I was standing in the empty bedroom looking around. I was so relieved. I was so grateful to get away from those ignorant people on the estate. I thanked god for his help. It was a new home and a new start.

I thought about my first home. It was a beautiful two storey stone house. Impressive though it was on the outside, it had been full of hate inside. I knew it was still standing but I would hate to go there ever again. I shuddered. I promised myself that would not happen inside our new home. That my children would not grow up like I'd.

Despite the move to the street, my children were growing up in a little Ireland. The people we were in contact with at their schools, mass and the club were mostly Irish Catholics. The stories that their Dad told them, made their history seem so great. Molly was desperate to see a leprechaun. Hugh had told her that if she met a wee mischief maker, he would grant her three wishes. Her wish was always the same, to go to Ireland, to go home.

I knew it was true, it would happen but there was no sense of urgency on my part. I'd nothing to add to the story-telling as I'd long forgotten the history of my family. My mother's family were all gone and I didn't want to think about what horrors were in my father's past.

Molly knew that Hugh's family derived from the Kings of Ireland. With her father's namesake being the chief that had battled but had been beaten in the Nine Years War, way back in the 16th and 17th century. Hugh told the girls that the English had won that war. He said that the O'Donnell's had fled. That they had planned to return but never did. Hugh was adamant. "We had to leave Ireland just like those O'Donnell's of old, but us O'Donnell's, we are going back."

When Molly had told her friends at the club that she hailed from kings of Tyrconnell, she was surprised to hear that the other children she met also had hailed from Kings of other parts of Ireland too. These other children of Irish descent came from all over the country with their parents. The club was well known for the dances with the travelling Irish bands. The kid's playroom was as busy as the hall where the adults danced.

There the children had discussed the wars in Ireland. They also knew that Ireland had been split into kingdoms and each Chieftain had battled to keep their part of the country.   Molly was disappointed to know The O'Neill's from Tyrone, who lived in North London, were the most powerful. She was happy that the O'Donnell's were better than the O'Reilly's of Cavan, who lived in Birmingham. As they had been taken by the English before the nine years war had started. It was all done in good spirit and it was just a game to play.

The similarities of the current situation with Ireland and England were thankfully not made. They were all proud to hail from kings. I told them not to tell everyone that they met, as some people especially the children on the street might think that they were showing off or making up stories. They never asked where my family were from so I never told them.

We still hadn't been to Ireland but I knew that it was only a matter of time. My anxiety was building inside me sending me back to being a child myself. The fear that always felt heavy on my heart of having to return. I sighed with relief when another year had passed and we had gone to the seaside for our summer holiday instead.

When the girls were fed up paddling in the cold sea, they ran back towards me. I dug into the large shopping bag that I'd packed for the day trip and took out a towel to dry their feet. They sat to put on their ankle's socks and shoes. They were chatting about the swing boat and trampolines.

I looked admiringly at their feet. They looked so smart with their white sandals and socks with lace edges. I was pleased that at least their feet were covered in brand new shoes as their dresses definitely were not new. I wished that we had more money to spend but I knew other things must come first.

The girls were being nice. I knew they wanted something. Jenny was being polite speaking in a grown-up voice. Kitty was practically on my lap saying how good she had been. Molly was smiling sweetly and talking rubbish as she was so excited. I smiled. I'd the money ready for them all to go on the trampolines. I gave Jenny the money as I trusted her with it.

I was brushing the sand off and repacked the bag. I would settle them in the Christian summer club and then meet Hugh. I wasn't sure what religion it was, definitely not catholic but they seemed very nice people. They were there every year and it didn't cost much. When I'd said goodbye to the girls, I headed off to find Hugh. He was bound to have met someone he knew. I couldn't remember a time that he hadn't.

I peered into the pub as it was dark compared to the sunshine outside, indeed he was in the first bar I found. He was sitting with another man laughing and gesturing so there was no doubt that he was telling a story.

He turned and he saw me walking in. He got up to get me a drink. He pointed across the table to man opposite "Hey Clare! You wouldn't believe who I met, look its Jonny from home. I haven't seen him for an age." Hugh was smiling at a man that I knew he played with as a child and grown up with like a brother. I smiled at the good-looking man with his long wavy blond hair so different to her husband's brylcreemed quiff.

He was Molly's godfather too. "We were just talking about the baptism now. He didn't even remember that he stood for Molly!" Both men were laughing loudly. "Good day it was though. Couple or three drinks partaken hey Jonny?" Hugh laughed remembering the had been an extended party as Jonny had been on holiday from Ireland at the time. He got up to shake hands with me and he kissed my cheek. I sat down in the empty chair next to my husband's newly vacated seat.

I smiled as Jonny was good fun. "Where have you been? What have you been working at?" Hugh returned with three drinks and set them on the table. Jonny's face paled and he stopped smiling. "Only just got back." I could see now that he had lost weight. "Were you home?" asked Hugh sitting back down obviously not having got to this story yet. Jonny looked like he didn't really want to say anything but he continued, "Not through choice."

His whole demeanour had changed. "I was picked up so I was. No reason but the sound of me voice." Hugh looked annoyed "When was this?" His friends voice had changed it was a bitter man that replied. "When do you think?" Hugh shook his head in discontent, "Birmingham." Hugh whistled quietly "Heard it happened to a few." They were now both shaking their heads.

Jonny explained "Well me gaffer didn't take kindly to it and I'd to go. Not just because of the time off. High and dry I was. I didn't want to go back home but sure what could I do. Peter had said 'lie low'."

Hugh interrupted his friend in disgust, "Peter Devlin!" Jonny continued. "I know. I don't know why I listened to him at all. What was I lying low from? It must have made people think that I was guilty!" I was confused and enquired. "Guilty of what?" He replied "the pubs of course." I couldn't believe it. "Why would they think that? He stated "Wasn't I in the area. I was Irish so it must be me so."

Hugh was nodding as if he'd heard it all before, but I was shaking my head in incredulity. "I can't believe it. That's so wrong, especially you Jonny." Hugh confirmed, "No Clare not just him. It's happened to the best of us." I was shocked, "Us?"

"Clare you know loads of lads were lifted." Hugh was bewildered that I didn't know. "No, not people we know." Both men's eyes met and raised their eyebrows. Jonny was shocked when he looked back to me. Hugh explained. "Yes, Clare, people we know." I was upset and it must have shown on my face. "Who else then?"

Hugh seemed eager to respond as I never normally wanted to discuss the troubles, like everyone else he knew.

Jonny was also interested to know, leaning forward "Yeah who else, if it weren't just me." Hugh reeled off some names. Some Jonny and I were more shocked about than others. "Not one a member but sympathisers like us all." I didn't agree and decided to leave them to their conversation. "Not all," picking up my gin and orange, emptying my glass. I needed to clear my head. I put the glass back on the table and was getting up to leave.

"Well, they have them now, so you could have come back before." "Clare....." Hugh's voice was tired. "I told you that they didn't do it either." I didn't agree, "Well that's what they say." As I turned, I saw Jonny and Hugh look at each other in dismay. I headed to the door and heard Jonny "She still won't take a side then? Even after everything that has happened?" then I heard Hugh "it's more complicated than that." "What is it then?" Jonny was keen to understand but Hugh shook his head, "I don't really know..." I hurried out and wished that I'd never asked.

Now I was hearing the news from friends of unjust arrests, sackings for no good reason and general abuse. Thankfully living on the street meant the daily abuse had stopped for me. I'd not made any new friends with the neighbours. Next door was polite but didn't invite confidences.

I also heard that it even harder to get digs, not just from Hugh but the mothers at the school, church and the club. I felt glad now that Hugh could help others into digs. I told the women to let him know if they needed help for young one's coming over. I knew that their families and friends were leaving Ireland because they had nothing to stay for. They didn't want to emigrate but had no option.

Not like me, I seemed to be the only person that was happy to be here and take on English ways. It was not the same for everyone else so I still knew that it was best not to repeat that. I could understand their anger now and I knew that it was different to my father's anger. I'd thought to believe in *The Cause* was to believe in him. I knew that as much as I was happy to be here and grateful, the people around me were not. If I wanted friendship and support, I'd no choice other than to immerse myself into the Irish community. I didn't like to take sides but I was slowly recognising that I'd to.

#

The girls were really looking forward to the party at the club. Molly was getting overexcited. I'd to shout up "Molly!" so many times that Hugh said "Clare, she might not be able to go in that state." Molly calmed down when she heard that. Hugh would have taken any opportunity to stop the kids going. They all had new rigouts so it would be a shame if they couldn't go. Molly seemed to think it was the queen's birthday, not the silver jubilee. It didn't really matter to her as she was happy to get biscuits and cakes for any reason. I thought it was nice to have a party. Hugh had seemed bemused by it "Would you believe it? In the Irish club." Shaking his head in wonder.

When we entered the hall there was loads of children that the girls knew. There was a long table down the middle of the big hall with lots of cakes and biscuits set out. Molly looked around the room. She saw the old ladies from the church pouring drinks, already telling the other children off. Taking in the scene, "Are the grownups having a party somewhere?" I nodded and smiled, not wanting to get into politics with a five-year-old child.

Kitty looked particularly happy as they often didn't have cakes at home. Molly was looking at the fig rolls smiling but she seemed disappointed that it was orange squash, not coke as She'd have preferred, as they didn't get it at home.

I thought it all looked wonderful from my position by the door to the hall. Molly had run away from her sisters to sit down with her friends. I looked around and saw decorations that were not usual; red, white and blue, not the green, white and gold that they sometimes had. Other children filled the seats. No one from their street was there but lots of children from the school.

I saw Molly's friend Jacinta sit down next to her. I smiled at her and she waved back. Even from here, her violet eyes were noticeable from where I stood. Such a beautiful child with her dark hair and porcelain like skin, she was like a flower. It was always nice to have her to stay. She was always a quiet, thoughtful and respectful girl that seemed somehow to keep her girls' calm.

I thought I would suggest it to her Mum that she might come over later to stay. I could see from all cake they were having I would have nothing else to quieten them down. I always tell them that this was the reason that we had no sweet things in the house but it wasn't the truth.

Jenny knew of course and helped lower her sisters' expectations. I sighed wishing we had the money for treats but then I smiled as Hugh always brought sweets on pay day and even if they were only spangles or something similar, the girls were always so appreciative.

The girl across from Molly, was someone that she didn't like from her class. As usual the girl was talking loudly, practically shouting so I could understand the dislike Molly felt. Her Mum was the same. I'd heard people say "She's English so what would ye expect." I heard her talking about the day and not letting anyone else speak. Though the other children's mouths were so full of food that they probably couldn't have spoken anyway. So they all just listened to what she had to say. The boy that was sitting next to her looked like he would be sick but he was watching the girl aswell.

"Do any of you even know what this is all about?" The girl looked around waiting for someone to answer, like a teacher. She obviously felt a level of superiority, "I knew it. It's the Queen silver jubilee." She looked around with a sly smile, "huh, you don't even know what that is. You are all so thick."

The girl continued "My Mother was going to take me to a proper street party. It should be on a road not inside. It should have proper decorations. This one is pathetic." The other children were looking at her with disbelief. I knew that they were having a great time and there would be music afterwards too. Someone down the table shouted, "Why didn't you go then? Instead of spoiling our party." The girl responded "I wish I'd," but she didn't explain why she hadn't gone to the other one. I left the hall to sit in the bar with the other parents.

When I looked into the hall later, the children were getting up from their seats. They had eaten everything that had been laid out in front of them and they could hear some music. The old ladies were telling some people to get up and others to get back to their seats. I could see that Molly was half way up when she heard one of the old ladies shouting.

The music was switched off and one of the old ladies announced, "We will now sing the national anthem." They all stood up and Molly looked confused as she must have expected *"Faith of our fathers."* Which was what the people sang at the end of the night when they were at the club. It wasn't our national anthem. It was actually a hymn in memory of Catholic martyrs. A reminder of the Tudors reformation attempts in Ireland.

When the music started, I could see that Molly didn't know the English national anthem. I wasn't surprised as they probably would not be taught it at school. Hugh nor I would hardly be singing it or know the words either.

Jenny was standing but not singing. Kitty was chatting and one of the women shushed her. A couple of the English children were singing the words but the rest were looking around at each other or mumbling something. Molly screwed up her face in confusion and the loud girl sang loudly "*God save our Queen*." The old women weren't happy but they weren't really singing either. There was bellowing laughter during the singing, which stopped abruptly in the silence that came after. I knew it was from the bar next door where the parents were waiting.

A song that Molly did know came on so she ran away from her chair to join in with the dancing for "*Save all your kisses for me……*" The Brotherhood of man song that won the Eurovision contest last year. This year's entry was no great shakes; England nor Irelands. Neither country had won which meant it would not have to be in England next year.

I was thankful for that as this year we had been scared that it might not be on at all, with all the strikes at the BBC. I sang along, as you couldn't not. I left them to it after they started the *hokey cokey*. I was amused to think that the children were singing a song that actually mocked the catholic church. It was amazing how much you could learn from working in a pub.

When the party was over the girls joined them in the bar, including Jacinta whose Mum was happy as usual, for her to stay the night. There was a woman that was singing the, "Oh, the *Crystal Chandeliers...*" Which was my favourite Charley Pride country song. The girls loved it too and sang along. Molly liked to hear her Dad sing the rebel songs and she sang loudly with him, *You could hear the din... ... of Johnston's motor car.*

We left soon after, as the girls were all shattered. Later, I looked in on them to make sure that they were all in bed, and to stop them from giggling, as I often had to do. I didn't have to scold them tonight, as Jacinta was fast asleep already, the poor creature, looked worn-out. Her skin was whiter than normal and was practically translucent.

Molly was laid down in silence looking at the coin that they had been given at the party, and then she put it under her pillow. There was no school the next day and Molly would be able to play out and hear about the other parties. I was sure that it was a day that She'd remember forever.

When I came downstairs Hugh was sat in the living room but the TV was off. It was late and there was probably nothing on. He looked like he was with his own thoughts anyhow. As soon as I sat down, he started to talk about the silver jubilee. He Couldn't understand why or how it had been allowed at the Irish club. I was unsure of the reasons why myself but told him that the kids had a great time, a party to remember.

"hmm, I can't believe they sang the English national anthem." I'd to admit to him that they didn't actually sing it, which made him smile. After a pause, "Clare, when are we going to Ireland?" I was taken aback; I didn't expect this question now. "Well we have a holiday all booked, at the chalet. You said you wanted to go."

I was being careful with my words, "Even you spoke about the man from the supermarket who was killed, you said that it was a difficult time at home at the moment." I thought the use of the word home would appease Hugh as I didn't like the way the conversation was going. Hugh responded "I know, I was worried about that, thinking it was a terrible thing too but I've heard more things now. You know that he was shouting his mouth off saying he knew things to the customers that he didn't." I exclaimed, "Jesus Mary and Joseph, this is all news to me. When did you hear that? Do you think he was an informer?" He didn't seem sure, "Yes, maybe, no. Someone from home told me. It is not as close to me as I thought, it's way up the country right near the border."

I was thoughtful, "The poor fella, it just sounds like he was boasting, though not enough to die for." Hugh shook his head "We all know to keep our mouths shut, that's just the way it is. If you don't, you get what's coming to you." I was shocked and annoyed, "Have you no compassion Hugh. If that's how it was, it was probably unintentional. Where's the forgiveness of "Holy catholic Ireland!"

Hugh was still shaking his head, "I keep telling you, they are casualties of war. Why won't you understand that?" I was slow and clear, "and I keep telling you, I just don't like it. If you have to be careful of what you say it's not a good location for a holiday, is it?" We stared at each other, wishing the other would understand their view. Although I'd taken a side, I didn't have to agree with it all.

#

We had been to the chalet for our summer holiday and had a lovely time. Then it was the August bank holiday weekend. Hugh had suggested that we go to Margate, and if we found somewhere, we could stay the night. Hugh had had a windfall, which probably meant a good day at the horses. It was brilliant knowing they could stay the night. I took Molly with me to look for somewhere, while Kitty and Jenny stayed on the beach.

45

Lots of places had signs up saying no vacancies. When we looked inside one that was available, I whispered to Molly, "It's no wonder, the sheets alone could kill you." I was shaking my head and I could see that Molly was scared that I would change my mind about staying the night. I thought of the cash Hugh had given me. I knew that we could get a proper hotel, not just a B&B or a guest house. With the amount of money, I'd, I knew we could try the proper hotel nearby.

I pushed my shoulders back. Looking at Molly, I pointed, directing her gaze to the big hotel looking over the sea. I was smiling with more confidence than I felt, "let's try that one." I walked into the lobby and up to the reception desk with Molly behind me looking scared. The woman who turned to me was fully made up and looked sophisticated compared to me, where I just had a touch of foundation. Her hair was held in a bun, while my short hair had been blowing in the sea wind. She looked down at me and took in my clothes. I was feeling self-conscious now. As soon as I started to speak, the woman's face changed. I realised that it was my Irish accent. The woman looked at me in poorly concealed disbelief.

The woman was shaking her head before I got to the end of my question. She spoke loudly, "there are no rooms available." Then she leaned in closely and murmured, "Do you think we let the Irish in, knowing their intentions." I was angry but in a normal voice as possible "What intentions?" The woman sneered, "If it's not just that you get drunk, it's to plant bombs. And you are stupid enough to think you could get away with it. I think you had better go. And quietly as so not to disturb or scare the guests." The woman turned away to greet the person beside me.

I was so shocked that I couldn't move. I hoped that Molly hadn't heard. It took the woman to look back at me, for me to turn and leave. How dare the woman judge me like that and how unfair it was to stop us staying there. Molly was pulling

46

on my cardigan, "So we can't stay there then?" I shook my head. I turned quickly and half ran to the door. I tried to hide my tears and stopped outside to take deep breaths. I looked left and right until I got my bearings.

I then remembered the pub that Hugh was in and we walked straight there. I was holding Molly's hand and had pulled her close to me. When I got to the pub, I forgot where Hugh was sitting and I was just looking around me. I felt like I was stuck to the spot, in front of the door.

Molly dropped my hand and smiling she ran over to her Dad. Her pig tails swishing behind her, she was so happy to see him. I still didn't move until a man nearly knocked me over coming into the pub.

Hugh was on his own, finishing a pint. Molly was telling him what happened and my fear that she had heard, was real. Hugh's face was getting redder, "I've got a mind to go and tell them about themselves." He was looking at me and continued "but I won't." He could tell that I was upset.

"There's no craic here anyhow. There's a dance at the club tonight. We'll go back now. We should be in time for the band and we can all sit in the hall." We never sat in the hall which made me smile. It pulled my mind away from the woman in the hotel and the worthlessness that she had made me feel.

Hugh rubbed his hands together, "We will have chips before we go though. Let's get the girls and tell them what we are going to do." Molly clapped her hands. When we got to Jenny and Kitty, they were sitting on the wall and swinging their ankles in an uninterested way. They were not talking and just looking at the sea.

When Hugh told them the plan, they smiled and seemed pleased. Overall, it hadn't been a successful trip but hopefully the day would end better. We missed the traffic as most people were still at the beach. So, the journey back was quicker than usual. We even had time to go home and change.

In the hall, a young man was moving through the tables and people were giving him money. I knew why they were doing a collection even before he spoke, "For *the Cause.*" The young man nodded at Hugh. I'd an idea that he had already given him some money. I was glad Molly didn't see us giving anything. I saw Molly trying to look inside the pint glass that held the money. It was dark in the hall and her forehead was nearly touching it. I moved her head away but from the wide O she made with her mouth, she must have caught sight of all the notes inside as it was passed to my friends' husband.

Molly's eyes were round. When she spoke, I thought She'd ask about *The Cause.* "The collection plate at church is never that full." I knew that was true. As I normally gave ten pence from us and kids two pence each. Most people didn't give notes at all. I lied, "There's more people here tonight." She didn't look convinced but thankfully she didn't ask any more questions. As I didn't want to think about what they did with that money. The band started up again. We all got up dancing even Hugh. We were all having so much fun that I forgot about the collection and so did Molly.

Later when the band were packing up and the visitors had gone, the regulars sat in the bar. With the doors shut and no windows it was the perfect place to have a lock in. The singing started immediately. Everyone sang with great passion, even the kids.

The night had turned out so much better than the day. We would never have had as much fun in Margate. The sad songs were being sung even though we were all so happy. Jacinta was sitting with Molly and she was going to stay the night again.

It was the girls who asked for *Nobody's child*. I'd felt a bit like Nobody's child in the Meaney's so I didn't like that song as much as they did. They were all crying as soon as it started, I tried to squeeze my ears closed when Hugh sang having mother or father wanting them.

I was even glad when they started to sing the rebel songs. I knew all the words to them but I never sang them myself. They used to make me think of my father but now with friends and family singing them, it seemed more about hope, love for their home and family. Not the hate and anger as in my own childhood home.

Jenny was smiling and was singing along. She obviously didn't take to heart what the women had shouted at her, when she had been praying with the legion of Mary outside the church last week. I told her that she wasn't to go back after hearing what had happened, "Go home you IRA scum." Jenny had been very mature about it, "They don't understand, just because you are Irish doesn't make you a terrorist."

She had sighed, "It was the same with those women on the estate. I know what they said was not true, so that's all that matters. I've watched the news, it's not just about religion but people's rights. They aren't rioting because they want to. Protests just turns to violence because no one is listening. As Dad says it is war. I'm learning about old wars at school, and it is all about people fighting for freedom. Some people want freedom and some people want things to stay the same. Knowing the truth doesn't make you a sympathiser but a nationalist."

Hugh must have discussed these events with her. Jenny was a secondary school, asking her own questions and would be making her own decisions now. I was just glad that she hadn't been taught the way I was by my father. What he said that he had seen and done, had given him a perverse pleasure in his teachings to his family. Which was definitely supported by his friends.

One of the young ones over from Ireland, who was staying with his Aunt until he got work and digs, said "Have you heard the Boney M one? Belfast?" and he sang "...*cause the children are leaving*... I knew it wasn't the sort of song they sang in the club as I'd heard it on the radio. It seemed then a good time to end the night.

The club manager had been wiping down a nearby table and said "let's be having ya then. Have you no homes to go to?" He looked tired so I stood up and called "Girls, come on now." I could see the clock above them and it was nearly 2am. Everyone followed suit and the goodbyes started, good god didn't they take forever, they'd probably see each other tomorrow, especially the men.

I thought of that Boney M song when the news came on about the restaurant bombing in Belfast. It had nothing to do with that really, but I couldn't get the words out of my head, "...*cause the people are leavin*...." I questioned whether the country was really changing and if they were talking about immigration or death.

#

Hugh was determined to reinforce his opinion, "I want it known again, that the ruling in the European court was wrong. Internment was torture not just mistreatment. If they had got it right then this bombing would never have happened." He was sitting reading the newspaper before he went to the club. It was Saturday night but we weren't going with him. I was glad as I knew the talk would be about the bombing. It was so awful. I would not have been able to agree on the benefits of retaliation. I did know that in some cases, internment had been torture but this sort of revenge attack made the mistreatment of protesters likely to happen again.

There was a silence until Molly came running in to the living room singing the Happy Days theme tune, asking if it was on tonight. Hugh patted her on the head as he passed her. I lifted the newspaper from his chair so that Molly wouldn't see it, if she was trying to look at what was on the TV. She was dancing and singing *Happy.. and Free... ..Those Happy Days....* and I wondered when that would be true for Ireland.

All the talk was about the blanket protests in the prisons of Ireland. It was on the news too. It was shocking to hear and gladly I didn't see the photos but I did read the descriptions. So many men and women going on to the "dirty protests," as the "Blanket protests" hadn't worked.

Still though no one seemed to be listening, even the Catholic Primate of Ireland was being ignored. He had been inside the prisons and seen for himself the excrement they were spreading on the walls, until they were recognised as political prisoners. I was worried about the talk of hunger strikes being the next steps for the prisoners. Hugh kept muttering about human rights and shaking his head.

The kids were too enthralled by Grange Hill, which was on before the news and they weren't bothered about much else. The girls would be doing the dishes now when the news was on. They didn't have to hear about it every day. This was alongside Hugh's commentary which so often differed from the newsreader.

Hugh's mother came over for the summer and stayed with us for a week. She was staying with her other sons and daughters aswell so was here for the whole summer. This was good news to me as there was no talk of going to Ireland this year.

Mrs O'Donnell was impressed with the house and sniffed when she said "Thank god Hugh got you out of those flats." She seemed to want to get a rise out of me, but in a way it was true. Hugh did work hard and we were always able to pay the rent on time. I smiled sweetly trying not to respond. It was just such good luck that the flat had to be demolished and we ended up here.

Mrs O'Donnell continued "Could you believe it? There is not one Irish family in the whole road." Shaking her head. "You know Clare, it was the same for us in the North. Full of protestants ready to throw you out on the street. Hugh's father had to travel for any sort of work, as there was surely none in the free state. Not having any land to farm ourselves, and that's how we were treated."

It definitely was not the same for us now in England, compared to the situation in the north and I'd to speak then. "God no, we have no trouble here like that. Not at all, and of course we pay the council so no private landlord can throw us out. It would tear the heart of you just to think about it." My mother in law's face softened, she was truly distressed and vulnerable for the first time, I'd ever seen, "It did tear my heart out certainly....." I felt for her but only for a moment as she quickly returned to her bitter self. I'm pleased to hear that poor Hugh doesn't have to go through all that again."

There was one good thing about his mother staying, as there was no talk of the Blanket protests. I would have thought She'd be all for it, considering her history. As it wasn't constantly discussed, it was good for the rest of us. It wasn't so much on the news now or in the papers. If Hugh was getting any information on it, he didn't tell me.

The woman was a terror in winding up Molly. She had decided that this was the only grandchild she liked from my family. She told her stories of Ireland, her cousins and friends she could play with at home. It was a great way to persuade me to go to Ireland through her grandchild.

By the time Mrs O'Donnell had left the country, there was no doubt in her mind, that our next holiday would be in her house. So, it was all agreed and we were going and that was that. I was shocked that I'd gotten away with it for so long. Hugh's patience had finally run out and so with the support of his mother, Molly was finally going 'home' to Ireland.

Part 1: Chapter 3 - The Funeral (1979)

There was a knock on the front door, it was five to nine in the evening. Hugh looked up from his newspaper with a quizzical look. "Clare, are you expecting anyone?" I'd my dressing gown on and was ironing, so I looked at myself up and down in answer. "Fair enough!" He said getting up from the armchair nearest to the living room door. The girls were on the sofa, not at all interested in who was at the door.

Hugh opened the living room door and father Tom followed in behind. He was without his normal smile. His black hair looked windswept. Hugh turned off the TV and then I heard the wind howl, as I asked the girls to make some tea. "All of you now." They trooped out of the room. Jenny unperturbed, Kitty annoyed and Molly inquisitive. I was intrigued aswell. Father Tom did pop in the odd time, but usually after his dinner when he was having his "Constitutional", as he called the walk around his parish.

"How are you Father? Would you like something stronger?" Hugh's face was worried. He had missed Mass with the all overtime he had been doing. Not that Father Tom was like that. A wonderful man, compared to some other priests, I remembered and I shivered.

As Father Tom made himself comfortable, he still hadn't spoken. He always had lots to say in his jovial voice. He was small but his voice carried well at church. "Maybe a drop for us all Hugh, and the girls to bed?" I was really worried now. I'd

never heard that tone before. Not stern but authoritative. Hugh got up from the
sofa, past the priest in his armchair and walked through the living room, looking
over his right shoulder at me with a questioning look. When he blocked my view of
the priest as he passed, I shrugged my shoulders in response.

Hugh went out of the living room door and I heard him walk quickly down
the short hallway. Father Tom was saying "Come Clare, switch off the iron for a
moment and sit over here." His midlands accent was stronger than hers, but she
had been away from Ireland for over twenty years now and Father Tom for only a
handful. He called it home as did Hugh. Hugh was surprised to see me sitting on
the sofa.

He went to the wall divider and pulled down the cupboard door where they
kept the whiskey. On the shelf above it, he placed down the bottle and he reached
behind the glass panels to the right for some good glasses, he filled two fingers in
each glass but left the bottle out.

He turned and passed a glass to Father Tom first, who was behind him and
then brought over his and my glass, and sat down next to me. Before Hugh could
say his normal "good health," Father Tom spoke again. "Now Clare, remember we
had the chat the other day at the Club." I was racking my brains as to what he was
referring too but he answered for me. "Us being from the same homeplace." I
nodded, surprised that should be important. "Yes Father."

He continued "and you have not been back for a long time I believe. "No I
haven't Father, you know the expense, with the children." I felt very guilty lying to a
priest especially a nice one. I bit my lip and looked at the floor. I didn't want to look
at Hugh in case he disagreed with me. He had been home himself a few times to see
his mother, since the girls were born. He was nodding.

The priest continued, "Well now, Father Michael is the parish priest there and we keep in contact, sure we were in the seminary together. I told him about you of course and he told me that he had seen your sister there." I wondered which one; Maggie or Anne. I knew that I probably wouldn't recognise either of them, it being so long. No letters or photos either. "Maggie was at mass and they prayed for your father."

Father Tom was looking at me with concern, but I was more worried about what he would think about a daughter that didn't even know that her father was unwell. He made no comment about it. No offers of prayers were made by the priest. There was a very long pause. I didn't know what to say next. I took a large sip of the whisky and Hugh and father Tom did the same.

I placed the glass by my foot and wished we had a coffee table. I wanted very much for the priest to say what he had to say. I liked him well enough but wanted him to leave, I was feeling very uncomfortable talking about my family, such as it was. "I see that they haven't been in contact, you have no telephone do you Hugh?" I looked at my husband and he said "Your right father, the coin box is fine for us."

Father Tom continued "Well then Clare I've some very sad news for you, your father passed away. I'm very sorry for your loss." I thanked him automatically. Father Tom knew that something wasn't right, he reassured me, "You wouldn't have even known. He took bad on the Thursday and was dead by yesterday. He was a good age I believe, seventy-seven and still worked every day till then and he went to mass on a Sunday." I was upset now. The hypocrisy of it all!

The priest was fishing in his pocket and took out his rosary beads, "Shall we say a decade now? "We all started with *Eternal Rest*. I said the words even though I couldn't care if he went to hell. I closed my eyes quickly so the priest couldn't see my

thoughts but god himself would know, so I would still need to say something at
confession.

Instead of thinking about the words of the prayers, I added up the years and
realised, that bitter twisted nasty man, had lived for so many years longer than my
beautiful, lovely, kind mother. Then I cried not for him but for her. How unfair. The
tears poured down my face. I was really angry at myself and didn't want to look like
a hypocrite and so I wiped my tears and took a deep breath.

Hugh was looking at me as I carried on with the prayers thinking about my
mother as I said the words. Father Tom stopped after one decade and I was pleased.
He got up and walked over to me "bless you my child" and patted me on my
shoulder. "I will leave you to make the arrangements." Hugh stood up and led him
to the door saying "Thank you for coming Father. We really appreciate it." Father
Tom kissed his finger tips and placed it on the bottom of the crucifix as he passed by
as it was to the left of the living room door. He was saying he would pray for us all
as he was leaving the house.

Hugh exhaled as if he had been holding the breath inside him as he returned
into the room. I reached down for my drink but the glass was empty. Hugh side
stepped and picked up the whisky bottle from the shelf looking concerned. "Are you
okay Clare?" He poured me a larger glass this time. "How long since you saw him?"
I looked at him, "1952." He whistled, "Twenty-seven years!"

Hugh was careful with his words, "Do you want me to come with you?" I was
confused. I wanted to go to bed not out. He saw my confusion "to the funeral?" I
laughed. Hugh was not laughing, "Clare, are you going to the funeral?" I answered,
"why would I, I hated him." He was shocked, "Tell me why then. Explain. He is
dead finally, surely you can tell me now."

I realised that it was wrong that I'd never explained my family to Hugh. I was embarrassed not just about the physical abuse but about his beliefs. Hugh asked, "Was he a drinker?" I responded "No more than anyone else…" Memories popped into my mind. I thought about the pushing, shoving to get me out of the way. That was the norm. The pulling of my hair hurt but it had upset me more when he swung a handful in my face and for everyone else to see. Not just his jeering face but my brothers and sisters to. What could they have done anyway?

Mammy was not there on that occasion and I'd not told her as what could she do, get a slap or punch too. I didn't laugh when he had taken his belt off to Patrick after he had kicked over the bucket of warm milk or when Emmett put his hands in the butter. Him being the baby, it had upset everyone, when he had lifted him out of the chair and part pushed, part punched in the head and he had fallen on the floor and went still. Then the was lots of blood. Mammy rushed to him and sat on the floor with him. She gathered him in her arms and was crying. Emmett was silent so Mammy kissed him. A clean cloth had been found to wipe his head. Fathers voice cutting the atmosphere, "Don't baby him, he did wrong.

"Ye" pointing at me. "Clean up that mess. The rest of you eat your dinner." I was glad when Emmett smiled but worried when Father looked at my Mother in disgust. It showed in her face that she was too scared to look at her husband when she picked up her son and taken him carefully towards the fire. Then she had found a bandage for his still bleeding head, knowing there would be a punishment later. I didn't know what to say about him to Hugh, I didn't want to remember anything else, but I needed to say something.

"You know that there was seven of us, four boys and three girls brought up on a farm. We went to the National school, then I got a job and came to England like you did." Hugh was perplexed, "it's obviously not the same. There are five of us and you know them all. You know my Mother and remember my Father. We didn't own a farm. We moved from rented house to house going where the work was, in the west and north aswell as Scotland." He waited for me to reply.

His childhood hadn't been a bed of roses but he spoke of his family and Ireland with love. He didn't go on about being thrown on the street when a landlord took their fancy or when their catholic money was no longer good enough. They had been abused for their religion but the whole lot of them had never let it get into their blood. I could never see where the whole anger thing of her father had come from and was unable to make sense of it.

Hugh shook his head slowly, "Father Tom is right we need to make the arrangements. You need to go whether you want to or not." Hugh was not negotiating today. "I can get my sister to look after the kids if you want me there." Just as I didn't want to see them, I really didn't want Hugh to be meeting my family. "No." I acknowledging now that I didn't have a choice "I will get the mail train and boat in the morning. I will be there by tomorrow night. The funeral shouldn't be until Wednesday, should it?" I know Hugh knew more about it than me. Having left so long ago and not going back since. A life time ago and I'd forgotten as much as possible.

I didn't want to relive his madness nor go back to the place that I never felt as home. Hugh enquired, "Will there be room in the house?" I thought of the two-storey house and nodded my head. My Mammy's house to replace her Dublin home when she married my Father.

At the very least I'd followed her wishes. I married a man that I loved not forced as I know she was. She'd no choices. I find it so hard to believe that such a beautiful house would give me no pleasure. There was no one to call to confirm my coming so we went to bed. Hugh went to sleep and me to remember.

As I lay in bed, I thought of them all in turn and wondered about them. Mammy of course I still missed every day. There could be more family for the girls. Molly was always wanting more. Would anyone care if I came or not? It would look badly I supposed if I didn't but there maybe questions from neighbours as to where I'd been. I wondered if they cared. I pondered on whether did I either.

The next morning was going to be a busy one so I got up much earlier than usual to have all the clothes ready for Hugh and the girls for a couple of days. kids were going to school. Jenny was old enough to make dinner but they might have fish and chips as a treat. I packed a small bag. The I stood at the bus stop. I didn't care how long it would take but the thought of getting back home, to England, would keep me going. I'd a long boring journey ahead.

My stomach jerked remembering the previous crossing over the Irish sea to a new country and life. It had been an awful journey when I headed to England, the waves flowing onto the decks. The rain and the wind had been the worst weather I'd ever been in. I'd also been terrified of leaving Ireland. It hadn't leaving home as I'd not been back to the house in the previous four years since my Mammy's death.

Not one on them had visited or written. I'd felt invisible. I hoped that they wouldn't make me feel that way again. I thought about Bernie, my friend from working in the pubs. She was the only one that knew my story as I did her own. It was a shame for me that I couldn't talk to her about this now, but I would see her when I got home and tell her all about it. She knew more about my life than Hugh did, She'dn't think badly of me, or anything I might say about my family.

I slept on and off on the train. Having an empty seat next to me was good, but if I only had a normal family, Hugh could be there too. I was welcomed into his family. There was never any awkwardness there, they were a proper family. I loved being included. Everyone had seen each other for all the christenings and holy communions. Distance was never a problem for them. Mrs O'Donnell of course had been frosty but was like that with her own daughters, showing preference to her sons. Even at funerals there'd be chatting and laughing, tea and scones of bread not like her Mammy's funeral which had been the worst day of my life.

A man nearby was humming a song that I recognised and the words were forming in my head. He wasn't any great shakes, but it was clear that it was *Do You Want Your Oul Lobby Washed Down* and then I was singing too, "*She sighs every day... as she passes this way...*" I clamped my hand over my mouth in shock. The man smiled at my embarrassment. I laughed to myself and was glad we were at Holyhead.

I moved straight up the ramp and into the middle of the ship, even though there was blue sky without any clouds. The Irish Sea was known to have a mind of its own. I rushed for a seat. It would be a long journey. The cars were driving on, the noise was so loud but this meant that it would be my best chance to sit down. Alot of people had the air that this was not a holiday. The summer was over so there were very few children around. Other people were going to visit sick relatives or to bury the dead. My long black coat didn't look out of place, other people would need to rush to churches aswell.

The worst thing apart from getting there itself, was the waiting. I looked at the magazines in my bag. Woman's own didn't interest me today. I remembered that I'd brought Mammy's book. Jenny is so like her with her love of reading. Only

Molly had seen this book though. She was always asking about "home" and so proud of being Irish. She definitely didn't get that from me.

The book was different for me, it always gave me the hope that Mammy had when she read it and her remembering the first part of her life. I'd a life of two halves like her but thankfully this part of mine was the better one. Molly loved the fairies and the myths. I didn't believe in them but I let Hugh, who of course always confirmed to Molly that they were true stories, even saying that he had seen faeries himself in the green hills of home.

I'd not even opened the book when a woman dressed similarly smiled, indicating that she wanted to sit next to me. There were many empty seats but I understood that she didn't know who She'd get, and I was near the window so no one the other side either. I smiled back. I hoped that She'dn't want to chat all the way.

Irish women can be so nosy and I couldn't face the questions. She seemed to be checking me too, looking hopeful that a smile was enough. There was agreement on both sides that we wouldn't be talking, and we knew that even a hello may break that. The woman took off her coat but I kept mine on as I was feeling the cold sitting by the window.

I looked down at my book and touched the front cover gently with my fingers, and then as usual I looked at the inscription inside. When I looked up, time must have past as the seats were full and I could hear the ferry doors closing. Of course, it was a rough journey after an hour I was wishing that I'd taken the plane. I knew it had been my need to prepare myself that I'd not chosen the quicker route.

A man nearby was talking about the last trip saying he was taking a wee drink in case it happened again. He told everyone that the boat he had been in had hit the pier in Dun Laoghaire last year. I turned to the woman next to me, "would you mind my seat for me?" She responded with a twinkle of understanding, "Oh yes, I'm fed up of his story too." I smiled and picked up my handbag. I'd left my other bag on the floor, there was no need for a suitcase as I would be away for such a short period.

When I returned to my seat the man that had been talking must of had another wee drink as he was starting to sing. As I sat down, the woman next to me was getting up saying "Do you mind if I do the same." I nodded and she walked away leaving her much bigger bag on her seat.

Another older woman was walking around obviously looking for a seat, she was complaining as she walked. She was coming towards me and I knew what She'd say. She looked at me and then the bag, "Would you not lift that bag off and let me have that seat?"

People were looking as she was talking loudly from four seats away. I was apologetic in tone but not in reality, "I'm sorry but there is a lady sitting here, but she has gone to the toilet." I was just guessing that and hoped that She'd be back soon. The woman pursed her lips, "I will wait to see." She put her bag on the floor and her hands on her hips. "if she's not back in five minutes I will lift the bag myself!"

She clearly thought she deserved a seat. I felt like telling her to get on earlier as I'd done myself, but She'd just want to argue the toss. She was mumbling about the plane and I wished that she had got that too. I also heard a few words of her ramblings "Would you believe the cheek... Jesus Mary & Joseph... God give me strength..."

I was nearly praying myself to get the woman back to her seat, so I didn't have to sit next to this old witch. I looked all around, but couldn't see the woman, she was about the same age as me, with short curly brown hair and was short woman like myself, and I straightened my neck and looked around again. She was leaning down talking. I couldn't see if it was a man or a woman as the chair had its back to me. I was half off my seat waiting for an opportunity to catch her attention. The woman that was waiting was making a show of looking at her watch.

I pointed, "There she is, she will be back any second." The standing woman, turned her neck to see her adversary. Her scarf had become detached and was sliding to the floor. The man who'd had a wee drink, and a couple more since made a grab for it, but his coordination was not great as he grabbed at her tweed coat instead.

She screamed unnecessarily loudly in my opinion. As she did so my companion looked over to see the commotion. I waved and indicated that she needed to come back immediately. She half ran back though it was difficult as there were bags and people everywhere.

The English barman was also coming over as the older woman was becoming hysterical. My companion slipped passed the entwined couple and I moved her bag so that she could sit down. We were both then watching what was going on to the side of us.

The barman was looking like he didn't need this, on top of the crowd at the bar he had to serve. He took a deep breath and was calm, "What's all this now. What happened to you." The woman was shouting and words like "attacked" and "assaulted" could be heard. The man was good and mad now "Argh Jesus Christ. Didn't I just try to help her and she moved and I touched her coat." The wasn't strictly true, but the worst of them both was the shouting woman and I was on his side for the moment.

This heated discussion continued for a couple of minutes. My unknown companion was smiling, "Thank ye so much, did I nearly lose my seat? I was only gone for a moment, what happened?" I told her about the seat, the scarf and the man. She laughed, "Oh my, the trouble I caused," I laughed in response.

Then the old woman was pointing at me. The barman looked over. I could see he was losing his patience. "This lady here" though I could see that he was not convinced of that, "says that you saw it all." I was sure that, what was actually said, was that I caused it all, but the barman wanted it dealt with as soon as possible. The queue at the bar was getting bigger.

I explained that it was an accident but the lady was upset that she didn't have a seat. He turned to the man "Okay, apologise and I will assist this lady with a seat." He had a warning look in his eyes to the man as if to say, just do this.

The man although slightly worse for wear, copped on quickly and he said sweetly "I'm very sorry to have upset you." Lots of people were watching and she had no choice to grimace in response. The barman waved his arm in a gesture to move her on and as he turned, he lifted his head and had a wry smile, and he seemed thankful for it to be over.

The man that had been, in his opinion, falsely accused was shaking his head. "what an old goat." The man next to him commented, "A Meath woman?" The man nodded in understanding and said to his new friend. "Where are ye from?" The new man responded, "Dublin." He was pleased, "good man, I'm from Wicklow meself." There was a bottle taken from a plastic bag and a clink of glasses heard. It was good for him as that barman wouldn't be serving him again.

My companion was saying, "Oh my." Then she caught my eye. "Are you alright there?" She was thinking I was upset by the incident but being a bar lady in the past, I'd seen much worse. I smiled in response, "Oh yes." She sighed "Funeral for me. Ye?" I nodded. She continued "me grandfather, he was a good age, 97." My voice cracked, "Father," not in grief but anger. She had a sympathetic look on her face, not simpering as some might be. "I'm Clare, after the poor Clare's." I laughed "me too." The Irish certainly didn't have much imagination when it came to names. Repeating them from generation to generation.

Not too long later the singing began as expected. The Irish national anthem first, which got a choir going, it was the Irish version so I didn't know it well. *Seo dhíbh a cháirde duan Óglaigh, Cathréimeach briomhar ceolmhar* . Then "the *Green, green grass of home*..." It was nothing like Tom Jones though, before the calls for other songs.

Another man started on *"When Irish Eyes Are Smiling..."* but people were talking over him and arguing.

One called for *Bold Robert Emmett,* another voice shouted for *James Connelly* which made me shiver, which they did decide upon.. *When they murdered James Connolly. The Irish rebel....*and I could hear and see my father unbidden and an unwanted vision. I shivered seeing him standing by, and holding the mantel piece, holding court with his family surrounding him. Some in wonder, some in agreement and me in terror.

Now they were singing about Kevin Barry, *"...High upon the gallows tree.. Kevin Barry gave his young life... For The Cause of liberty.."* I was concerned as it hadn't been long since the murder of Lord Mountbatten, but no one else was uncomfortable. Clare was saying "Sure it's only a bit of fun."

"Isn't it amazing, that the pope is coming to Ireland!" I nodded and wondered out loud when he was coming to us." Clare looked at me oddly, "You're the only Irish person that I've met, that doesn't call Ireland home and has no connection to it. Each to their own, I suppose." She was confused by me, but it didn't stop the chat and I was glad of it.

The journey went a lot quicker listening about her life in Birmingham. She was going to the railway station too and had done her journey many times before. "A holiday every year back home without fail. Me mother would kill me otherwise, but I'd miss it too meself." We parted and I was glad that I'd met her. For that short period as I'd forgotten the reason for my visit.

The train journey was fine but I was worried about actually getting to the house. I looked at my good shoes and bag and wondered how far I could walk. I tried to think of something else but it was nagging at me the whole time. It was easy enough to get a bus to the town but after that I was not even sure that I would remember.

The bus was easy enough but I kept thinking about what to do next. The bus was emptying, the driver called to me when he stopped at a junction. I acknowledged him, "where are you headed?" When I told him, he smiled, "Surely, can't I pass by the end of the road, if that helps." I was smiling and thanked him when I got off. I could see the house when I was at the junction. It was still light and I felt happy to stretch my legs and breathe in the fresh air.

I stopped a few hundred yards away from the house as two men were entering the front door. They were elderly men hunched over, by the cold or by age. I squinted but I couldn't see their faces, with their collars up and caps pulled down. I didn't recognise them. When I got in front of the house, my feet stuck to the road. I wasn't moving. To me it was not the grand house that others saw. It was just as I remembered. Unchanged a two story four-bedroom square house. Whereas most of the neighbouring properties were cottages. It was well maintained. Seamus must still paint the front white every year.

If Hugh would see this. He would think that I was of a different class. They had lived in two rooms where they had laid their heads. Wherever they had lived it was filled with laughter and songs. Just the same as now when they met. This house was richer in possessions but poorer in love. The words of a hymn that we sung at mass came into my mind. "Richer than gold is the love of my Lord. Better than splendour and wealth."

I'd not foreseen this panic on seeing this place again. There had been a time when I'd prayed to go back, but that was when I'd first moved to the Meaney's. There were very few happy memories. They were mostly with my Mother and she was long gone. I worried if I'd dreamed her. Someone so good in a place that was so bad. I had to remind myself that he was dead. I knew his body was still there inside. His presence would still be felt.

I'd come all this way. I knew now it had been the wrong thing to do. But I had to go in. I took a deep breath lifting myself on to my toes. I didn't know whether to go in through the front door or the back door. I felt like a visitor even though it was my childhood home. These thoughts went around my head. The whirling was making me feel sick.

A woman came from around the side of the house. I recognised her immediately. I was so glad it wasn't a family member. Veronica also recognised me aswell. She came forward and I met her. She had her arms open, "Welcome home." She'd been like that before when my Mother had died. Her and her mother had

68

made me feel safe. I was happy to accept a hug from her. I was not usually a hug person. I realised how much this was all affecting me. Just being back. She didn't say *I'm sorry for your loss*. The usual refrain in death, which strengthened my resolve. She of all people would know that I would not mourn him.

"Wait while I get some more milk and I will walk in with you." I was so grateful. I knew how unlikely it was that I would have moved of my own accord. She was back in a flash with a bucket. "No time for niceties. It's heaving in there. Lots of people coming and no one going!" I touched her arm "Your Mother and Father?" She smiled weakly. "Both dead a few years now." She paused and I offered my condolences. They were sincere.

She continued "I'm the farmer's wife now. I'vefive boys to help me. Not a girl among them. Come on, they will be gasping so they will." She took the decision away from me. We went through the back door into the scullery.

"Look who I found." I recognised Maggie immediately. I wondered if I looked the same. She ran the few steps to where I'd remained at the back door. She was crying "Thank god you are alive. I'm so happy you are here." She stepped back and was smiling and seemed genuine in her response. "I'm so so sorry. Will you ever forgive me? What a terrible sister I'vebeen."

My mouth was open but I didn't know what to say. "Daddy never did say where you had gone. It was like he didn't know himself. When we did find out, we heard that you had gone to England." She was crying. I realised I was crying silently too but I let the tears fall.

Maggie passed me a handkerchief and I pressed it to my face. "I wish you had seen Daddy before he died. I'm sure he would have loved to see you." I couldn't speak now as I was scared that I would shout at my sister, who was being so nice to me. My hand covered my mouth to physically stop me from talking.

I wanted to shout that he did know where I was. How he had taken half my wages each month. I wanted to tell her that he hated me and I hated him. That I was glad that he was finally dead. I knew that would be a terrible thing to say at a funeral. Especially before I was even reunited with the rest of the family or at all.

She pulled my arm to sit at the same small table with the rickety chairs. Though still scrubbed and as clean as my Mother had kept them. I sat still not speaking. "How are you Clare? Are ye well. I hope ye are happy." I nodded and smiled because it was true. "Tell me the news."

I was happy to hear of her marriage to Liam who we had played with when we young. She had two girls and a baby boy. I heard that Seamus was still a bachelor. He had still worked the farm with their Father. I felt sad that he had never gotten away.

That Anne had gotten a great job in the bank. She had given it up of course when she married. Her husband had worked in the same bank and they were doing alright for themselves. She had one boy and they lived in the city so they didn't see them much. There was no evidence of a friendship with her as she just rattled off the facts.

Patrick was on the buildings in England. He'd left as soon as he was eighteen. Not long after me but he came home for his holidays. He was single too. That surprised me as he was always the most handsome of the boys. Emmett was working with their uncle at the garage as I'd suspected. None of the boys were courting. It was very strange and unusual that none of the boys had married.

She didn't mention my other brother, "and Vincent?" She just shook her head and changed the subject quickly, asking what happened to me. "Well, I left the Meany's when I was eighteen." Choosing not to explain how awful that part of my life had been. "They had been very nice but strict. I only went out for church. I decided at the start to get the boat to England as soon as I was eighteen. I went on my own." Maggie was surprised and seemed sadden by that. In reality I'd felt liberated but scared.

"I'd started to earn as bit more when I was sixteen (not mentioning that he had stopped taking money then) and saved enough for the ticket. When I got to London, I was a barmaid at first and now I work for the council." This news seemed distasteful to her but she let me continue. "I married Hugh and have three girls; Jenny Kitty and Molly."

Veronica was indicating for me to take my coat off. She took it away to hang in the press, I assumed, then returned with a cup of tea. My bag was already gone from the door. Veronica must have left with it whilst I was talking to my sister. I hadn't expected that. I didn't think the others would be as receptive to my being there as Maggie.

I drank my tea appreciatively. Then a butter scone and cake were brought, which I ate hungrily realising my sandwiches were still uneaten in my bag. I looked around at the small room. Clean and bright but with all the same sink and cupboards. No changes had been made at all.

When Maggie returned, she nodded for me to go towards the parlour. I walked through the kitchen. There were so many people standing and sitting. Heads bent in conversation. Mostly men of my Father's age but a few younger ones too.

The mantlepiece was still the same. Polished and empty apart from a framed proclamation.

Maggie saw me looking. I got that one for Daddy for his birthday. The old original one was yellowed with age and smoke." The cold tiles still covered the floor but the mat was gone. There were more sofas and chairs. They looked new and probably more of Maggie's taste. I looked ahead and in case of any stares that I may get.

I walked through the door into the hall. It was being left open as people were moving in and out of the parlour. That door had always been kept shut to keep the heat in. Woe betide you if you forgot. I could still hear the shout of *Dun an doras sin*, always with a smack which was the punishment. I looked up the stairs. I couldn't understand how the same wallpaper could have survived all this time.

More people were coming in. I knew that I would have to see him but I would not touch him or say a prayer as I passed. As required, I went to the open coffin straightaway. I didn't look to see who was in the crowded room. It was too dark anyway. I felt eyes on me as Maggie evidently had informed the others of my arrival.

I stood with my eyes shut trying not to see his face. I stood for the minimum time required and had to open my eyes before I turned. He was long and thin and white. He had his hair still long and black with some grey. His skin was stretched on his face, and his nose was still prominent and eyes bulging with anger in death aswell as life.

I turned and saw my brothers stand. I shook hands with Seamus, he kissed my cheek then Patrick and Emmett did the same. I didn't see Anne yet. I sat down next to Emmett as his smile was the widest to allow the other mourners to talk to us as they passed.

Patrick leaned over Emmett and touched my arm and smiled. I smiled back. I'd always got on best with him. As I was here, I wanted to catch up with him. The pain of losing my family so young was melting away seeing them again. Emmett whispered in my ear about the old woman standing at the coffin reminding me who she was, and told me to get ready for the rosary. "She's a devil for them." This made me want to laugh and on cue the old woman started a decade.

A few dozen hands were shaken but there were not many conversations as there was too many people to greet to do that, some people were surprised to see me others passed no notice at all. When I saw the clock, even though it was covered, I could see that the time was nearing midnight.

Emmett whispered again "I, they will be all gone by midnight." He was right. They were getting up to leave. I was trying to see if I recognised anyone but many were very old, their faces ravished by the wind and some had definitely hadn't even been born when I'd left the place.

Maggie, who had been sitting on my other side had gotten up and was directing people to the door saying goodbyes and thankyous, her knowing them best. Seamus as the oldest wasn't taking the lead as tradition and he just stood still looking sombre in his new suit. He was letting his brother-in-law Liam, follow the people out of the room.

I was eager to leave the body of the man I could never forgive, so I made to leave the room too. Seamus pulled me back and shut the door behind Emmett and Patrick who had gotten there first. I was alone with my brother for the first time in over twenty years.

There was no civility with him, no welcome. His face was twisted in anger. I felt that he looked very much like Father tall but broad. His hair the same black as him but shorter and I felt afraid. Afraid of my own brother! He indicated that I should sit. I didn't want to so I remained standing. He stayed standing aswell.

"why are you here Clare?" Not knowing what to say, I was honest. "I'm not sure but I didn't want to come." He said "You were so upset about Vincent but you did the same to us. You left and never contacted us again." He was making me angry. I didn't want to lose my temper but I had to respond, "what do you mean? I wrote every week for a year but not one of you replied."

His expression changed but he was not convinced by me. "No, you didn't." I was surprised that he should say something that was so untrue. My face must have shown my astonishment but he went on to say "Were you with Vincent?" "No" I was a dressmakers assistant, didn't you know, didn't he tell you at least, as the oldest." Evidently by his face their father hadn't.

"How did you get here?" I told him by train, boat and bus. He told me Veronica had put my bag upstairs and there was a bed made for me. I was glad that I'd somewhere to stay. He grimaced a smile and I felt relief that the encounter was over.

I was now concerned about seeing Anne as I'd not seen her yet. I rushed out of the room as I realised, I was alone with my father and either alive or dead I couldn't stomach that.

There were still some old men drinking whiskey in the kitchen. Maggie had said that we could leave them to it. Seamus would stay with them. The bottle was beside them. They were happy to talk in low tones to themselves.

Maggie was suddenly gone and Anne was at my shoulder and directed me upstairs, "You must be tired after the travelling today." Indicating I should go to bed. No greeting or recognition of who I was. There was no feeling at all towards me.

I wasn't tired but I was glad to escape. I didn't want to be there at all. There had been mixed reactions from my family. I went up the stairs on my own. I'd dreamt about returning. Firstly, at Meaney's and then in London. But then only when I'd been scared to be in a new country. I didn't think I would be able to sleep in a house full of ghosts. Then Maggie was touching my shoulder and it was morning.

The journey to the church and the requiem mass went fine. The priest was talking as if my father was a great man. It was quick as I remember now not like the funeral's at home. There were lots of shaking of hands, which was to be expected. Not as many questions about me but definitely inquisitive looks. The weather was cold and I was glad of my coat at the graveside.

The sky was blue though not a drop of rain. This pleased me no crying eyes of god or whatever that saying meant. It must have rained the day before as the ground was slippery.

People came to the house after the funeral but not as many as at the wake, and they had fizzled out by dinnertime. There were seven adults and five children in the house so the grandchildren and my brother in laws were eating first. I'd not been introduced to Anne's husband but I assumed it was him.

We sat in the dining room waiting to eat. Not speaking. All with our own thoughts. There was a smell of damp that you get when rooms are unused. I doubted the fire had been lit in a long time before today. There was a knock on the front door. Maggie went to answer it without question. Everyone seemed unsurprised. Seeing my face Patrick explained, "it will be the solicitor come to read the will."

I wondered if it was the same man who we had seen with our Father in that meeting. Surely, he couldn't still be alive. He had been an unlikely friend for our father. He had come from nothing as he always said. It is strange what things draw people together. I'd not seen him for a very long time. It could be his son or employee but it was the Mr Sullivan that I knew. Still tall and thin and with some grey hair. He stood upright in the entitled manner of those people with money can. He was officious as he came in. He took off his coat which Maggie hurried away with.

Seamus offered him a glass of whisky which he accepted with a nod. Seamus passed around a glass to each of us that partook in alcohol. We were sitting on the chairs in the dining room. We sat around the oval mahogany table left from Mammy's father. It was beautifully made. I'd forgotten about it. We had never used them. I imagined not since either as they were in the same good condition as the day I left. The parlour had remained Mammy's domain. She had loved polishing the furniture and silver framed photographs which nether inhibited the rest of the house.

The solicitor nodded to me, "Hello Clare, I'd heard you were back." He didn't acknowledge the rest; he obviously must have seen them recently. I was surprised that he even remembered my name. He was curt but not unkind. We did a small toast of good health. After he had taken a sip of his drink, he set the glass down. We all did the same. He took a small sealed envelope from his leather briefcase. He took his glasses from his pocket and put them on.

I looked around at my family. Seamus was looking at his hands which were twisting in his lap. Anne was agitated, she was eager to leave. She hadn't even spoken to me yet, apart from the instructions she had been providing to everyone.

Patrick looked bemused, his blue eyes giving me a sly wink. He had taken my address and we were planning to meet up in London. Emmett was nervous and was fidgeting in his chair so I couldn't catch his eye. He'd taken my address and promised to write. He would stay with me in London for a holiday. I'd told them both that I would be delighted.

The solicitor seemed unwilling to start as if he was rereading the letter to himself. There was one sheet of paper, obviously he had reviewed it so I was surprised at the delay. He cleared his throat, "Your father was of sound mind when he wrote this letter. We discussed the contents at length." I thought it was a strange way to start though I'd only seen will readings on the TV so I'd nothing to compare it with.

Maggie was glancing at Seamus but Seamus was still looking at his hands. He continued then "this is my last will and testament…. I leave the house and contents to my daughter Maggie. I leave my savings to The Cause."

Anne smile was twisted in disgust but looked unsurprised. She didn't look at anyone. I knew that she wanted out of the house as quickly as me. I was shocked. Surely there must be something else in it. I was not upset for myself, I'd never expected anything.

Seamus had gone white. He must have worked his fingers to the bone with their father telling him what to do for all those years with no recognition. Neither Emmett nor Patrick seemed to care. Patrick even laughed, saying wryly, "well, what would you expect."

I felt a sharp pain in my heart. I knew my mother would not like the Fitzgerald family home to go to one child. Her own father had grown up in it. The house had given her no joy though. Her thoughts were always of Dublin where she had lived a happy life.

I was pulled back to reality. My eyes were wide. I covered my open mouth with my hand. I wondered how much savings he had. I couldn't comprehend how that money would even get to the IRA.

Part 2

1980's

Ireland

Part 2: Chapter 4 - Welcome Home (1980)

"What are you at Molly? We are going in a minute!" Mum was shouting up the
stairs. I took one last look at my dolls lined up in bed under the covers and knew
they would be fine when we went away. To go to Ireland, finally! For the whole of
Christmas! It was so exciting. My Mum started shouting again. I flew out of the
room and down the stairs. We were going to the pickup point and then all the way
on the coach to the town that Dad had been born. Going on a coach would be fun
aswell. Mum and Dad said it would take a whole day with crossing the Irish Sea.

The thought of leaving England was scary but as Dad had said we were
going home, and there was nothing to be frightened of at all, except the cows. I only
remembered them standing still in a field, when we passed them to go to the
seaside. They didn't look like anything that I should be worried about.

I stood next to my Dad, "Will it be like when we go to Leysdown? With the
roads surrounded by all the trees?" My Dad winked at me, "Yes, but far better than
that. Are you excited?" He knew that compared to my older sisters and mum, that I
was. Jenny was reading standing up as usual. I'd tried to do that but can't
especially the walking too. Kitty was complaining to Mum again about the
hairdresser who had cut her hair too short. She definitely wanted to stay at home.

Mum wasn't saying much. She didn't have a smile on her face like me and
Dad. She wasn't even listening to Kitty who had bored everyone about her hair.

Mum had the same dark look as when she had come back from Ireland last year. I remembered that her father had died, so maybe she was sad.

I went over to her, "Can I sit next to you Mum? Dad can sit with Uncle Michael. Then Kitty and Jenny can be together?" Mum turned her head and was thinking about what I was asking. Kitty's face was red, "No one is listening to me." Jenny moved her book away from her face, "We've done nothing but listen to you." Kitty started shouting at my older sister. I agreed with Jenny, but I didn't want Kitty to shout at me too. Jenny sighed and continued to read. If Jenny or I behaved like Kitty we'd get a smack on the back of our legs, but Kitty was always allowed to rant and rave and stamp her feet.

I repeated, "Mum?" she looked at me confused; Kitty had made her forget my question. "We'll see" she replied. Her saying that always meant that the answer was "No." I shook my head in frustration, deflated, taking away my cheerfulness, like only Kitty could. I definitely didn't want to sit next to Kitty now. We all knew that Kitty was Mum's favourite. Mum said that this was not true, but Kitty always smirked because she knew it was. Kitty said I was Dad's favourite, but I didn't think so. Jenny was certainly Uncle Michael's favourite, so if it was true it was all fine.

After an hour into the journey, I was bored and hot. It was noisy on the coach. I was finding it hard to read my library book. I was under strict orders not to lose. I couldn't even see out of the window as I was on the aisle seat. Jenny was at the window seat and not even looking out, as she was reading as usual.

"Can we play a game?" She put down her book and smiled "Eye spy?" I nodded. She told me that it could only be things inside the coach as outside was going past too quickly. She started with the letter "S" and that passed the time for a while, until the coach stopped. We could get out and go to the toilet. It felt like we had been travelling for days already. Everyone laughed at me when I asked, "how much further?" but they didn't answer my question. I was allowed cola today. I didn't want my Mum to take it away. So, I stopped asking questions.

It was dark and windy when we finally got to Holyhead. The coach was driving on towards the boat. There was a long queue of coaches and cars. I was standing in the aisle to see. Uncle Michael who was in front of me turned and looked very serious. He touched my arm. "Molly now, don't be going off. I know what you're like. Gerald Tuite could be going over the sea to Ireland aswell."

I knew I looked confused. I didn't remember that name. He looked concerned that I didn't understand him. "Ye know the Irishman, who is no longer at your majesty's pleasure." He turned to his brother saying "Hugh, why doesn't she know about him." My Dad was looking behind at mum as if not wanting her to hear, "Well why should she know, for god's sake, she's only eight years old!" I didn't like the sound of what was being said, "Dad, could he be here? He was matter of fact, "Well, he could of course be here so do as your Uncles says. Don't be running off." I was really scared.

My Mum had moved up behind us as we waited to get off the coach, she looked concerned and annoyed, "For god sake will you stop, she'll be having nightmares. Molly now be a good girl and don't take a blind bit of notice of them both." Mum turned away and my Dad and Uncle Michael looked like they had been told off by a teacher.

Uncle Michael was humming and singing, though not loud enough for Mum to hear. I did catch some words by The Dublin City ramblers. *For another three prisoners jumped over the wall.* Mum seemed to get some of it and turned and stared at him until he stopped singing.

When the coach got to the ramp the noise it made underneath made me think that it couldn't take the weight. I was scared that we would drop into the sea. The creaking noise was extremely loud. No one else seemed worried they all seemed happy to be getting off the coach.

I heard people tutting and muttering *Tis terribly uncomfortable... God I hope we get a seat on there..I, ..I just want to stretch my legs...Jesus Mary & Joseph didn't I say we should get the plane.*" Everyone was Irish here. Just like at mass. Mum was saying we needed to be quick onto the boat to get a seat.

Jenny and Kitty were being instructed to run on ahead. They were to get seats together in the bar. "Now Molly stay with me. We don't want you getting lost." I scowled at my mum. I hated it when they all treated me like a baby. We were squeezing through the other cars to get to the stairs. It was very noisy. The howling of the wind could still be heard above the engines and the shouting men that were in charge.

We were walking fast up the stairs and Kitty and Jenny had already sprinted off. When we got to the top there was a sign for the bar. My Dad and uncle were behind us. When we got inside, they had gotten six seats together. It was filling up fast. We had to sit down until everyone had found a seat.

I sat for a minute then I needed to go to the toilet. Mum sighed "What a surprise.... go with her Jenny... the queue will be as long as your arm but never mind." Jenny didn't seem to mind. Kitty was looking mischievous but not to Mum's face and followed us.

As we left the bar she pointed, "There's signs near the stairs saying that people can't be on that loading deck, when the boat is leaving or arriving. Let's go down there now to see what happens." Jenny wrinkled her brow but shrugged.

Kitty was walking towards the stairs that went down to the cars. There were people everywhere but not going down.

There was talking, laughing and singing. There would be alot of that I should imagine. Dad had told me that everyone would be so happy to be going home. That we should all join in the party.

A girl about my age was singing "*what's another year*." Hearing that song made me smile. I remembered how we all had felt when Jonny Logan had won the Eurovision song contest for Ireland. We were in the club; everyone had been asking the kids for the news. The song contest was on the TV. There was only one in the club, in the children's games room.

All the boys and girls had been running into the bar with the scores. Normally some of the adults would shout at them. Children aren't allowed in there but they had been smiling and then cheers when we won. We got to stay there later too.

Kitty was saying "Come on." She pulled me towards the staircase. It seemed further going down than coming up. It was deadly quiet now. It seemed like all the space had been covered with cars and coaches. We weaved through the cars. The boat doors were still open so we hadn't left yet. The wind and rain were driving towards us. I could see men on the ramp.

The boat started to move. There were loud toots on a horn. We were moving even though the big doors were still wide open. The men didn't seem worried or in a hurry to shut them. I was scared and grabbed Jenny's hand, she looked a bit shocked, but you could see by the smirk on Kitty's face that she thought it was great. She was always the naughty one but somehow this made everyone laugh.

We could see the dock and then the sea. I was relieved when the doors were shutting. I was pleased to hear the loud creaking noise. A man saw us and shouted "What the hell are you doing there, get out of it will ya!" We ran as fast as we could up the stairs. We were breathless when we got to the top.

We ran out onto the deck in case the man had followed us. The wind took my breath away. It was pushing me in all directions. I was shocked at how cold it was. My hair was blowing everywhere even though it was tied up in pig-tails. The rain or waves was soaking me.

I didn't like it, I shouted that I was going back inside. When I got inside, I'd to manoeuvre around lots of people to get to the toilet. I looked around for my sisters, they weren't with me, they mustn't have heard me. I knew I was in trouble now!

I bit my lip, hoping that they would follow me to the toilet. I wasn't surprised that it was very difficult to walk around especially after coming in from outside. Dad had told me about the Irish sea so I was ready for it. Lots of people didn't seem to have their sea legs and were holding onto the wall. When I got to the toilet there was a very long queue, just as my Mum had said. There was a line of people snaking along the wall to the open toilet door. I wished I'd gone earlier.

I was annoyed with myself, as usual Kitty was going to get me into trouble with her foolish ideas. I was now doing exactly what they'd told me not to do. It happened all the time never planned and then never believed.

I sighed loudly without meaning to. The lady standing in front of me looked down," have ye lost someone?" I nodded. "Don't ye be worrying; I will get you back to your family." She smiled encouragingly and I was relieved.

A girl in front of the lady was then peering around her. She smiled too. "It's easy to get lost on here. This is my first time on the boat, what about you?" I nodded, "it's my first time too." She walked around the lady who must have been her Mum next to me. The queue hadn't moved. She was the same height as me but that probably meant she was younger than me. I'm so small and called titch by the kids at school. She was the complete opposite to me with pale skin and short curly blond hair, though her eyes were the same as mine.

She was probably thinking the same about me as she was looking at my long straight brown hair and dark skin. "I'm Rosie." I told her my name. "How lovely, ...Mammy?" as she pulled on her mother's arm, "This is Molly, what a lovely name." Her mother smiled "It surely is. Who are you named after then?" I knew what my Mum had said but I didn't want to say.

Everyone was called after their granny or their aunty. They were very nice and felt ok to tell them, "After a film." The lady nodded "Oh yes, now is it Molly Malone made good?" I was pleased, no-one had ever seen it as it was so old.

Rosie looked confused. I raised my eyebrows and smiled. She knew that I didn't know either. The queue moved on. An older woman came out mumbling "would ye look at the state of the place...I hope that they don't live like that at home but mark my words they do." She looked both ways with the look of disgust still on her face as she walked towards the stairs.

I dreaded what the toilets upstairs would be like if she'd come down here. Rosie and I were giggling. "Well," Rosie's Mum shook her head "you won't be laughing when you get in there." She tutted loudly. Some of the other women tutted in agreement and nodded their heads. Someone was saying "would ye believe it..."

I saw a man stopping to light a cigarette. What if he was Gerald Tuite. I covered my face with my hand and sank into the wall. Rosie looked at me with concern but when I suggested this, she reassured me as her Dad had said that he definitely wouldn't be on the boat. He would be away to America or somewhere like that. I was pleased to hear this. The line was moving then and we finally got inside the door of the toilets.

Kitty pushed her head around the door frame, "so this is where you have been hiding." I was infuriated with her, where else would I be. Rosie looked at me sympathetically, "Sister? I nodded sadly. Kitty was gleeful, "You're in alot of trouble." Rosie's Mum turned to me "Don't ye be worrying, I will take ye back to explain." Kitty's interest waned when she heard that and turned away in a huff.

When we got back to the bar, Mum was shaking her head, "well you lost your seat now." It was so unfair especially as it wasn't my fault. They should have kept it for me. I looked at the floor nearby, knowing I would have to sleep next to the other people already settled in for the night. Rosie's Mum was explaining what had happened and my Mum laughed.

Mum turned back to me, "Well would you like to do that Molly?" her words were unsure. I'd missed what she said but Rosie had heard, "Wouldn't that be great if you shared a cabin with us." Normally I would be scared to go with strangers. We had been told not too by the school policeman. Kitty was fuming so I said yes just to annoy her.

Rosie's Mum introduced herself as Mary. She was very friendly and it was clear she was very happy to go back home. Mum was nodding but wasn't agreeing. Mary was explaining that she was going to her husband's home place first, as he was from the north but she was not as excited to go there. When Mum nodded it was in true agreement this time. Mary was eager to know where we were going, "Oooh still a bit of trouble on the border, but more for the soldiers than our boys. Wasn't there one shot down that way this Summer?"

Mum didn't respond, she didn't discuss the troubles with anyone, so I took my chance before she changed her mind. "Shall I take my coat?" Mum nodded. I was feeling a bit anxious. "Bye then." I looked at Kitty first, she was pursing her lips. Jenny looked up from the newspaper and mum raised her hand and watched me leave.

As I was walking beside Rosie, my tummy rumbled very loudly. Rosie's Mum turned to me and smiled. "Come on we have got some sandwiches and crisps." I was really smiling then.

When we got to the berth, there were other younger children with another woman, already eating. Rosie explained that they were her Aunt and cousins. Her Dad and Uncle wouldn't be back to sleep there.

I was eating quickly. Rosie's Mum said I was a good eater and that She'dn't need to remind me about those that had to go without. I thought they were talking about the babies in Africa as that's who we prayed for at mass. As I listened, I realised that they were talking about Ireland. They knew one of the hunger strikers in a prison in the north. That's why they were telling us all to eat up.

The light was turned off but seemed to be back on again soon after. Rosie's family packed up their things and took me back to my family. My Mum was thanking them and she looked at me to speak. "Thanks for having me." I didn't have time to get Rosie's address, it would have been nice to have her as a pen pal.

It was such a long boring journey on the coach. I thought we'd never get there. It was snaking around the border with the north, which Dad commented on with his brother "Wouldn't it make you vex?"

The driver let us off at the end of my Granny's Road which was good. I didn't mind the walk up the lane as I was so excited. Granny was happy to see Dad. Less so to see my Mum or my sisters. She smiled smugly at Mum, "Well at least Molly's glad to be here." I didn't care what was being said. I was so desperate to get inside. My sisters and Mum didn't look happy.

I couldn't believe how cold Granny's house was. I tried to get near to the fire but she only had a big cooker in the living room. Mum was laughing, looking at my face. She said that it was called a range. It burnt turf. It was the fire and the cooker. "What's turf?" Uncle Michael laughed at me too. He bent over and picked up a lump of dirt from a bucket. He waggled it in front of my face. I tried to understand how that would work.

We sat down in our coats and drank tea for an age. Granny said we would be going to Aunty Geraldine's when we were settled. She was going to cook us some dinner. Dad was excited, "Are you ready to meet your cousins, Molly?" I forgot about the cold and was excited to see what they would be like. I ran down the lane. I had to be careful not to fall. It had lots of holes with big puddles. Mum would kill me if I ruined my new coat. I loved it, it swirled around as I twirled.

When we got to the house, my Dad and Uncle didn't go to the front door but around towards the hay shed. I was confused but I followed them. He turned again towards the back of the house and entered without knocking. I heard a woman shout out. I thought she was scared but she was just happy to see her brothers.

We all trooped in behind them, in to another room called the kitchen. It looked like a living room but it had a range too. This one was big and white. A man stood and shook my Dad's hand, "Welcome home."

A tall girl with long black hair, put out her hand for me to shake. Like in church. She was formal, "Céad míle fáilte." When she smiled, I felt very much at home. I guessed this was Saoirse. She was so much taller and older than me. I knew from my Dad that she was only born a couple of months before me. She looked me up and down. I thought that She'd be disappointed that I was small.

She said she was excited to meet me. She was reassuring that being born in England hadn't made me less Irish. I was pleased with that but I didn't really know why. "I love your name, Molly..... *Good Golly Miss Molly*" she sang pleased with herself.

I wondered if I would be able to pronounce her name properly even though I'd been practising. "Mine is a difficult one. Its pronounced Ser sha but call me Shea if you like, that's what the kids at school call me." I was relieved. "It's an amazing name. I've never heard it before. My Dad told me it's the most Irish name you can get and the most impressive one. I agree with him!"

Everyone was shaking hands and saying "Hello." There were older cousins too. They were the same ages as my sisters and I was glad for them. They were all very friendly and pleased to see us. There were younger boys running around us. Even though it was cold. We went outside to meet the cows. I was the only English cousin that wanted to milk them.

On Christmas day the room was so packed. Chairs were brought in from the parlour and it was very noisy. It was warm in their kitchen. There were so many people. Not like in Granny's house which never did heat up. When I went to the toilet, it was cold on their stairs though. It was cold on my stairs at home but not this bad. When I came down Saoirse was sitting on the stairs waiting for me. "I'll teach you some Irish while you're here so everyone in England will know you have been home." I hoped it wouldn't be too hard, I'd French lessons at school and I could never get the hang of it.

When we were eating dinner, we were bumping arms as there were so many of us but it was great fun. By the end of the meal, we were all getting restless. We started to chat. Grannie was telling us to shush.

Saoirse had a glint in her eye and then started singing "*Grandma we love you.* We all joined in, *there's no one like grandma...* It was the Christmas number one in England by St Winifred's school choir. I was surprised that she knew the song at all. Granny was stern, "Will you stop that now," but her eyes showed that she was pleased.

When the table was cleared, they made a space in the middle of the room. Annie was the first to stand to recite a poem; *There's many a strong farmer....Whose heart would break in two,... If he could see the townland ....An old man plays the bagpipes ...In a golden and silver wood; ...Are dancing in a crowd...*

I'd a feeling that there was more but was all she could remember. My Dad was smiling as if the townland she spoke about was his. He was so happy to be home. Even Mum was smiling. My younger cousin took out his tin whistle. He played a tune that I didn't know. It was really good but very sad. I'd never heard of this instrument before.

It sounded so much better than a recorder that we practised at school. I supressed a yawn. I was enjoying myself so much I didn't want my Mum to catch me and send us back to Granny's cold house.

My Uncle called out "now you Jonny, in solidarity with those prisoners of war in the H Blocks, the great James Connolly poem by Liam McGowen." Jonny smiled, pleased to have been chosen. He stood to recite something that was vaguely familiar to me;

A great crowd had gathered, outside of Kilmainham...............There was many a sad heart....When they murdered James Connolly, the Irish rebel

Mum had a strange glazed look on her face. When she saw me looking at her, she caught a hint of a yawn. "Oh my god, would you look at the time. We had better be heading off." Dad wasn't too happy but readied himself to leave saying "now he really was a great man, who lived and died for The Cause."

Part 2: Chapter 5 –Being Irish (1981)

When we were back from our holiday, I kept bothering Dad asking for stories of
Ireland. If Mum was there, he would pat me on my head, "go on and play Molly."
So, I learnt to ask when she wasn't around. He told me that he had gone to school in
his bare feet. That they never had meat and chicken was a treat.

Mum overheard once, "You would only want chicken if you didn't have to watch it
be killed. See it run around without a head before it died." I shrank back at that. The
hens in Saoirse's farm had been lovely and had let me pick them up.

I asked "is that why you prefer liver?" I knew that I'd the look of disgust on
my face. Mum looked annoyed at me, "you should be happy with what you get."
She looked tired so I thought better of saying anything else. I felt bad as I knew we
didn't have much money. That must be why we didn't have chicken or meat much
either.

That night it rained and I came in and sat by the gas fire to warm up. The
news was on. Mum and Dad were both watching intently, shushing me when I
began to talk. The newsreader read about how a man in prison was on hunger
strike.

It reminded me of Rosie from the boat to Ireland. I couldn't imagine
someone giving up their food. The newsreader said that he had been doing this for
twenty days and that he was also going to be a MP at the same time.

They showed a picture of the prison. My Dad was shaking his head. Even my Mum seemed upset, "why would he do that?" Dad responded "it's the only way they notice us." I didn't understand, "who?" My Dad was annoyed, "the British government. He is a prisoner of this war." I still didn't understand where this war was as they didn't talk about it on the tv like that.

Dad looked directly at me now, "Molly, see now what is happening in Ireland?" "What?" I was eager to know. Mum was cross, "don't you dare fill her head with that old tripe! We live in England you can't say those things." His chest had puffed out. "I have and I will continue." "I'm only here as I was pushed out of my own country. Our people are dying Clare, why can't you see it?" My Mum's face was concerned, "I don't want anyone to die." I felt sad aswell.

Dad was firm, "You're just like the British government, you won't listen either." My Mum looked upset and she went red. She looked at me and I was frightened. It seemed so serious but I didn't understand why. She didn't say anything back to Dad. I'd not known things were that bad until I heard about it in my Aunt's house. In Ireland my relatives had talked about the suffering of the Catholics in the north openly. It seemed more real now because of how my Mum and Dad were acting.

Mum turned to me with fire in her eyes. "Go to bed now." I jumped up and ran out of the living room. I shut the door and stood to listen but I couldn't hear anything. I ran up the stairs in to Jenny's room. She was reading. She sat upright when I came in. "What have you done now?" She was smiling and sighing at the same time.

I was annoyed "Nothing! It's this man in prison in Ireland not eating. Jenny nodded, "Oh... Yes, Bobby Sands." She wasn't smiling now. I nodded and sat down on the single bed. I liked it in here even though it was the smallest room. Jenny was lucky that she didn't have to share with Kitty.

I sat crossed legged and waited for her to speak. "What's it about?" Jenny was very clever so I knew She'd know. She looked unsure. "Well Ireland was split into two parts. The south, which is where we went. They want the English to leave the north and for Ireland to be a whole country again.

But there are lots of people in the North, the other part of Ireland, that want the country to be English. They are mainly Protestants. The Catholics are fighting with them because they are not getting the same rights with housing and jobs. They protested and it led to violence. Our Government sent the soldiers there but it has made things worse.

It is against the law to protest or fight with the army. So, people are being put into prison for their beliefs. They say they are prisoners of war. Others say they are violent criminals that need to be punished." I was frightened, "Is it a war then, like Dad says?" Jenny considered my question, "it's how you view it." I asked "what do you think?" Jenny was unsure, "It was wrong what happened in the past but I don't like what they are doing now either."

I asked her what she meant. "The bombs in Guilford, Birmingham and Marylebone. Well, you may not remember but innocent people died." She turned back to her book. I sat on the bed and thought about what she'd said. I still didn't understand. I would write and ask Saoirse. She'd be able to tell me. She seemed to know a lot about this stuff when I met her.

#

I was really excited about the Eurovision song contest as it was in Dublin. Dad's usual cheerful tone was gone, "there are more important things going on in the H blocks." When we watched the news, Bobby Sand's photo was on the TV again. Next to his face it had the number of days that he had been on hunger strike. Mum looked worried and Dad was angry. "they will listen when he steps up and wins the election for Sinn Fein."

He went out and we stayed at home for the Eurovision song contest. England was great and had to win. We were shouting at the TV and jumping up and down when Bucks Fizz won, *You gotta speed it up, And then you....*" Mum had to tell us to shut up and calm down before the neighbours complained.

The song was great and I couldn't stop singing it. I was singing it and doing the dance with Lizzy and Amy in the street. "*see some more.*" The bit where the skirts came off which made us laugh. Then we noticed the man who lived at the top of the street walking towards us. He was swaying as if he was very drunk. He usually was and his sons only came out when he was in a good mood.

We moved back to the fencing to let him pass on the pavement. He was laughing and mumbling to himself. We didn't say anything. I looked down my long hair covering my face. I was hoping he would go away. He stopped and pointed at me. I lifted my head slightly. I was scared as I'd been told that he hit his children with a belt when they were naughty.

He leaned towards me. Amy ran off calling for her Dad. He leaned in closer, "I'm glad he's dead." I was confused but I didn't say anything. I didn't know who was dead. He was laughing "that Irish bastard, Bobby Sands." He leered into my face "I know who you are, the runt of the ole Irish Mick." I was crying but I couldn't get away. He seemed to be all around me. His breath smelt dirty and it was hot against my face.

Suddenly the man was pulled away by my friend's Dad. "Big man aren't ya, picking on a child. Go on home before I get angry. Come on girls" indicating Lizzy and me. Amy was already on their doorstep watching us. I didn't go in to their house. I ran across the road and into my house. I went into the kitchen to find my Mum but she wasn't there. I turned back down the hall and into the living room.

Mum was watching the TV. When she saw my face, she put out her arms. I went to sit on the sofa next to her. I was shaking and crying. I was so scared. She hugged me and asked what had happened. As I told her she was stroking my hair. She was shaking her head. Her voice soothed me and I stopped crying, "This is what makes things worse." I didn't understand that but I felt better.

Then Mum said "my god your hair is knotty." She went to the mantelpiece and took down the brush. "Come on and I will get those knots out." I got up and stood beside her. She brushed her fingers through my hair aswell as the brush.

Then we heard the front door open. Dad called as he popped his head around the door "Clare, is Molly here? I've just seen the man across the road." he stepped into the room when he saw us. Mum stopped brushing my hair. She seemed to speak to my Dad without words. He looked down at me and smiled. "Who's the girl with the beautiful hair?" and I smiled too.

Mum was very clear that we were to stay away from the nasty man up the road. She told us all not to be running around the streets but to play in the garden or the park. Jenny and Kitty turned away not very happy with me. It wasn't my fault what had had happened. I asked again, "why was he so pleased that a man was dead?" I really wanted to understand. Mum shook her head, "it has nothing to do with that." I was ready to ask another question. "Molly, be a good girl now and stop bothering me."

I followed Kitty into the living room and asked her what it was all about. She sighed, "it's only the boys up the road Dad, just being drunk again." which didn't explain anything.

I went upstairs and stood at Jenny's bedroom door. When I asked her, she shook her head, "Molly, he is just a horrible man. Don't think about it anymore." She smiled sadly at me. I knew that it did have something to do with the man that died. I wished there was someone that would tell me.

We watched the news and they were talking about Bobby Sands death. Dad was shaking his head, repeating "66 days." The newsreader stated that there had been riots after the hunger strike. Dad tilted his head upwards, "what do they expect." He was pleased that so many people attended his funeral. It made me feel sad. Dad was angry and Mum seemed upset but not in the same way. I couldn't work it out. They were both troubled with what happened and with each other.

It was just something else that didn't make sense. I wished that I was clever like my sisters but they were older. They seemed to know what was going on too. Though no one would tell me. I hated being the baby. Mum became more tight-lipped and white-faced especially when the news was on. She didn't like us watching the news anymore. I only really liked to see it as it meant I was staying up late.

Mum was being strict about it now. On one Tuesday night she seemed to forget. Men had escaped from prison. Dad felt that it was justified. My Mum was distraught, "for god's sake, they had guns and were shooting guards. They could've killed someone." Dad's response was always the same. "What do ye expect this is war!"

Mum sighed. She saw that I was going to ask a question and was adamant when she pointed at me, "bed." Kitty was happy that I was being sent to bed and smirked at me. This time Mum did catch the look on her face, "All of you."

Jenny looked up from her book and then stood up. Kitty was arguing. "That's not fair I don't even care about Ireland. I agree with you Mum." Mum was not placated. Kitty's pleas didn't work this time. Kitty pulled my cardigan and lifted me up and half dragged me to the door.

Dad wasn't happy. "This is their heritage. You're hiding it from them is all wrong." As we left the room, Mum was sighing again, "We live here now and I haven't the good memories that you have." Dad was saying "oh I, us being thrown out onto an *ol boreen* was grand was it?" I shut the door and thought I would ask Dad what he meant, when Mum was not there.

#

There was news about rioting in England now. Some not far from us. Shop windows were being boarded up at the end of each day. It seemed the British government was upsetting the people in England too. As well as the fighting, there were lots of job losses. The news said that it may all be linked.

The new woman prime minister seemed to be making the situation worse. No one seemed to like her. Everyone had been happy that a woman had got such an important job before. I heard then that she had been sent a letter bomb, though luckily was not hurt.

Our teacher asked us to write a story about all the good things that happened that year. I struggled to think of anything as it all seemed liked bad news. I remembered that the London Marathon had been a huge thing. It had never happened before. I'd been in awe of all those people who could run that far.

I couldn't really think of anything else and I looked forward to see what other people might have written. The Eurovision song contest had been good but that just reminded me of the man up the road. I didn't want to think about that.

#

There was so much on the news now about the Royal wedding. Apparently, Lady Diana's dress was going to be amazing. Dad was deflated "It's wrong talking about weddings when hunger strikers are dying." Mum was cross, "Would you let her alone, let her just see something nice for a change." She was also worried about the rioting, it was all over the country and nothing seemed to be able to stop it.

People everywhere were really angry. We all watched the wedding and the dress was amazing, the train was so long. I wished that we were going to Ireland again this summer. As we had gone at Christmas, we just had a week in a chalet. It was a good holiday but I hoped that next year we would be going back home.

#

I looked for Lizzy and Amy on the street after school but they weren't there. I knocked on their door to ask them to play out. Their Mum opened the door. She told me they were not going out to play anymore. I thought she might ask me in. Which would be great, they always had lots of sweets. She seemed conflicted, "People will start to think we are sympathisers too." I must have looked confused and screwed up my eyes as I do when I don't understand.

I was looking up at her. I pushed my fringe out of my eyes thinking I need a haircut. She smiled, "it's not you but Molly people are dying." I didn't know what she was talking about. "Who died", there hadn't been any funerals at church recently. "Molly the bombs in London." I remembered the soldiers that had died.

Then there had been a car bomb. After the wimpy thing, I'd been worried we wouldn't be allowed there for a treat again.

I didn't know how I was to blame. It didn't seem fair that I couldn't play with my friends because of it. "Molly we can't associate with the IRA." I turned away not even sure what the IRA was. I knew it didn't have anything to do with me. I saw my Dad coming back from work. I ran up to him "What's the IRA?

Part 2: Chapter 6 - War in England (1982)

I was so excited being back on the ferry and this time it was summer. Jenny looked unimpressed. Kitty was not happy and she got annoyed at my excitement, finally shouting at me, "Will you shut up Molly." Mum intervened but with no real conviction, "Will you leave her alone Kitty. And you, Molly, calm down." Then she suggested that the three of us go and look at the sea. I knew she had had enough of us.

Jenny left her book on her chair as we knew someone would take her seat otherwise. We went to the door to the side of the boat. It was hard to open as the wind was strong and it banged behind us. Other people were walking quickly along the deck, heads down.

We looked over the side and the waves were really high as usual. The white of the waves was being churned up by the wind, it looked very angry. Kitty was gleeful, she grabbed my shoulders, "don't fall over the side." I was scared that she might push me in so I ran inside.

I slept for a while but my Mum woke me as she knew I wanted to see the boat going into the harbour. She came with me and when I leant on the barrier, she pulled my hair back to stop it flying in the air.

She looked wistful. With tears in her eyes "You know your name means star of the sea?" I didn't know that but it made me happy. I was not sure that I liked the sea. I was worried I would disappoint my mum if I said that. My mum wiped her eyes. It must have been the salt in the air, not tears as what she had said couldn't make her sad. I looked into the half-light and watched the boat being drawn in by the arms of Dun Loaghaire, welcoming us home to Ireland again.

The weather was not much better on the land but there was some blue sky under the grey clouds. The journey was long and boring but we did get off the coach so we could get some food. Dad was smiling and stretching his arms towards the sky and he pointed out a rainbow, "With a bit of Leprechaun luck you will be able to go swimming at the beach this year."

#

We did get to the beach but not the next day or the day after. I stopped in awe to look at the spectacular scene. The beach was so wide and long. I could see for miles and there were mountains in the distance aswell. I was mesmerized by the sand, the long grass and the blue sea. It was by far the best beach I'd ever seen, although it was really cold and I had goose pimples.

The sun was shining today but it was still windy though, there was no rain, yet. I expected it as it had been raining every day before. The weather didn't seem to bother anyone apart from me. As I shivered, I saw lots of children running around in their bathing costumes, not bothered by the cold in the slightest. The waves seemed so far away as the beach was vast. The Atlantic Ocean was wild but lots of people were swimming or rather bouncing in the waves. Looking at it I didn't think I was the star of that sea.

I was so busy looking at the sea that I didn't see anyone approach me until I heard, "Ye name is Molly?" There was a boy standing on the beach to the side of me. I could hear that he was sneering at me, I didn't want to talk to him. I didn't look up at him, hoping he would go away. He continued to stand by me so I had to look up. I saw that he was taller than me with brown hair and he had piercing blue eyes. He was staring at me, "Yes, what's wrong with that?" He rolled his eyes "and ye are English too." I shrunk back at that.

So, I'm Irish in England and English in Ireland. I didn't know what to say and was pleased to see my cousin appear. She was angry and her eyes were flashing black, "Sean, Molly is as Irish as you and me." He shrugged his shoulders and turned away. Saoirse smiled at me, "beat you to the waves." She ran off and I looked at her long legs running in front of me and knew I wouldn't beat her but I tried anyway.

In the sea, it was freezing and there was lots of splashing. Saoirse was swimming far out in the water. I didn't try to follow her. I had my 100 metres certificate but was not a confident swimmer. The other girls and boys were all friendly so that didn't matter.

After a while I went back to the beach to sit for a minute and a girl followed me to do the same. I was putting the towel around me, "Hello, I'm Mary, what's your name?" I smiled, "Molly." She was smiling, "You're from England" but the tone was not accusatory like the boy's had been. "Yes, we are over from London visiting our family."

Her face was so white underneath the freckles on her face. Her curly ginger hair was wet and shrunk to her head. She pulled me up to my feet, "Let's play catch. My brother is there. Let him catch us."

I put my towel down thinking running would warm me up. The boy obviously heard us as he ran over to where we were standing. He was very tall and had brown hair, brown eyes and the same pale face as his sister. He smiled at me. Mary said, "This is Molly, catch us." I ran away as fast as I could.

I was out of breath and had a stitch so I sat down. I didn't realize anyone was behind me so I was surprised when Mary's brother touched me on the shoulder. "Got you." and he sat down beside me. He was out of breath too. I knew I was defeated and smiled in confirmation of this.

He told me his name was "Robert Elliott." He paused after he said his name and was studying my face. Then he smiled, he seemed pleased by something. Then he told me a joke. I was still laughing when Mary flung herself beside me and then we were all laughing.

I noticed that it was getting colder when Sean appeared. He sneered at me again, "Molly what are ye at?" I was unsure of what was going on. Robert stood up "Sean we don't want any trouble." Sean stared up into Robert's eyes and laughed, "there won't be from me but Saoirse is coming now." I turned and saw Saoirse just behind him. Saoirse didn't acknowledge the Elliott's but it was obvious they all knew each other. She was curt when she said her Dad was waiting. I quickly said goodbye to Mary and Robert as I moved away.

I wrapped the towel around me, and I picked up my bag. I followed my sisters and other cousins who were walking in front of us towards the sand dunes. Saoirse didn't talk while we walked. I was glad that we didn't have to walk all the way back to Granny's house, even though the walk there had been fun. It was colder now and it had taken a very long time. Even the bus seemed to be parked very far from the sea.

Saoirse didn't look happy as we sat on the bus. I wondered what was wrong with the people that I'd been playing with. She looked at me quizzically. "Molly, did ye not know that they are Protestants?" I shook my head not really understanding why I should know that and why it mattered. "If you ever meet anyone called Elliott, just remember he's orange." That didn't make any sense either.

Before I could ask, Sean got on the bus too. He sat on the seat behind us. Saoirse told me that he was a close neighbour to her house and that's why he was there. They exchanged a glance before he spoke again. "This Molly Malone has a lot of learning to do."

My cousin Jonny was laughing and sang "*Molly…my Irish Molly…my sweet acushla dear…I'm fairly off my trolley… my Irish Molly, …when you are near…*" My other cousins laughed too. Annie said "I saw you speaking to the Elliottt's. I think Robert is sweet on you." Saoirse's eyes were blazing and Sean didn't look happy either. I knew I was blushing. I opened my mouth but decided not to say anything.

Then someone else said she could be a Molly McGuire! Again, I didn't have a clue what they were talking about. "*Make way for the Molly Maguires. You'll never see the likes of them again.*"

I couldn't believe how many songs seemed to have my name in them especially as I'd never met anyone that had the same name as me. Annie intervened, "Come on now, she doesn't know anything about land ownership." The other kids didn't seem to know either so she changed her tact. She smiled "and you can see there isn't a bad bone in her, so leave her alone now." Heads were lowered and I knew then that no one argued with Annie.

#

Sean seemed to be everywhere after that. When we went to collect the eggs, he was in the barn. He was looking at us as we entered as if he had been waiting for us, "I think ye need some lessons in Irish history, if ye do want to be Irish." I ignored him and carried on looking for eggs. I turned and was walking past him.

Saoirse sighed "Would ye not give it a rest?"

Sean shook his head. "No, there are things that she needs to know." Saoirse said "Where would you even start, the Nine Years' War?" He nodded, "Well yes, Molly did you know that was when Ireland came under British rule in 1603?" Saoirse laughed, "Jesus, Sean ye have been listening at school then."

I'd gathered all the eggs and had turned to look at him. He seemed different now not as grumpy as he had been before. Saoirse seemed to find him funny not horrible. I decided that he must not be as bad as I first thought. As he seemed eager to talk to me, I sat down to listen.

The bale of hay was scratchy but the floor had some hen poo on it so I thought it was safer. It did seem exciting, what he was saying and in parts he even smiled. Saoirse didn't join in but seemed to know the stories. Some parts sounded familiar to me too. At the end he seemed sombre, "we have had alot battles since and ye will learn them yet."

We had left our cousins on Dad's side to see my Mum's homeplace in the midlands. We drove past the house Mum had lived in when she was a child and it was grand in comparison with my granny's house. We went to see my Mum's neighbour's. The families of my Mum's neighbour's that we met were very welcoming. There was more tea and biscuits. It was raining outside and when we got to the last house it was dark outside.

Mum was smiling reminiscing about her childhood. I was interested as she never talked about this at home. She remembered summers when they were children and when they had been running around together. They talked about the trouble they gotten into with neighbour's farms for going on their land. When they started talking about finishing primary school she didn't join in anymore and I wondered why that made her sad.

Someone said "Sorry, Clare sure that was the year your mother died. God rest her soul. She was so young. It all changed then, eh?" He was looking around but no one spoke and my Mum's childhood friends seemed to be in deep thought. I wondered if that's why she didn't like to come to Ireland. More tea was served and potcheen was offered to the adults. The chat turned to debate, and I knew they were discussing the troubles, again. I was tired and wasn't really listening anymore.

My Dad told them about an English man, who met with the mother of a hunger striker in prison. This Livingstone man had publicly proclaimed his support for those prisoners stating it wasn't terrorism but a colonial war. This seemed to surprise people and they gave wry smiles. My Mum's childhood friend, Jim spoke, "I'm glad that some Englishmen understand *The Cause*."

My Mum spoke for the first time and her voice was raised, I looked up and saw her chin tilting forward which normally meant one of us was in trouble and she had moved forward in her chair too. "I understand *The Cause* but why do people have to die. Hyde Park and Regents Park should never have happened." Jim disagreed "I don't think ye do understand *The Cause*. These acts are necessary to carry on what was started in the partition. This is war and soldiers die." She shook her head, "I know more than you think!"

She paused and swallowed, "And anyone could have died in Belleek, we could *have* been there, we were there last week. Landmines in Ireland; for god's sake!" Her friend responded "Well that's the point, it isn't Ireland, is it? Its British."

My Mum shook her head and looked round, "We need to be going, Maggie will be waiting for us." I knew this wasn't why she was leaving but I didn't care, I just wanted to leave too. I was so bored with the constant talk of *The Cause* which despite all the talking, I thought I would never understand.

My thoughts wondered to my midland cousins who I hadn't met yet. I hoped the weather would get better, from what I could see through the window and the howling of the wind from the chimney, I knew we would be stuck in my Aunts house if the bad weather continued and I was sure *The Cause* would be discussed again.

#

The weather did change and when we got back to Granny's the sun was out. Saoirse was waiting outside; she was swinging on the five-bar gate across the lane. Saoirse asked me about my midland cousins and what I'd done there. I told her that we climbed an Ougham Rock and played with their puppies.

I climbed up on the gate too and as I turned to sit. I could see Sean walking along the hedge towards us. I sighed but Saoirse laughed, "Don't tell Sean about the Ougham rock, he's bound to have something to say about that." I knew this meant something important about Ireland. I was disappointed as I was in no mood for a history lesson.

I greeted him and he acknowledged me with a lift of his head. He then started talking about Gaelic football. I listened to them talking but I didn't join in. I'd never even seen a match. Then I heard Sean sneer, "Wasn't that the day of the Royal wedding?" I was fed up about talking about Ireland all the time. "That was a great day." They just stared at me open mouthed.

As no one spoke I started to hum my favourite tune by Captain Sensible "*Happy talking...Happy talk.....*" Saoirse joined in and we were singing the words then. Sean shook his head in disgust and Saoirse was laughing, "Ok then Sean we will sing something you like instead... U2... *If you walk away,... I will follow.* I heard you singing along on the radio yesterday and you seemed to know all the words." He laughed then joined in, singing loudly.

Saoirse changed the subject and we spoke about TV. Fame was the most popular show. I laughed "I definitely couldn't see any of us in a dance school." Saoirse nodded but then said mischievously "Maybe Molly would though, with the history of her name."

She smiled, "You know Sean, Molly's Mum told me why she called her Molly. Can you guess why? Seeing as you know everything." I joined in with the joke, "Despite all his knowledge, he would never know that!"

Of course, with all the Irish references to consider he would never imagine it was linked to a silent film. As time went on, we were crying with laughter at all his guesses as he got further from the truth. He continued to offer ideas as we walked down the lane. Finally, he gave up and we didn't tell him either. He shook his head, he hated not being right. I wished that he could be fun like this more often.

The next day though the talk returned to Ireland but it was about the history of my surname. It pained him to say that both Saoirse and me, not himself, were related to Red Hugh. This was a story that I did want to hear. He told me about the castle in the next town and fighters losing toes in the bad weather. I easily understood from visiting here in the winter. Sean didn't annoy me as much now with his constant story telling as they were actually interesting.

Later that day, we left Sean and went into town with our families. We were going to do some shopping before we went home to England. The others left me in the book shop as they knew I would be ages looking at the books and stationery. I saw a book about Red Hugh. I was checking it out see if Sean's version was correct, then I laughed to myself as I was a bit disappointed to know Sean was right.

When I looked up, I saw Mary Elliott and wondered if She'd remember me. I was too shy to say hello to her but she looked up from the book in her hand and smiled at me. "Hello Molly, how are you? Are you enjoying your holidays?" I told her it was my last day here and she asked if I would be back soon. I told her that I hoped to be back again next year.

She asked if she could write to me. I loved having pen pals and I was happy to agree. She had a lovely note pad and pen in her pocket. I wrote down my address and she wrote hers on the note pad that I'd just bought. I suddenly remembered what Saoirse had said about protestants, I felt a bit guilty and put the notepad away quickly. I looked around but I didn't see anyone I knew.

Then Robert was at his sister's shoulder. He was a lot taller than us both, he seemed much older. He shook my hand and smiled but I needed to get away quickly. I was hoping that I'd not been seen by any of the cousins through the window. I knew they would be annoyed but I still didn't really understand why.

We were back at Saoirse's house for the last night with my Dads family. I smelt the turf, it seemed more noticeable when it rained. I knew the range must have been on full as the room was warm or it could have just been because of the amount of people in the kitchen. Saoirse was in her normal place on the stool at the range. I was crossed legged on the mat near the range.

My Dad and her father were talking intently again and I could see Saoirse listening to them. I could hear my Mum talking to my Aunty Geraldine in the corner by the window near where I was sitting. I was not listening to either conversation. I could tell that my Mum had half an ear to my Dad's conversation. I could see her sigh and frown at Dad sometimes. The conversation turned to the Birmingham six as it often did. There had been a piece in the newspaper that day and my Uncle was showing it to my Dad who nodded. "Oh I, your man Chris Mullin. He's the one who is going to prove that the six are innocent." Uncle Peter nodded "I, your right there."

Dad was pleased. "He is a great man all together. Has he any Irish in him himself, do ye think? He surely has with his name like that." They all pondered this and there was quiet for a moment as no one seemed to know the answer. My Uncle brought my Mum into the conversation. As he was at the opposite side of the room, he spoke louder and all the other conversations stopped. Even my younger cousins stopped messing about and turned to my Mum. "Isn't your brother in Birmingham now Clare?" They must have been talking about my Uncle Patrick, I'd not met him yet.

Before she could speak my Dad answered, "I, we saw him not so long ago." My uncle Peter leaned forward, "how is it there now? with all the anti-Irish feeling." My Mum answered him saying, "He has made a happy home there. We are all going to see him soon." Indicating me and my sisters. Even I knew that she hadn't answered his question. As to be expected, my Dad stated, "This is his home though. We are all home now." This was something my Mum and Dad really disagreed about. My Mum just sighed. They would never see each other's point of view.

My Dad turned back to my Uncle "Sure, there are certain places that you cannot go in Birmingham so we stayed nearby him. T'was great craic in the Irish pub there." My uncle leaned forward "Still? "as he shook his head. After what they had they had been saying, it might not be a good place for us to visit and made me shiver.

After a long pause, my Uncle Peter was aggrieved, "The English government don't get it, they have never understood that they will never win the war in England if they don't deal with the troubles here first." My Dad was agreeing with him, "How many more people will have to die before they sort this all out. Only when Ireland is whole again, will it all stop." I looked at my Mum as I knew She'd be biting her tongue. It always worried me when she looked like that as I thought that she might not want to go home to Ireland the next year.

Part 2: Chapter 7 – Clare's mother (1952)

I stood next to my Mammy's bed and looked down at her face, it was pale and clammy. She woke and saw me and gave a small smile "Clare?" I nodded. "I've brought you some soup." With the effort of speaking, it seemed to drain the little colour left from her cheeks. She was getting paler by the day. She couldn't even lift her head now. She was so weak; it was awful to see. I struggled to smile too.

It was hard as I was sad. Also, in disgust which I hated myself for. I'd to say a small prayer, may god forgive me, each time I felt like that. She took a deep breath to fortify herself, "I will try." She had done this action many times before. Though no longer with the conviction that she had before.

I sat down. "The doctor said, you need to keep your strength up and that I need to look after you." I was proud that I'd been picked out to nurse Mammy. I prayed every night that I could make her better but my wishing and praying was not helping at all. I brought a spoonful of chicken soup to her lips. She didn't open her mouth but she did taste it.

I was upset but not surprised as she hadn't eaten anything in weeks. The doctor said that he didn't know what was wrong with her but she just had no strength left. I didn't tell him but I knew she was dying, dying of a broken heart.

It made me so upset about how my older brother, Vincent, could have left her without saying goodbye. I'd never told her or anyone else, what Patrick and I saw.

Even though she was sick Mammy was still very proud of us all. Seamus and Patrick working on their farm. Anne was at Secondary school. Now that I was finishing primary school, I knew that I could look after her properly. Maggie and Emmett would have to go into town without me. Mammy had said "you are making a good little nurse for me," that was before she got so sick. I so wanted her to eat and I tried another spoonful but the soup remained on the spoon. I put the still full bowl on the dressing table.

Mammy moved a bit to look at me so I knew she wanted to talk today. Mammy touched my hair. Long, wavy and brown like hers used to be. "Did I tell you that I wanted to call you Molly." I didn't know so I was very surprised. Mammy gave a little laugh "Your father didn't like it so we named you after the Poor Clare's where your Father's sister had entered. It's a closed convent so you have never met your Aunty Angela." This was all news to me. "It also means bright so I liked it anyway."

"Why Molly?" She smiled "you know my name?" Of course, I thought, its Maggie. "It's Marguerite." I responded enthusiastically, "How wonderful." She continued. "I was named after Marguerite Gale. She was a beautiful actress. She was in a film the year I was born, *How Molly Malone made Good.* I saw the film years later at the Grafton Street Picture House. I'd so many dreams then." She sounded very wistful when she was talking.

Then suddenly she grabbed my hand, "What are your dreams Clare?" I was caught off guard, "I don't really have any....." Mammy was upset by this and so I replied quickly "I would have loved to see the Abbey theatre. I can still see plays at the new theatre. I read in the Champion that Juno and the Paycock is on their now." I'd remembered this in case Mammy had wanted to talk about something.

I smiled "It's so good that you got to meet Yeats. I would like to meet him too." She smiled and her eyes became wistful, then sad again. "Do you still have my book?" I nodded, "O yes Mammy. I will never let anything happen to it." It was true, I treasured the only book that I owned.

"Do you remember the inscription?" I nodded and then we both recited Yeats, The Land of Hearts desire, "*Faeries, come take me out of this dull world, For I would ride with you upon the wind.*" I pondered on the story. "Mammy, why did you love *The Stolen Child?*" Mammy looked like she didn't want to answer. Her lips were moving but she didn't speak. I said a line that she had recited many times before "is it because *Come away, O human child! To the waters and the wild. With a faery, hand in hand, For the world's more full of weeping than you can understand.*" There were tears in her eyes and I was sorry that I'd upset her.

I stood up embarrassed not knowing what to say and she lifted her hand. "You need to rest." Mammy seemed more like herself now. "Be a good girl and sit down." I did as I was told. "Promise me that you will only marry someone you love." I nodded, knowing that meant that she didn't love my father, which I could very much understand.

"Clare?" someone shouted from downstairs. I jumped up "I will be back." I was happy to leave. I was feeling very uneasy hearing her secrets. As I moved away, "is there any post?" My answer was always the same, "not today." The disappointment was etched into her once beautiful face. "Can you help me with a letter later?" I nodded, "Of course," but inside the knots in my stomach tightened.

Not another letter to Vincent, that I'd no address to send too. I went downstairs to finish the stew and do the washing.

When I returned with the pencil and paper, Mammy opened her eyes but shut them again. "Mammy" again she only blinked. I was very scared; this was the worst she had ever been. I ran downstairs calling "Father, father?" He wasn't in the house so I ran out into Mammy's small garden and saw him walking towards me, in the field beyond.

I was shouting his name but he didn't seem to hear me so I ran towards him. When I was close by, I shouted "Mammy's worse." He shook his head "She'd be better off if she got up and did some work. Is the dinner on?" I nodded. "Go ye and get things ready." I was upset, "But father please, its Mammy" I begged. He bellowed "Go on, ye lazy girl" and then he swiped at the back of my legs, where it really hurts.

I knew to shut up then. I ran back to the house crying silently for where my legs hurt but more for my Mammy. Maggie was in the kitchen when I got there. I asked her to sit with Mammy as Father would kill me if I didn't do what he said. I got all the bowls and spoons ready. I cut the soda bread that I'd made with trembling hands, knowing it was not the same as Mammy's. I knew Father would be bound to notice and not be pleased.

At six o clock we prayed the *Angelus* led by Anne as Mammy was not at the table. Father had a great appetite for the stew but no one else was eating much. We were all worried about Mammy but father took the opportunity to say "Eat up children, it may not be nice but ye need to keep your strength up." He looked at me. He laughed unkindly as I would have expected.

They all started to eat, accept Maggie who spoke to father, "Mammy's alot worse, do we need to get the doctor again?" He was indifferent to this news, "I will look in on her when I'm finished." We all ate silently until Father was finished and went upstairs. We all stayed in the same position and waited as we knew he wouldn't stay long above.

On his return, "I, Maggie she is worse. The priest is cheaper than the doctor, he can't do anything with her anyway. Emmett run down and get Father Bryan." He didn't seem to understand the horror of his words.

I turned to Anne and whispered, "Can you clear away whilst I sit with Mammy?" She agreed and I ran up the stairs. No one else felt able to look at Mammy now. I sat on her bed and touched her hand and it was cold. She didn't speak when I called her name but she did stir.

I looked at her glass of water that I'd left this morning. It was still full. I was scared, sure that Mammy would never wake up. The thought of this loss made me shudder with terror. The fear of being alone. I whispered, not a prayer as I should have but Yeats *"Come away, O human child!* I said this over and over as I didn't remember the rest and didn't want to leave Mammy to get my book.

I must have fallen asleep as I saw the light come on and it was darker outside. Father and Father Bryan were in the doorway. They were talking in undertones. I was looking at Mammy but she was still. The Priest moved his arm pushing the air to the left, to let me know to get out of the way. I moved to the window as I wanted to know what was happening.

The priest stood over Mammy and straightened up and confirming "She's gone. Too late for the last rites. Get the children." He looked at me, "Go on then."

I was crying but I hasn't realised until I felt the tears on my face. I wiped them away as I passed father in the door way. The priest was shaking my father's hand saying "my condolences." As I got to the top of the stairs, I heard him say "What are you going to do with all these children?" I couldn't hear Father's reply.

Everyone else was in the kitchen. It was clean so Anne had cleaned up as I'd asked. I didn't say anything but Seamus asked, "Has she gone then?" I nodded and I looked to the floor. I didn't want to see anyone else's grief, its private.

After a few moments to take in this terrible news, I swallowed "We are needed upstairs." Father Bryan was outside the bedroom door and father was standing by the bed looking at us trooping in.

When we were all inside, the priest lead us in a decade of the rosary. "*In the name of the father, the son and the Holy Spirit ...*" and we all continued I believe in *God the Father Almighty, Creator of heaven and earth... Our Father, who art in heaven.... Hail Mary, full of grace.... The Lord is with thee... Glory Be...."*

After the priest had gone and before the visitors came, we needed to ready the body. Mammy was dressed by Anne, Maggie and I. The boys must have lifted a bed into the parlour as it was ready to be made up when we went in. I opened a window and closed the curtains.

Maggie was at the bed with the sheets and I went over to help her. We never said a word. We somehow knew what to do. I think Anne may have remembered Grandma's wake here in this house but I didn't. Then Anne covered the mirror and pictures.

When we had made up the bed. We moved the chairs to the sides of the room so people could sit around. We had been to enough wakes to know this was needed. Then we went into the kitchen to get some food ready. I was glad to see

Eamonn's wife, Biddy and their daughter Veronica already in there. They had brought more food and cups and plates. I was happy that we had someone who knew what to do.

Biddy wrapped the three of us girls in a hug and kissed our heads saying "You poor girlins." Eamonn stood at the fire with father talking in a low voice. Father said nothing in reply.

Later we were called back into the parlour to pay our own respects. I kissed my mother and squeezed her hand. Father Bryan was back and we were praying again. The Hail Mary washed over me and I could only think about the words *now and at the hour of our death,* though I continued saying the prayers with my family automatically.

A telephone call had been made to America to Aunty Mary. I think she and Aunty Anne wanted to come for the funeral but father put her off. I heard him say that they needed no help at home which confused and worried me.

The flow of other people was constant. Making cups of tea and cutting bread. I heard people wonder about why such a young woman would die. "Only thirty-seven!" I heard lots of people say. They deliberated on the cause of Mammy's death. I listened to see if I could hear why they thought she had died. I heard no other reason to suggest that it wasn't a broken heart.

Vincent didn't come home and there was no word from him either. People commented about that when Father wasn't around. Some of them men that had been at the meeting talked in corners and I thought they knew where Vincent was but I could never hear what they had to say.

As I moved around, I saw a couple talking to Father that I didn't recognise. They kept looking at me and the woman approached me "Is it Clare? I nodded. She

was looking at me, which was more in consideration that giving her condolences,
"I'm sorry for your loss." I thanked her and walked away, gathering up cups as I
passed through the house.

   After the funeral, when everyone was gone and the tidying up was done, we
spoke with each other about what might change. Seamus the oldest said nothing.
Patrick said we'd get a woman in. Anne was worried about school. Maggie and
Emmett were less concerned.

   The day after the funeral, there was a knock at the front door. Father
answered it so he must have been expecting someone. They went into the parlour. I
made tea as my father had directed me too. I brought the tea tray in and put it down
on the side table. I set out the cups and plates for the soda bread that Biddy had
made and poured out the tea. As I turned to leave, I saw the unknown couple who
had been at the funeral.

   No one had spoken until that moment. I stopped when my father said my
name. "Mr & Mrs Meaney, have offered you a job." I was surprised but I was off age
so I turned and smiled, "Thank you." I was scared but the woman seemed nice, "We
were not blessed with children and we need help with our business." I was very
confused but waited intently keeping my smile wide.

   I must not show any weakness in front of Father. She was continuing. "I
know your mother was good with a needle, people have told me that she had ye all
turned out nicely." She noted that I'd not a clue what she was talking about. "We
need an apprentice seamstress."

   Mr Meaney turned to father "Is she ready to leave now?" Father replied "Of
course, Clare pack your things you will need to leave when they have had their tea."
I nodded and walked slowly out of the room. I hurried upstairs then ran onto my

bed and cried. The tears wouldn't stop. I didn't understand why I was being sent away. I didn't even know where I was going. I heard a noise on the stairs and rubbed my eyes.

I got Mammy's book from its hiding place and held it to my heart. I whispered "God give me strength to carry on…" as I used to hear Mammy whisper too. I said on the edge of the bed and took a deep breath and vowed never to forgive him….

Part 2: Chapter 8 - Being English (1983)

I never told Saoirse about meeting Mary or that I'd started to write to her. Everyone laughed at me in my house and called me "Molly, the prolific writer." I didn't even tell my sisters about Mary. It probably wouldn't have bothered them, though my Dad may have been upset or told his family.

I worried about what it would be like when we got back to Ireland. Mary was keen to see me. I knew it would be hard to arrange and definitely not acceptable. I was constantly vague with Mary about dates of our holiday, even though I knew when we were going in January.

I hoped she was away as she was talking about a holiday herself. It was just her and her brother which I thought was unusual for an Irish family. They could probably afford to go around Ireland or even a trip to Europe. Saoirse never went away. Dad always said "Sure, why would she need too."

Mum had started saving the new twenty pence pieces to pay for our travelling and spending money as soon as we got back home. When she had quite a few she took them to the bank in plastic bags. She seemed more open to going to Ireland this time. She even said "going home," once after she received a letter from her sister.

She seemed to be getting a lot of other post too. My Mum was planning to spend more time in the Midlands with her family this time. It was a good reason not to make any plans with Mary. The likelihood of meeting her otherwise was slim as she obviously didn't go to mass where we saw Saoirse's other friends and neighbours.

I'd met alot of Saoirse's other friends there as they were in the choir too. Saoirse said that I could sit in the choir this time so I was looking forward to it. I knew my sisters were not happy to be going back to Ireland but me and my Dad were talking about it, whenever they were not around.

#

When we were back at my Granny's house, Saoirse came to find me straight away. She had to go to the shop. When I got outside Sean was there too. He was kicking stones. Saoirse was stern, "Stop that now, what would your Mammy say?" She laughed, "He's lucky that he's the baby otherwise, how would they replace them." I was sure that he wouldn't like that. I didn't when people said that to me.

He looked at Saoirse and he seemed used to her comments. He was smug, "I'm the seventh son of the seventh son and you're just a middle child." Saoirse responded "Well that's an old wives' tale obviously, there's nothing special about ye."

She whipped her round her hair and her body turned, with her nose in the air in an exaggerated pose. She walked tall down the hill. I looked at Sean "what's that about the seventh son?" There was such a lot of Irish things that I didn't understand.

He started walking behind Saoirse and was talking but not looking at me. I'd to run to catch up. "Some people like me have special abilities." He didn't say anymore but I thought he seemed upset that he didn't have any special gifts. I was unsure what they could even be. Saoirse was still in front but obviously listening. She laughed again "Arr now, ye are good at telling stories, tell Molly another one!"

I was still behind but Sean stopped "Ok, I will. I wanted to tell Molly about wool-carding anyway." Saoirse had stopped and turned around. She exhaled "Who's been filling your head with that rubbish?"

He stopped in front of her, his shoulders were pulled back, lifting his head so he was taller than her, though there was only millimetres difference in their height. He matched her superiority, "My father." As if that meant it was definitely a true story. I stopped next to Saoirse and she whispered in my ear, "He's old and senile but Sean seems to forget that." They stared into each other's eyes both thinking they were right.

There was a gap in the brambles and Sean turned into it. I walked behind him and saw him climb a six-bar gate into a field. He was directly in front of me on the gate. I climbed up on it too. I was nervous as I sat on the top bar. I was swinging my legs trying not to show it, when Saoirse started to push it open. I'd to hold on tight with both hands either side of me but even then, I didn't feel safe. Sean jumped off.

I didn't know whether to follow him. He was grabbing the gate from Saoirse and shouted "Did you not see the bull inside." From the smile on her face, I guessed she had. Saoirse tossed her head, "It doesn't scare me." It did scare me; I didn't look around to see it.

As the gate had stopped moving, I climbed down into the field and I as I turned, I saw the bull. It was enormous. I'd never seen anything like it. I turned and ran around the gate that they both were holding. Saoirse pulling it open and Sean pushing it shut. I was in the lane and I called out "Shut the gate."

I stood close to the bush on the opposite side of the lane. My breathing was heavy not from the running but in fear. Saoirse pushing it open, laughing. She was strong and was winning the battle of wills. I looked at the bull and he was looking at me. He seemed to sense my fear. I backed away forgetting how close I was to the bush. I was in the ditch now.

Saoirse and Sean were so busy arguing they didn't see the bull start to walk then run. I screamed and they turned to me and they looked confused. I pointed at the bull. Saoirse was laughing with tears in her eyes but she did let go of the gate allowing Sean to shut it. He was shaking his head and mumbling to himself. The bull was still running but slowing down. His means of escape had gone and it was panting heavily. Saoirse's whole body was shaking with laughter.

I turned away fed up with their bickering and them taking the mickey out of me. She had known it would scare me. I carried on towards the road, to go the shop as intended. Saoirse ran behind me "Molly, I'm sorry." I looked at her face to see if she meant it and she seemed too. Her eyes were no longer sparkling and were concerned.

Sean came on the other side of me. "Now Molly, the Oak boys were Protestants just like your friends Robert and Mary...." They both laughed not believing it possible that I could be friends with them. It also felt like a warning to me, to know what was the right thing to do. I hid my face under my hair as I felt red and didn't want them to guess that they really were my friends, well Mary anyway.

#

On our way back from the shop, when we got to the cross roads instead of going back to my Grannies, Sean ran ahead. Saoirse shouted, "Come on now or we'll be late." I didn't know where I was going and it felt like I was constantly confused

126

around Saoirse. When we got to her house, I expected to see my sisters. I saw my Aunt and moved through some boys that were milling around the bus.

I asked her where my family was. "Well, your father's away to meet his friend and your mother went into town on the bus with your sisters. Your Father told me you would love to see a Gaelic football match." That was news to me. I didn't even know much about normal football so probably wouldn't know what the difference would be and I was not sure that I cared. My shoulders drooped; the start of my holidays hadn't gone well.

I took a deep breath and smiled and followed Saoirse onto the bus. I saw Sean running out of his gate from the next house further up the lane. He was changed into team colours. I realized it was a match as my cousins were also wearing the same jerseys. I did start to feel excited to see the match with the buzz on the bus.

I was cheering on my cousins and Sean, even though he was a strange boy. I laughed at first as they ran, kicking and carrying the ball. Someone was telling me that it was a cross between football and rugby but that didn't help me as I'd never seen rugby either. Someone else was talking about hurling which I'd never heard of saying, "It's much better altogether."

I continued to cheer them on, even when it rained. I was well used to the weather now. It was great to see them win. Sean was smiling for a change as he had actually got a goal. My cousin Jimmy, had scored a point. I realised that everyone I met here was sport mad. Even Mary wrote about Rugby, probably only as her brother played it. She had told me about Ireland winning the Triple Crown, she had been excited but I didn't have a clue about it. I didn't mention sports to Saoirse or Mary in my letters unless it was to congratulate them on their wins.

127

I didn't want to ask anyone on the bus about rugby in case they guessed that I'd heard it from a protestant. It seemed that protestants didn't play Gaelic football. I thought the teams might be related in some way to their parishes. I realised that I could be caught on, the little things. This made me sigh and wondered why everything was so difficult.

There was a lot of mud but Uncle Peter didn't seem to mind that his bus was filthy. They were all singing a song. The boys talked to Saoirse but not me. I asked her why when we got off the bus. She looked at me and said nothing but I could see her looking at my hair. I asked "It's the pig tails isn't it? She was sympathetic, "I know you can't get all your hair in a ponytail. That's not your fault. You do wear runners and jeans so they will get used to it."

I looked down and laughed, "Don't forget the jumper. We hardly ever need to wear these in the summer at home in England." She laughed to "You just need an Aran sweater!" She paused, "Remember you are home when you are in Ireland." I smiled at her as if in answer. Then I promised myself that I wouldn't wear pigtails ever again.

It was late and everyone was having tea and bread before bed. We were at my Aunt Geraldine's house again. I was looking forward to going to bed. It was cold in the kitchen even though there were so many people in the house. My younger cousins had gone to bed now but I was still far away from the range so the room wasn't as warm now.

My Aunt asked me "How is wee Jacinta? I've sent a mass card of course. I'd a short note back from her Mother. We were good friends at school you know. Just like the two of you are." I was sad for Jacinta that her Dad had died. She had taken some time off school and was very quiet, which was to be expected, I supposed. I'd not seen much of her except at mass of course. I'd not even known her mother was

from the same place as my Dad, until then. My Aunt must have seen my surprise.

My Aunt explained, "Sure didn't she used to come every year but not since

her father got sick, god rest his soul." Lowering her head as she did the sign of the

cross. "They haven't been for a good bit of time now." Saoirse was nodding her

head. My Mum was sombre, "I think she will be taking in lodgers to make ends

meet. It will be good for them as it's just the two of them in a big house."

There was a pause as everyone was thinking about the Cullen's. Then we

heard Uncle Peter say, "I agree Hugh, it was a great day altogether when Gerry

Adams was elected." My Mum tutted in disagreement. She normally didn't express

her feelings at Dads homeplace but she obviously couldn't stop herself tonight,

saying. "He's a terrorist, he should be in jail."

The room went quiet and there was alot of shaking heads. Dad looked like

he wanted to say something but at the same time he didn't want a row. It was my

Aunt that responded, "Clare, he's a member of the IRA for sure but anything he has

done, has been for The Cause." Mum half whispered "We will never agree." She

stood and said "Its late we'd better be off now."

The next day Sean saw us sitting on the stonewall in the field next to

Saoirse's house. Saoirse was explaining about Sinn Fein to me. To try to make me

understand the conversation from the night before, about Gerry Adams. Sean sat

and listened too. He was studying my face as Saoirse spoke. I was uncomfortable

but didn't want Saoirse to see that. When she finished, I didn't ask any questions

even though it hadn't made much sense what she had been telling me.

Sean was exasperated with me. "It's obviously time for more lessons. This

should explain it better." Saoirse seemed pleased, obviously it was also clear to her that I didn't get it. I sighed and my whole body was sinking down on to the wall, I was defeated, "What else do I need to learn now?" He didn't notice my response but he looked very pleased with himself and told me "I've only just started... now, The story of James Connolly...

A great crowd had gathered Outside of Kilmainhaim,

With their heads uncovered they knelt on the ground,

For inside that grim prison lay a brave Irish Soldier,

His life for his Country about to lay down,

Then he shouted "T'was the voice of James Connolly, the Irish Rebel.

I was shocked that they remembered all the words. I was sad, it was a terrible story. I didn't really understand what it had to do with this Gerry Adams though. I just listened to Sean as he was enjoying telling me. I watched him talk, he was aminated. His enthusiasm was infectious. I still didn't understand everything he was saying. There really was alot I that didn't know.

After a while, my mind wondered and I started to think of my school uniform for my new secondary school. I was starting in September and this was making me want to go back home. It was boring listening to them both, when they did this.

On my way home I thought of Mary, I hadn't seen her around town so I thought she might be on holiday herself. I felt really guilty as she was meant to be my friend. I was hiding from her and her from everyone. I wondered whether she was doing the same with me. I wished that I could pluck up the courage and ask her about it all. How she felt about Catholics and if she felt she was being treated differently.

I was looking forward to telling her that I'd finished the first book in the Chalet school's series that she had written to me about. I'd read it on the way home. They were similar to Malory Towers which I'd read over and over again. Alicia reminded me of Saoirse. Her friend Darrell was a bit like me. I hoped we could be friends for a long time too. I hadn't read the book in Ireland as I didn't want Saoirse to ask me about it as it was Mary's suggestion. I much preferred these stories to Sean's Irish lessons.

#

It was September and I was scared to be starting secondary school. I walked with my sister up the steep hill. I was pleased that so many classmates from my primary school were also coming too. I was scared of the thought of nuns teaching me. I knew the ones up at the church were very strict. I'd kept away from them as much as possible.

Jenny had got on with them when she was in the legion of Mary but everyone loved her. She had laughed when I'd asked her and Kitty about them, saying that the nuns were praying for me to be like her, not like Kitty, who was always in trouble. Kitty hated the nuns at the church and in school as they were horrible to her. "You will need to grow up quickly and stand up to the nuns."

Jenny told me not to do that. Kitty went on to say that I was too easily swayed and I needed to make my own decisions. Jenny agreed but was nice about it. She said being naive is something I would grow out of. I didn't know how I could do that but swore that I would.

I was so pleased that the form teacher was not a nun. It was a man that taught science. When I got home on the first day, Kitty asked me who I'd got. She was approving "You can get away with anything with him." He didn't seem that way to me. Most of the girls from my primary school were in the same class as me

so it felt normal going in the next day. I'd been glad that I'd not needed to speak to

anyone else on the first day.

When we came into the class, Mr Connor said he wanted to split up the St

Brigid's girls. He directed me to a different seat. I sat by a girl that I didn't know.

She had short ginger hair like Mary's but with no curls. She smiled at me,"Your

school are mad!" I could see what she meant they were very noisy and the teacher

was trying hard to calm them down. I replied "I." The girl looked confused. "Sorry,

I'vebeen in Ireland for my holidays and seemed to have caught some words."

I knew I was pink in the face. I remembered Saoirse getting me to practice

copying her. I was scared that this girl would be scornful. She just laughed "Yeah I

was at home too." Which made me feel ok.

She introduced herself, "I'm Maria Quinn." I told her my name. She smiled

and sang "Molly Malone, ... Singing cockles and mussels...alive alive ohhh. I

laughed even though I'd heard it loads of time before. "I prefer Club Tropicana" She

smiled, "I love Wham too." That made all Sean's stories forgotten for now.

One day, we were watching Grange Hill and my Mum offered me and Maria

a drink. After she came back with the orange squash, she handed me a letter on the

mantelpiece saying "that came today from Ireland." She turned to Maria, "Nonstop

she is, writing to her cousins." I looked at the writing and knew it wasn't from

Saoirse or my Midlands cousins. It was from Mary.

I felt guilty and I was blushing. After my Mum went back to the kitchen,

Maria was curious, "what's going on? Is it from a boy?" I laughed," no" but she was

waiting for an answer. "I write to another girl too." Maria was nodding, "that's great

I have an Irish best friend too."

She looked at me closely "What's the problem?" I told her that Mary was a protestant. Maria's eyes widened "oooh, do your cousins know?" I shook my head. She shook her head too, "well we are in England so don't worry about it now." She did look a bit concerned which worried me.

Part 2: Chapter 9 - Irish History (1984)

We were all watching telly. When Coronation Street finished a newsflash came through. A British soldier had been killed in an IRA bomb attack in Newry. Then the newsreader was also talking about the artillery barracks and the Harrods bombings.

Then he was reminding people that the Governor of the Maze Prison had been shot dead by the IRA not long before. I opened my mouth and Jenny shook her head so that I wouldn't speak or look at Mum or Dad.

When things were reported on the news, English people were reminded of the troubles in Ireland. Dad had said in the past, that some ganger men would use that as an excuse to give Dad and other Irish men their cards. I'd heard them talk about one ganger man holding his wages back. This always which made my Mum anxious and she always warned her Dad to hold his tongue.

Even the ganger man now called Dad names but he laughed it off. "Ol thick Irish mick, "why would it bother me as I'm an uneducated, catholic Irish man so he was only stating a fact." I knew it would bother me but he was more used to it than us. When he was a child there had been a lot of name calling. He had laughed that had been the best of it. He didn't seem bitter which surprised me. I never asked what was the worst. I knew Mum wanted him to move on from that job but Dad had explained there wasn't anything else.

It reminded me of something that had happened to one of Dad's friends in the catholic club, not long before that. I'd slipped in to the bar to get crisps and coke. I heard him say that he had been given his cards and punched in the face for arguing back. The other men at the bar had alot to say about it too. They had shaken their heads saying that it had happened to them all at one time or another. Then they had called the barman over to get him a chaser.

As children weren't really allowed in the bar, I didn't want to be shouted at for being in there. I decided that it was not the best time to ask for anything and I ran out before I was seen. They must have bought the man a few drinks as he had to be practically carried out at the end of the night.

I knew this news would make Mum worried about going to Ireland but that it also would mean that Dad would want to go more. I knew it was dear and hoped that Mum would let us go. If Dad lost his job then we definitely wouldn't go. I was praying every night for Dad and that he would not be shouted at.

I also prayed that we could go on holiday. I knew it's not something that I should ask God as it was selfish. I was really looking forward to my holidays as the letters from Saoirse and Mary really made me want to go back again.

Maria came over to watch the Olympics with us. The athletics were great. There were so many English winners. We were shocked when Zola Budd was running without shoes! It made me want to do my cross country running more. Daley Thompson was winning everything. None of us liked Sebastian Coe as he was arrogant.

It made Dad angry, he didn't like any of it because Ireland had no winners. "We were all forced out of Ireland, in the famine and the war, and we hadn't been able to go back." Mum shook her head and her voice was strained, "that has nothing to do with it at all." Dad raised his eyes. It was the only thing they disagreed on. As he left for the club, he sighed "I'll leave you all to it."

I wasn't embarrassed or worried that Maria had heard the argument. As usual, she just smiled and raised her eyebrows telling me that her Dad was the same. My friends across the road would have told their Mums and they would have stopped us playing for a while.

Despite the news Dad kept his job and we were finally "home" again. I was so excited. It was just me, Mum and Dad this time. Kitty was on holiday for the summer with her friend and Jenny was staying on her own. She didn't seem to mind but I did worry about her. Mum had said she was sensible and had a job now so she didn't want to miss work. Jenny didn't like Ireland so I could see that she was happy to stay home.

It was the same with Kitty, "ergh, it's so cold, wet and full of cows!" She screwed up her eyes and nose at the same time as shaking her head. "I can't even believe you like it!" I couldn't explain to anyone why I did. It just made me smile and give me a rush of love into my heart. I didn't say that to anyone either as they would think I was odd.

Saoirse came to get me straight away. I was so happy to run down the lane with her. The next day they said that we were going shopping in the North. I was worried when I heard that. I could see that Mum was concerned too. We knew that British soldiers had been recently killed.

Saoirse explained to me that we were just going over the border as things were cheaper there and that my Dad needed to get petrol. This was the first time that Dad had driven over to Ireland as we had gotten the coach up from Dublin before.

On the way to my Grannies, Dad had told me that we couldn't go into the North even though it was a quicker way. Mum didn't say anything when he complained, "I can't even drive in my own country." Then he had smiled at the same time as it meant that we were nearly at his home. I was confused that we could go into the North now but not before. I really wasn't looking forward to it at all.

The car was slowing down and Saoirse leaned forward, "Uncle Hugh, wouldn't it make anyone vexed now." "Dad agreed "I, it would now." I looked out of the window and saw tall wooden gates and someone standing at the top. He had a gun, I gasped. I wasn't expecting that. It was much worse than I could ever have imagined. Another soldier came to the car window and Dad rolled it down to answer questions. I heard a couple of words "holiday, shopping, visit."

Saoirse was moaning to herself and sighing alot. We went through the gates and Mum was upset by the encounter aswell as me, "God, I thought they were going to search the car then." Dad joked, "it's a good thing they didn't as I'vea bomb in the back!"

He turned and winked at Saoirse and she laughed. Mum was annoyed, "Hugh don't even joke about it." Her face was both bright red and white at the same time. I sunk back into my seat as I could see how angry she was. Dad turned to look at the road and we were all quiet.

When we got into the town we stopped and Dad let the three of us out. Mum wanted some china. Saoirse wanted to go off on our own but Mum said no. When we were walking along the street, we saw more soldiers. They were really big men with serious faces. Their uniforms really stood out. They walked towards us with their large guns in their hands in front of their chests. I was shocked and scared, Mum looked worried too.

Saoirse was watching them, not in horror but in disgust. I hoped that she wouldn't say anything. We walked past them and I was panicky. There was an eerie feel to the place and not too many other people around. I didn't enjoy the trip and was happy when the door of the big gates closed behind us. Dad was shaking his head and mumbling to himself. Saoirse leaned forward to talk to him as Mum leaned back to smile reassuringly at me.

When we were back at granny's house, Dad was talking about his trip to his mother and Mum was looking concerned. She seemed to be considering things. She was probably as torn as I was feeling, about what we had seen. We had heard about it and seen it on the telly but it was the first time in real life that we both had seen it. I felt really upset about the soldiers being in town. I was scared and uneasy about the trip. I didn't want to go back again.

Sean seemed to find us as usual. It surprised me as he had his brothers and Saoirse's brothers too. I asked him about it, "mine are all older and yours pointing at Saoirse "are a bit younger. It's about the football with them." I thought that he would have liked that too but now that he was older, they didn't play in the same team anymore. He didn't really answer my question but I couldn't always explain things either so I didn't push him. Instead, I looked at the lush green fields and hoped it wouldn't rain today.

Saoirse was quick to tell Sean about our shopping trip. He was looking at me when she was talking, "Are you getting the idea now." He wasn't angry when he spoke but expectant, waiting for my confirmation. I'd twinge in my stomach that hadn't been there before. I remembered when he had told me about the war.

After what I'd seen, it seemed real. I could understand their feelings about the North more now. Sean was looking intently into my eyes, to make a judgement on how I felt. I didn't have to speak my expression seemed to be enough for him to nod and look away.

He turned back to Saoirse, "I saw Robert and his sister in town." Saoirse seemed to groan without making a noise. He turned back to me and gave me a searching look. I knew he was remembering that I'd played with them both at the beach.

I was feeling uncomfortable again as Saoirse still didn't know I was writing to Mary. It definitely was not the time to say we were friends. It made me more unsure about being Mary's friend. I knew she was protestant but she really hadn't anything to do with the war. I tried to justify myself, "I've friends in England that have no religion at all." Thinking of the girls across the road "and they are nice."

Saoirse shared a smile with Sean and they shook their heads. Saoirse explained, "Molly, it's different in London." I felt that I needed to defend my decision, to myself, to have a protestant pen pal. "It's a shame though as I liked Mary, she seems a nice person."

Sean was disdainful again. "That's different Molly. It's what the Elliott's represent, the British and what they did to this country. They stood by and watched and even helped. They took all the land and money and they still have it."

I thought about Saoirse's small house for all those children and Mary's big house. We had passed it when we had gone in to town. I realised now that there was a difference, not just in the history that I heard from Sean. I felt conflicted and ashamed. I didn't say anything in return. Saoirse instructed us, "come on it's raining, let's get inside. They ran to a stone wall and were vaulting over it. I felt the wet now and looked around. I'd not even noticed the rain until then.

I thought we must be miles from Saoirse or granny's houses as we had walked for so long. It could also be somewhere just over the hill or near the village. I could never tell. I would definitely be lost without them. I ran after them. I couldn't work out where we could get shelter. Then behind some trees was a stone house, derelict and missing a wall and part of what would have been a thatched roof. Both Sean and Saoirse were inside.

They were standing up as there was nothing left inside. It must have been very old and not used for many years. I looked around me and knew my Mum would kill me for getting so messy but my trainers and jeans were in a state already from the mud and rain. There were some boxes so I sat down as the rain seemed to be getting worse not better. Sean was moschiferous, "Careful where you sit Molly, the IRA uses this place to store ammunition." I was horrified. Saoirse laughed "I doubt that. Molly, will you look at the state of the place. God, Sean you're so full of shite sometimes."

She turned to me "Don't worry Molly, he sees the IRA everywhere! He will probably tell you he is a member and involved in secret campaigns." He didn't look happy, "well you'd be surprised" in a knowing voice. But neither of us believed him and we smiled at each other.

Sean sat down on the floor in front of me, which looked surprisingly dry. Saoirse moved a box next to me to listen. "Molly, now let me tell you about another Robert. A protestant that would have been worth knowing."

Saoirse leaned forward. Despite my dislike of his story telling, the way he was smiling with pride made me lean towards him too. He started to sing, Saoirse joined in. It was a song that I'd heard before and I knew that I would hear all about it afterwards.

I even sung along to some parts as I realised, I knew it too. .".*And I, Robert Emmett...awaiting my doom,... hung drawn and quartered, sure that was my sentence... the darling of Erin....will die with a smile......but I was arrested ...and cast into prison,... tried as a traitor, rebel and spy. Hero, I live and I'll die.....emerald isle*

Sean sang the whole song. It was longer than I'd heard at home, no one must have remembered all those words so it made me listen more intently. He sang on his own even though Saoirse sang in the choir and had a better voice. It was a sad story. He sang well in the tone of ballads that I knew so well...*Hark the bell is tolling,... I well know its meaning,...... A hero I lived and a hero I'll die*

When he finished the song, he paused and then he began with "on 19th Sep 1803 Robert Emmett was hanged and beheaded.........."I'd to admit that he can tell a story well. I felt the sorrow and could understand why people did feel so passionate about it all. We walked back slowly and in silence after my very long history lesson. I'd enjoyed it but wouldn't want to be tested on it. I supposed enjoyed would not be a word to use. I remembered Sean's mantra it's *our heritage, we cannot forget.*

The dark clouds had passed as we walked back to Saoirse's house. I was still wet. I wondered what my Mum would say about the state of my clothes. Saoirse explained that we were all having dinner together as we walked to her house. Sean walked through the backdoor with us, he went to the tap and took some water in a mug at the sink. He drank it down in one. Then turned, "I'll be seeing ye" and left the way he had come in. I was still surprised even now that everyone came in the unlocked back door.

I was thirsty but I waited for Saoirse to ask if I wanted a drink. "Molly you can get yourself a drink, if ye want one" but she opened the fridge. "Ooh we have red lemonade. That must be because your here!" She wasn't really excited as She'd drink tea which was always on the go.

I poured myself a drink and followed Saoirse who then headed straight into the living room or as they called it, the kitchen. Which must have been because there was a cooker in it. It still confused me as we had been in the scullery which it was far too big to be called that. Saoirse leaned on the side of the range with her cup of tea. I went to the stool beside it and sat down, taking care not to spill my drink on the floor.

As always, the room was full with more people than seats. The arms of the sofa and the floor were being used too, some were my family and some were neighbours. I recognised some of them but didn't remember their names. I'd to search to see my younger cousins. They were sitting with their backs to me crossed legged on the floor with two other boys facing them, who must have been their friends.

My Aunty Geraldine told them "Get ye to the bathroom and you boys' home." I saw the football boots by the press and the mud on their tops which completely covered their team emblem. I realised that it must have been a match and as they were smiling it looked like they had won.

They must have been playing in the rain that we had seen by their dirtied faces and legs. I couldn't even see their socks for all the dried mud. I supposed that they were used to those sorts of weather conditions. At home a netball match would have been stopped if we had the same sheets of rain. Saoirse had told me it was because of the Atlantic Ocean. I didn't really understand that as the beach was not that close.

The dirt on me was obviously nothing that my Aunt would mind but she sighed, "I'll need to wash the floor again; we have visitors coming." I was drying off by the heat from the range. Saoirse was filling it up with turf. She liked to stoke it and to put her hand right inside the hole to the flames, to scare me. She never got burnt though.

"Molly, where were you at, why didn't you come to watch us play?" my cousin Bryan asked as the boys were getting ready to leave the room. Saoirse answered, "sure weren't we in the north with Molly for the first time!" everyone looked at me.

My Uncle Peter who was sat in his usual seat in the corner turned towards me. He interrupted his own conversation with someone who looked to be Sean's Dad. "Well now, what did ye think about that Molly?" I didn't know what to say. I wondered if my Mum and Dad were coming. My answer would depend on whether they were there or not.

I was looking out of the window instead of all their eager faces. I could see the sky darkening again. As always Saoirse started to speak for me. I wasn't sure I would like her answer but I couldn't put into words the way that I felt. I'd been scared and thought it was wrong. "Well of course she couldn't believe it. Nothing like that on the streets of London. The war is being fought here. The British don't care that they are killing the likes of us." Aunt Geraldine interjected "Saoirse... go on into the scullery. I need you to do the potatoes."

The boys had lost interest and were filing out of the room. This time using the front door, baffling me. There were shouts of "I'll be seeing ye"...."Good luck now.".. and "mind how ye go there" Among other strange versions of goodbye as I heard the front door closing and my cousins' footsteps on the stairs.

Two of the men got up. They were much older than my Uncle. Sean's Dad said "If I don't put a hurry on, me dinner will be on the table before I get there." He saluted those of us who were left. Then I followed him and then Saoirse into the scullery. Saoirse was smiling at me knowingly as I still didn't get the door situation.

We were eating the roast beef and boiled potatoes for our dinner. My Mum was saying how Irish potatoes were so much better than English ones. She wasn't just saying that to be nice. She said it at home all the time. When I was very young Dad had always told us about the famine but he had stopped now. The O'Shea's took their opportunity when they could. My older cousins were back and they had alot to say about it.

I thought about what Sean had told me. I remembered that it started in 1845. It had ended seven years later with one million deaths and the same number leaving. Not only for a better life but for food. I knew my Mum would have wished that she had never said anything and would be careful in the future. She didn't like talking about Irish history. I wondered again why that could be. I hoped one day She'd explain like Dad always did.

The hurt in the tone of the O'Shea's could be heard. I understood all about the Corn Laws and rich English landowners who had made a terrible situation even worse. Even Mum seemed to be listening this time although she must have heard the story as a child like the rest of them.

Later after the food had been eaten the usual debate started. Uncle Peter was talking about the IRA and the Maze Prison escape but he didn't mention the man who was killed or the others that were injured. I knew this story from home but this was another version entirely. It continued like this until they started to discuss the Brighton hotel bombing, they were talking as if Margaret Thatcher had escaped death as if it was a bad thing. I didn't like her much myself but felt that was wrong. Again, they didn't mention those people that were hurt.

I was fed up listening to this talk so I went into the scullery and sat with the younger cousins at the table. They were clean now. They told me how the team were doing. They told me they were going to win the league this year.

I agreed to go to the next match and was excited for them as from what they said they were in with a chance. Saoirse had followed me and she didn't scoff but was offering them advice. I knew that she didn't play but she seemed to know what she was talking about. I knew Jonny played too so it obviously was in their blood but I doubted it was from our side of the family.

Yet again, it was raining and I was covered up for the weather on the touchline. I never needed the summer clothes I brought on holiday. I was shouting for my cousins and also cheering on the rest of the team, knowing them from being around Saoirse's house. Saoirse and I were running up and down the pitch following the boys as they were kicking and throwing the ball to each other. It seemed natural now.

Saoirse was directing the boys as if she was their teacher but it was working. They played on and on in the mud and the rain. My hands and feet were wet and cold and getting stuck in the boggy field. The final whistle blew and the boys were so happy, they were in the final. I was excited too, jumping up and down. Bryan had scored a goal to help them win so the O'Shea's were pleased with themselves.

Later that day, Saoirse and I were sitting with her brothers in the scullery. My Dad came in the back door, he was whistling and was in a good mood. My cousins were eager to tell him about the match. He sat down at the table to hear about their victory. This tale buoyed him up more. He smiled and then was singing

145

his favourite song and I joined in *It's my party, and I'll cry.....You would cry too if it happened to you*...It made me laugh because it wasn't really a happy song at all. It made me think about the night before. It had been a nice evening except for the politics as it had ended with songs and the tin whistle. I wished I'd been able to sing along but they were all too good.

Saoirse sighed, "We had better get ready if we are going to the disco." I was taken aback. I didn't know about this disco. I looked at the clock, it was already getting really late. I usually went to bed at 9pm and it was past that already. I was on holiday so I thought that it would be ok.

As Saoirse got ready, my Dad took me back to Grannies to get changed. My Mum and Dad were coming too but they didn't need to change. They said there was a bar at the front of the function room overlooking the Atlantic sea.

Not long after we got back, there was tooting from the bus outside Grannies. My Mum and Dad were already inside it when I got to the front door. Saoirse was hanging out of the back door. She was waiting to close the door of the bus for me. I was glad it was heavy and I couldn't close it myself.

I saw Aunt Geraldine on the front seat of the bus. None of my cousins were there but Sean was at the back on his own. He had changed and washed his hair and looked cleaner than I'd ever seen him. I ducked my head and headed to the back with him. Saoirse joined us. This was really weird. I'd not expected this. I wondered if it would be like the school discos and what sort of music they would play.

As we walked into the small room behind the bar there were lots of teenagers, all about our age. *Prince Charming* by Adam and the Ants was playing loudly. A girl was coming towards me and then dragging me to the dance floor. It was Mary. I was pleased to see her. I didn't know where Saoirse was and I didn't want to look. Most of the songs were in the charts. I listened every Sunday and there were only a couple of songs that I didn't know.

Saoirse found me after a while and tapped me on the shoulder. I waved at Mary who smiled back. We walked towards a table where there were drinks. Saoirse looked perturbed. She handed me the red lemonade. I smiled a thank you as the music was so loud. I was glad as they Couldn't ask me any questions about Mary.

Sean was next to Saoirse, she said something in his ear but I was unable to read her lips. Then in the pause of the music I heard her say "Molly's too polite for her own good." They were laughing and as I turned away, I smiled with relief.

I was standing with Saoirse and Sean and we sang along to some songs. Saoirse laughed at my attempts. She promised "next year if you come for longer, we will get you into the choir to teach you properly." I didn't take offense as I knew it to be true. It would be nice to sit upstairs with the other girls at mass in the big church on the hill.

The slow songs were coming on and the three of us sat down. A boy appeared. I thought he was going to ask Saoirse to dance but it was Robert. He was looking down at me. "*Careless Whisper*" was playing which was a wham song that Maria and I loved. "Molly, would you like to dance?"

I knew if I said yes, Saoirse and Sean would be mad. If I said no, Robert and Mary would be upset. I knew it would be embarrassing to dance anyway. I couldn't say no, just because he was a protestant. I knew he was being brave facing Saoirse and Sean.

I agreed and felt their eyes boring into my back. I didn't know if it was just Saoirse, Sean or both of them. I was uncomfortable dancing but he was being nice and was asking if I was having a good holiday. He had heard I'd been to the match. I agreed that both were great.

"Hello" by Lionel Richie started to play then. I tried to forget Saoirse and Sean. I was thinking about the steps of the waltz. I was looking around the others that were dancing, they weren't doing it properly either.

Then it was the *Irish national anthem.* At home they played *faith of our fathers* at the end of the night but this was the real thing. Everyone stood up. I turned and looked at Saoirse. She was singing as was Sean. I knew they were surprised and disappointed in me. I wished that he hadn't asked me to dance. I hoped Saoirse understood that it was common curtesy by my delaying saying yes. I knew Maria would be excited to hear all about it. I'd never danced with a boy before but I wished that he wasn't a protestant.

Part 2: Chapter 10 - Going Home (1985)

Maggie's stopped to take a breath, "Clare did you hear me? I know it's unbelievable isn't it. "I didn't know if she meant it was because Anne was dying or wanting to see me. Whatever the reason, I just wanted to put the phone down to let myself hear my own thoughts.

My mind was whirling with memories of our father's funeral. Anne hadn't spoken to me then, even though she had had the opportunity. I was very confused. I didn't even know where she lived. Now Maggie's continued chatter showed how intrigued she was by it all. Too curious for my liking. I didn't know if the meeting was for a reconciliation or confrontation.

My mother's face swam into my thoughts. Maggie was chirping away. I really needed to get off the phone. I search my mind and heard a car toot outside. I found the lie that I was searching for. "Sorry Maggie that's the oven, I will have to let you go."

I sat on the stairs and pieced together the snippets of conversations with Maggie, complaining that Anne had changed after going to secondary school. A snob, a madam with ideas above her station! Nothing good. Maggie must have seen Anne but didn't mention her health at all. I sighed. Even being back in contact didn't seem to make us a family that I'd so craved.

Maggie had invited me to stay at her house so I could visit with Anne. It was overwhelming. I went to the kitchen and automatically made the tea. I carried the cup to the back step. I sat down to think about what was the right thing to do. I thought of my mother again, how sad that such a lovely lady had children who behaved like us.

Our years apart just reminded me how I felt in the Meaney's small attic work room. I'd missed my sisters and brothers then and dreamed of us being friends' again. There had been no letters from home despite my weekly updates to them, not that I'd a lot to say.

The noise from the actual sewing machine had been quite soothing or at least it prevented me hearing my own thoughts. It had been my first time not sharing a room. There was no chatting or giggling or shouts to be quiet, just silence when I tried to sleep.

The Meaney's told me when Anne had finished school and got a job in the bank, and when my oldest brother, Seamus was engaged and then it being broken off by his fiancée. No one came to see me and I couldn't get to them. I'd gone to a small town that I'd not known. There were no green fields to look at or the sea.

The couple, my employers, sometimes had to stop me working but it was because there wasn't anything else to do. I reread my mother's book and the books that they had around the house. I saw people on a Sunday at mass but they were strangers and no one was interested enough to talk to me nor I to them.

I'd counted the days to leave since the day I got there. I knew I'd to wait until I was old enough and that it would take a long time to save especially with what they paid me. Also half went straight to my father and I'd gritted my teeth through it all.

I went back to the hallway and sat on the stairs to make a call to Bernie. We had worked together as barmaids and she was more like my own sister. I knew She'd have an opinion.

Bernie didn't work so unless she was shopping, she should be at home to take the call. Bernie didn't like the sound of either of my sisters. Bernie was scornful and cursed the family that she felt I was unfortunate enough to have. When she had had her say, she paused "go and find out what the ol goat wants."

I agreed but I thought about the money, if I went now to Ireland, we probably wouldn't have a summer holiday and I saw Molly's disappointment in my mind. I knew Hugh would not mind me going and he would get in some overtime if he could. He would definitely think it was right that I went to visit a sick family member as he would do so himself. "Thanks Bernie, I will go to the travel agents now." I decided that I wouldn't do the boat this time after the experience of my father's funeral, it would definitely be the plane.

Hugh of course was happy for me to go. Jenny and Kitty could look after themselves, Molly and him too. He was just as curious to know what it was all about especially as he had never met Anne. "Clare, I can understand why there is bad feeling between them all, after that Maggie turfing her own brother outta his home." He felt affronted on behalf of Seamus even though he hardly knew him. The family home had been sold and Maggie moved in with her mother-in-law.

He smiled, "but your brother Patrick was great craic all together." They had all met since her Father's funeral. Once in Birmingham, where he lived and then in Finsbury Park as it was near to Bernie. They had been great nights without any talk of the family.

He also commented "It was grand meeting your man Emmett, last year when he was over, although he is a frail sorta fella, you couldn't find a nicer man if you tried." Hugh was eager to put my family back together as he couldn't imagine falling out with his own family.

His brothers and sisters were so important to him and he wanted me to have the same. I knew that Hugh also thought that more contact by me, with my family would mean more trips home. Especially as that's the only place that Molly wanted to go to as well. I heard all that Hugh had to say but I thought there was more too it with Anne. She didn't seem to care about any of them, not just me.

I didn't want any of my own family to see or feel the tension in the O'Callaghan's so I was happy I was going on my own. The hospital was not far from the station so I could get a bus there and my brother-in-law, Liam, had offered to collect me and I would stay at Maggie's home for the night. I was amazed how quickly things can be arranged, when necessary. The journey over was a good one but the question did keep sneaking in my mind "What did Anne want?"

When I got to the hospital it was strange asking after a sister as I was only recently getting to grips with having a family again. I'd sometimes said that I'd no family in the past as it was better than explaining that I'd no contact with them. I knew that now that was changing but it didn't stop me being nervous about the change.

The nurse was expecting me and knew who I was. She smiled at me, "isn't it grand that you could come all the way over from London, to see your sister. The rest of the family have left so that you could visit with her alone."

I steeled myself and went to Anne's bedside. My older sister looked terrible. She had changed so much since the funeral five years before. I didn't know what was wrong with her and I wouldn't like to ask her directly. I hoped that Maggie could explain later.

I didn't think a kiss or touching her would be right. I just sat down on the only chair there and called her name as she was sleeping. Anne's eyes fluttered open as if even that was an effort. She didn't move her position but her eyes turned towards me. She swallowed and there was no introduction. I understood that there was to be no small talk, about the flight over or about my family, which would normally be expected.

Anne said slowly, "Please be honest with me." I nodded and agreed that I would. I'd no idea what She'd say. "Were you with Vincent?" I was so shocked. I almost shouted "No!", but I knew that this was not the right place or time. "When?" I was confused. "When you left, after Mammy died." I repeated myself and explained that Father had sent me to be a dressmaker's assistant. "I sent you letters! No one wrote back so I stopped writing."

Anne was looking at me closely, obviously unsure of my answer. She shook her head and her lined face got more crumpled. "We never got a letter from you." I shrugged and sighed. "I don't know how but our *loving* father must have intercepted them somehow." I was scornful and the anger for my father must have shown in my face. I hoped that it was obvious, I desperately wanted my sister to believe me.

Anne seemed more able to speak after that. She was galvanised and she was obviously pleased as I could see she had more questions to ask or things to say. "Tell me about it." I told her from the day of the funeral. I left nothing out. I told her how I'd felt and found strength in the telling as I'd gotten through it. Soon though I was crying so I ended it with the boat over to England. I'd nothing to cry about, looking at this woman before me so near the end of her life. Not much older really, than our own mother when she had died.

I stopped "I'm sorry, if I've spoken out of turn. I was angry that no one believed me, about why I left. I was forced." My sister swallowed and said in a low and weak tone. She was shaking her head. Taking a huge effort even with the small movements she was making. "No, I'm sorry. I should have believed you...... but all the whispers and gossip. I thought you have joined Vincent."

This time I did allow myself to express my feelings, "No!" I've no idea where he is either. No doubt somewhere that our twisted father had sent him. Just like him sending me away. He had no heart at all."

Anne now looked even worse than when I entered and I felt annoyed at myself for putting this on a sick woman. I reminded myself that it had been at her request that we meet and that she had asked for the truth.

I started to speak again but Anne sighed heavily but then said quietly and slowly. "I understand. I just felt the whole family was riddled with our father's passion. I was so embarrassed and didn't want to be associated with him or any of them. The singing of those rebel songs. The stupidity of what they had to say about a forgotten Ireland. The violence; particularly against Mammy, you and Seamus. I always wondered why he picked on you three. Anyhow I couldn't bear it and I left as soon as possible for as a faraway place as I could."

I took an intake of breath. I understood her estrangement, which seemed also to be down to our father. First Vincent, then Mammy, me, Anne and Patrick, if you counted him going to England himself so young.

I shook my head, it seemed that my oldest sister didn't have much time left. I needed to gather as much detail as she could express. I listened to her talk about her husband. Then having a son which showed in her eyes of the pleasure they must have given her.

The conversation had really taken its toll and the passion she had expressed had sapped away all her energy. It was hard to see her like that but much worse for her, of course. I was relieved when the nurse returned with Liam. The nurse suggested that we leave after Liam spoke to his sister-in-law.

I listened to their very short conversation. It was between two people who didn't know each other well. Anne had also played with Liam as a child but he must have seemed like a stranger to her now. He was saying, "Maggie has been asking after you. She'll be in the morning, if you feel up to it. Have a good night now."

He turned to me "Come on now, Clare we'd better head off." I repeated the same rejoinder, wishing her a restful night sleep and telling her, "I will be in with Maggie in the morning." I smiled and Anne looked at me intently as I was walking away. Not with the same attitude as before, there seemed a softening and an understanding with just one look.

When we were in the car, I looked at my watch. I was shocked at the time. Liam noted my face "I, its late, the kids are in bed but you can see them in the morning. Maggie is waiting for ye. I'd say it will be a long night so I'll be saying goodnight when we get in the house now, if you don't mind. The milking won't get itself done."

"How did you find her?" I didn't think he meant in her health but meeting her again. Given our conversation, I was unsure what to say. When I didn't answer he shook his head, "She's a puzzle alright." He told me what I suspected. He had known her as a child but she'd gone from the house at a young age too. Before he had started walking out with Maggie and they had no real contact since.

155

I was surprised that Father had let anyone marry Maggie at all. Liam smiled reading my thoughts, "I, I'm from good stock. A true Irish man!" I understood what that meant. I remembered that there were many nights that Liam's father had talked about *The Cause* with my own father. With a bottle of something of course.

I decided not to encourage that subject further. The more information that I was hearing, was explaining what had happened in the gap of my own family history. It scared me and I shivered. To now fully understand that the family's estrangement was orchestrated or due to their father in some way. Maybe I was one of the lucky ones.

Maggie seemed happy to see me. She was full of energy. I knew then what Liam had said about a long night was true. She was busy getting food as she knew I would be hungry. "You must be famished ye poor girl and need tea." She also put the potcheen on the table aswell even though she didn't drink herself. The pioneer part remaining in her still. Liam had the same badge so he must not partake in any alcohol either. Maggie had been around Father longer so she probably only saw that type of drinker. He had been a violent drunk.

Working in the pub I'd seen lots of different reactions to drink. Most of them were happy and singing. Some just came for one in on a Friday to get their wages to hurry home with the fish and chips to their families. Some obviously got themselves into fights and arguments over cards mainly or associations with other people. I was hungry and ate all before me. I listened to Maggie chatter on about her family and then our own brothers.

It was when the tea had been drunk and dinner eaten, that we went into the parlour as in my last visit. The kitchen with the range was overheated but the parlour was cold in comparison. I didn't miss the weather in Ireland, that's for sure.

Liam had already taken my small bag saying, "I will leave it in the room below." I didn't know where that was as the last visit had been a short one. I'd chosen to do the rounds instead of staying in any place to long.

I knew the talk would be of Anne. Maggie asked how she looked and if she was in pain. She didn't linger on that subject and was quick to get on to the real business of why Anne had asked for me. I needed more information first, about our own family history so I asked Maggie about Anne leaving home and how she saw the situation.

I needed to understand how it looked from Maggie's point of view. As expected, Maggie said that after she went to the posh school, getting educated, she just felt that Anne was a snob. Maggie explained her estrangement in the terms that Anne had been responsible for it. She had been I suppose but her reasons were different.

Maggie didn't seem that she had tried much either. There was a gap in their ages but also in the opinions of our father. Maggie being the baby girl had never felt his wrath. She had been his favourite. She had hung on his every word.

I decided to remind her of my story first as it linked into Anne's own disappearance. It was easier to tell now. I didn't care if she believed me or not. I knew that I would not agree, with what Maggie's response. Anne's take on it was very different. I told her to speak to Anne herself as it wasn't my story to tell.

"Is it cancer?" I was unsure of how much time Anne had left. Maggie nodded, "It apparently started in the lungs and spread everywhere." Maggie had no feeling in the telling. It seemed that it was just passing on information to or from a neighbour. I wondered how it would affect me. Someone that I didn't know anymore, was dying.

I put those thoughts aside for later as I'd to continue what I'd started saying, "Anne thought that I was with Vincent, after Mammy's funeral, did you?" Maggie was shaking her head, "I'veno idea why she thought that of you." So, I said "Where did you think I was, did you even ask?"

Maggie shook her head but I think she was the only person their Father would have told. I was angry now. Maggie didn't seem to care about Anne, or me, or her brothers, even though those that were close in distance seemed to be far from her heart, if she had one. She seemed like her father's daughter.

I felt then that I'd to tell her the reason, why Anne had said that she had left. I looked deep into my sister's eyes to see what the reaction would be of Anne's version of events and about why she had left. "Sure, that's alota old tripe, just an excuse. Everyone around here is the same, she just thought she was better than us."

I was disappointed with her response and worded the question differently. "Why does Anne think you are all connected to *The Cause*? Enough for her to want to leave forever?" Maggie looked surprised, "sure we all believe in *The Cause*, don't we?" I didn't know what I believed in. I told her about living in England. How being angry at the English was not right.

Maggie had the same stock answer. That the Irish were only there as they had taken their land away from them. "Did you not listen to Daddy when he told us what he went through? Did he not make ye see the importance of this all is?" She threw her hands in the air to illustrate this point. "The treatment of Ireland by England was wrong, you have to agree that and the treatment of the Catholics in the North is no better now, we still have to fight for our country."

I couldn't disagree with either statement, "but I don't think violence is the answer." Maggie shook her head, "but we have tried everything else and no one listens." I could see Maggie's shock and disappointment on her face that I didn't fully agree with her. I understood Anne's decision now. I was forced to leave and she chose to leave. In our own way, we had both come back to see if we made the right decision, to stay away.

Anne didn't have to worry about keeping in touch as she was dying but I would have a decision to make about my family now. I'd got them back and needed to choose if I wanted to keep them. Maggie had been watching my face but said nothing, maybe my internal struggles were showing on my face. When she finally spoke, it was to suggest that we turn in for the night.

I tossed and turned in the different bed. It was freezing even with the extra blankets. It was easy to tell this was a guest room. I thought about everyone around me believing in *The Cause* to the core of their being. I realised that I'd taken Mammy stance about life and this was why I was different from Maggie. I wondered about the boys and what they thought.

Anne had made her feelings clear she had decided that she had made the right choice with her family. I prayed that she could at least see that I was different. That my beliefs didn't mirror our Father's. I didn't know if there was enough time before she died. Which I was sure would be very soon.

I also prayed that she was pain free. I doubted that. Being unable to breathe can cause panic. Therefore, more distress. I hoped that I'd not added to that distress. Just so that I could make her see that she was wrong about me.

I awoke to the news that Anne had died in the night, which meant I would never know if she had really been reconciled with me. I was sad. I was not heartbroken like when Mammy died. I'd already grieved for the loss of my family when I was in the solitude of the Meaney's. I'd another chance. I decided now that I would take it. I would not be going home as planned. I would stay for the funeral.

The first place to go the next day was to Anne's home to meet her family for the first time. I wished that this had been dealt with sooner. That we had been reconciled. As Anne had left to get away from the family beliefs. I doubted that would have been possible.

They would never believe Anne for the reason why she had left. They would always believe that she had felt that she was better than her sisters and brothers. I knew that there was no point in arguing with Maggie about it. I was also concerned about Maggie's beliefs. The more I knew. The more concerned I got.

My oldest brother Seamus was at Anne's house when we got there. He was standing away from the crowd as he obviously knew no one. The discomfort showed on his face and in the way he stood. Not just because he was wearing a suit but he just looked out of place. I wondered if he had discussed The Cause with Anne and his own response to her. I'd no idea of his political opinions. I thought that it would be unlikely to get him to open up to me.

I was surprised to see Maggie go straight over to Seamus before meeting Anne's family. She gave him a hug which he didn't reciprocate. Even I could see that she had a cheek to expect him to be happy to see her. She had put him out on the street, so to speak, in selling the family home.

Seamus didn't seem too happy to see me either. Liam stepped forward as Maggie moved to stand next to her brother. He offered Seamus his hand. Seamus was forced to accept the handshake. He hardly touched his brother-in-law as his hand was pulled away nearly immediately.

I was not surprised that he just nodded at me. I did the same in return. He seemed to have something that he wanted to say to me. He was holding back. I felt a conversation was needed. I guessed that things hadn't been even sorted out with Maggie yet, otherwise the situation would not be so strained. We were in a semi-circle by the door. It would have been hard to speak to him even if I'd wanted too. Being between Liam and Maggie I seemed as trapped as the tie on his neck, that he kept trying to loosen.

I was on Maggie's left and first to see Emmett come in from the cold. His pink face smiling as he joined the group. Seeing Emmett was a joy. He lived near Seamus. He seemed to have no issues with him. Emmett came to stand next to me. He gave me a huge smile and hug. He stepped forward to hug Maggie and leaned across to shake his brother and his brother in law's hand. A big smile for each of them that they both returned. He obviously harboured no ill feeling to any of them. Which was welcomed by everyone.

Emmett was full of good wishes. He apologised that he had only been over once since their father's funeral. He said he was planning a trip to London and asked if he could check dates later. I smiled thinking my decision so far to give my family a chance seemed to be getting better. He changed the atmosphere of their family party.

Patrick didn't come. He was working in Birmingham. He said he couldn't get the time. He really wasn't expected to attend. Considering everything, it was a good turnout from the O'Callaghan side of the family. I wished that it could have been like that in her life time. I hoped a new connection could be made with the family for me. I was glad that I'd decided to put the past behind us and build our relationships.

I knew it was my Father's fault. Now that he was dead, I wanted to disperse the divide that he caused. To not keep thinking about his rage that we had lived in fear of. I would welcome Emmett to my home. I would keep in contact with Patrick in Birmingham. I would come to Ireland as planned in the summer. I would see Maggie again and try to build bridges with her.

I turned to look to Seamus, I knew that he would be the most difficult. He was angry, bitter and twisted. Their Father and Maggie had mistreated him. Seeing the pioneer badge on his lapel meant that he had taken the decision not to drink aswell. It was very likely that he didn't drink in case he behaved like their father. He seemed so unhappy and unwilling to let anyone in. I would try but I thought it was too late to change his opinion. Being withdrawn was his protection.

As we waited for Anne's family to greet us, I decided that I would find Vincent. I needed to know exactly what had happened to him. I thought that *The Cause* had torn my family apart so it was no wonder I found it so difficult to believe in it.

Part 2: Chapter 11 - Being Catholic (1985)

Saoirse sent me a letter for my birthday with a card. She mentioned the Band Aid Christmas song, saying everyone was still singing it at home. Mary had said the same so I knew that was true. We were too. *Feed the world* had settled in everybody's ears.

I still hadn't told Saoirse about Mary writing to me. I knew that I should but I also knew that She wouldn't be happy. I didn't think that Mary was responsible for the troubles and she never moaned about Catholics. Mary talked about books and music which Saoirse didn't. Saoirse was mad on sports but although I liked cross country running, I hadn't made the netball team so I didn't have much to contribute. Mary and I were so excited that there was going to be another Maeve Binchy book.

Mary talked about brother's sports a lot. Although we had danced at the disco, I'd that no real interest in him. I was definitely worried when Mary suggested that I marry him, for us to be sisters. This thought frightened the life out of me so I tried hard to never mention him. I didn't want to give either of them the idea that I wanted that. The thought of how Saoirse would react to even a hint of a relationship, made me shiver. Me, having protestant friend was bad enough but a boyfriend was definitely never going to happen.

Both of them had mentioned Knock airport opening and they suggested that I fly there next year. I hadn't even been on a plane and I knew that would also be scared to fly. Although the Irish sea was rough, the ferry was the start of me being nearer to Ireland.

I thought it would cost a lot of money too so I didn't even suggest it. Even though it would be just me and my parents again this summer I knew it how expensive it would be and was happy to go with them in the car and come back on the bus and train with my Aunty Mary. I was staying for the whole summer with my Grannie. I couldn't wait.

There were lots on the news about Ireland and the difference between the news about the IRA in England and from Ireland was huge. In March two IRA members were jailed for 35 years for bombing campaign a few years earlier. This news was not taken well by our Dad, he ranted about the war. My Mum looked really worried too but she didn't say why.

The kids in street even made comments about it so I didn't play outside anymore. I either went to Maria's house or she came to mine now. When I told Saoirse about my neighbours, she had alot to say. She was offended on my behalf. If the anti-Irish feeling was bad then, it got even worse. As later in June the IRA had been found to be planning a bombing campaign. Luckily it had been stopped by the police.

Lots of people were saying "Why don't you go back to your own country" Dad didn't seem to care that they were saying it. Instead, he always said to us "I wish I could, nothing for us there now!" I only went places that there were Irish people; to school, to church and the club. I didn't hear it said much to me except in the street from my old friends and their parents.

It did get really bad when Patrick Magee was charged with the murder of the people who died in the Brighton bombing. Even at school, the English girls talked about it. Not too loudly as there was alot of Irish girls there. Sometimes they would taunt us about being in the IRA. Some people responded "yeah we are so you'd better watch out!" Which didn't help matters. Saoirse told me her opinions in her letters but I didn't agree or disagree. I didn't know what to say or think.

My Mum seemed to be taking alot of interest in the news now. Her brother, Uncle Pat, was coming down for weekends. They talked about Vincent who must be another Uncle. I'd no idea who he was. It was unusual as it used to only Dads family visiting but now it was our Mums too. Also, Mum and Dad would go to her family at the weekends. We didn't go to the club as much.

Jenny and Kitty would "babysit" me which really annoyed me. Once when Kitty was out, I asked Jenny where Mum and Dad had gone. She looked at me intently as if to see if she could trust me. It was obviously as secret. I wondered if Kitty knew. I probably was only me that was not being told. I was sick of being called the baby. They even sent me to bed when they stayed up late to play cards. I know trumps is for four people but they never let me play. Jenny sighed and I asked if it was a secret.

Jenny said "not really but if I tell you, don't say anything to Mum, ok?" I nodded in agreement. Jenny told me that Mums brother, our uncle, had left home really young. He hadn't been seen since or even written or rang anyone. They hadn't investigated it before. Since our Aunt Anne's funeral, Mums family were now looking for him.

I wondered why they hadn't told me. In my opinion it shouldn't be a big secret. I asked "Is that this Vincent they are always talking about?" She nodded I asked some more questions about him. I thought it was sad for Mum but didn't really think it about again.

#

Maria had come for a sleepover. Mum and Dad were visiting Bernie. Jenny was in charge. We had taped my favourite song from the radio, Frankie by Sister Sledge. We were singing it at the top of our voices. Kitty had shouted at us and said if we're going to sing, to do it outside.

We knew all the words.... *Frankie, do you remember?* Maria stopped singing. She was laughing and saying that she bet Robert felt that about me. I thought that this whole thing was being so exaggerated. I promised myself to definitely not have anything to do with him this summer. I shook my head as Mary and Maria seemed obsessed with Robert.

Maria was screaming with laughter. My next-door neighbour burst out of the backdoor. Maria stopped laughing. When he came to the fence, we backed away from him. He looked really angry. He was shouting at us for being loud. He was really drunk. He told me to get my Dad.

I didn't want him to know that my Dad was out. We were frozen in fear. We knew he was a very violent man. We had often heard screaming from his wife and son. I saw his son looking out of the window. His Dad followed our gaze. He looked up at the window. He shook his fist at his son and shouted "Get away from that window or you can get my belt."

He turned back to us and shouted "get that Irish bastard out here now. Big man isn't he. I don't care if he is IRA. I will knock his block off for not controlling his children."

Maria and I were looking at each other and neither of us knew what to do.
Luckily Jenny came to the back door and beckoned us in. She was standing back so
the man couldn't see her. We ran inside. Jenny shut the door and locked it. The
man was still shouting and we were scared. Kitty was standing in the kitchen. She
was telling us off for being noisy.

The shouting stopped from outside. He had obviously gone inside. Then he
was shouting for his son. We all looked at each other. I knew the boy would get a
beating because of our behaviour.

Maria asked "Jenny, why is that man so angry?" Jenny answered "He has
just come out of the army." Maria seemly understood immediately "Not Northern
Ireland?" Jenny nodded. I looked at Maria and she looked as scared as I felt.

We heard crying from next door. Jenny said "come on, let's all watch
something on the telly. We can have coke floats too." We all smiled weakly. We were
still worried about the boy next door.

Later when we were in bed, Maria was earnest, "Molly is your Dad IRA?" I
was surprised by the question and said no immediately. Maria said "It's just
something my Dad said..." I waited for her to finish what she was saying. Then she
shook her head, "Fooled ya!" and laughed. I was not sure she really meant it as a
joke.

Maria could talk of nothing other than the live aid concert. She hoped to get
tickets. I was excited as there were so many famous people going to sing. I was
spending the summer in Ireland so there was no way I would have the money for
something like that. We were careful not to talk loudly and only giggled quietly. We
didn't want to get told off again.

Maria was surprised that I liked to go to Ireland for such a long time. Her family went for a week each year to the festival in her Dad's hometown. She had no cousins to go out with as her Dad had been an only child. She joked "Is it to see Robert? Maybe to cause trouble between Mary and Saoirse?" We had talked these subjects to death. I agreed I was mad and needed to "catch myself on." Which made as laugh as our parents said a form of this all of the time.

The journey on the boat was really rough this year. The wind and rain were unbelievably bad. I asked my Mum, "Is it like this on the plane?" She laughed, "Well it's quicker anyhow. Would you like the plane do you think Molly?" I doubted I would and said so. "Your no Molly Malone then?" My Mum was smiling.

I asked her to tell me about it again. I knew that it had been my grandmother's favourite film but I wondered why. She explained that although it was a silent movie, the star was vivacious and determined. Things that her grandmother had admired. She had wished she had had the same sort of life. My Mum looked wistful not for herself but sad. It was probably that her mother had died such a long time ago. I knew I wasn't like Molly Malone. I wished I was more like my namesake.

#

This year we had more freedom. We could go further afield. Not just the village but into town. To the cinema and the diner. We still went for long walks too. For the first few days Sean wasn't there which was unusual. Saoirse said he was around the place. I didn't understand what that meant. I wondered if they had had a row. I was pleased as he could be gloomy sometimes. There was no bickering when he wasn't around too.

When we did see him, he looked bored. He explained that his cousin was staying and said that he was a real pain. Saoirse asked, "Where's he at now?" Sean pointed to his house. Saoirse marched off towards it and we turned to follow her. She was in the house before we had started walking. We ran behind her.

By the time we got there Saoirse was in conversation with Sean's mother. I'd only really seen Sean's father before. His mother was very old looking indeed. I knew that Sean had lots of older sisters and brothers but I was still surprised.

Mrs McDermott was happy to get her nephew out from under her feet. She looked at Sean, "See now, didn't I tell ye that the girlins would be fine with it." She was mumbling about him being inside on a good day. I didn't agree that it was a good day. It was grey and cold but she probably just meant it wasn't raining.

Sean was looking mad and staring at Saoirse. She laughed as she stood behind his mother who was giving out to him for not looking after his cousin who was visiting. We went outside leaving Sean looking furious. When he came out of the house he pointed at his cousin as he followed him. In a pained voice Sean introduced his cousin as Jack. Jack greeted us with a big smile. He had a face that made you think that he smiled all the time.

I compared the cousins. Sean, was tall and stocky. He had pale skin and freckles. Brown hair and blue eyes. As Maria and I would say, very Irish looking. Jack couldn't be more different in looks. Although he was about the same height as his cousin. He had darker skin, lighter hair and brown eyes. Maria and I would never guess he was Irish at all.

Jack must have thought the same about me. Saoirse and I didn't look similar either. Especially as she was so tall and I was so short. I felt sorry for Jack as he must have been bored in the house with only Sean to talk to. Sean suggested we go for a bike ride. We were still outside Sean's house. He had his bike leaning on the wall. He pointed to his shed. Inside there were a number of bikes. They were a variety of sizes. They had probably belonged to his older brothers and sisters.

They looked a bit worse for wear. Sean and Saoirse had a job getting one that would be small enough for me. As they were bickering, I heard Sean complaining about Jack being there. Which was so rude.

I spoke loudly to Jack to cover for Sean's behaviour. He seemed unconcerned about what his cousin was saying. I asked him about where he was from. He told me he was from Dublin. He explained that he was an only child and his Mum had sent him down to his cousins, for company. I laughed when he said that. I thought Sean would be no company at all. He seemed to guess what I was thinking. He raised his eyebrows and laughed too.

Jack asked me if I'd watched the Live Aid charity concert. This was a conversation that interested me. I smiled, "Of course, it was great." He said that he liked U2. This seemed to impress Sean as he looked over his shoulder to appraise the cousin, that he had been living with the past week.

It seemed as if this was new information to him. I wondered if they had even spoken up to now. They started talking about U2s songs. I remembered that Irish history was part of some of their songs too. I groaned internally. Not that I didn't like them but now they reminded me of Sean's storytelling. I was eager to get on a bike then even though I was not confident on a bike, not having one of my own.

Saoirse was putting a bicycle seat down to the bar for me and was agreeing with them about U2. She said that Queen were great too. I'd enjoyed Spandau Ballet the best. From what they were saying, they wouldn't be fans of them or Wham so I didn't mention my preferences to them. Maria and Mary were fans. I always felt more comfortable talking about music with them. I felt a bit out of place and wondered if I would see Mary this year. I doubted it. It was so hard to get away.

Sean was talking about Bob Geldof organising it all and telling us how Ireland raised the most money. Even Saoirse seemed bored with his story, "come on will ye now, let's go to the beach."

I hoped that it would take less time on the bikes as walking took hours! The others were riding off ahead of me. I'd not even got on the bike. I'd passed my cycling proficiency test but I wasn't very good. They were far ahead but they stopped at the crossroads to wait for me.

Everything was going ok. I was keeping up with them until the steep hill. On the way down. I found out there were no brakes. As I turned with the lane, I came off the bike. My knee was dragged along the gravel as I tried to stop. I jumped up quickly and got back on the bike. I'd scraped my knee even through my jeans and there was a hole. It was really stinging. It was bleeding. Tears sprang into my eyes. I couldn't show that it hurt. Sean always said I was a baby. He was far ahead but had stopped to laugh at me. Saoirse had stopped too. She had called back, asking if I was ok. As I said yes, Sean and Saoirse carried on.

Jack stopped and turned to look at me. He rode over to me. "That looks bad, does it hurt?" I nodded but smiled back at him. It was nice that he wasn't laughing about it. "I know he's my cousin but he can be really horrible, eh?" I certainly agreed with that. I nodded in response. When he asked if I was okay to carry on. I took a deep breath and nodded again. We started riding to catch up with our cousins. I was really sore but I didn't want to tell anyone.

It started to rain on the way to the beach. Saoirse decided that we should head back home instead of going the whole way there. I was glad. I was tired and

171

cold. By the time we got back, my knee really hurt. I needed to wash it. I followed Saoirse into her house. Jack went towards Sean's.

Jack called goodbye. I smiled and waved goodbye. Sean just rushed through his backdoor without looking back. Saoirse had shouted out loudly, "It was nice to meet ye Jack. I hope to see ye again soon." I thought it more for Sean's benefit than Jacks. When we got inside, I rolled up the right leg of my jeans. I looked at my knee. It was starting to scab over. It had grit inside so I wet a towel to wash it. I sat on a chair and held my leg out. I could see Saoirse watching me. Saoirse's eyes were dancing.

She seemed to be considering what to say, "well Molly, was it nice to meet Jack?" She was smiling and laughing. I said "yes, I suppose." I was being casual but I knew I was going red. She started to sing Dead or alive song, *You spin me right 'round, Like a record, 'round, 'round,* ' I shook my head but didn't have any response. I looked down at my knee. I didn't want to see her face as I knew that She'd be smirking.

The weather got better and we were finally able to go to the beach. I wondered if Mary would be there. I wondered if there was any possible way of talking to her without upsetting anyone. Particularly Saoirse. I questioned myself whether talking to her or not, would be worse. I decided that if she was there, I couldn't ignore her.

Jack was coming too. He and Sean didn't have too much in common. Sean mainly just spoke to Saoirse. As Jack and I were outsiders, we were left together. It had been hard talking to him at first. Going to on all girl's convent school meant I didn't have much contact with boys. Sean was more like a cousin so he didn't count as a boy. Jack was really easy to talk to. Thankfully, he didn't have the same fascination about the war with England. Sean and Saoirse were leading the way. There was a mix of cousins, neighbours and school friends between us and them.

I hung back from the crowd. Jack waited for me. He asked why I was quiet. I looked at his eyes and I believed I could trust him. I told him about Mary and that I'd been writing to her. I waited to see his response from his face. He looked annoyed. I was mad with myself for telling him. Now he would tell his cousin. Sean would be unimpressed to say the least. He would definitely tell Saoirse.

When Jack spoke though it was with concern for me. He spoke about the futility of the religious divide. He said things had been getting better so the fighting was no longer necessary. If there was peace, the British army would leave the North. He shook his head. "We should be celebrating you trying to breach the divide, instead of having to hide it."

Then he was smiling, "We'll find a way round this, I'm sure." He looked mischievous as if he was forming a plan in his mind. Jack didn't speak immediately. He agreed with me that if Mary was at the beach that I should talk to her.

He knew the problems it would cause so he said he would create a diversion. I laughed with both relief and what possible diversion he could arrange. The possibilities we both suggested were outrageous and obviously unworkable. I was clutching my sides. I was really smiling. I was happy that Jack was here as Sean especially and Saoirse could be serious at times.

The whole group had stopped for a drink. Saoirse was leaning on the wall of the bridge. Under which a small river was running towards the sea. Sean was hanging over the wall trying to touch the water. Saoirse called us over. We made our way through the crowd to them. I didn't lean on the wall as it was low, I didn't think they repaired these roadways at all. I was scared that I might fall in.

Saoirse was eyeing me suspiciously. "What was so funny, what did we miss."

I'd forgotten to have a cover story. I didn't know what to say. I'd my mouth wide

open. I shut it quickly and looked at Jack. He was smiling, "I was guessing what

type of books that Molly reads. She was not impressed by my suggestions! Though

I'm still sure "Milly, Molly, Mandy" is a great book altogether."

I was impressed with his story until someone started singing, *Milly, Molly,*

Mandy sweet as sugar candy I'm in love with you." I was mortified. We both went

red and Saoirse laughed. I'd never heard that song by Glyne Poole before. I just

Couldn't believe that there was another song with my name in it.

When Saoirse stopped laughing. She was humming the tune. I knew She'd

be singing that forever. To make it worse, "I think all those *Sweet dreams books* that

she reads are like that song." I was even more offended as I did read other books

too.

Jack said "I don't know them. When we go to the bookshop in the town you

can show me them. I could maybe show you some other ones that you might like."

Saoirse said "well I won't be with you." "Nor me" Sean agreed. I understood what he

was doing. I knew that I could meet Mary there. When Saoirse looked away, I

smiled at Jack to say thanks.

Saoirse shouted, "Come on will ye, the sun we'll be gone before get there."

She started to pull people onto their feet. She stopped and looked over her shoulder

"We'll leave you too it, to plan your date." She was laughing as she moved on. I was

happy and disappointed at the same time. I was pleased that we had a plan for me

to meet Mary. I wished at the same time that it would be with Jack. Especially as

Saoirse already thought that was what it was.

I told him I was really pleased. I smiled widely with more effort than it should have needed. I felt bad as I should have been happy to be able to meet Mary. I thanked him again more graciously. "Tell me about these sweet dreams books then." The way he smiled, made me think that he knew about them. I was embarrassed, "I definitely don't think there your sort of thing."

I changed the subject and told him what Mary looked like so he would recognise her, to be able to create the diversion. "Pale skin, freckles and ginger curly hair...we might have a problem. We are in Ireland you know." I said "well then, how come that doesn't describe you?" He laughed, "I've Spanish in me." Open mouthed, "That's what my Granny says about me!"

"Not wanting to give a history lesson." Which I understood to be a comment about his cousin, "It's thought that when the Spanish came to Ireland during the Siege of Kinsale or even during the Spanish revolution. Then some people stayed and had families. I think is unlikely to be true... but of course it's similar to the seventh son of the seventh son myth, wouldn't you think." I agreed "Don't tell Sean that though as it is one thing that always sets him off. I wish that the Spanish had left the weather behind!" Jack also nodded at that.

"Now about Mary..." We agreed, that if I saw her, I would sit on my towel. Then he would challenge Sean and Saoirse to have a race into the sea. I was happy with the plan. Also, that I wouldn't have to race into the cold, wild Atlantic sea. The beach was so long and the tide was usually so far out.

I did see Mary straight away. I sat down on my towel. I told Saoirse that I would sit awhile. She was surprised but became uninterested when Jack challenged her and Sean to a race. Jack knew that she was competitive and this was a great diversion.

Jack looked back at me and tapped his wrist. There wouldn't be that much time. I left my towel and ran over to Mary. She was surprised to see me and was smiling. I said the wind was cold. I suggested that we chat in the dunes. We walked over the mound. We Couldn't be seen behind the grass. It was less windy too. If Mary did understand the reason, she didn't say anything about it.

We chatted about books, school and films we had seen. We both loved the Karate Kid and we both sang *You're The Best Around... Nothing's gonna keep you down, ..."* We kept repeating the same words as we didn't know the rest.

We were laughing so much. It had been good to see her. "I'd better find Saoirse now or she will think I'm lost. When are you in town next? We could meet in the bookshop." She thought about it and said Saturday. I said I could get my Mum and Dad to drop me into town at around 1pm. She agreed.

She gave me her telephone number, in case there were any problems. She took my Grannies telephone number too. It was easy to remember as there were alot less numbers than at home. I hoped that there wouldn't be a problem. I didn't want to get caught out. The plan was going well so far.

I ran towards the sea to paddle a bit so Saoirse would think that's what I'd been doing all that time. A big wave got me; it was freezing. I ran down the beach looking for my towel. Saoirse, Sean and Jack were standing there with their own towels around them.

Before they could question me. I asked "Who won?" Jack started telling a story about how he had won. Both Sean and Saoirse were strongly disagreeing with his version. We ran back into the sea again. We were all splashing each other. Sean and Saoirse still argued about the race on the bus on the way home too.

As Saoirse and Sean bickered, Jack raised his eyebrows in question about how it went with Mary. I smiled in response as I'd met her and it hadn't caused any issues with our respective cousins. They dropped me off at Grannies and they headed back to their houses.

My Mum was having a cup of tea when I went in. She asked if I'd fun and I nodded. "It's only that you seem a bit down." I decided to tell her about Mary. She nodded; her face was concerned. "I can see your predicament Molly. They definitely won't like it here but what they don't know won't hurt them." She said that she wanted to go to town on Saturday anyway. We were going together and Saoirse wasn't going to be invited. I was feeling better now that Jack and my Mum thought it was ok to be friends with Mary.

#

I knew that Saoirse would be asking me lots of questions the next time we met. We were going to the shops for Granny. Saoirse was laughing "so then what's going on with ye and Jack?" I looked innocently at her as nothing was going on between us. "Nothing, why did you think that?" with a twinkle in my eye.

I wanted her to keeping thinking along these lines and know nothing about Mary. I looked slightly disappointed, "Nothing but I do like him, he's fun" which was true. I hoped he was nice enough to keep my secret too.

"Well, he's away home on Sunday so I will set something up for ye both." She looked thoughtful and then started humming." *You spin me right 'round....* I opened my mouth to say something but I was too embarrassed. "What are you planning?" She said, "You'll just have to wait and see." I wasn't sure how Jack would feel about Saoirse's intervention. I knew that he only considered me as a friend.

177

My Mum and Dad were going home on Sunday so there were no questions asked about us all going to town together on Saturday. Saoirse wasn't upset not to be invited. We spent all morning looking at the shops especially at the Aran jumpers. We all laughed as I said I needed one now, referring to the weather. It was also a joke as the prices were so high. We could get one similar in C&A for alot less money.

At lunchtime Mum and Dad went to the pub and I went to the bookshop. Mary was hovering at the cards looking anxious. She smiled looking relieved. "I didn't think you would be able to come." I knew that she meant Saoirse. I intentionally misunderstood her. "My Mum wanted to come shopping anyhow."

We went for a burger. When we were leaving, Mary saw her brother and waved to him. Robert walked towards us smiling at me. My heart had sunk when I saw him. "It's great to see you again Molly. I've heard everything you have been up to from Mary. Are you having a good holiday?" I nodded and tried to smile back.

It made me feel uncomfortable to know that he would know so much about me. I told Mary nearly as much as I told Maria. Jacinta had a different friendship group at school so we didn't talk as much anymore. It was good to have someone else's opinion on things. Saoirse's letters were not the same as we talked of football, my cousins and Sean too.

I didn't like the interest that Robert showed in me. I also thought of Saoirse and Sean's anger, if I was involved with a protestant boy. It definitely wasn't worth the trouble that might cause. I felt that I should move on quickly, now that we were out in the street. I didn't want to be seen with Mary.

"My Mum and Dad will be waiting for me so I will have to go. I will write to you Mary." She said She'd write too and waved goodbye. I didn't want to hug her in case Robert expected one too. I walked towards the pub to see if I could find my parents. I thought with concern about Saoirse's and Sean's feelings on the Elliott's. I wondered if Jack would be bothered, I hoped that he would be for a different reason.

I appreciated his cover story but was disappointed that was all it was. Jack was so nice; he would already have a girlfriend. Saoirse's promise about Jack didn't happen as he left early. With him gone, it left me with Sean's stories. He never preached in front of Jack.

I dreaded more and more about how they would react if they found out about Mary. Sean's stories were becoming more about the present and what was on the news. It wasn't just Irish history anymore. He seemed more interested in that than anything else now. Not music or the football which he had at least spoken about before.

I still had fun with Saoirse when Sean wasn't there. I was glad that he had to help his father on the farm. It was only him and one brother left at home now. Sean must be listening to his father's stories more now as he was working alongside him.

I knew his Father's opinions from hearing him talk to my Uncle Peter. They were certainly pro-IRA. I was starting to suspect that his Father may have been involved in *The Cause* in the past. Which didn't bode well for Sean. I hoped that I was making a mountain out of a molehill. As everyone always said I did.

Part 2: Chapter 12 - Mary (1986)

I smiled at my younger brother as he got off the train. His smile was wide. He kissed me on my cheek and I hugged him. "Thanks for having me Clare, I really appreciate it." He wanted to see the sights but not today. He would be tired and hungry after the boat and train. I'd food waiting at home. I knew Hugh would want him to go down to the club to meet everyone but he wasn't much of a drinker.

He was still slight compared to his brothers. Their father had often called him the runt of the litter and said he was more like a girl than a boy. Their father also mentioned the death of his brother Padraic, who died in the Black flu. He'd always sneered, "he was weak and anguish looking too."

Emmett had seemed to let it go over his head. I doubted that. If I still remembered every word. He must too. I remembered the beatings my father gave me for such silly things. No one had said anything for the fear of it happening to them. When I didn't cry, he got bored. It was hard not to but I'd too. If Mammy could do it so could I.

I could tell how excited he was to be in London. I wanted to look after him and protect him like any sister would. He didn't have much baggage so he carried his suitcase easily onto the tube. Hugh would have been with us but he had overtime that would mean Emmett would have a good holiday.

We had been in correspondence. I now knew what had happened to each sibling. Some of the stories I was not impressed with but this was not the time to discuss them. It was all going to be about finding Vincent. Hugh had asked at the club, of course and the pubs in the area. We had already checked with the Irish Centres in Camden Town and Wood Green. No one had heard of Vincent O'Callaghan. I thought that he must have changed his name.

Emmett knew some of the older lads, neighbours, that had left Ireland from their village and the surrounding towns. Vincent had been to school with them. Emmett was going to try and catch up with them. They didn't have many addresses. That was fine as they knew the pubs and clubs they went too. I hoped that they may have seen or heard something.

It was not unusual for an Irish man to change his name. Work was hard to come by and a name might hold a reputation, that needed to be forgotten. Emmett was an instant hit with the girls. He had remembered my updates about them. He smiled and gave them compliments. Jenny so clever. Kitty was the life and sole of any party. Molly with her sweet disposition and dark skin like her Dad. He said to her, "you're like meself." He spoiled her as they were both the youngest.

I included sightseeing with the pub visits as that's where the information would be coming from. I was glad we were looking now as the girls were older. It seemed like I was out of the house all the time. Thankfully, Jenny and Kitty were working. Molly spent all her time in her room listening to Capital Radio. Sometimes with Maria now. Jacinta was in a different class and had new friends. I was sure they would come back together again; childhood friendships were very important.

She was constantly talking on the phone about this junior best disco they were going to. Molly had been ecstatic when her Uncle Emmett had given her

181

enough money to buy an outfit. He nearly choked when he saw what she bought, illuminous green cords and a bright yellow blouse to go with it. We didn't laugh to her face but afterwards we did. It was a godsend as these trips around London were not fruitful. The week was up and he was going to Birmingham to stay with Patrick. They all hoped he would have better luck there.

Hugh drove Emmett up to Birmingham. Emmett promised to update me on any progress he made in finding Vincent. There was a big Irish contingent there aswell. "You know Clare, I didn't want to say anything till now. I asked around and there's a job in Kilburn and digs too. I can be a mechanic anywhere. I fancy it to be London now. Great fella the owner. He's from the next town along to where I work now. I think he asked about me. I got the thumbs up." I was so happy I was crying.

"That will be great to have you here. When are you coming back?" He was smiling, "a couple of weeks maybe. We can spend more time looking for Vincent. We must be able to find him somewhere." He looked confident. I was concerned about the little progress we had made. I knew that Irish men talk in the pub and on the building sites. If he's out there someone will know him. That's if he wanted to be found.

#

Saoirse wrote to me to tell me that they had the whole week planned. It was the Mary of Dungloe festival. I'd never heard of it but I was looking forward to going. The Drifters were playing which was great. Everyone liked their songs. There was going to be a disco in town and the open-air cinema too.

When I told Maria, she was envious. She said nothing like that happened where she went in Ireland. Her eyes were twinkling and I knew what she was going to say. "Well, is it going to be Robert or Jack or someone new this year." She was giggling. "As well you know, there's never been anything with Robert or Jack. Especially not Robert. The older I get the more he gives me the creeps." I shuddered "erg."

"You'll never get a boyfriend if you act like that." I rolled my eyes. She conceded "I know. I'm one to talk. Robert seems nice. He may be your only chance." I threw my pillow at her. "If Roberts my only chance then that means there's no chance. Imagine me saying that I'd a protestant boyfriend. I can't even tell them about having a pen pal." Maria nodded and we laughed. "Is Jack going to be around at all?" I said "I don't know. I'm not asking Saoirse as she will have to ask Sean. That would be sooo embarrassing."

We carried on playing the game of life. "My Mum and Dad aren't staying the whole time with my Granny this year. They will be visiting more people. I don't have to go with them. Which is odd, don't you think?" Maria shrugged "thank your lucky stars. Think of all the tea that you won't have to drink. And those horrible cakes." She made to throw up. The thought of the tea made me gag. I grimaced "those pink biscuits too"

Maria started to laugh again, "and your other problem?" I knew she was referring to Mary. "How did you even get to this stage at all. "I said "hum....err, with your advice!" Maria had to agree that she had had a lot to say about the situation. She definitely enjoyed the letters from Mary more than Saoirse's. I read them all to her. She preferred the things that Mary did.

Saoirse's were more serious. She talked about sports, politics and religion. I knew Maria was annoyed with Saoirse for putting me under this unnecessary stress. I bit my lip and Maria said "Surely Saoirse wouldn't be as upset as you think?" I sadly shook my head and wished that I told Saoirse from the beginning.

I was in the queue for the junior best disco looking at everyone else's clothes. I was so happy that Uncle Emmett had given me the money for the new rig-out. Lots of people had the same green and yellow on as me. I was very happy to fit in, as often my Mum couldn't afford the clothes I wanted.

We were singing and dancing already. Maria and I were in a group of girls from our class. I saw Jacinta in front of us with her friends. I smiled and elbowed Maria to let her know that she was there. I shouted her name and we both waved.

Chain reaction by Sister Sledge was playing when we finally got inside. We rushed to the dance floor to sing We talk about love, love, love. They played "it's a kind of magic by Queen after. It made me think of Saoirse and my trip to Ireland. She had written saying she loved the song.

Uncle Emmett was living here now but coming back with us to Ireland for a visit. He was happy when he came around but tired really easily. He was frail looking. I wondered if he was sick. I shook my head and thought that someone would say something if he was. Wham was playing so I forgot any concerns I may have had. I enjoyed every second of the day.

#

While Molly was at the disco, I took the opportunity to meet Emmett for some more investigation into finding Vincent. I met him at Charing Cross. We were going to St Catherine's House. When I'd gone to see the Salvation Army they had said to work backwards and check if Vincent had died. I'd had to sit down as the dread inside me had grown. I'd had these unwanted thoughts before. I'd feared this was true. The nightmares that had awoken me at night. That had plagued my past and had increased with our new investigations.

The man that worked at St Catherine's House was sympathetic towards us. He said that he got quite a few Irish in, looking for loved ones. He was realistic with us. The indexes were only yearly for the past two years and before that it was quarterly which he explained to us was alot to view. He suggested that we start from the date that he left. I really appreciated the help I was getting.

I started the search with a heavy heart. It was not only the scale of the task but what it would mean if we did succeed. We knew that his name might be an issue. We agreed that we would work to his own name and hope that he hadn't changed it along the way. We were tired at the end of the first day. I didn't look forward to going back again. By the end the day the checks were taking less time to do. Not finding anything was a blessing. I prayed every night to god that he should be found safe and sound.

The visits to St Catherine's House in our search for Vincent hadn't produced a death certificate. We hadn't yet met anybody who knew about him. Someone must know if he was dead or alive. We had decided that our next step was to use the holidays to check at Roscommon registry office. We hadn't told Maggie about the search. We would now as we were starting the checks in Ireland. The aim was to leave Molly with her Granny, when we went to the Midlands. I'd to go to my husband's homeplace first or Mrs McDermott would give out. Otherwise, it would just add to the list of her gripes about me.

#

Before they left for Ireland Molly had gotten herself into a state again. It was about her protestant friend, Mary. I'd found her writing a letter to her friend a week before we were going on our holidays.

I was at a loss what to advise my daughter. I knew that Saoirse would likely never speak to Molly again if she found out now. It wasn't just about the religious divide but the betrayal of all these years of keeping this secret. Molly's friend Maria had made light of it sometimes, which hadn't helped.

I was concerned because I knew that Hugh's relatives and friends were sympathisers. Molly's link could be a real problem. I wanted to be wrong but it nagged away at the back of my mind. I was a coward. After years of keeping my own secrets. I was letting Molly do the same. I advised her to either tell Saoirse or tell Mary that they could no longer be friends. It was all because of *The Cause*. I worried that people we knew were more than sympathisers. I wondered if it was being kept from me. I would surely have seen it by now.

I understood that those people living by the border were subject to day-to-day experiences which I'd not had as a child. There had been no protestants near me to get involved with. We owed our own home and farm. Paid for with my mother's money. There was never a question of us being put out on the road by protestant landlords.

I thought about the house being left to Maggie, which had been sold. Since then, Seamus had been helping on a neighbouring farm but it wasn't the same as toiling on your own. Seamus had looked very down on my last visit. I wondered if I could help him. It was unlikely that he could do anything but labouring in London. Hugh would help if that's what Seamus wanted. He was the only one who hadn't opened up to me so I couldn't gage how he felt about things.

#

My Dad was driving us down from Dublin. We were going to the open-air cinema that night and I didn't want to miss it. Mum was irritated, "Will you calm down Molly, we will get there." Dad was saying, "if we could just drive through the north it would be quicker." I knew the drive around the border was longer but it meant that they didn't have to see the soldiers at the checkpoints.

We eventually got to my Granny's house, As I rushed inside my Granny hugged me, "Don't you be worrying now. Saoirse said they would wait for you if they needed. You have plenty of time so. Now, let me look at ye. You look so skinny." Slapping my bottom in disgust at the sight of me. "I'll get some fat on you while you are here." I raised my eyes to heaven and smiled at my Mum. I was so relieved not to miss the film that I could breathe and laugh now.

I just had time to quickly change and was brushing my hair when I heard a beep. I could see Sean but I didn't know who was driving the blue car. Saoirse was in the back seat. The window was rolled down. She was waving and smiling shouting, "Welcome home Molly! Then she started to sing her favourite Molly song, "*Good golly Ms Molly!* She jumped out of the car. "Get ye in the middle, you're the smallest."

I looked inside and saw Jack smiling at me. I was surprised and happy to see him. My stomach rolled and my breath caught in my throat. "How are you doing Molly? It's really good to see you." He sneaked a peek at Sean. I guessed he was more fed up with his cousin than seeing me. Anything for a distraction.

Sean turned and nodded at me as would be his normal greeting. "How are you?" He ignored me and was listening to Saoirse humming. Sean said "hmmm... let me think of what's my favourite Molly song?"

A man turned around from the driver's seat, "There's sure alot of to choose from. It's nice to meet ye Molly. I'm Sean's brother and your chauffeur for the

187

evening." He was putting on an English accent. We all laughed. I thanked him for the lift.

I turned to Saoirse, "what are we seeing? Saoirse smirked as if she was going to say something she shouldn't. "Well not *Milly Molly Mandy* even though it's yours and Jack's favourite." I groaned so did Jack remembering last summer. We both had found out the lyrics to that song in front of everyone.

Saoirse started to sing it now, *sweet as sugar candy... I'm in love* .....and it had been so embarrassing, I went red thinking about it again. Sean said "will you stop with that right now Saoirse." She apologised but in a tone that meant she didn't mean it. Sean didn't respond, he couldn't stop Saoirse doing what she wanted, just the same as the rest of us.

To reduce the tension that was brewing between Sean and Saoirse, which was not unusual, his brother said "what about this...?" He put on a cassette. He started singing it's a kind of magic. Sean and Saoirse sang loudly with the words *This rage that lasts a thousand years, will be soon.... will be soon.... will soon be done.*

It didn't take long to get there. I was so excited I'd never been to a drive-in cinema. Sean's brother wasn't staying so we wouldn't be sitting in the car. He told us that he would be back later to collect us. Luckily it was warmish with my jumper on and I'd my coat ready aswell.

We all got out of the car and he waved, "have a good one." I waved back thinking that no one had even told me his name. I knew Sean had loads of brothers so I would have to ask Saoirse later. Saoirse said indicating Sean and herself "We'll get provisions. Ye" pointing at Jack and I "can find us some seats. "We turned and made our way down the aisle past rows to get four seats together. It was really busy.

The adverts were on. The film looked like it might start very quickly. We were careful not to block people's view or stand on their feet.

Jack put his jacket on two of the seats and then sat next to me. I was asking how long he had been at Sean's and what he had been up to. He answered as he shrugged "Not long. Nothing until now."

"What about Mary? Are you still friends?" I nodded my head. I said "we have been writing all year." He said "and .... Saoirse and Sean, do they know yet?" I shook my head. He laughed as he knew I wouldn't tell them.

He whispered in a conspiratorial tone "Well I should tell you off but it will keep me busy coming up with another plan." I said "but it's mainly so you can block out Sean's stories isn't it?" He laughed, "Molly, how dare you suggest such a thing. My cousin is a knowledgeable young man with lots of principles. We could stand to be more like him!" His eyes danced as he spoke.

Then he paused and his forehead wrinkled. He shook his head, "when you listen to him, you'd think he was a fully-fledged member of the IRA already." He sighed so I worried whether that was likely.

I saw Saoirse and Sean coming with some cokes and popcorn I stood and waved at them. Jack made to move for Saoirse but she said "Don't bother yourself, it's fine." Sean seemed happy with the arrangements. I thought he must really hate Jack to not sit by him but I also thought maybe he liked Saoirse.

I pondered on that thought. He was always around which was odd especially as he didn't seem to like me much. I knew that She'd never like him. If that was true, I felt sad for him. Then a little sad for myself because we seemed to be in the same boat.

Another thought popped in my head, about Sean's beliefs. I hoped that Jack had been making a joke. I shook my head to forget as the film was starting. I was really looking forward to seeing Top Gun. Everyone had been talking about it.

The next day Saoirse and I were on Sean's farm watching him work. They couldn't go anywhere until the chores were done. Jack was also helping with the cows. Sean's father was very unwell and didn't come to Saoirse's house anymore. I think Sean and his older brother had to do all the work now.

Sean had told me that his brother was leaving as he was going to university in September and would be stay at their aunts. That meant Sean would be the only one left to do the work. I didn't know how he would study and do that. I think Sean felt the same. Sean was tired when he had finished and sat down for a rest. It seemed to cover up his worries. After a pause, normal service resumed. "My cousin from Clogga Strand, you don't know him," looking at Jack. "from my Mother's side. He told me what happened down there with the shipment. He was helping of course; all the men were."

I'd heard that the IRA had brought in weapons by the sea so he must have been talking about that. "Jesus Mary & Joseph you talk shite." Saoirse said, "You'll be worrying her Mother, if you tell Molly that stuff. She's already worried about all the talk about the rebels." He said "well it's important that she understands." I assumed that this was about me, not my mother.

We all looked at him. Saoirse with annoyance, Jack with disbelief and me, hoping it was not true. Particularly as I knew my Mum would not be happy if this had really happened. He could be stopping me coming here again. He turned to me and said "have you been keeping up with your studies?" I knew that he didn't mean my school work.

He continued "I've been putting a little test together for you Molly." We all knew what that meant and we groaned. Saoirse said "Will you not leave her alone this year?" Sean shook his head. "I want to test ye both as well. I feel that we are forgetting our history and why we are fighting." We all raised our eyebrows at him and I noted his use of the word "we."

Sean was not put off. "Molly, do you know who was the last king of Ireland?" I knew it was James II but Saoirse's response was to stand up. "That's it, we're off!" Saoirse was walking towards the gate even before I'd a chance to move. "Come on Molly and ye too Jack. You don't have to listen to this shite either, just cos he's a relation."

We looked at each other, got up and followed Saoirse. Sean said "Don't get huffy now because you don't know. Saoirse shouted over her shoulder "James the second!" but Sean continued to question me. "whose son was he though. He was pleased as he thought I wouldn't know that either. I said over my shoulder, "Charles the second." I smirked. I wanted to change the atmosphere.

Sean ran up in front of us walking backwards. He shouted "Who was James the second's son in law then. Jack sighed, "William of Orange. Are you happy now?" Sean laughed. "I suppose you all know that James was catholic then" but he was laughing now, overriding our groaning.

He continued, "ok so you do know he was catholic then... and that he didn't enforce the penal laws?" Saoirse said "Of course we do! Now ye know, we know. Will ye shut up, Sean? Ye can be such an eejit sometimes." Jack and I looked at each other. I know we were both thinking that he's an eejit most of the time!

I didn't know where we were walking but Saoirse was leading the way. She was walking next to Sean and they were bickering away as normal. We came to the same broken house that we had been to in the past. As we walked towards it, it seemed different. I realised that there was some boarding on it now as if it was being protected. I wondered if the owner had wanted to do it up.

We still went inside but I was wary now. When it was derelict it didn't matter that we were there. I said this and Saoirse replied "You are always such a worrier Molly. But you don't need to. We know the owners so we won't get into trouble." She and Sean shared a knowing smile.

I remembered the last visit and Sean telling me about Robert Emmett. I just knew he would be telling me more stories. It was about the Easter Rising this time as it had been the seventy-year anniversary. I let him tell me the story. As usual he had us all enthralled. He told us proudly "My Mothers uncle had fought at the Rising. His name was Sean too. She had known about another Sean McDermott who was executed at Kilmainham Jail on May 12th, so that's why my mother called me after him."

I was surprised that he hadn't mentioned this story before. I wondered if his mother had felt that strongly why she hadn't called one of his six brothers that name. Then I felt bad for thinking that as my Mum had left Molly until last. I remembered that most Irish families were called after their Grandparents, Aunts and uncles first until they ran out of names.

Sean turned to me now, "Another exciting name is your uncle Vincent." I wondered how he knew my new uncles name when I'd only recently found out about him. "There was a Vincent O'Callaghan who fought in the Williamite war. He lost all his land even though he was nobility at the time. That's the English for ye Molly."

"I know now what I said about you was wrong. Ye are as Irish as the rest of us. It's not your fault that you were unfortunate enough to be born there. It's those who pillaged and destroyed our land that are responsible." His chest was puffed out and his shoulders were pulled back. He smiled proudly and the look in his eyes was excited and wild.

I was being facetious, "Don't you always say, you are where you live?" He said "Well you know I've been thinking about that. So many Irish had to leave unwillingly so I will include you in that too. Also, there is something special about you Molly, that I only found out recently." I was surprised to be getting praise from Sean. "You were born on Bloody Sunday. While those protesters were being unjustly killed. Their passion was reborn through you."

I wasn't sure how this passion had impacted on me. I knew that I should be happy that he had finally accepted me but what he said made me nervous at the same time.

Jack looked uncomfortable too. Which didn't help my sense of foreboding. I felt what he was saying was dangerous. I knew that I was being ridiculous. He was just Sean, being Sean. I was proud to be Irish. It should not have made me concerned at all. On the walk home, Jack and I held back. We discussed out plan for me to meet Mary. It also stopped me from worrying about Sean's stories.

I was asking Saoirse what to wear for the festival as I didn't have a clue. She didn't seem that interested so I thought we probably didn't need to dress up. I wanted to look ok so I got out my favourite jeans and a light blue top that was new. When Saoirse saw me, she smiled and was on the verge of laughing. I turned away as I knew that she was going to say something about Jack. I'd my camera with me. It had been the best confirmation present ever and I knew I was lucky to have it.

I explained "I will be taking more photos so I want good ones." That made her smile more "Will it just be Jack, or me and Sean too?" I shook my head and raised my eyes to heaven. I actually wanted one of Mary as she was coming. I'd told Maria that Mary had the same shade of ginger hair which she didn't believe. Maria had said "If she does, I feel sorry for her."

Jack had hatched another plan. He had been smiling when he had said *"If you have a problem, if no one else can help, and if you can find me, maybe you can hire me......* I laughed at his enthusiasm.

As soon as we got there, I'd taken some photos. Saoirse was the only one who seemed to mind. She was quick to take one of me and Jack on our own. She smiled when she said she had seen us chatting separately but as that was about Mary, I was able to deny what she suggested because unfortunately it was true. The Drifters were great fun and we were all singing along as we all knew the songs. *Saturday night at the movies...*

#

When the interval began, Jack jumped up quickly. He volunteered us to get the drinks. At his suggestion I'd called Mary to meet up in the interval. He was as pleased about this as me. He had enjoyed putting his idea together and keeping this secret. It wasn't the same for me. My guilt had increased as the hours ticked by. I was glad the band had made me forget for a short while.

I did enjoy spending time with Jack and away from the politics. He went to the bar and joined the long queue. He waved, "Good luck!" smiling with anticipation of the success of his plan.

I rushed to the stage where the local groups sang. It was alot smaller than where the Drifters were. Mary had suggested the place. I saw her waving when I was still a distance away. When I got to her, she was so excited. She gave me a big

hug "argh it's so good to see you Molly. Aren't the band great live?" I smiled and we

sat down to have a catch up. After a chat I said "Let's have a photo together. I've my

camera here. Who can we ask to take it?" looking around.

Robert seemed to appear from nowhere. I should have known that and it

made my heart sink. He was smiling "I can do that for you Molly! It's great to see

you." He had taken the camera. He was taking a few photos. I'd only brought one

film for the camera. I'd taken some photos already.

To get him to stop, I quickly said "Shall I get one of you two?" Mary agreed

eagerly. She thought her brother was the best brother in the world! At least Maria

could see a picture of him now. Then Mary was saying "Let me take one of you both

and she grabbed the camera from me."

I moved to stand by Robert. He looked down at me "You are looking very

well Molly." I thanked him for taking the photos. Then Mary called to us to smile. I

turned to the camera so I didn't have to say anything else to him. It was great to see

Mary but Robert seemed never away from her side.

The band were started up again, "I have got to go now. I'll send you a copy of

the photos, bye!" I ran fast to the bar. Jack still hadn't been served but he was at the

front of the queue. I went to help him with the drinks. His eyebrows raised in a

question. I nodded. He rubbed his palms together and said as expected *"I love it

when a plan comes together!"* I laughed with relief as much as what he said.

When we got back to Saoirse's house my parents were there. My Mum's

face was drawn. I knew they must be talking about the troubles again. My Dad was

nodding as I listened to my Uncle say "It's just what ye'd expect from the English,

they incarcerate Patrick Joseph Magee for the 1984 Brighton hotel bombing but there have never been any arrests ever made for the Dublin and Monaghan bombings in 1974. More people were injured and killed there but that's ok with them."

There was a pause while everyone thought about what he had said. Sean was shaking his head too, "This is what I keep telling ye Molly?" I wished he hadn't as I'd stupidly told my Mum about his Irish lessons and his boasts about the IRA when he had annoyed me.

Hearing Sean, my Mum's face looked grim. She took the opportunity to say, "Well, Molly's back from the festival now so we'd better get some sleep. Hugh has alot of driving to do tomorrow." Saoirse said "Aunty Clare, can Molly stay here tonight as she's not going with you?" My Mum replied "Well I've been thinking, it's probably best if Molly comes with us. You know, to see my relations too. So, no, I'm sorry Saoirse, she can't stay." I was shocked and upset as we had made plans for the rest of the week.

My Mum saw the disappointment in my face, "It's only a few days and then you'll be back." Saoirse was annoyed and looked at Sean in disgust. My Dad was not happy either but smiled "I, we'll be back in a few days. Good luck to ye" and he followed my Mum out of the door, saluting everyone sitting around.

I followed them and Saoirse came to the door with me. We were leaving by the front door this time as the car was parked at the gate. "Don't worry, we will rearrange things. I will speak to that eejit." She pulled a face at me.

I knew Sean would be in for it now but it wasn't just Sean's fault. If he stopped at least it might help. It was everyone else too but my Mum Couldn't stop them all talking in their own home. Saoirse waved as I got into the car and smiled

calling "Have fun with your other cousins. Seen ye soon, Molly Malone!"

My Mum and Dad we silent in the car. I felt there would be a row when we

got back to Granny's house. Granny was in bed already. I went straight to my room.

I heard low voices, my Dad said "you have really disappointed Molly. You're

spoiling her holiday, for what reason?" She replied in a slow quiet voice. I knew the

signs well. She was trying not to lose her temper. "I don't want Molly listening to all

your talk. About *the war on England'* or *'the troubles in the north'* or 'The Cause'

from anyone especially not that Sean. Have you heard him? I hope to god what he

says about his relations and himself are not true. I just can't take that chance!"

I moved closer to the bedroom door. This was the one occasion that I

appreciated the gaps around the door frame. They kept me cold at night no matter

how many blankets I'd. In an equally low voice, I was now able to hear my Dad say

"She's only hearing the truth. You knew we were sympathiser's when we met. Why

are ye acting so surprised and upset about it."

His tone changed when he revealed, "Just to let you know, I do help find digs

for the lads 'on holiday' so I can help your brother Seamus as you asked. I know I'd

said I stopped. We were both keeping secrets, weren't we Clare? You never told me

that your father was an active member of the IRA." He paused "I wonder what else I

don't know."

I stumbled when I turned away to get ready for bed. I needed to think about

what my Dad had just said. I stood at the side of the bed. My hand covered my

mouth even though there was no one to tell. I would not be able to tell anyone. Not

Maria, Not Mary. Not Jack. I wondered who else knew. I didn't like to think what Sean and Saoirse's reaction would be. I pictured them smiling and looking smug.

My thoughts were whirling around as I got ready for bed. I knew I wouldn't be able to sleep now with the buzzing in my head. I didn't think helping Jacinta's Mum would be a problem, though I did know that my Granddad being a member of the IRA was wrong. It was disturbing to think what he may have done.

I tried to digest this and I was reminded of Sean's stories. I tried to work out when my granddad would have been a member. There was a civil war in the past...I sat up and held my head in my hands. I shook my head. As my Dad had said "What else don't I know?"

Part 2: Chapter 13 – Uncle Vincent (1987)

I'd been so disappointed that we still had had no news on Vincent. At least there was no death certificate in his name in Ireland or England. The pubs hadn't brought much news either. I couldn't believe that there was not one person that knew him or why he Couldn't be found in Medway, Birmingham or London where they knew so many Irish people. I found refuge at Mass and was lighting candles every week and praying every night.

Hugh was helping me but he was still not happy that it was Emmett that had told him about her family's history. Emmett was not much help now. He had found a lovely girlfriend. I liked her very much even though she was a bit younger than himself but she was from a good Irish family.

During another argument, Hugh said "you only care about Vincent at this stage." I took it that he was insinuating that I was not looking after my family. I was angry about that. I'd two grown daughters working and one at Secondary school. None of whom needed that much attention. I still worked part time at the council, washed, cleaned, shopped and cooked for them all, including him.

He shouted, "Go to the priests, get them to say a mass or something. Anything is better than this." I stopped and looked at him. I thought about it and decided that I would try as I'd certainly tried everything else. I nodded and said ok. I was so tired of it all now. Hugh looked surprised that the argument had ended that way.

The next day I knocked at the Presbytery and Father Tom himself opened the door. He smiled and welcomed me in, directing me to the holy water. As I blessed myself with the *sign of the cross*, he indicated for me to go to the parlour behind the normal meeting rooms. I'd only been in the priest's house to get mass cards before and that had been in the front rooms. I was surprised and wondered why.

Father Tom told me to take a seat and asked me if I wanted tea. I shook my head and he began "I'm glad you have come to me. I know you have been troubled." He sat back to listen and I did something I never did and told my story. The priest didn't speak but nodded and shook his head as necessary to confirm that he was listening. When I finished, he said "let us say *a decade of the rosary* for your intention to find your brother." We knelt and Father produced his beads as although I'd some at home, I never carried them or used them. The familiar words rushed over me and they were a release from my worries.

When we sat on the chairs again, Father Tom said "Bless you my child, put your trust in god. We will do a mass for your intention. I will speak to my colleagues here and in Ireland to see if I can help you. You know us priests love to talk." His eyes twinkled. "

Let's do the mass next Saturday evening when you are there. Its shame that we don't see much of the girls now they are working and I know Hugh does too, of course." I was glad that the priest didn't pass comment that Hugh could find time to go to the club. The priest had seen us there a few times.

"It is good to see Molly there every week. She is a lovely girl and doing well at school I hear." He paused and smiled "Clare, I've always wanted to ask you, why Molly?" I felt strange to tell a priest that Molly was a character in my mother's favourite film. When I did, he clapped his hands together. He smiled, "I hoped it was that. It was my mother's favourite film too. God rest her soul. *Molly Malone does good.* Am I right?

I've never seen it, have you?" I nodded. "I did once but not many other people have. I saw it in Dublin before I came over to England. I don't think it's been on anywhere else since." Father Tom thanked me for coming. As I left the house, he said he would pray for me.

All the O'Donnell's were at Saturday evening mass at my request. They could see in the newsletter that the mass was for my private intention. After mass we all lit candles. Father Tom came to find us. "Lovely to see ye all. I have you in my prayers. Clare, I will pop in one night this week, if that's ok?

Not Thursday though, I know you like the old bingo." When I was young any gambling was a sin but as it was played in the catholic club hall here, he would hardly be able to complain. Hugh said "We will have a whiskey waiting father." He replied "Thank you, Hugh that will be grand, so it would."

Father Tom came to the house with no news but another decade of the rosary was said. It was only Molly with me as Hugh and the girls were still at work. He said that he had just popped in before his dinner but would be back again another evening for his drink. He said he was going back home to Ireland for a holiday. He promised to do some investigations for me. I was so happy with all the help I was receiving. I could see Molly was pleased to be in the know and have more understanding of the situation. When the priest had left, I told Molly as much as

201

she needed to know. "I will pray to *St Anthony* as he is lost." I thanked her. That prayer was for lost things not people but I didn't say that.

A week later there was a telephone call from Father Tom. He was excited and said he had good news. Another priest had met Vincent a while back. I was so shocked that I nearly dropped the phone. "He had certainly been alive when Father John left Balham in 1980. Father John said he was going to talk to some parishioners that he kept in touch with from that parish."

He advised me to do a *novena* and I agreed to do the nine days of prayer for my special intention. I continued to sit on the stairs for a long time after I'd replaced the receiver. I was numb. I didn't know how to process this news. We had been looking for so long now.

Hugh was really pleased for me. He was glad that his idea said in the heat of the moment seemed to be inexplicably working. The arguments stopped. The constant talk of Vincent was now being diverted directly to god; in all the prayers I was saying. Hugh said "I, I thanked god myself for his intervention but I'll you let you do the rosaries and novenas. It's been so long I've forgotten how to do them." And then we were both laughing.

When Father Tom came around on Wednesday evening, he accepted a drink. Hugh had one as well. He didn't suggest saying a prayer to the obvious relief of Hugh. The priest sat back on the sofa and smiled thanking them for the drink. I wished that the sofa wasn't so old. We needed a new one. The priest practically sat on the springs. The shame of it.

He didn't seem to mind. He smiled "I think our prayers have been answered. We found someone that knows him. We are getting a message to him. I've given your address and telephone number; I hope that's okay? He travels alot for his job I believe but he should be back soon."

The priest looked at me, I couldn't speak, I was crying without a sound and my body was shaking. I was just repeating "I cannot believe it." Hugh had stood and walked across to the priest and offered his hand. "Thank you so much Father." The priest took his hand and shook it. Hugh turned and walked to the armchair that I was sitting at and placed his hand on my shoulder as if giving me strength. He didn't seem to mind that I continued to cry.

When the priest left, I couldn't even say thank you to him. I was in such a state. I heard Hugh talking to him then the door close. I hoped Father Tom didn't think that I was. I took a fortifying breath, wiped my eyes with the back of my hands and heaved myself up using the arms of the chair to help me rise.

I went straight to the telephone to call my family. I hesitated on who to call first but as I put my finger to the dial, it was Emmett's number that I called. As Hugh passed me, he smiled and stopped to touch my cheek. I looked into his eyes and I was as pleased for him as he was relieved for me.

#

I watched my Mum frantically cleaning the house. My Dad said "sure he couldn't care less what the place looks like." He was shaking his head and then raised the newspaper in front of his face as if hiding as he continued to sit in his armchair.

I slipped out of the room in case my Mum asked me to do something else. I would read until she called me down. It wasn't long until there was a knock on the door. I stayed upstairs, I thought that it's a big thing to meet your brother after all this time and felt that they needed time to chat.

I was still reading an hour later when my Mum called me down. Uncle Emmett had also arrived. Maybe he had come with Uncle Vincent, I didn't know for sure. I'd been so engrossed in my book. I was so lucky to be the first person to get the Firefly Summer by Maeve Binchy out of the library. There had been a long waiting list. I was there all the time so the Librarian knew me well which meant I got the new books first.

I shook Uncle Vincent's hand. "it is nice to meet you." My uncle Emmett fluffed my hair. I said down but they ignored me. I listened to their conversation. They had obviously discussed where he had been for all this time already and were talking about my other aunts and uncles now.

I was really bored and glad when the phone rang. I ran out of the room to get it but no one else moved anyway as they were so intent in their discussion. Thankfully it was Maria. I asked her if she was coming over still. "Yeah, I'll be there in a bit, how's the prodigal uncle?" I thought for a moment, "okay I guess." She told me She'd see me soon.

My Mum came out to the hall heading to the kitchen, when I was putting down the phone and she asked who it was. I reminded her that Maria was coming around. "Oh yes of course, that fine, we are going to the club; do you want to come." I shook my head as now that I was older, there was less people my age there.

When Maria came, my Mum answered the door. "Now, Maria, no singing *Nothing's gonna stop us now*" but she was laughing talking about a song by Starship. "Molly hasn't stopped, since that disco." Maria said sweetly "I know Mrs O'Donnell. God knows I've tried already." I responded "well your just as bad." We went upstairs. We were talking about this junior best disco as it was the best one yet!

We put on the radio and *Stand by me* by Ben E King was playing. As we sang, Maria looked at the wall beside her and started laughing. I looked at her quizzically. She pointed, "What is that?" I thought that much was clear. "It's a poster of River Phoenix." She was teasing me but I didn't understand why. "I thought it was Jack, it looks so like him?" I went red. "No, it doesn't."

Maria sat back and was rolling around on my bed in hysterical laughter. I stood up shaking my head. As I looked at the photo, I saw what she meant. I was infuriated with myself as I really hadn't thought that when I put it up. I wished now that I'd not shown her my summer holiday photos. I knew that She'd never let this go.

My Mum and Dad were arguing again. I wanted to go to my Granny's for a month in the summer. It had been agreed in principle but that was before the news of two IRA attacks near my Granny's house. My Mum was not happy, neither was my Dad but for seemingly different reasons.

I was listening from the hall. "Why take it out on the child? She'll be fine. The men that are dead are the other side, casualties of war. They'd never pick on a young catholic girl on her holidays with her family. Especially not my family." I thought about what he said. I was not sure I liked the sound of it. I knew my Mum wouldn't either.

Sean was still a worry to her but I hoped She'd see that he is just a fantasist and would grow out of it. I knew though that keeping in touch with Mary was the wrong thing to do. I didn't discuss it with my Mum this year as I knew her view already. In Saoirse's letters, her opinions were even more negative against protestants than ever before.

I dreaded to think what Sean would say about it all. I couldn't tell my Mum about Sean and Saoirse opinions as She'd never let me go. My Mum eventually gave in. "Ok I will talk to her. Molly is still so naive. She sees the best in everyone and needs to be more aware of the potential risks."

#

When Mum spoke to me, it was about Sean and Mary aswell as the violence. She was emphatic, "you need to be aware of where you go. Don't wander off, stay with Saoirse." I was exasperated, "Mum I'm not five you know!" I was indignant at the warnings. "Also, you need to take what Sean says with a pinch of salt." I sighed, "I do."

Mum continued "I know that you must still see him as he's Saoirse friend but just be wary of him." I was rolling my eyes to heaven "ok, I will." Luckily, she didn't notice. "Now, I hope Jack is there. He is a nice boy. He's the only one of them who does not go on about religion and the troubles." I agreed with that.

Then came the question that I didn't want to answer. "And what have you decided about Mary?" I was conflicted, "I don't know yet." I was looking down as I didn't want to see the concern in her eyes. I knew the best decision was to end our friendship but I just couldn't do it. I prayed that it would all work out okay, but my feelings of guilt worsened the nearer I got to Ireland

I was so pleased to be on the boat. Dad was fuming about "the never-ending war." Mum was worried about "the terrorism." I'd been scared that it wasn't going to happen this year.

The weather was bad as usual and I expressed my concerns to my Mum, "it's like the hurricane last year." She laughed shaking her head at me, "it's not that bad!" She was smiling and seemed happy to be going home.

I picked up my library book to reread the new Maeve Binchy. Maria and Mary loved it too. I'd to be careful with it. Mum and Dad would bring it back with them. I wanted to finish it again before I got to Ireland as Saoirse didn't think much of these books, even though they were set in Ireland.

She always laughed, "you want to be in the books!" I didn't, especially not these ones as they didn't generally end well. There was a big house near my Granny's but no one lived there. There were no similarities with my own summers. They were all set in the past but I don't think Saoirse even knew that.

I was in a quandary whether to see Mary. Everyone said it was a bad idea, even Maria. She knew I would be there as I came every year. Even though she was not Saoirse's friend, she was a neighbour. She'd hear when I was there. They all knew everyone's business. Even if it was just having visitors from England. I decided to wait and see if she contacted me. I was putting my head in the sand and just hoping it would turn out ok.

I'd missed the Mary Of Dungloe festival this year. I wondered what we would do instead. The weather was so good when I got there, that I didn't even have to wear a jacket. When I'd walked over to Saoirse's house from my Granny's, I saw her talking to Sean and Jack. My heart seemed to rise up to meet my throat. I was so happy to be back.

Seeing Jack again, reminded me of Maria laughing about my River Phoenix poster. I took a sharp intake of breath. She had been right. I imagined what Saoirse would say if she saw it. I walked a bit faster to mask my embarrassment, looking away from Jack, scared he would guess.

The welcome was the same as usual. Just like they had seen me only minutes earlier, not a whole year. Saoirse kept me up to date in her letters so I knew what was going on with her and Sean. She always joked that She'd find out about Jack but never did. Saoirse called out, "we're going into town to do some sightseeing. It's Sean's idea!" I was suspicious but she didn't elaborate.

My cousin John shouted, "Its grand to see you Molly. What's been going on with you?" I smiled. He explained that he was going to drop us off in town. Sean was very pleased with himself, "I'm really looking forward to this." Saoirse got into the front seat laughing. I followed Sean into the back of the car and Jack sat on the other side of me.

I turned to look at Jack reluctantly but when I did, he greeted me with a smile which I returned. I was relieved. I raised my eyebrows expectantly but he shrugged his shoulders to show that he didn't know the plan either. I asked them what they had been up to as they had been off school for a whole month already, getting two weeks school holidays more than me.

Sean didn't respond but looked tired. I thought that he must have been busy on the farm. Saoirse was her nonchalant self, "Not much." Jack said "I was away with my parents to Spain for a couple of weeks." I was impressed, "wow, what was that like?" Sitting close to him now, I noticed that he had a tan. I would have known that he hadn't got that in Ireland. I said this and we all laughed. I noted that Sean and Saoirse were pale as ever. I waited for Jack to tell me what Europe was like as I'd never been.

Sean sighed and I turned to him, "Have you heard this already?" Saoirse answered for him, "of course he's not. Sean would never ask about Jack's holidays. Besides Jack only got here today himself. Now, wasn't that grand timing Molly?" I could hear her facetious tone and ignored her. I looked at Jack he was eager to talk about his holidays. Saoirse and I listened to what he had been up to. It sounded great. We also knew that it would annoy Sean to allow Jack to speak so I asked lots of questions. When I did look at Sean, he was scowling.

When we got to town, we went right through it and over a bridge. We turned up a lane that I hadn't noticed before. John gave us a thumbs up, "Have a good one" as he drove away.

Through some metal railings there was a ruin of what would have been a castle. We walked towards it. The grass was as green as ever but dry as it must not have rained for a few days. Which was good news as I took it that Sean had some information to impart to me, if not all of us. "Ok then, tell me everything."

We walked through the ruins and I listened to the story of the O'Donnell's. I'd heard it before but in the grounds of the castle it did seem more real. We sat down after a while as there really was not that much to see.

Sean was really enjoying his storytelling as usual. Saoirse who, like me was a descendant of the last kings of Ireland listened intently too. As did Jack, even though they obviously knew the stories from school. It was interesting and I was happy to let them chatter on as they all chimed in. It had been a long journey over so I was happy to be out in the fresh air.

In the pause, Saoirse stood up, "I'm hungry." As she expected we all followed her. It was a short walk back into town. Before we crossed the bridge, Sean pointed, "Let's walk by the river first." We made our way down the riverbank. There were bushes and trees near the water so I'd to bat away a lot of midges that were flying around me.

We walked along the river. It was not an easy walk having to negotiate fallen branches and bushes. Saoirse and Sean leaned over and put their fingers in the water and they splashed each other lightly. Saoirse said "Shall we go swimming?"

but laughed. There was lots of stray branches and leaves, we all agreed that was never going to happen.

We walked down by the river's edge for about ten minutes and then turned back. When we got near the bridge, I could see the other side of town. Which is where I normally saw the river from. We went back up the bank and headed to the burger bar.

I was hungry and was looking forward to chips. I laughed as Saoirse ordered curry sauce with hers. We would never do that at home. Sean ordered the same but both Jack and I'd ours with salt and vinegar.

That night my Mum and Dad had a dinner at Saoirse's house as we usually did on our first night. When dinner was finished, Saoirse slipped into the scullery. She indicated with her head, for me to follow her. "Come on, we're going to the forest." I'd never been to the wood behind her home and didn't particularly want to go in the dark but as usual the choice was not mine to make.

She ran up the road to Sean's house. I looked at the hill and it was darker than the sky. Sean and Jack followed her back down the lane. She saw my face and laughed. "There's nothing to be scared off, just a few rats and foxes." I didn't like the sound of that but as usual I did as I was told. I didn't plan to be in there for long.

Sean and Saoirse ran off ahead. I dawdled at the edge of the trees. Jack stayed with me, "You'll never live it down if you don't go in. Come on, I will walk with you." He led the way. It was eerie as we moved inside. It was pitch dark and very difficult to see. There were alot of noises that I didn't recognise. When I looked at Jack he smiled encouragingly.

I could hear Sean and Saoirse running around and expected them to jump out at me any minute. It wasn't fair as they lived here and had probably been in here hundreds of times before. As expected, Saoirse crept up behind me and roared. I screamed as she had expected. I turned on my heel, "I'm off." She ran back into the wood laughing. Jack followed me towards the field below.

We still could hear the pair of them making loud noises as we moved away. They would stay to see who would scare the most. When we got to the stone wall between the field and garden, we Couldn't see them at all. We sat down to wait. Jack looked mischievous, "So do we need to make secret plans for you to meet Mary this year?"

I shook my head slowly, "I really don't know." He acted disappointed and hung his head as if he was upset. "Oh no, I've been thinking up ideas all year." I doubted that, "ok, tell me." To my surprise he had come up with some plans. I was really pleased. I didn't know what to say. I was glad he had thought about me or the situation at least. "Well, let's just wait to see. We have options." I swallowed as he chatted on.

We were so engrossed that we didn't hear Sean and Saoirse creep up behind us. We both shouted out when they jumped up from behind the wall as this time, it was unexpected. Saoirse was laughing at my shrieking and then considered us both, "so what were ye whispering about?" I was relieved that she hadn't heard the conversation. I was concerned that we were so nearly caught out. We both shrugged innocently.

I knew She'd think that meant something else. She was breathing heavily, "Let's all get a drink." Jack and I looked at each other. We were both relieved. We followed them through the backdoor. I heard Saoirse warn Sean to watch what he said around my mother. Reminding him what happened last year.

We took our drinks into the kitchen to sit by the range as we were cold now. My Mum was telling my aunt and uncle about finding her brother. Saoirse, Sean and Jack seemed very interested in the story too. Everyone was smiling and nodding their heads at the good news.

My uncle asked "Where's he been at then? My Mum was unusually relaxed, "working all over apparently. He never settled anywhere." My uncle continued "but where did he go straight after he left your family home?" She was vague, "We only saw him the once before coming away. We will catch up again when we get back. I'm just so relieved that he is alive and well." My aunt said "why wouldn't he be?"

My Dad changed the subject saying "We are planning to go to the seaside tomorrow. A few amusements should be fun. Do the four of you want to come? It might be a squash in the car though." They were nodding in agreement but I was confused, "there's nothing near the beach."

My Dad explained that we were going to the seaside town where he had his first job. I nodded in understanding having heard about that place before. It would be nice to see the hotel where he had worked.

"Will you be going into O'Neill's Hugh?" My Dad smiled at my uncle, "I, I may pop in." My Uncle was concerned, "maybe not with the kids eh?" My Dad nodded. "The tri-colour is still flying in there, then?" My uncle nodded "the same as ever. You might see a few you recognise especially as it's the summer." My Dad nodded and "I, I'm sure I will. One of the young ones from the club is from the town so I do hear the news."

Sean interjected, "Sure I've been there meself Hugh." Saoirse laughed "I'm sure that ye have not." Sending him a warning look. He looked affronted and didn't seem to get the hint. "Oh I, with me father."

Saoirse was intrigued now as he was so adamant, "ok what's it like so you can tell Uncle Hugh. He can say if it has changed at all." My father agreed with what he described and Saoirse was disappointed not to catch Sean out.

Aunt Geraldine suggested "Perhaps you could go on Sunday instead. Tomorrow is the community day, down the way. I don't think Molly has ever been for some reason or another." Saoirse groaned, "that's because it's so lame." My aunt was looking at my Mum, "and there's a band in the pub after which should be good."

Again, Saoirse groaned. "Jesus, Saoirse will you stop at that. There is a DJ in the room behind for you kids, but if you'd rather have an early night, that's fine by me." Saoirse didn't answer as she usually would, just in case she got made to stay in as it did sound really good.

Sean actually smiled, he seemed pleased with the weekend plans too. "I, that's grand so. Good night" he was looking over his shoulder as he left. Jack followed him to the back door, "Night. See you tomorrow then," waving to everyone. My Dad called, "Good luck lads!" My Aunt shouted, "Take care up the lane now." I said goodnight but only Jack heard as Sean was already gone.

After they had left, my younger cousins came in the back door. There was a beep as we heard a car pull away even though I hadn't heard it coming. Suddenly there was alot of noise with opening of cupboards and my cousins getting some food. "Get ye in there, to help them or they'll make a mess of the place that I just cleaned."

Saoirse and I went into the scullery and she automatically prepared the teapot. She had filled up the kettle and taken in back into the range to boil. I sat at the table and listened to what my cousins had been up too. They had been

213

swimming in the next town and had chips after. We debated curry sauce and vinegar.

They told me about the community event the next day. They were looking forward to it. They had their tea and during that time Saoirse had prepared more for both of our parents. I washed up the cups and plates that my cousins had used.

We all went through to the kitchen and Saoirse had poured another cup of tea for herself. I couldn't believe the amount of tea that she was able to drink. Everyone else was still drinking theirs but I'd turned down the offer of tea as usual, the smell was bad enough.

Aunt Geraldine and my mother were chatting about people they knew. "How's Finola, now? Her husband dying was terrible sad. Then the shock of her brother's murder." My aunts face was full of concern. My Dad said "I, ok, I think. Lots of family visiting." I realised that they were talking about Jacinta's Mum and I remembered that Jacinta had been off for a while after her Uncle had died. I wasn't quite sure how he died so I tuned into their conversation.

I remembered that her father had died many years before when we were at primary school. We had been good friends before that. My Aunt asked. "Do you still see Jacinta, Molly?" I said "Yes, she is in my school." I realised that it was a long time since I'd actually seen her. We had all been revising for our exams. I felt guilty. I would go to see her as soon as I went home.

My Aunt said "Sure you remember her Saoirse. Didn't you play with her too when she was over on her holidays, when her Dad was still living. She was a lovely sweet wee girl." Saoirse nodded solemnly. Mum was nodding aswell, "Sure she was always around our place when she was younger too. She loved coming to stay, the four of them had a great time altogether. Molly used to go there aswell." My Aunt looked at me, "Do you be staying there with her at all now?" I shook my head, "I used to but not for a long while. I know she has alot of people staying, now that it's a digs."

I still wanted to know how her uncle died but I didn't like to ask. I hoped someone would say. Mum explained "Finola's not working so it keeps her going when visitors pay her to stay. Luckily, they own their house. Not like us we are renting." I knew my Mum was stating a fact. She was not upset or angry about it.

She was very much appreciative of being in England not like my Dad, who said "No change there." I knew he was referring to Ireland and he repeated, "us being put out on the road every time a protestant landlord had the inclination." It did make me sad to think of that happening. So horrible not being sure of where you would be living.

I knew that as a family they had followed my grandfather's work where it was available, whether it was in the republic, the north or Scotland. There was a pause and everyone was remembering that. Although my mother hadn't experienced having nowhere to live or abuse from protestants, she hadn't had a happy childhood herself. She hadn't said it to me directly but I heard her discussing it will Uncle Emmett recently.

My Dad returned to our previous conversation, "Sure isn't Clare's brother, Vincent going to be staying there now. It was good of her to take him in." My Mum nodded "I wish he could stay with me, but you know how it is." My aunt nodded.

We had a three-bedroom house for three children and they had the same for five children. Saoirse had been listening and agreeing. "and isn't it still the same here for the protestants. They still have all the money. Look at the Elliott's, down the way, with their big five-bedroom house for just Robert and Mary. Robert is off to Belfast soon of course, to follow his father's footsteps to be a solicitor I hear. Then he'll be able to stay here and have no worries about having to immigrate."

My Aunt reprimanded her, "It's not the same now Saoirse. Sure, won't you be staying here yourself, when you leave college. You don't need to emigrate either. Aren't your brother and sister doing just fine."

She turned to mother, "Clare, I doubt a one of them will leave Ireland but I'm not sure about the younger ones yet. It's just great that they can stay if they want to." Turning back to her daughter, "It's different now Saoirse but we should never forget how it was."

Saoirse turned away from her mum, "Aunt Clare, how was it that you found your brother? I heard you were looking for years." My Mum explained "Thank god for the priests. Didn't Father Tom find him. There's alot of things you can say about the catholic church but Father Tom is a great man altogether.

He was on his holidays and speaking to priests here. He met another priest that had been at Balham but is living over here now. He knew my brother when he was staying in the parish. It's a great relief altogether. I was out of my mind with worry."

My Dad was nodding, "Sure he's had a bad old time with it all but he's great craic alright. He has been down the club and he fits right in there. He has some stories to tell, I can tell ye, He might drop in here, when he's on his holidays.

I don't know how we didn't find him before; sure, don't we know alot of the same people. I must have been asking the wrong ones, but I think he changed his name for a while there." He shook his head "it's quite common place now, you know for jobs, mistaken identity sometimes and still hard to get in some digs too."

My Mum seemed surprised by some of that information but didn't say anything. "Come on now, Granny will be wondering where we are. She has hardly seen Molly at all. We'll be seeing you tomorrow then, we'll drop off Molly for the fun day." I wondered what was the bad time that Uncle Vincent had. It was the first I was hearing of it.

The community day was in a field near Mary's house. It had a few stalls and some competitions including an egg & spoon race. It was like a school sports day. The tug of war was men versus women which ended predictably. There was squash, sweets and cakes for sale. The weather was good so it wasn't as bad as it could've been. Lame was a good description of the event.

I was sat on my own drinking some red lemonade when Jack sprinted over to me. "Mary has spotted you; she's coming over." I indicated for him to sit down, "please stay with me, she might not stay to long then." He agreed and then I regretted it as I'd mentioned Jack a few times in my letters.

I didn't want him to know that I'd. Luckily, she just asked about my holidays and didn't mention my letters at all. She was chatting about the disco and if we were going to the pub later and I swallowed, "I think so." She smiled "great I will see you there then."

She ran off and I looked at Jack for divine intervention but didn't see it in his face. I was surprised that She'd be going tonight. I remembered the last disco I was at. I squirmed thinking about dancing with her brother. I hoped that he wouldn't be there but I'd an awful feeling that he would be.

I rubbed my forehead. I was anxious about seeing Mary later but more that I might see Robert too. I could feel Jack looking at me but I didn't want to meet his eyes. I wondered what he would think about my previous meetings with Robert.

217

*

Saoirse told us all to go and change as we were going to the pub. We were all wearing shorts so it was a good idea aswell as an instruction, especially as it had turned colder again and it was starting to rain.

As Sean and Jack were a year older, I was anxious that they might want to go to the disco at the hotel in town with Saoirse's older brother and sister. When I asked Sean, he said he was happy to stay with us. Though he probably meant that he didn't want to do anything alone with his cousin.

The back room of the pub was full when we got there. I saw Mary in the crowd but she didn't see me. I couldn't have got to her even if I wanted too. I went to the toilet. Mary came in when I was washing my hands. She stood next to me.

She looked nervous, "I'm so sorry Molly. My cousins have come to stay so I'm with them tonight." She bit her lip. I smiled "That's fine, it's the same for me. I'll write to you when I get home." She looked relieved, "I'm glad that's ok. Robert said to say hello and that he was sorry that he missed you today at the field."

I was not sorry to miss him. I felt obliged to say, "I hope he is well." I was glad and I was hoping that it didn't show on my face. She replied "He's studying hard. Have a good holiday and tell me all about it when you get home." I was relieved too, "Thanks, you have a good summer too, bye." I left the toilet while she went into a cubicle.

It was really warm inside so I decided to get a drink and go outside. I made my way through the crowd. As I was going out of the door, I saw Jack standing beside it. "Where are you off too?" he was grinning so he must have seen me struggling to get to the door. I pushed my fringe away from my face. I knew my face was red, not just because of the heat or Mary. I explained unnecessarily that it was hot and was going outside." He smiled, "I'll come with you."

We leaned against a stone wall near the gate. I was pleased but worried about what I should say. Normally Sean and Saoirse led the conversation. I didn't have to worry as Jack was eager for an update. "I saw Mary follow you into the toilet, what did she have to say for herself?" I repeated the conversation. He grinned and so did I. "That was lucky." There was a lot to be pleased about.

We could still hear the music from where we were. Not long after we saw Saoirse and Sean make their way out of the door. Saoirse seemed suspicious. I looked at her innocently in reply but again felt the heat rise in my face, more in guilt this time than embarrassment, which She'd assume it to be.

Then a song we all knew came on and we all started to sing along. I could hear people inside singing too.... . *Everybody take a stand   Join the caravan of love by the Housemartins... ... She's my sister, don't you know...*Whilst I was singing, I thought of Mary and wondered why this song couldn't be true for us. I knew in my heart it would never be. I'd to end our friendship but I didn't know how.

Part 2: Chapter 14 – Robert (1988)

Sean shouted "shite!" I looked up in horror and thought we were going to crash.

Saoirse was sighing. "Ye're such an eejit." I bent over to look through the gap in their

seats to see what was happening through the front window. Saoirse was shaking

her head at Sean, "Sure, it's only the guards."

Then she turned to me. "It's nothing to concern yourself with Molly." I was

worried. Being stopped by a policeman in England was a big thing, especially as I

knew that Sean didn't even have a driving licence.

The music was shut off. Sean had parked on the side of the road as the guard

indicated. Sean wound down his window and was casual, "How are ye, what's

going on?"

The Guard bent down and looked in the window. He was smiling. His round

face was shining with sweat but no exertion showed when he spoke. "Grand so. Oh,

I, there's a tractor turned over in the road away up there. It's best for you to be going

around the other way now."

The guard looked away from Sean, inside of the car. He saw Saoirse an

nodded, "Oh, how ye doing Saoirse? I didn't see ye there. How's your brother doing

in Galway now? Saoirse was mischievous as usual, "oh you know up to all sorts I

imagine." The Guard grinned, "Like meself. Sure, what am I like, telling ye that for."

We all laughed at his mock embarrassment.

"Off to the disco eh?" We all nodded and he turned to look at me. I was surprised at the way this was going. He smiled at me, "So ye must be the cousin that's always home from England. Good to meet ye." He started to straighten up, "take care of yeselfs now. Good luck." He patted the car roof before putting on his hat as he walked to his car.

He sat inside his car but didn't drive off. I supposed that it was his job to warn other cars too, though none had passed us throughout the conversation we had. He waved us through and gave a thumbs up as well. Sean gave a sigh of relief and took a deep breath before driving off again. This was the first Guard I'd seen in Ireland and the difference between them and the English soldiers in the North was stark.

The diversion made Sean more cautious than before. He had learned to drive on tractors so we had to keep to the back roads. We seemed to have been driving forever. It was starting to get dark now.

Saoirse had turned off the music saying that she'd had enough. She put the radio on instead. I felt like a child but I did have to ask, "Are we nearly there?" Sean nodded, "Oh I." Saoirse was not as confident in his answer as I was. "Where are we, exactly?"" Saoirse swivelled her head from me to Sean.

She was laughing, "we're lost, aren't we?" Sean shook his head. "Sure, I know well where I'm." I could see in the rear-view mirror, that he was sweating and there was concern in his eyes. Without any street lights and no houses, it was even darker outside now.

I could make out the stone walls so I knew we were just surrounded by fields. The trees along the way seemed to be getting taller and closer together. I was scared of how dark it got here, but I definitely would not be telling either of them that, and I concentrated on looking bored.

We followed the curve of the road and then Sean said in relief "Now, are we not in Ballyfinney?" Saoirse was laughing so much she was in tears and the more she laughed the more worried I got. I could see that she was trying to speak.

She composed herself enough to state, "That's not where we are meant to be!" Then she carried on laughing loudly. Neither of us joined in. Sean was agitated, "well you'll see now; we are coming up to a village soon."

How soon seemed to be very vague as we continued for some time. Saoirse was turning back to me and I saw laughter in her eyes, but unusually she was not saying anything to Sean. It was the right thing to do as his driving was a bit erratic already. I was looking out of the window but couldn't discern any shapes now.

When we turned the corner, he stopped the car. I could see relief in Sean's face. "Didn't I tell you now." But it was just a row of houses. Saoirse was annoyed now, "No it's not. We are lost, aren't we." Sean's forehead was creased in concern, "I, maybe. I will knock on that house with the light on."

Sean was mumbling to himself as he got out of the car. He walked up to the house. He tentatively knocked on the door. Saoirse rolled down the car window and shouted, "knock louder." He did as she said. It was a solid wooden door; it didn't have a bell or a door knocker. There was still no response.

Finally, we could see someone pulling back the net curtain at the window. Saoirse pointed to the window. There was an old man looking out. Sean turned towards the window but as he did, another old man opened the front door and beckoned him inside. It seemed only a matter of seconds before he ran back to the car.

I was surprised, "Sean, what's wrong?" He looked embarrassed. The old man followed Sean outside. He was chuckling as he opened the door fully and the light flooded out. Saoirse cried out in laughter, "it's a pub." I could see the small bar and the men inside. Saoirse was howling and I was giggling too. Nobody knocked on a pub door. The old man saw us laughing and saluted us, with a smile, He went back inside, to no doubt retell the story.

When Saoirse stopped for breath, "Did you at least ask them where we are?" Sean shook his head and then we were all laughing with tears running down our faces. The more we laughed the funnier it seemed. It was a while before Sean was able to drive off. The journey had taken us far from the coastline that we should have followed. Sean was as relieved as me when we eventually arrived at the town.

The next day Saoirse was working in town. Uncle Peter had said that he would drop me in later on. I was tired as we had got in late or early as the younger cousins always said. I was happy for the lay in. I didn't know how Saoirse managed. When I got into town, Uncle Peter said that he had some things to do but he would be back later, if we wanted a lift home. I'd arranged to meet Saoirse, to go for a burger after she finished.

I thought about Mary. I was still writing to her even though I knew I shouldn't. She knew I was on holiday so I thought I would call her. Saoirse was working in the bakery and Sean was on his farm. I'd my diary in my bag and went to the phone box. I'd the change I needed and rang her number.

As the phone rang, I was nervous as I didn't want to speak to Robert or even her mother. If it was them, I decided that I wouldn't speak or put the coin in. I didn't want to explain who I was. They would never know it was me.

Luckily, Mary answered. She was delighted to hear from me. When I asked how she was, she told me she was very bored. "How was last night, did you have fun?" I wondered how she knew where we were but everyone seemed to know everything here.

She suggested a day to meet and as it suited Saoirse's working hours, I agreed. I could hear the pips. My money was running out and we quickly said our goodbyes.

I went into the bookshop. I was looking at the cards, thinking that I might send one to Maria. I heard a voice from behind me "Hello Molly, I heard you were here." I turned but I already knew it was Robert, Mary's brother. I didn't know if he meant in Ireland or the shop.

I was suspicious to see him in the bookshop so soon after my call to his sister. He must have guessed my thoughts, "I'm getting notebooks for my father, we ran out. I'm working with him this summer. I can't be out long but would you like to get a drink in the café?"

I really wanted to say no as I didn't like him and I didn't want to upset my family. I knew it would be rude and more importantly I thought that Mary would be disappointed if I didn't go, so I agreed. Though I was still suspicious despite what he had said. I told myself it was just a drink. We didn't go to the place where Saoirse worked but to the burger bar. e asked me what I wanted to drink and to get a seat. He brought over two cokes.

We chatted about Mary, his job, his school and rugby. I didn't want to talk about me. He said Mary was reading a lot. That didn't surprise me as the new Maeve Binchy book was out. He told me about his father's firm and that he was expected to study law at university and follow in his footsteps. He was older than me so he talked about the study that he would need to do this year to pass his leaving cert, to get into Queens College Belfast.

I let him chatter on. Then he was taking me into his confidence by admitting that he would have preferred Galway. I was concerned that he was sharing this information with me and tried to lighten the mood. "My cousin is there. He loves it. You should ask him about it." Then I quickly realised my mistake. There was a pause and he mumbled, "I don't really know him well enough."

Talking about studying made me wonder about my exam results. I got home the day they came out. My mind wandered off as he spoke, I was hoping that I would pass enough GCSEs to get into sixth form college. I let him talk while I made plans.

When my mind came back to the chat, I was annoyed with myself. I knew that this conversation needed to stop right now. I looked at my watch, I feigned worry, "Oh no, your Dad must be wondering where you are." I finished my drink and thanked him as I was getting up. He got up too and smiled at me, "it was great to see you Molly. I hope I see you soon."

My stomach churned. I didn't say the same as it wasn't true. I was so angry with myself. I walked around the town aimlessly not noticing my surroundings until it was time to meet Saoirse. We went straight to the burger bar. We both ordered burger and chips. The man was smiling at me. "Back again?" Saoirse laughed, "You stand out like a sore thumb." I laughed too and didn't correct her that he was talking about just an hour earlier.

When I met Mary, it was in a cafe that I'd never noticed before. I was a bit worried as it looked fancy and I didn't have much money. Mary read my mind, "It's my treat. It's so lovely to see you." She was full of excitement about me going for a drink with her brother. She seemed to think the chance meeting as a date. I was exasperated with myself.

She invited me to her house for dinner and I was horrified. I thought it was a terrible idea. It made me feel extremely anxious. I was trying to think of an excuse. I stared at the pink patterned china cups and fiddled with the napkin with the lace edges but my mind was blank. I'd to say something, "maybe next holiday, I'm going home soon."

I continued to look down and was noticing how white the tablecloth was. I just wanted to shout No. But it wasn't her fault that Robert was her brother. She was smiling now, "wouldn't it be great if we were sisters Molly?" She really meant it. I didn't agree and just said "your mad" laughing to cover my true feelings.

I changed the subject quickly to the new Binchy book. After we had eaten, I heard the tinkle from the bell on the door again. I looked up. I'd been checking who was coming in throughout the meal. I did know it would be highly unlikely to see any of my family in here but I couldn't be sure. I couldn't believe it, it was Robert.

This was ridiculous. I knew Mary had set this up. I was feeling suffocated. Mary so wanted these meetings and I was so worried about them. Robert was smiling and my stomach sank, as I definitely felt that he liked me. I felt out of control not just because I didn't like him but because he was a protestant. I looked at my watch, "Oh, I'veto go now." I jumped up and walked around the table and I hugged Mary thanking her for the cake and coffee.

Robert was still by the door. He held out his hand for me to shake. He was so formal and strange. I shook it without looking at him. "See you soon." I attempted a smile but prayed that we would not meet again.

I was elated to be leaving. When I got outside, I suddenly felt a sense of danger. I tried to rationalise it as just having a pen pal and me being polite to her brother. Then I remembered the words that I'd heard so often, You're so naive Molly!

That night Saoirse and I went with Sean to his friend's house. Sean was driving. Saoirse and I'd laughed but agreed despite our last excursion. Saoirse threatened to tell Sean's friends about our trip out. Saoirse was laughing and Sean was infuriated with her. I'd no doubt that She'd. Sean must have expected it too. I felt sorry for him and changed the subject.

I asked him about his Dad. I'd heard he was getting worse. I could see that Sean had been taking on alot more farm work with his brother away at University. He told me that his brother was back now and was taking on the slack for the summer.

His tone had changed, "My Fathers old now and very unwell. He will never work the farm properly again. My Mammy says he's not long for the world." I didn't know what to say. I was worried about him. "Oh no Sean, I'm really sorry, I didn't know it was that bad." As he turned his attention back to the road, I pulled a face at Saoirse. She should have told me. Saoirse just shrugged and turned away.

He didn't say what was wrong with his father so I asked a different question "so, what will happen about the farm then? You're the last one left at home. Your Mother can't look after the place."

I was thinking that she didn't look to well herself, "especially when you go away to college." His face was sad, "me Mammy wants me to stay and look after the farm." I exclaimed, "but don't you want to go to university." He smiled weakly, "someone has to stay home."

227

I was upset on his behalf. "Don't do it, go away like you planned." Before I could say anymore, Saoirse mocked "that puts pay to the seventh son of the seventh son rubbish that you have been spouting all these years." I thought that was heartless especially as he hadn't said it for a long time.

His Dad was old, not even Jesus could stop him dying. "Will ye, get over yourself, Molly is here on her holidays she doesn't want you being maudlin." He nodded at Saoirse and I knew that the conversation was over.

Saoirse turned to me, to further take advantage of Sean's low mood, "John, Sean's friend is really looking forward to meeting ye Molly." Sean's shock could be seen in the mirror, "He never said anything about that to me."

Saoirse raised her eyebrows, "You never notice anything that's going on around you. Molly has liked Jack forever and you haven't even noticed." I was mortified but neither of them was looking at me. He was disgusted. "I wouldn't even want to notice that."

"Where is he at this summer, he hasn't been around at all?" Saoirse was really taking advantage of Sean's mood now. Sean shook his head and turned to me, "Jesus! Molly have you no taste at all. Why would ye, in the lord's name, be bothering with him?" Saoirse was enjoying our discomfort and I wondered if she even knew how Sean felt about her. None of us seemed to know each other at all. Thank god that Mary and Robert weren't known about either.

Saoirse and Sean continued to bicker as usual but I wasn't listening now, having my own issues to contend with. Sean had parked the car in front of the white stone house. He was so quick out of the car and was already walking into the side door, when I'd unbuckled my seat belt. Neither of them had had them on as usual. Saoirse laughed at me as she followed him. I knew she thought I was mad to put it on in the first place. I knew it was compulsory in England for a few years now but didn't know if it was in Ireland yet.

I went into the house last. There were two boys inside and they shook hands with me, saying the normal greetings, "It's good to meet you Molly, how are ye? Are you having good holidays?" John went to get us some drinks, we had all just sat down when we heard an almighty bang from outside.

We all rushed to the door and window, but we Couldn't see what had caused the noise. Saoirse pointed to her right. Sean's brother's car had hit the wall of the house. Sean pushed through us and went to the car.

We followed him, standing behind him, in a line along the side of the car. No one spoke. I turned to look at Sean. He was looking at it in disbelief. His hands settled in his brown hair. It was long at the front now so I couldn't see much of his face, but the bit I could see was whiter than normal and his freckles more pronounced.

John turned back towards his house. His hands were on his hips, surveying his wall, "Don't ye be worrying, the wall will be fine." We all laughed in relief, the shock had left us and we knew the house was solid. He showed no concern for the car.

We turned around to check the damage. Sean wasn't looking at the car but the driveway itself. I could see the issue too. There was a very low slope down towards the house. He realised what had happened but was still confused. "Did ye forget to put the hand brake on there now, Sean?" John had a smile playing on his lips.

Our attention returned to the car. Luckily there was no evidence of physical damage to the car so we were all able to let rip. Saoirse was elated, the scorn showing on her face. "What an Eejit ye are." Sean was dazed. He had turned scarlet but then he laughed, in relief more than mirth.

Saoirse got into the car and reversed it. When she stopped, she shouted out of the car window, "Hand brake going on now." We spent the whole night laughing but when there was a gap in the conversation, we kept going back to the incident with the car.

Sean took it in the same good spirit as the rest of us. I liked the relaxed version of Sean, especially as he had so much on his mind, including what his brother's reaction would be. What could have been and some very good imitations of the owner of the car, were on the agenda. Saoirse must have felt the same as me, as she didn't mention the trip to the disco on the Saturday before.

Saoirse and Sean said they were both free on the same day which had been unusual this summer. Saoirse was working most days and Sean was on the farm. Saoirse told me that Sean's Aunt and uncle were down for the weekend so he didn't have to be on the farm that day.

We waited for Sean to walk down to Saoirse's house. We were going to get the bus to the next town to play pitch and putt. I was not looking forward to it. I was so bad at any type of golf and I could hardly hit the ball with the club. I explained this to Saoirse. She nodded, "I know you are rubbish but how will you ever get better if you don't practise." I'd to agree that it was true, but then said "mmm, or maybe you just like beating me all the time." Her smug face said it all.

It was warm enough to wear jeans shorts. I'd my new Fido dido t-shit on, I'd got in town. They never had Fido dido stuff in England. Saoirse laughed at my new top. "I don't know about Fido, more like Molly is for Molly. Molly is against no one!" I shook my head ignoring her jibe.

Sean was very eager to get away, "come on will ye, we will miss the bus." I retorted "erm ... Sean we were waiting for you." He didn't look happy, "No we were waiting for him," indicating behind him with a toss of his head. When I saw who he was referring, I knew the delight would show on my face so I turned away quickly.

I ran on ahead, to make sure that we didn't miss the bus. Surprisingly, on this occasion it had been me who had stopped the bus. The driver had to wait for the others to meet me. I was pleased to be the fastest. I knew my cross-country running must be getting better. We were all breathless though. I couldn't say hello to Jack until we were sitting down.

We all took a two seat each as the bus was empty. Jack's smile was genuine as usual. "It's good to see you both. Sean has been as welcoming to me as ever." Sean turned away to stare out of the side window. I was pleased that it was this Aunt and Uncle that they had been talking about. Jack pointed at my t-shirt approvingly, "I like Fido dido too." Saoirse was smirking at us, I ignored her.

She started humming and then was singing, *"you spin me* turned to stare at her until she stopped. I knew it was her favourite song, when Jack was around. If he noticed he never showed it.

When she did stop, her eyes narrowed as she questioned Sean, "How come you didn't say Jack was coming down?" Sean was looking ahead but I could see him scowling from where I sat, "he wasn't meant to; he just turned up with his mother and father." Saoirse took the opportunity to give a true sardonic response, "Well how dare he visit his relatives." Jack looked across at me and raised his eyebrows.

Sean was being ruder to his cousin than usual. I was offended on his behalf. "So has Sean caught you up with the news and places we have been?" Jack smiled in a way that River Phoenix never did. Maria should see him now.

Saoirse hooted at my rhetorical question, "well I never thought it would be you to spill the beans Molly." I smiled sweetly when Sean turned to look at me, his enraged look plastered on his face, "Well Jack would normally have been here so it's only fair to be told." Saoirse chose to do the telling, even I was interested on her take on the recent events and how She'd perform them for Jack.

Sean was eyeing me with annoyance, but he did join in our laughter when Saoirse told the stories. Jack chuckled but didn't try to embarrass Sean. Jack and I were both on the aisle seats to better watch the dramatics.

When he had the chance, he caught my eye, "Have you seen Mary?" his low voice showed that he was still sympathetic to my situation. I nodded, not wanting to draw anyone's attention. He looked both pleased and concerned, mirroring my own feelings, "tell me about it later."

I shook my head in dismay when we got to the pitch and putt course. It was on a hill. There was no chance that I would get any balls into the holes. I was honest, "Let's agree on a number to stop at as I don't want to keep you back."

I knew both Saoirse and Sean had already played some golf at the nearby golf course. They had also been paid to collect lost balls in the rough, or those left by the players who couldn't be bothered to go back for them.

I looked at Jack hopefully, "Are you good too?" Jack was apologetic, "I play with my Dad most Sundays." I pouted and stamped my foot, pretending to be upset by the news. I laughed with them when they did.

It turned out that Saoirse was right, the practise was good for me. I did learn as Jack was a good teacher. Although I came last, I did get the ball in the hole within six every time, even with them laughing at my attempts. I was pleased with my performance. The golf club wasn't whirling around as much and I hit the ball more than the grass. Though it took many attempts to get near the hole.

I knew that I made the game more interesting. As they were all so good, we would have been there for less than twenty minutes. At the start Sean had said "Surely you can't be that bad," but by the end he had to agree "you really are terrible." I was smiling but I was pleased that I'd gotten better. Sean and Saoirse's banter had kept me and Jack entertained all day as it was all in good spirit. The craic really was mighty.

This time we went to the night club with Saoirse's boyfriend, Cillian. I hadn't met him before so it was a bit awkward. He was a lot older than us. He had long dark brown hair and dark brown eyes. He wasn't pale skinned or have freckles which surprised me.

He was already sat in the car when he met us so I didn't know his height or build but I suspected he was tall and athletic. He drove his own car and Saoirse had been happy to inform me that he had a British driving licence as he was living in the North.

I suspected that Sean hadn't come as he did like Saoirse and didn't want to see her with her boyfriend. He was still embarrassed about the two car trips. Even though he had laughed with us at the time, he hadn't driven since. I was disappointed for him as listening to Saoirse and Cillian's banter they seemed to be a good match.

After only a few minutes, we stopped outside a house and the atmosphere in the car change. His body stiffened and his speech was stilted. "I still can't believe he's dead." His face had gone white now and he was angry. Saoirse was shaking her head silently.

Cillian turned to me. "Sure, don't you know his niece." I didn't know who he was referring too. Saoirse saw my confusion, "That's Jacinta's mothers homeplace. Her mother's sister lives there. Didn't you know?" I didn't. I could see in their eyes as they both leaned in more through the gap in the car seats. I knew this was very important information that they expected me to know, "How did he die?" They both looked horrified.

Saoirse was clearly embarrassed in front of Cillian and quickly informed me, "it was connected to Milltown." I still didn't know what that meant. I shook my head and raised my shoulders. My face must have been blank as they continued to stare at me. "At the Gibraltar three's funeral." She was shaking her head at me in astonishment, "and the murders in the cemetery."

It did sound familiar but I'd not been watching the news because of my revision. My Dad hadn't told me and my Mum wouldn't have said anything to me if it was linked to the IRA in any way.

As I didn't know, Cillian took me through the timeline of events, it was really shocking. He explained to me of the link of the murders to the British government and how the truth had been made to look like a conspiracy theory. I couldn't speak, especially with the connection to Jacinta. No wonder she hadn't been around as much recently. I couldn't believe that Sean hadn't told me but he was so busy now.

I could see Saoirse's boyfriend looking in the rear-view mirror at me. Saoirse said "Now will you see?" She knew that I'd tried not to take sides on this as I lived in England but this, it made it so real. I didn't say anything. All I could think of was Mary. I could see how wrong it was to continue seeing her given the strength of feeling particularly right now in the car.

"You know Hugh is Molly's Dad, don't you?" I knew she was trying to mollify him as he didn't look happy at all. Cillian replied "O I, of course. He is great craic when I see him in London. A great supporter *The Cause* he is too." He continued to watch me in the rear-view mirror. I could tell that he thought I was letting the side down. The look in his eyes made me feel very afraid. I knew that was overdramatic and turned to look out of the window.

My Mum had been uncomfortable when she had heard where we were going that night as it was so close to the border. Saoirse had told her that we weren't going into the North and her reassurance that "Sure the British soldiers would probably be happy to hear Molly's English accent, if we did go. They probably wouldn't get up to their normal carry-on." I very much doubted that was true and it didn't seem to help my Mum either.

I realised that we hadn't been into the North that year. I was glad as I didn't like the checkpoints or seeing the soldiers on the street. Saoirse of course had always thought that was all part of the fun. Cillian said "What do you think about the prods, Molly?" Even Saoirse seemed surprised by the question and answered for me "Sure she doesn't know any here or in England but she understands the way things are, don't you Molly?" I nodded as I certainly did understand.

My lie was getting bigger every day. Saoirse said, "Now." Which meant the conversation was over and she turned her attention to the radio. That suited me very well. The Human League was playing. *Don't, don't you want me? You know I don't believe you* She switched stations very quickly as I doubted, she liked that band.

When we arrived and as I was getting out of the car, Cillian said "have a good night. I might see ye again before you go back." I was shocked he wasn't coming in after driving all around the place to pick us up just to drop as off, but a bit pleased too. I didn't want to spend an evening talking about politics.

When Saoirse met me on the side of the road, although I didn't care I was still interested, "Why's he not coming in?" She was nonchalant, "Oh, they are all a bit young for him in there. It's just I told him about Sean and he offered to drive us here." She was laughing remembering our last nights out and I laughed with her relieved that it was just the two of us.

As I walked to the club, I saw a sign back home to Grannies, it was miles away. I thought how the hell are we getting back. Saoirse saw my face and was a bit impatient with me "Sure, there will be loads of people going back to the town." I realised that was true when Saoirse was stopped by numerous people on her way in; family friends, people from church and from her school.

I was trying to follow her, but had been stopped by the crowd. I heard someone call my name. I turned and Couldn't believe it was Robert. He was slowly making his way in the crowd towards me. I couldn't pretend that I'd not seen him. Thankfully I could no longer see Saoirse in the crowd. I felt like he was stalking me as he seemed to be everywhere this summer.

When he got in front of me, he was laughing at his effort to get to me. Then he smiled which I returned weakly too. He commented on the crowd and enquired after me, I nodded and I gave him the same greeting. He told that me that he thought I might be out as there as it was the last night of my holiday.

I was perturbed, I was sure that I'd been vague about that date even with Mary. I looked around for her. He knew what I was thinking, "Are you looking for Mary? She's too young." I knew she was a year younger than me but I could see girls from the church and they were the same age as Mary. I was surprised but thankful, it definitely worked out better this way.

He asked me how I was getting home and I explained that Saoirse had arranged something, hoping that was true. He offered to take us back as he was driving. "Come and find me if you need a lift." I thanked him and even though he was a close neighbour, I doubted Saoirse would accept the offer.

Saoirse appeared in front of me, not best pleased. Robert offered a "Hello Saoirse," She acknowledged him with a curt nod. She directed me towards the dance floor. I replied to his "Have a good night," with you too, as Saoirse led me away. I was happy that she noted that I was really glad to get away.

I'd a great night but the thought of how we would get back to my Grannies was playing on my mind. Saoirse knew lots of people so I tried to be positive that it would work out okay. I'd met Sean's friends again but they left before the end.

As we were leaving Saoirse was bidding people goodnight but didn't look as sure of herself as usual. By the time she got to me, she was biting a lip, "Everyone from town has left already. I suppose they thought we had a lift home."

She was looking round and her gaze stopped behind me. I turned and saw Robert; he was saying goodbyes himself. Saoirse was thoughtful, "what did Robert say to you before?" I didn't want to mention Mary, "He just asked about my holidays." She shook her head but was smiling, "What did I tell you about talking to Protestants?" I didn't know if it was a joke or a warning.

Then she was hesitant and talking more to herself, "I wonder if he is driving? I don't think he takes a drink... Hmm...He obviously likes ye, he seems to remember you from the beach all those years ago. It will ok, if you ask him, everyone knows how anxious you get about these sorta things."

When we got to the car, Saoirse jumped in the back obviously not wanting to be seen. Robert had been delighted to take us back. A bit too excited I thought but it was great to get a lift, especially all the way home. I knew that Saoirse wouldn't want to stop in town now. She usually liked to watch the boys who did laps in their cars around the square, at the end of a night out. I knew by now that this happened even if the disco hadn't been in town.

Robert was chatting away but not about Mary or about seeing me in town. He probably knew what Saoirse's reaction would be to these meetings. He was asking me about my holidays, and what I'd done, and what I was doing when I got back home.

I told him about getting my exam results when I got home. It made me nervous so I prattled on telling him about going to sixth form and looking for a Saturday job. I was sure that none of this was news to him as Mary would probably have told him this already.

Saoirse didn't say a word throughout the whole journey. Robert didn't do laps around the square. He was too careful for that. Saoirse thanked him when we got to her house. I must have told him that I was staying at my Grannies so he had offered to drop me there.

Saoirse's eyes flashed at me as she turned away. I took it as some kind of warning, but as I didn't understand I shrugged my shoulders. She didn't turn to see my reaction. I wasn't going to get out and walk at this time in the morning. She didn't even reply to me when I called goodnight and that I would see her the next day. I hoped She'd be over it by then.

At the crossroads we went straight across on to my Grannies lane. There were no other cars around. When we got to the parking space across from my

Grannies house, he stopped the engine and got out. I was feeling uncomfortable. It seemed like we were ending a date. Which we definitely were not. I followed him up the path. He had stopped on the doorstep, in front of the house. Thankfully I wasn't going in that way as I didn't have a key. I would be going in the back door so as not to wake anyone.

I thanked him for the lift and was genuinely grateful. He wished me a good journey home and before I could say goodbye he smiled, "I really like you Molly." I was horrified, I didn't know how this night had manifested into such a terrible situation.

My stomach sunk as it always did when he spoke to me. I wanted him to stop talking as I could feel some sort of speech coming on, "I've liked you since I met you on the beach all those summers ago. I think about you all the time. I love to hear your news through Mary."

I was dismayed and I didn't know what to say. I felt sick. I knew I should say something but if I spoke, I might shout something horrible. Not only because he was a protestant or that Saoirse would go mad but just that I didn't like him.

He leaned down towards my face. I turned to get away but his kiss caught my cheek. I mumbled "goodbye" and rushed around the side of the house and in through the back door. *Don't, don't you want me?* was playing in my mind. I really didn't want him. The situation was escalating out of my control. I was gulping for air, I couldn't think of anyone who would be happy about this. Except Mary and Robert.

Part 2: Chapter 15 - Our last summer (1989)

It wasn't until after we had our exam results and we were at sixth form college that I finally got the courage to tell Maria about Robert. She thought it was hilarious. "Your first kiss cannot be with a Protestant!" I knew that was true.

She was pensive. Then she told me that her boyfriend had a friend called Jamie and that he liked me. This was news to me. "You really need to go out with him. Then you can write to Mary and she will tell her brother. That way you won't be lying and I know how much you hate that." Which set off her laughter again.

"Jack seems great but he just doesn't like you, not the way Robert does." The tears were running down her face now, in delight of my situation. I didn't find it at all humorous and didn't join in with her. I'd not even met Jamie but she was right, it definitely was the best thing I could do.

When I'd got home, I'd tried to contact Jacinta to say sorry about her Uncle. She had been on holiday. I mentioned it to Mum as she'd always liked her. Not about the details that I'd heard from Saoirse and her boyfriend but she seemed to know as she was adamant that I shouldn't go there again, because it was a digs. I hoped Dad would override her but surprisingly he agreed. I tried calling Jacinta but she never seemed to be in.

I was relieved when Maria said they were on the same BTEC course and she was doing fine. It was strange not seeing her anymore. I hoped I could meet up with her again through Maria. I'd not realised that we had family from the same area.

I did write to Mary. I wanted to tell her about Jamie. Jamie was nice and good fun so I wasn't lying to her. It just meant that I was still in contact with her. I knew I shouldn't be. I tried to write less frequently but that just meant Mary wrote more.

The fact that I was still in contact with Mary was not good. She was so nice that I found it hard to find an excuse. I wondered again how this situation had occurred. I should have been braver from the start and just told Saoirse about Mary. It was too late to tell Saoirse now and I worried what would happen if she did find out. If she knew about Robert, she'd be even more angry. I'd been so naive about the situation.

I was still being naïve, thinking that it was okay, just because it should be. I knew my family in Ireland and maybe some in England might be upset about it. Even my Mum thought with all the recent trouble, that it wasn't right anymore.

The Ballygawley bus bombing last summer seemed to change things. We had all experienced more taunting. I hated being called a terrorist. Most English people seemed to think we were murderers.

It had been shocking that so many soldiers had died. It was understandable that people would feel angry. The belief of *The Cause* was being reinforced because of it. I asked myself the same question; was it war? or was it terrorism? I could hear my Dad's answer, "If they hadn't invaded Ireland, they wouldn't be dead."

I'd written to Saoirse about a new Irish band that Maria and I'd seen. I told her that the Saw Doctors had been great live. When I saw the letter from Sean, I was shocked as he had never written to me before. Saoirse had told him about the band. He wrote that he had met them as they were friends of his brother. They were playing in Galway when I was over on my holidays. He offered to take us to see them.

I was flabbergasted and wrote to Saoirse. She was as shocked as me. She told me to wait and see, obviously not believing him. I was even more excited to be going on holiday then. I was already pleased as it meant time off work. I was working full time this summer and not getting out much.

Maria had been really jealous when I told her about seeing the Saw Doctors. She hadn't been pleased that I'd split up with Jamie. She was still annoyed even after I explained to her that it was because he was going to University, and we had both thought it would be for the best.

Saoirse had found it amusing when I told her. "What a coincidence that it happened just before your holidays and exactly the same time as Jack's decision to stay for the summer."

Maria was thinking along the same lines though she didn't find it funny. She was sighing, "You never listen to me anyway." I knew that she meant Mary and Robert aswell as Jack. I'd not told Mary that I'd split up with Jamie. I didn't want to risk Robert asking me out if he knew.

Despite what Saoirse had said, it seemed like Sean's brother did know the band. I couldn't wait to see them again. We were on our way to Galway. I was so excited. "Thank you so much Sean. I'm so excited about this." Sean was smiling and smug. Saoirse rolled her eyes, "We can see that. Now Sean drive carefully. Even though you have passed your driving test, Molly still doesn't trust you." I didn't know he had and laughed. "How come you took the test? No one else seems too."

He was very pleased with himself, "O you'd be fine around town but I wouldn't be able to go to other counties."

Galway was a long distance away so he was concentrating on the road. This was the furthest I'd been in Ireland without my parents or aunts and uncles. I laughed again at the fact we were in a *Red Cortina* and I wished that song had been released already by The Saw Doctors. *N17* was brilliant too.

Sean put on the tape when I asked. The night I'd seen the *Saw Doctors* with *The Waterboys* at the National in London had been amazing. Maria and I'd never even heard of them before that night.

I started singing again *And I wish I was on the N17, Stone walls and the grass is green..*

Saoirse groaned again but was smiling, "Thank god you're in the back." I could see that some off my excitement was rubbing off on her and that pleased me as she was always so nonplussed.

When I finally stopped singing to the relief of my fellow travellers, my mind drifted back to Mary. The words of Waterboys song the *whole of the moon* came into my mind. They meant something new to me now, *I was dumbfounded by truth,* and wondered if that's how Saoirse would feel if she found out about Mary.

It was a long drive but it went by quickly. As we were passing the turnoff for my midland cousins, Sean announced that we were on the N17. I was excited as I'd never needed to be on this road before. Maria would be green with envy. I'd not even thought about how we'd get there. Sitting in the back I never noticed the roads except that they N not M.

I requested for *N17* to be played again and Saoirse covered her ears. I was pleased that Sean didn't have to drive back tonight. We were all staying at his Aunt's house. "It's very good of your Aunt to put us all up." Sean looked at Saoirse with surprise and then at me, "Sure doesn't she know your Father well. He's sorted out digs for all her sons aswell as my brothers, when they went to England."

I was surprised as it was my Mum who normally organised everything. I couldn't believe that my Dad had done that. There again, it was probably just sorted out in the club over a pint.

Sean was confused, "Haven't you met anyone going over to London to work or for their holidays." I shook my head, "not that I know of, but I may have seen them at the Club and not known they were your relatives."

Sean looked back at Saoirse but she turned to look out of the window and didn't say anything. I always worried when Saoirse was quiet, it always meant she thought I wouldn't understand things. At that moment I didn't care. The gig tonight would be great and I didn't want to spoil it.

Next thing I was shaking hands with Sean's Aunt, Uncle and cousins that were home. They were very pleased to meet me. They were interested in my Dad, saying what a great man he was, and to tell him they were asking after him. I always thought that was such an odd expression and it made me smile, and I just nodded as they spoke.

As expected, the tea was flowing within seconds of our arrival. Saoirse looked at me and her twinkling eyes meant she was looking forward to this, as she knew I hated tea and never drank it.

Even the smell of it reminded me of my childhood. Stirring the tea leaves in the teapot endlessly, morning, noon and night. I used to fill the cup up with sugar just to cover the taste. I'd given sugar up for lent last year and I'd not had tea since. I'd to have it without sugar today. I felt like retching. Saoirse felt it was an over-reaction but it was true. I knew it would be rude not to have it so I quickly drank the cup that was given to me.

I covered the cup with my hand in case someone thought that I wanted a refill. I'd learned this lesson the hard way. The teapot always seemed to find me. The obligatory homemade apple pie was being offered. I accepted a slice just to cover the taste of the tea. I was pleased when Saoirse turned to Sean, "Shouldn't we be leaving now? We want to get Molly a good spot." Sean looked at me too with laughter in his eyes and agreed.

Sean's Aunt was concerned that we were not staying for some dinner, but Sean was explaining that we would get a burger. He told her what time we would be back. She nodded, "The door will be unlocked for you and the beds are made already. You know where things are Sean so I will let you go now. Have a grand time." I thanked his Aunt, she was beaming, "Sure it's a pleasure to have you and you're welcome at any time. You're a great girl all together so like your father."

It was the right time for me to be going out, but very early for Saoirse and Sean. The bar was just as it had been described by the people that had already been there. It was packed. It was dark but with some bright lights in the high ceiling. The mezzanine was as impressive as I'd heard. I knew there would be no way of getting near to it tonight. The atmosphere was great. There were so many people to meet. I was shaking hands and hearing names that I knew I would forget.

The drinks were flowing. Sean was having pints of Guinness, but I couldn't bear the stuff and asked for vodka. I didn't usually drink with Saoirse as she was a pioneer, but I felt it was okay tonight. Maria and I always had a drink when we went out. Soon I was jumping around with the other fans shouting N17 with them. There were a few new songs. The tin whistle and mandolin were new sounds to me in pop music.

I met the band afterwards. When I said hello, I told them that I'd seen them at the National. Pearse, Sean's brother's friend laughed, "The Waterboys were something else, eh?" then I smiled at the rest of them and we sat down again.

I was thirsty and tired from the dancing and singing. I'd another drink and sat to listen to the post gig singing. "The craic was fierce" as Saoirse always said on a good night. Later we were in a car, I was not sure whose but it got us back to Sean's Aunt safely.

I slept late and when I woke up Saoirse was not in the room. I checked my watch and realised that I would miss mass if I wasn't quick. I didn't want to upset Sean's Aunt.

I washed quickly and dressed. I looked at the bed not knowing whether to strip it but decided to make it instead like Saoirse had done. The house was quiet compared to yesterday evening. It was a big house but I'd heard that most of them were away in England and America, though some had been visiting for their holidays.

Saoirse was sitting in the kitchen having a cup of tea with Sean's Aunt. It was very quiet compared to the night before. Sean's Aunt explained, "Everyone else is away to Mass." I was very upset to have missed it, my own Aunt, Saoirse's Mother would be livid. She read my mind. She smiled at me, "Sure no one needs to know. If anyone asks, I will say you came to early mass with Saoirse and I." I was surprised at her response and sat down at the table with them. She got up, " Ye'll have a drink and a spot to eat." The thought of tea made my stomach turn. So, I was very pleased when she brought me a cup of coffee. I was also relieved that I wouldn't get into trouble for missing mass.

As I was eating, she asked me if I saw much of my Uncle Vincent. I remembered all the trouble my Mum and her family had gone through to find him. I didn't know how to answer as I'd only heard about him a couple of years ago, and I'd not really got to know him since either. When he visited, they would go to the club. Mum didn't like this, she wanted to cook him dinner. She said he had no wife to look after him. He had no children so that meant no cousins either.

I'd not known Uncle Emmett long either but I liked him a lot more. I thought it best not to say that. I shook my head, "not much at home but he does go to the club with my Dad." She seemed satisfied with my answer. "He would I of course. Well when you see him say we were asking for him." Saoirse stated, "My Dad enjoyed meeting him too, when came after Easter." I thought that was weird and I wondered how they all knew each other.

I slept in the car on the way home. I didn't ask for any music and the journey back went quickly. Nearer home we talked about the night and we agreed that we'd all had a great time.

Saoirse was sincere and disappointed, "It's a shame Jack had to miss it. He'd have enjoyed it." I'd thought the same but didn't vocalise comments like that. I knew he had wanted to come too but there'd been no one else to do the milking. Sean's brother was away on his holidays so it was just the two of them now. Sean's father was still too ill to work the farm.

Sean did the milking all year but Jack had come to help him for the summer. Sean's Mother still wanted him to be a farmer but it seemed that she wasn't aware of Sean's plans. He was trying to persuade his father and mother to get some help, or sell up as he wanted to go to Dublin as soon as he got his exams. Jack was planning to go to university so he couldn't help out anymore either. I was upset for Sean as they didn't seem any further along in making it happen. He just stated that they needed to sort out the farm situation very quickly.

The next day, Saoirse and Sean had tickets to the game in Dublin. Jack and I'd discussed whether I should see Mary. He told me that this was an opportunity to be honest and discuss my concerns with her. I rang Mary and although she was surprised at the short notice, she agreed to meet. Jack had offered to drop me into town in his Uncle's car, and then pick me up after as I wouldn't have any other way home.

Jack had never questioned my friendship with Mary. He didn't agree with Sean and Saoirse's beliefs about protestants. He did agree that he hadn't been affected by the troubles in the same way as they had. He could see that I was concerned about the situation now. He understood that there had been an escalation in the affects the troubles were having on me aswell.

I'd explained that I didn't want to lie to Saoirse anymore. He told me that he would support me in any decision I made and he looked concerned. He knew I would be unhappy to end a great friendship but was also aware of the risks it entailed.

Maria had urged me to end my friendship with Mary. She had also advised me to seek Jack's friendship, as he was not obsessed with republicanism like Saoirse and Sean. She didn't like the way they could be so forceful in their beliefs. Over the years I'd told her about the teachings and it had worried her. I didn't tell Jack about Robert; Maria had agreed with that decision. I was too embarrassed to talk to anyone about it, especially him. It would be a deciding factor in my decision whether to continue my friendship with Mary.

Jack dropped me off as close to the bakery as possible. Mary was already there and she gave me a quick hug. She spoke quietly, "can we go back to my house?" Her face was drawn and white making her freckles more pronounced. Her red hair was more noticeable aswell.

I was surprised, "now?" She nodded and swallowed, "Can I explain when we get there?" It seemed that she didn't want to be seen with me. I was intrigued but didn't take offence. I knew that I'd done the same in the past. I thought that it was odd but I agreed.

She turned quickly and I followed her. She pointed to a car explaining that it was her Mums. I was surprised that Mary could drive especially as she was younger than me. I got in as she was checking the mirrors. Then she moved off so fast thatI hadn'teven put my seat belt on.

It wasn't until we were out of town that we spoke properly. She was more relaxed and was interested in what I'd been up too. I told her about The Saw Doctors. She could see I'd an amazing night and was smiling with me.

I'd driven past her house before, and written to her there but I'd never been inside. She could see I was uneasy, "My Mum is home but Dad and Robert are at work." I hoped her Mum would be okay with me, even though I was a catholic.

Her Mum came to meet us at the front door. She smiled and shook my hand. She was genuinely happy to see me, which let me breathe again. "It's lovely to meet you Molly. I'veheard so much about you from Mary and Robert." I replied appreciatively for her welcome, "it's nice to meet you too Mrs Elliott." Though I didn't like the sound of Roberts name in her sentence. She pointed to the room to the right of the front door saying "Go on into the living room. I think Mary has a film for you to watch."

The first thing I noticed was that the room we entered didn't have a range, which surprised me. It looked more like home than any of my relative's houses. I was pleased that she had a video recorder. We didn't have one at home. Maria had so I'd watched lots of videos at her house. I saw my favourite film *Pretty in pink* on top of the TV and I smiled. We had written to each other about Molly Ringwood as she had my name but Mary's features.

Mary's mother brought some red lemonade and tayto crisps. When she left, Mary was apologetic, "I'm sorry about rushing you here." I was curious but unconcerned about the change of venue, "That's fine" I responded. "No, it's not, you came to see me, and would have sat with me in town, even though you know that your family or their friends may see you with me. I didn't offer you the same consideration."

I thought of the plan I'd put together to arrange this meeting myself, "Well Saoirse doesn't know I'm here. All the family and Sean have gone to the game." I pulled a face in apology. "Jack drove me right to the door and he'll come and collect me."

"Oh, I don't feel so bad now." She was relieved and thankfully not upset. I was glad that this came up. It sounded like neither of us wanted to offend the other. We laughed in relief but she stopped quickly and she became pale again. I waited as I knew that she had something serious to say. She sat down on the sofa and leaned forward and I mirrored her, we were each sitting at the end of the sofa facing each other.

I was worried now as she seemed to have some sort of speech prepared, "did you hear that there was a shooting near your Granny's house after Christmas?" It definitely was not what I'd expected her to say. I thought about it and did remember hearing it on the news and talking about it to my Dad. I'd been surprised by his response so I didn't want to talk about it. He had felt there was a justified reason for the murder, knowing the area so well. I didn't say this to Mary but nodded in answer to her question.

She took a deep breath, "his girlfriend is my relation. She saw it all." I was about to say how sorry I was, but she'd taken another deep breath before I could speak. "Also, there are some people who live around here who seem to agree with what happened." She didn't say Catholics but I knew that's what she probably meant. When I looked at her more closely, I could see in her eyes it seemed even more personal than that.

I looked away thinking about what my Dad had said. I thought that it was most likely that Saoirse and her family aswell as Sean may be of that opinion too. Not that I'd any idea why that could be. I started to talk but she was eager to carry on. "Molly, I know you aren't involved in the divide in this country. I'vealways appreciated you not taking sides. Especially as I know your family have had completely different experiences than we have." I agreed, "well I don't see you like that. I just think we have a lot in common. We like the same things." I indicated the video box on the TV, I smiled but she didn't return it.

She took a very deep breath and I could see her chest rise. She nearly lifted up from her seat. "There are two really big issues. One is that I've heard rumours that the O'Shea's were involved." I jumped up, upset at this idea and exclaimed, "No!" She carried on "and there was a suggestion that the responsible person…" She swallowed. Maybe remembering what happened or her choosing not to use the word murderer. She was looking down so I couldn't see her eyes. I didn't know if she was sad, angry or torn in deference to me.

I called her name. I wanted her to look at me. I needed to gage her mood. I waited. After a few moments, her breathing had returned to normal and she did look at me, "there is an opinion that it couldn't have happened unless information was passed. There is a suggestion that someone either sought that information and it was unintentionally given, or worse, willingly given."

I sat down again in shock. I told her I didn't understand. She looked intently into my eyes. "It is said that there is information being shared between a protestant and a catholic. They are looking for that relationship." I was getting very concerned at her words and at the consequences of what she is saying. "Who is saying that?" She ignored my question, "I'veonly told Robert and my Mum. What about you?"

I licked my lips as it was my mouth that was dry now. I realised how this would sound. I was beseeching her, "Well my Mum and Maria of course ... and Jack but none of them would say anything." I was hesitant at giving his name. I was right to be concerned. She was horrified. "Jack McDermott?" She looked at me in disbelief. I tried to explain, "yes but he wouldn't say, honestly he wouldn't." I was leaning towards her now, pleading with my eyes. I needed her to understand that he wasn't like Sean, and that he'd definitely not be able, or want to get involved.

My mind was whirling over the enormity of the situation. I tried to rationalise the allegation, "Also, wouldn't that have to mean I'd asked you something about your relative, who I didn't know about, or you told me something, that I passed on without your permission. We didn't discuss your relative at all." She wasn't looking at me. I couldn't see if she was listening or like me hearing her own jumbled thoughts.

I felt tears in my eyes. I was begging now. My unconsidered words were tumbling out of my mouth. "and who would I pass it on to anyway?" Again, Mary only answered part of my question, "I know but people might think we had if they found out we were friends. It could look like we did then, or could do that in the future."

I explained truthfully that my own worry was that Saoirse and Sean would find out about us being pen pals, for all these years, and that they might be upset for me not telling them before. I was angry at my naivety. I'd never considered the validity of this issue. "Not this. Nothing like this."

I was panicking. "Do you think I passed something?" She smiled weakly "No. But other people might think that we have. We are putting each other at risk by seeing or writing to each other."

I was desperate now, hearing the seriousness she was placing on this. I closed my mouth that had been static while I listened, to enquire, "what sort of risk?" I didn't understand. She seemed perturbed by my question, "well, if the IRA or the UDA thought that we were passing information..."

She paused and didn't continue, but I knew she had an idea. I responded "but we're not." I was annoyed at myself. At my stupidity. It reminded me of what had been said earlier, "And, about Saoirse?" She spoke slowly "Yes even if it's not us, they could still be involved..."

This was overwhelming me; I'd never anticipated any of this from our overdue discussion. So much worse than I could have ever imagined. I couldn't speak as my mind was still whirling with the different issues. I needed to leave. Not only were there these risks. Extremely serious risks but she seemed to believe that Saoirse and my family were involved aswell.

I stood up quickly and had to right myself by grabbing the arm of the sofa. "I need to go. Now." Mary stood and move towards me, her arms outstretched as if I would fall. "No Molly, I will take you or my Mum will." I shook my head "No... no I will walk."

I was at the front door now. I deserved the anguish that I felt. I was anxious to show my understanding and responsibility. "I'm sorry." With my head falling forward, I stumbled down the garden path realising two things; it was raining and that I didn't know where I was going.

Mary ran down the path "No. It's my fault too. I should have known better. Molly come back in and if you still want to go, call Jack to come and get you." I agreed and Mary led me inside to the phone.

I looked in my pocket for the piece of paper that had Jack's telephone number written on. I hoped that he would be at home. He had said that he would wait inside, though it was a lot earlier than we had imagined. The phone rang a few times and Jack did answer eventually. When he heard my voice, he was apologizing saying he hadn't expected it to me as the call was so early. I didn't explain but asked him to come to the house as soon as he could.

The phone was on the hall table by the front door and I stood beside it waiting. Mary was sat on the stairs. Her face showed the tears that I'd not noticed before. The pink of her cheeks showed her own distress, "Are you angry with me Molly?" I shook my head slowly, "No. Of course not. I'm worried. I should have taken this all more seriously."

Neither of us spoke. Mary's mother came from the door by the stairs which I assumed was the kitchen. She looked from Mary to me, "what's happened?" Mary was brief, "Molly has to go." But Mary's mother seemed to take in the whole situation. She stood at the stairs as if to support us in our pain. Her eyes flickered between Mary and I. They showed concern and not placing blame as I feared. My family would not be as sympathetic.

There was a beep from outside. I turned to Mary's mother and thanked her for having me. I stopped fleetingly at the front door. I looked over my shoulder to see Mary knowing I wouldn't see her again. She was hugging herself still in the same position on the stairs. "Take care Mary."

I didn't know how else to say our final goodbye. Then I walked as quickly as I could to the car. Jack was looking concerned through the side window and it was only after we drove off that I started to cry, a waterfall of tears I'd never experienced before.

I couldn't tell Jack. It was all too much. He didn't push me. I doubt he had any clue how serious this was. He probably thought it was that we had decided it was for the best to no longer be friends. How could I tell him about Mary's suspicions? Not just about me, Saoirse's family and Sean, but about him too.

He took me to my Grannies. Sensing my pain, his compassion was easy to feel, "Molly you need to rest. When you get your thoughts together, we can talk, if you want to." I knew I'd to calm down for Saoirse and Sean's return. I couldn't tell them Mary's fears as I couldn't tell them about Mary. I appreciated Jack's offer but I didn't know if I could take it.

I looked forward to going to bed that night to think things through. I was tired and drained from the emotional turmoil of the day. Saoirse was knocking at the door before I been able to go to bed. She told me as part of the celebration of the win, we were all going out for the night. They would wait in the car whilst I got ready.

I didn't want to go out but I couldn't think of an excuse not to. I didn't expect Jack to be there but Sean explained that one of his older brother's was visiting and had agreed to do the milking. Jack looked concerned and was watching me. Jack didn't seem to be excited about the night either.

Sean was driving again and Saoirse was in the front seat, so Jack was next to me. We discreetly tried to talk about earlier. His eyebrows were raised in question and concern, "Are you ok?" I shook my head, "It's really bad, so much worse than I could ever imagined."

I was watching Saoirse but her and Sean were going through the game second by second and our low tones didn't seem to carry over to her. I wished that I could just tell Jack all about it. He wouldn't blame me. But I blamed me. How could I not even have thought about this? I'd heard so many times the stories about what happened to informers, from both sides. Why on earth would I be exempt from that? It was not just naive. It was stupid. It had been reckless.

No wonder my Mum and Maria had been growing more concerned. There was no way to find out what was going on with the murder Mary had talked about. No one to ask. *Unless I told Saoirse about Mary.* Which I couldn't. She'd be the first to say that Mary and my friendship was dangerous to each other and those around us.

I'd a very good idea about how She'd react to that. I'd seen Saoirse angry and I would not like to be at the receiving end. Also, I wasn't sure I wanted to know how far Saoirse and her family's beliefs ran! I really wanted to ask Saoirse about everything I heard learnt today but She'd be suspicious as I'd never mentioned these attacks or types of rumours before.

The thought that I would pass information? It was horrifying. I would never do that, ever. No matter my concerns about war or terrorism. I understood the background of The Cause. I knew about Irish history, not just what Sean told me. I knew about the North. I knew about how Catholic's had been treated there. I knew there had been improvements but not enough. I knew it all. I could see my Mums shock. My Dad's disappointment and fear.

Should I be annoyed that Mary was insinuating things about my family? Should I be worried that Saoirse and her family were involved in the IRA as Mary seemed to be saying? I knew they were republicans but I didn't believe that? Jack was watching me. He had said that he understood, that he would feel the same way as me about Mary. Unlike me though, he hadn't made friends with anyone except his cousins, and my family. He was smart enough not to be in my position at all.

Saoirse pressed play on the cassette and the haunting tune of Simple Minds, Belfast child played and we were all transfixed. We didn't speak. Sean joined in and I'd forgotten that he could sing these traditional Irish ballads so well *Come back people...*Catholic people had had to leave because it was war. So many people had died. People were still dying. I could die. Mary could die. There was hope that it could get better but could it still be lost for us.

I was so distracted. I didn't want to be there. The club was packed with people, lots of them were also celebrating the win. I saw Saoirse's boyfriend briefly and then she disappeared with him. Sean and Jack were nowhere to be seen. I thought that they must have be at the bar. I just wanted to get back to my Grannies to sort out my feelings. This seemed wrong when Mary was suffering more than me. Her family being upset about the murder. She obviously knew this man that was killed.

As it was a warm night now and despite the earlier rain I sat outside. I wasn't drinking so I didn't need to get a drink. I could hear the music and normally would be dancing but instead I was looking at the people around me and wondered how they all felt about these issues. Living here all the time, it didn't seem to worry them at all. My Mum seemed to be the only other conflicted person that I knew. Either they were passionate about what they felt or it didn't concern them at all, like my sisters.

Someone approached me and it wasn't until he was in front of me that I realised it was Robert. He pointed to the wall that I was sitting on, "Can I sit with you?" I nodded hopeful he may be able to answer my questions. I forced myself not to look around for Saoirse or Sean. I didn't want Jack to see me with him either but that was for another reason entirely.

Before he could speak, I enquired "how is Mary?" The words rushed out of my mouth, "I left so quickly as I just didn't know how to react to what she said." I didn't want to say that I also had concerns about what she thought of my family. It seemed wrong given the circumstances. My intake of breath was audible, "I don't know the details of what happened to your relative. I'm not sure whether I need too."

I paused to see his reaction, he was looking concerned too, not angry. "I tried not to take sides. To me there have never been any sides. I just got on with Mary and loved getting her letters, we are so alike in our opinions." I wanted him to know if was all about my friendship with Mary and that I didn't include him in that.

Robert didn't speak for a moment but he had also been thoughtful and deliberate on the other occasions that we had met.

"Molly, do not take on the responsibility for what the killers did. Also, what Mary said about your family, she does not have evidence. She has listened to other people. I know that Saoirse's experience has been different to ours. I know your family's opinion will be affected by that. I do not think you are passing information. This murder has made things real for Mary." I said "wouldn't I'veto be involved with the IRA to make her fears true?" Robert didn't answer me which made me think that's what he thought.

The sounds of the club seemed to have died away and Robert continued to sit there looking ahead. I needed more, "Robert, what do you know about this, is there a real cause for concern?" He shook his head unconvincingly, "I don't know. Do you not think, that you should discuss this with Saoirse and Sean?" The look he gave me made me think that he already knew that I didn't want to do that.

I thought if I knew more about what had happened it could help me decide. "What did my family say about the shooting, that Mary is concerned about?" He swallowed, his face was pink and clammy, not from the weather but as he was struggling to answer. He looked at his hands and spread them wide. He leaned forward to try to get his brown hair to cover his face but it was too short.

I could see him clearly now under the moonlight as there was a gap in the clouds. I could also see the stars. I was suddenly disappointed that there had been a change in the weather. If it had been as cold as usual or raining like earlier, I would have been inside. I would not be having this conversation with him. I didn't want to know his point of view but I needed to know. I was finding it very uncomfortable. Like a child I wished that I'd never started my friendship with Mary, to never have to hear what I was hearing or think what I was thinking.

Robert was speaking in a low voice and I missed his first words. As he was looking down, he didn't realise that I'd not heard him but when I told him. he looked up, "Sorry. I don't really know anything for sure but I've heard bits and pieces. Mary knows more as she goes to the Tech with Saoirse. I do know about Noraid for sure and that definitely does not fill me with confidence about Saoirse's family beliefs."

I'd no idea what Noraid was so this didn't help me but from his voice it didn't sound good. He saw my confusion, "It is meant to be an American charity for Northern Irish families, to help prisoners' families or send children on vacations. It's not, it is really a cover to fund the IRA." I said out loud a thought that jumped into my mind. "Like collecting for *The Cause*." Immediately I knew that I should not have said that.

He turned towards me. He made me feel even more uncomfortable than he usually did. He looked deep into my eyes. I shuddered. His eyes were searching mine. He looked disappointed. "What do you mean Molly?" I'd to lower my eyes from his stare.

I bit my lip and took a deep breath. "My family have always gone to an Irish catholic club. I used to love it when I was young. It was a great place to make friends. As often when the news was bad about Ireland our neighbours wouldn't be allowed to play with us. I remember at the dances when the bands came, the hall was filled with people and someone would be collecting for *'The Cause.'* I didn't know what it was then but now I think it was for the IRA too."

He was processing what I was telling him. I'd never even discussed this issue with Mary. "Your mother and father?" I replied "I never saw them give anything." I didn't see it but I couldn't be confident that my Dad hadn't. In fact, I was sure that he had.

I was glad when he changed the subject. He took a really deep breath. His shoulders lifted as he did, he leaned back and looked at the sky, in desperation it seemed. He was conflicted, "All we know is that there are rumours of informing. Mary says that you didn't discuss it so I know there are no links to you. But it could be suggested if anyone knew about your friendship and link to Saoirse. It's just suspicions. Maybe you and Mary could still be friends. You need to make a decision; you both need to make a choice."

He got up then, he looked sad, "I'm sorry that this has happened. I really like you. I wish things were different." He walked away with his eyes staring at the ground. This definitely was time to decide on my allegiances. I knew that I'd to sever all ties with them both. It was a harder decision about Mary than Robert. I didn't want any contact with him. I never had. My choice was made then. I would never contact Mary again.

I looked up and saw Jack standing outside the bar doors. I attempted a smile and he came over. He sat in the same spot that Robert had left. "I saw you talking to Robert, it looked intense." I nodded as it really had been. "I didn't understand the consequences of what I'd been doing before. I was acting like I would as if I was in London but it's nothing like that here. I need to stop it now. It's not a game, it's serious. I need to put my family first and stop worrying about the Elliottt's. I won't ever write to Mary again."

I took a deep breath. "Mary thinks my family have links to the IRA. Links to that murder near my Grannies house. She is worried that people will think that she had passed information to me and that I shared it, which led to the murder."

Jack's eyes were wide and his mouth was open, but no words were coming out, he obviously didn't expect this either. He shook his head vehemently, "Oh my god, Oh my god. I don't believe it." I didn't know exactly what he didn't believe. I waited for him to speak. "I understand why there would be suspicions about Saoirse's family. And my family. But not you. You would never do that."

I was glad that he believed me but I'd hoped that he would refute the allegations made against our families. He didn't say that he thought the suspicions were true though so I didn't push him on that. "Thank you for believing in me Jack. It's definitely the right decision to end contact with Mary. I'd been wanting to do it for a long time now. I should have done it before. It's the only option." I was nodding as I spoke as if to reinforce my decision. I knew that it was the right thing. Jack nodded too.

"What about Robert?" His tone was lighter and less serious reducing the tension. His eyes danced and he was grinning, "It's pretty obvious he likes you. Will it be a problem for you, if you stop talking to Mary?" I was horrified that Jack could believe that. I was squirming at the thought of Robert liking me. Reminding me of Maria's teasing that caused her such joy to see my reaction. "Definitely not. I only spoke to him so that I didn't offend Mary. Now I won't have too ever again." I was relieved about that at least.

Then I sighed about the suspicions around me and my family. He continued with the same positive attitude. "It's actually good to hear this about Mary as I've run out of ideas for you to meet up now, anyhow." Even given the circumstances, as

his family were also implicated his face lit up as he laughed.

There was a pause as I thought of the many plans that we had made to allow

me to meet Mary in secret. He seemed to be remembering that too. So many ideas

that we had discussed and had never implemented. He continued saying "I did

enjoy those times we discussed those plans. I'm pleased that the conversations

happened otherwise we probably wouldn't be friends now."

His voice changed and his dancing eyes closed as his gaze left me falling

towards his hands. The clouds had passed the moon and I was surrounded by the

dark now. I'd heard his words, of course I was glad we were friends but it just

reminded me of Maria's words of warning of my attachment to him.

I looked away behind me were some twinkling stars that lifted my mood. I

was making a fresh start and as scary as that was, I knew it was going to happened

whether I liked it or not. I turned to hear his words more clearly, "I know now

though that I shouldn't have encouraged you. I was selfish. I put you at risk. I'm

sorry. You are a very nice person Molly. Someone who would never want to hurt

anyone...like your Fido dido... but you are a bit naive though."

I nodded, "It's been said before." He elbowed me in the side gently and

laughed looking directly at me again. "I meant....you didn't really think that I came

here every summer to see Sean. Did you?" I didn't know what to say to that. His

smile was hopeful. He was nervous. I was surprised I'd never seen this look before.

Forever cheerful even when Sean had been mean to him. Nothing had fazed him.

I licked my lips to appease my dry mouth. I couldn't speak. The worries of

the moments before were overtaken by this revelation. I could see his face clearly

now as the moon emerged again. I saw a blush that I'd seen once before, a long time ago. It encouraged me to see this vulnerability and my smile was of relief as much as joy.

Saoirse and Sean came out of the bar looking around, they were obviously wondering where we were. They saw us and started to walk over. Now it was my panic which allowed me to speak, being drawn back to my conversation with Robert. "What should I say, if they ask what I was doing?" It seemed such a long time ago but it wasn't.

He turned momentarily to look at our cousins. I knew he would be able to answer their questions. I was grateful and expectant, "Tell them the truth, that I was asking you out. Do you want to?" My excitement must have shown on my face, not believing the way this terrible day was ending. I'd stopped dreaming of this moment a long time ago as I'd been advised to do.

When they were in shouting distance, Saoirse barked an instruction, "Come on, let's go swimming." They didn't ask what we had been doing and we readily agreed to the new plan. The thrill of the night made me feel that I could do anything. This time Saoirse sat in the back with me. I was glad for some moments with my thoughts without Jack's presence to distract me from the events of the night.

None of us spoke as Sean drove back to town but the air was electric. He parked by the river. We all knew the Atlantic was not the place to swim at night. Even I, swam or paddled really as it was shallow. I remembered the day years ago when we vowed never to swim here.

I laughed thinking about the fun that we had had over the years. It was so dark. We Couldn't see each other because of the tall trees. We were only able to judge where each of us was by our voices. Though they sometimes were drowned out by the splashing. We didn't want the night to end. It was like we all knew; we would never be all together again.

Part 2: Chapter 16 - The Free state (1948)

"Partition is not a celebration!" Clare's Father stood as if he was addressing a crowd of people. I turned to see my Mammy's reaction. Her head was down but I could see the tightness around her eyes. Mammy was sitting but working as usual darning the boy's socks. Father didn't like to see anyone idle. I went to sit by Mammy, to offer help.

On this occasion, my father wanted me to sit and listen to him. He grabbed me and pulled me towards him. I turned as instructed and sat at his feet. Mammy would be upset that father had pulled my hair again. He never did it to Maggie or Anne. Especially Maggie, his favourite of the girls who was happy to hear the stories and sing his songs about Irish independence.

I listened to what Father was saying; he was talking about the government. "Thank God the King is gone, but we have been fighting since 1916 to get our country back and I will carry on until I die." Maggie asked "Daddy, why is it wrong?" He returned to his position standing tall at the mantlepiece, buoyed again after my misbehaviour had distracted him. "I will tell ye again. Remember I told you the story, the true story about what happened at the Rising?" He looked around furiously as if we would not know what was coming next. How could we ever forget?

I was trying to squeeze myself onto the mat. I was the furthest away from the fire having tried to get away and the floor was cold as usual. I'd my head down hoping that I would not be "chosen" to retell the story. I much preferred to hear about Oisín who lived in the land of Tír na nÓg from Mammy than the horrible things that he talked about. I tried not to smile at the thought of the far-off land, given the mood their Father was in.

I was relieved when Seamus started talking. He leaned forward on the wooden bench he was sitting on. He was excited, "Father, you were the same age as me when you met James Connelly." Our father said "Don't be so happy about that son. It was a bad time to be in, so it was." Their father's face twisted in anger as it so often did.

My oldest brother changed his tack, "You were delivering a message and you saw innocent people being shot by men from the Castle, just because they didn't know what was going on." Their father sat down on the chair by the fireplace to relive the horrors. He repeated the story they had heard so many times before.

He had been running away from the Green, so intent to get back to the GPO. When he saw the soldiers in the street, they had rifles and were looking for rebels. He had pushed himself into the door way of a building, where he saw an old man smoking his pipe watching the street. The old man had shushed him and indicated with his head that he should stay there.

"The soldiers were strutting around the street even though they had no right to be there, so they were." They were looking around and saw the people turn in the street behind them. The soldiers looked at each other and smirked. They called out but were going to shoot them anyway."

Father again put his hands to his ears saying, "the gunfire was so loud and the screams of the lads were desperate. They all fell to the ground." He pointed at the floor as if they were there in front of him, "there was blood everywhere, even on the murderers themselves!" He was shouting again, spitting out his words, "The English Bastards!" as he always did. I hated this story it always frightened me, not about what happened, but him and what he would do next.

Their father was all riled up and his face was very red, though there were white spots too. He had clenched his fists high up in the air as he did when he was very angry. His black wiry long hair seemed to expand at times like this and he looked bigger and scarier than ever. He was very tall anyway but he seemed able to have lent in and gather them all up in one swoop. I was shivering as he often made me feel this scared.

My brother Patrick leaned forward excitedly, "Father, tell us again what Mr Connelly was like and Patrick Pearse when he read the Proclamation." I couldn't believe that my brother was asking for the same details that we had all heard a thousand times before.

Patrick did like this story, as the latter was told to be his namesake (Mammy had told me that her own uncle had the same name so I knew she didn't agree.) Their father looked up to the ceiling, "to see that sight and hear those words. I will never forget. I felt stronger and braver with each word. I was confident that Ireland would truly be free."

He was up again, walking around us, waving the newspaper now. "What fools were we, twenty-two years later and I'm meant to celebrate this. And my father and brothers are long since dead." I could hear the disgust in his voice though he wasn't as loud now, he was no less disturbing.

I couldn't bear hearing about the black and tans now or the Noble six again, but their father was saying "I, we suffered it here in our own county too." I wanted to put my fingers in my ears or run away but was paralysed in fear, one false move and I would be in for it. Even looking away could allow an outlet for his anger.

My older brother Vincent interjected, prolonging my fear, "What happened to Uncle Joseph?" My ears pricked up; this was a new story. Not a nice one if I'd not heard it before now, I was very sure of that. Seamus being the oldest seemed to have been privy to this information before. "I, children he was wrongly arrested and beaten to death by them toughs dressed in uniforms. Then didn't they burn the house down. Evicted again, by the flames.

Then didn't Uncle Jim and Jack have to leave straight after the wake. They would have starved to death if they stayed. Off to the America's! I stayed to look after the bit of land and my Mammy. They have a lot to answer for, them English politicians. Then the cheek of them boyos, coming into our towns. We would not stand for it. These are our lands. Then the uniformed FSA troops, nothing Free State about it at all were arriving in the town.............."

The details were horrific and I knew I should be sympathetic but I wondered what his brothers had done to cause this response from the army. Other families didn't have all the stories that he did. I couldn't let it show on my face but I knew Father would tan the hide off me if he noticed, or tar and feather me which he often said I could do with.

Mammy was getting up to make tea and I wished that I could escape from him to help her. She looked tired and thin. Her beautiful long dark wavy brown hair was hidden in a bun and her face showed no colour as usual. Just the same focused look she had, whenever he was around.

The rest of us being out on the fields were red or brown with the wind and sun aswell as the dirt! Mammy complained that it didn't always wash off us. Not for father to hear as he would say, "away with ye, ye gentry" I'd heard my Mammy say that she wished that was true but only under her breath and not to him, she knew better.

There was a tap at the back door and our neighbour was walking in to the room. The old man was wrapped up well and had his cap pulled tight on to his forehead with white tufts of hairs showing at the side and back. He was pulling it off as he spoke, "Oh I, Ben Bulben" as if he had been there for the retelling of the whole story.

Father stood and lent over us and shook his neighbour's hand saying, "Ye are very welcome. How are ye?" The newcomer nodded "and yeself." Father had calmed down but was still outraged by the news that had set him off initially, "it's a bad business" pointing at the newspaper he had been holding up earlier.

He shouted to Mammy, "No need now for tea, get the put-cheen for Eamonn." The man sat down and was making himself comfortable saying "Glencar. What would they be saying now"? Then they were both reciting a familiar verse, "*Six hearts that were true to old Ireland And died that their land might be free...*"

Mammy gave them their drinks and they toasted each other "Sláinte!" Her father raised his cup for more and after she poured more drink, he took the bottle from her and she turned away. He said to his friend "Eamonn, did you know that Maggie here lost her Uncle at Rahelly House there and not a sound from her."

Eamonn raised his glass to her "I, right an all, not getting involved. There were too many woman wearing trousers and caps in them times." Father sneered,

"She was a small child then so she doesn't understand the importance of his bravery but she was welcomed to the Midlands because of him."

Eamonn nodded, "Sure don't I remember well, her family dead and yours scattered and ye taking her in." Father continued "She was born in Dublin town and her father had been a teacher." There was a pause as if he had said something odd. "Her mother died so he sent her to stay with the Carroll's. She was meant to return home when the summer ended but didn't her father go and die too."

Father sighed as if he'd no choice in the matter, "She had no one so I married her. Ye can tell she's not from here though. Missing the town life and with no love for the green fields. But didn't it all workout for the best. T'was far better for the money to be spent on the head of cattle than on schooling. Sure, what would be the point? But there's still the dreams of the theatre and Yeats!"

Mammy still had her back to the conversation but I didn't think it worked out best for Mammy at all. How awful. How very very sad. Mammy must have been very young if she had only come for the summer. Eamonn was saying "I've never been to the theatre meself but Yeats now he knows how to write about the fight for a united Ireland. *"they dreamed and are dead..."* He recited.

As Eamonn whispered on, their father shouted "Away ye children to bed." I knew Seamus and Vincent would want to stay but I was so happy to get away. I couldn't care less if they would be allowed to stay up or not. My book, my only book was waiting to be read again. The Yeats I knew was not like the poem that Eamonn had recited. It was one of the Yeats poems that I didn't like.

As I scrambled up, I saw Mammy's sad face. I smiled not wanting to show my relief of getting away when she had to stay. As I ran out of the room, she was calling to us all. "Don't forget to say your prayers." When Mammy said that I found it restful but when Father said it to me, it was more of a threat that seemed to give him pleasure

I got ready for bed quickly, then kneeling down on the cold floor for the least time possible and took up my book. I looked again at the inscription and I wondered if Yeats had really written it himself. The words were engraved into my mind and I could recite them like a Hail Mary. I shut my eyes tightly to just think the words as I didn't want Maggie or Anne to hear me, "*Faeries, come take me out of this dull world, For I would ride with you upon the wind.*"

I could still hear the loud voices from below but not the exact words. I opened the book and found Mammy's favourite poem and I wondered again about it. I would ask her why she liked it so much. *Come away, O human child! To the waters and the wild, with a faery, hand in hand, For the worlds more full of weeping than you can understand.* I didn't understand it or many of the other poems. I found some quite scary but having been given the book was a great honour.

It's was unusual to be singled out, being the fifth child out of the seven children. Not the oldest or the youngest, just a middle child. But I knew that I was the only one that was interested. I wanted to go to the place's Mammy had talked about even if they were in Dublin. She'd never return to but I dreamed of going too. I turned over in the bed with a sigh when I heard the singing, knowing the song when I heard the words *A great crowd had gathered....* I knew that they were starting with *James Connolly*, just as they always did.

I woke early as usual and dressed quickly to help Mammy in the kitchen. The fire was lit and she had the kettle going. We were cutting turf today so we had to be up and out early. I handed Father a cup of tea as soon as he came into the room. He stood by the fire drinking his tea. He waited until everyone was sat at the table having their porridge before he spoke.

Father was in a very bad mood. I thought that he may have had too much pot-cheen last night. "We need to be quick today as meself, Vincent and Seamus have business to attend to tonight."

He looked over at Mammy and my eyes darted there to for her reaction but she had her head down. He sneered at her lack of response. I didn't know where they were going but I could sense Mammy's fear. Vincent and Seamus looked very pleased with themselves. Smiley faces and puffed out chests.

Patrick was not happy, saying "Father, can I not go too? Their father laughed, "no children allowed." Patrick was thirteen and still at school so not old enough for whatever it was they were planning. Father continued. "I can only take the children out today that I can trust so Clare you stay and help your Mammy, Maggie, ye are to do the chickens and Emmett, ye will clear the turf shed." Although I was pleased to stay with Mammy. I didn't want to show it.

Maggie and Emmett would be happy to stay and play at nine and seven they were really too young to be going to the bog anyway. Father would think he was punishing me as at ten I should be allowed to go. I didn't want him to know that I was happy to stay. I was getting good at hiding my feelings, just like Mammy did. Mammy and I seemed to upset him the most. Though he mocked Seamus, he didn't hit him anymore.

At least he didn't say something about the "poor Clare's" again, which he did when he was trying to upset me. I was sure that he thought it was the best place for me. But I would never join the nuns. The less attention I received from him the better. He called Mammy and me dreamers and I suppose he was trying to beat it out of us. It wasn't working and he knew it.

Anne was going with the boys but Father wouldn't make her cut the turf, just make sure they had food and drink. He usually made me cut the turf and I hated it. I was always scared that I would fall into the bog and that my father would just smile if I got into trouble. He was in such a bad mood that if I cut it wrong, I would have been in for it. I closed my eyes and thanked god.

When everyone had left, the workers to the field aswell as Maggie and Emmett to the garden, we cleared the kitchen table. Then we sat at the table before we did the work around the house and we were having a cup of tea. I was so pleased to have this time alone with Mammy. I was fed up of hearing father speak about the English and fighting.

I wanted to hear about the theatre in Dublin, "Mammy, the book you gave me, can I really keep it?" Mammy was smiling and nodding. "Won't you miss it?" I exclaimed in shock, that she was so ready to give it away. Maybe it wasn't that good after all.

Mammy was smiling now. Alive. Sometimes when she sat still, she had the look of a corpse at a wake, which always made me shiver. Her chin was raised so were her eyes which were shining. Although I liked to see her like this, I often wondered if she was happy or sad. "I know all the words, they are in my head, and my heart. My memory cannot be taken from me and if they are you can tell me." She spoke softly but her words were strong and meaningful.

As I listened to her, I remembered Father saying, "she thinks she's gentry." I didn'tice that she spoke differently from us all, slowly and without our accent. I was confused about the book but pleased at the same time.

Mammy touched me between the eyes as I must have had some worry lines. She smiled at me. I felt loved. It was a rare feeling as Mammy never showed any emotion around Father.

I continued talking quickly as we had a lot of work to do and I wanted to use every second of my time wisely, "How did you get the book?" Mammy wasn't annoyed at the enquiry I repeated often. That was the only trait that her Mammy and Father shared; they like to reminisce but for entirely different reasons.

"I was at the Abbey theatre with my mother and sisters; Mary and Anne. They were emigrating to America and it was a treat to say goodbye to them. I was scared as my Aunt Mary had died on the Titanic but they thought I was silly and laughed at me. They felt me naive but I was a lot younger than them. I would have been scared to leave home. We went to see the play it was more like a dream it was so lyrical. I can just close my eyes and think of Emer still."

Mammy closed her eyes so did I too but after a pause as short as possible, "So, is it not a sad story with his son being dead?" She could see that I didn't understand. She nodded, "But love saved him though." Then she looked sadder than ever. I said "Are you happy? Would you have liked to return to Dublin instead of staying here?" Mammy took a deep breath and said nothing but was getting up to do the work.

I was so angry with myself to ask something so stupid. It was obvious she couldn't say yes. It had taken a lot of energy for Mammy to get up. "Clare what does the pope proclaim about Mothers?" I looked at her and then recited "*that mothers will above all devote their work to the home and the things connected with it.*" She replied "Your right. Come on now, let's get on with it." She seemed fortified by the words and moved swiftly from the chair.

#

Later when dinner had been eaten, I watched my father ready himself to go out, and my two oldest brothers were doing the same. Patrick was gently pulling at my hair and pushed me playfully into the pantry. I was infuriated by him always coming up with these stupid ideas, and went to shout out but he put his hand on my mouth. As I was about to bite his fingers, he whispered "I'm going to follow them. Do ye want to come?" I scowled as I forced my brother's hand away; I couldn't call out as it would draw attention to us so I whispered, "No" near to his ear.

He replied "come on will ye?" I was shaking my head, just the thought of whatever it was and how Mammy would react made me not want to be involved or even interested. Patrick was teasing me, "Ye are a wee baby sometimes. I thought that ye were brave after climbing up the rock but now I'm not so sure." He cut his eyes at me as if exasperated but I could see that he didn't want to go alone.

Although I was a bit pleased that he had come to me and not Anne who was older, I really didn't want to go. "Father will tar and feather me himself if he found out." But he was patting my shoulder saying, "Go on will ye, he won't find out, it's just a bit of a laugh."

As I was considering this Patrick stepped into the kitchen dragging me with him, "Mammy, is it alright if we go out for an hour or so?" She was unsure, "Ok but be careful and back before dark." She meant get back before father and we both knew it. He pulled at my sleeve and pushed me towards the back door. I was trembling but not for the cold but at what I might see. Patrick made a funny face and he made me laugh, though I couldn't stop the ice running through me.

Patrick ran ahead, "Quick now." As their father and brothers were already nearing the end of the lane. They were heading towards the village. We followed in the fields whilst the "three men" walked on the road. It was windy and hard to make out anything being said. We needed to run close and low to the stone walls so as not to be seen. We both ran on ahead guessing where they were going.

When Patrick stopped to get his breath, he noticed that I was far behind him now and sat on the grass. The weather was still good that's why they had been saving the turf today. It could all change quickly so I looked at the sky but I couldn't see any rain thankfully. I said a quick prayer to *St Medard* for the weather to stay that way.

As I caught up with him, I could see that they had turned onto the main street. Patrick was standing now, his hands on his hips and panting as he looked down. I knew I was red in the face and felt warm in the cool evening air. I was breathing heavily too. "I think they are off to the pub!" He looked very jealous.

We climbed over the wall and could run along the road now as they were so far in front. When we turned the corner, they had gone into the pub. We stopped by the shop part of the pub and wondered what to do now. I wanted to go home but Patrick was eager to find out why they were here, not just where.

He told me to wait and he ran around the back. I saw some women walking towards me so I decided to head out of sight. I didn't want any difficult questions that could be hard to explain later as they would be bound to see Mammy at mass.

A call of "Oy," made me turn my head to look down the side of the pub. Patrick was beckoning me towards him. He was standing on a barrel. He was looking through the window. I was intrigued and hauled myself up too. There was plenty of men though no one of school age which seemed to make Patrick feel better about himself.

It must have been the back room of the pub. I'd never seen it before so I was having a good look around. There were at least thirty men dressed as if they were going to mass but it was a Saturday. They were shaking each other's hands and asking after people not there. They were commenting on the good weather and about the Fair next week.

Many of them had newspapers in their hands, rolled up under their arms or folded in their jacket pockets. I could see that most of them were from here as I'd seen them at Mass but there was a small group of men in the middle that I didn't know.

I looked at Patrick and he shook his head, he seemed not to know who they were either. From Dublin I reckon. Do ye see how smart they are." I looked again and the hats and suits were better quality to my family's and the other men there. I spotted my Father; he had a hand on Vincent's shoulder and another man with them all bent in together in a small circle near the door. Seamus was standing apart from them but he was straining to hear what they were saying.

Father was patting Vincent's back and had a proud smile on his face agreeing with everything the stranger said. Vincent was nodding. Another well-dressed man who was standing in the middle indicated the men to take the seats that surrounded him.

When they sat down, he said "Tráthnóna maith, gabhaim buíochas leat as teacht chuig an gcruinniú seo. Creidimid go léir go bhfuil Éire aontaithe, ceannasacht náisiúnta agus féinchinnteoireacht na hÉireann. Many of the men waved their newspapers. Then the man introduced himself as Tony and his colleagues as Sean and Connor.

I pulled Patrick away from the window and whispered, "why are they speaking in Irish?" He was animated, "It must be a secret society otherwise they would be speaking normally. They don't want the English to hear." I looked around quickly but of course there were no English there.

He must have meant protestants but there was none of them there either. As they could speak Irish it didn't answer my question. My heart missed a beat. I didn't like this at all. I wanted to go home but I also wanted to understand. Patrick put his head up to the small window again and I followed suit.

The man called Sean was very excited waving his arms and looking into everyone's faces. The men in the audience were sitting on the edge of their chairs and listening intently. The President of Ireland was getting booed alot. There was a mix of Irish and English being spoken. Questions were asked and some answers were given by the Dubliner's and some answered by their neighbours.

When the conversation was with the men of the town, the three strangers stood together and smiled watching their performances. Their father had alot to say about the Rising, the tans and the army. Many of the men had heard these before but were eager to listen again. He had been arrested himself and put in gaol.

I looked at Patrick in surprise, "Did you know?" Patrick shook his head. Someone else started speaking then so we didn't hear how that had happened. Seamus and Vincent had been listening intently to every word their Father said and to the other, mainly older men.

Tony took the opportunity of a pause to thank the men who had fought for Ireland in the past. Naming names and honouring the dead men of the families there. A short prayer was uttered under their breaths. He continued "Its new blood, young men that we need to carry on with *The Cause*. We must get Ireland reunited.

We must have the same rights for education, jobs and land. This political way is not working. We have to fight again. Like the United Irishmen and the R I B." the men cheered each name "against the Tithe, the tans and the FSA." The men called "I."

This Tony was having a great effect on everyone there. Patrick and I looked at each other impressed and then behind me. I noticed that it was dark now. It was colder too but I was more concerned that Mammy would be worried especially with Father out too. I could see Patrick wanted to stay and he knew I wouldn't go back alone.

"It's finishing up now anyhow." When I looked back inside people were leaving but Tony was talking to one of the Feeney boy's and Sean to our father. I couldn't really hear what was being said. As more men left, they were patting Vincent on his shoulder and I heard a few calls of, "God bless ye son" and "Good luck to ye."

Vincent shook Sean's hand. Then the Feeney boy and Tony came over to them. They all shook hands. Father was standing a few steps back. He looked very pleased with himself. Seamus's mouth was hanging open and he was looking confused.

It was less noisy now and we could clearly hear Tony say to the skinny Feeney boy with the short brown hair "How old are you son?" and he replied "Eighteen, next month Sir!" Tony said "and you Vincent?" "Sixteen" Vincent replied. He did look older and was strong as an ox and as big as one, people would say.

Tony and Sean looked at each other and our Father. Our Father said "He's nearer seventeen and no better man could you have. He's from good stock, you can ask anyone." Seamus touched Vincent's elbow from where he was standing behind him but Vincent pulled away. "I'm ready to take the oath." The Feeney boy nodded in agreement, he looked less sure than Vincent. Tony said "We know well what your

family has done for *The Cause*."

He turned to a door, "After you." When they left, the light went off. I could still hear

them but didn't understand "Geallaim go sollúnta seasamh le agus creidim i

gcuspóirí an IRA agus cloí le gach ordú a eisíonn Comhairle an Airm agus mo chuid

ard-oifigeach uilig dom" I looked at Patrick, "What was that about?" I was confused

and he replied "ye know full well. Come on. Mammy won't be pleased. We have

been away longer than we should've."

He jumped off the barrel and started running. I followed him immediately,

happy to be going home. We ran very fast and I kept up with him all the way. I was

so relieved to be home. We crept through the back door. Mammy was sitting at the

fire, her sewing on her lap, "Thank god, I thought something had happened to the

pair of you. Off to bed now." We both said sorry and good night.

We hid it from Mammy but we were both still out of breath from our run

back from the pub. As we left the kitchen, Patrick left the door open. He went

halfway up the stairs and then sat down. I stopped behind him, "aren't you going

up?" He shook his head, "oh no, I'm waiting for them to come back. Listen they are

coming now." I crouched down next to him. I was still really scared about what we

had heard and seen through the pub window.

Even though we couldn't see from where we were, we heard Mammy ask

"Where's Vincent?" Patrick and I were leaning over the banister now to see but still

we couldn't. Father was abrupt in his reply, "He emigrated." Mammy shouted out in

a shocked voice, "without saying goodbye?"

I couldn't see him but I was sure that he would be looking very pleased with

himself. "He got a chance and he's taken it." Mammy's voice was breaking, "but why, I don't understand, there's plenty of work on the farm for him. Who's going to help you?" Mammy was crying now. Father was sighing, talking as if to a child. "Argh sure Patrick is about finished school now and I've another son still here, even if he is a waste of space." I felt sorry that Seamus had to listen to the insult.

My Mammy sounded terrified, "Please tell me where he has gone?" When there was no response, "O no, please god no, don't say it has anything to do with *The Cause?*" Their father bellowed "and why not. He has taken the oath and he will do what they need him too. I would go meself, if I didn't have ye all, bleeding me dry but Vincent can keep up the family tradition instead. You should be proud having a son in the IRA." She cried "but he's only sixteen, he still a child."

I was scared, Mammy had said too much. Her sobbing made our father shout louder. His smugness turned to anger. "Ye bloody stupid, ignorant bitch. Why I married you is beyond me. Stop ye crying." After another loud sob we heard a slap, a scream and a bang, Mammy must have fallen to the floor. We didn't hear her get up and there was no more crying. Patrick and I looked at each other. He was biting his lip. His concern radiating from his eyes. I was silently crying.

We were torn about what to do. We desperately wanted to help Mammy but we didn't want him to know that we had been listening. Their father bellowed, "Leave her." This must have been directed towards Seamus and then we saw our father in the kitchen doorway and we ran upstairs to bed.

I was very scared. I was worried about Mammy and prayed she was alright. I couldn't sleep until I heard her come up the stairs. It was only when I heard her getting into bed, that I started to think about what Vincent had done. I didn't think that he had really wanted to go. I wondered where he was now and what they would make him do.

Part 3

1989

London

Part 3: Chapter 17 - Sean

Hi Molly

Sadly, my father has become very unwell since I saw you last and he is in the hospital. He needs alot of care and the Doctor has warned us that he may never come home again. As you know my Mother is a similar age, she had me very late, and she's not well either. I know she wanted me to stay with her and become a farmer so she was disappointed that I don't want that anymore.

When the rest of the family came to visit my father, I told them that I don't want to stay at home or go to university. They were not very happy but my sister Carrie, and her husband agreed to move in here for the time being, to look after my mother and the farm so I could look for a job elsewhere. They know I've been looking after the farm singlehandedly for a long while and that I need a rest, at the very least.

Jack and his father came down to the hospital too. Jack's father has got me a job interview which is really good timing so I'm heading over to London on 2nd September. Jack has an Aunt there so we are both coming over on the boat. Jack is driving us down from Holyhead.

The job is at a newspaper which makes me perfect for them! Hence the long letter, I'm practising my journalistic skills! I know that you will be surprised about me wanting to go to England but I'm older and wiser. I know now that I was too

black and white about England in the past.

I'm sure Jack will write to you separately and I hope that you will come to the

interview with me. Then afterwards we can go out to celebrate!

There's nothing like a bit of confidence.

See you soon

Sean

#

Dear Molly

I hope you are well.

I'm sure that you have heard that my Uncle, Sean's Dad, is dying and does not have

long to live. He has a few weeks at most. My Dad and I were back down to see him

yesterday. I don't think that he knew we were there but it was some comfort to my

father to see him.

When we saw Sean, he had just told his family that he wanted to look for a job in

London. Luckily my father was able to suggest a job as he knows the owner of the

newspaper. His friend had actually asked him a couple of days ago, if he knew

anyone that might be suitable. Sean jumped at the opportunity and I'd say that he

has a pretty good chance of getting it as my Father has put in a good word for him.

I offered to drive him as I hoped to be able to see you again before I start at UCD

and you go back to college. I know it's not long since I saw you last but we didn't

really get a chance to say a proper goodbye.

Sean told me that he was going to write to you but I wanted to let you know that I

was coming with him, just in case he forgot to mention it! I think Sean wants you to take him to his interview as he seems a bit daunted by London especially as he has never been there before.

I'm sure you were as shocked as I was to hear that he wants to move to England! I definitely didn't see that coming. I never thought he would leave here, considering how much he loves Ireland.

As Sean is visiting his family on Wednesday, it would be great if you would like to go out with me then. Please write back as soon as you can, to say if you do want to meet up.

Did you hear from Mary (or Robert)? Do we need another plan?

I saw a Fido dido keyring and I'd to get it for you. I will bring it with me when I come over.

Hope to see you soon

Jack

#

Hi Molly

Sean said that he was going to write to you himself so I'm sure that you already know the sad news about his father. This must have been the reason that it made him think about his own future. He didn't even discuss it with me first! I cannot believe that he wants to live in England, especially after the grief he has given you over the years. I'm pleased that Jack's Dad was able to arrange this interview. I hope that he gets the job but it will be strange without him. I will miss him not being just up the road, don't tell him that though. I do need to study hard if I want to get into College next year so this will mean that all his crazy capers won't be able to distract me. His sense of direction and parking skills have not improved so I hope

that he doesn't have to drive for this job. ha ha

I hear that Jack is taking Sean to London which is very nice of him considering how

he has been treated by his cousin in the past. I wonder if he has an ulterior motive?

I hope you can ALL meet up but don't have too much fun without me!

Write and tell me all the news as soon as they leave.

Love Saoirse x

#

Dear Sean

I'm sorry to hear about your father; I hope he is as comfortable as he can be.

It is good news about the job interview. I'm in shock that you want to leave Ireland

but I agree that your storytelling skills will come in handy as a journalist!

My Mum wants to cook dinner for you and Jack before your interview and I think

my Dad wants to take you to the Club too. So, if you are free, please come over to

me on Sunday about 12pm.

Call me when you get to London to let me know if you can.

See you then.

Molly

#

Dear Jack

I'm good thanks. I hope you are well too. I'm sorry to hear about your uncle and I

hope he's not in any pain. I'm really pleased for Sean but I cannot believe that he wants to move here. I never expected him to even visit London after all his talk. My Mum has invited you both over for dinner on Sunday, in case he doesn't mention it to you himself! Sean did ask if I could go to the interview with him so I hope I will see you then. I would really like to meet up next Wednesday aswell. It is very generous of you to take Sean over. I'm glad that you have the time to come as I know you are getting ready for University. You must be really excited. Thank you for getting me a present, especially Fido dido, I can't get it over here. I got something for you too. I'm glad that I don't have to send it in the post, it's quite big! Thankfully there has been no news from Mary (or Robert) so I hope she has decided that it's for the best not to contact me either. It's so weird finally writing to you, after all these years knowing you.

I'm really looking forward to seeing you.

Molly

#

Jack had called to confirm they would be able to come to dinner so I was excited and nervous in equal measures. I was even happy cleaning the living room to my Mum's satisfaction. Though it was a lot more than it needed. She had made me pull out the sofa and chairs for the hoover and clean the windows.

When I finally sat down in the living room to wait for them a Rick Astley's song; Never gonna give you up entered my head. *We've known each other for so long....* which made me scared to be seeing Jack as something other than friends. My stomach turned. I was dreading the knock on the door. I tried to watch the TV but of course there was nothing on and I couldn't concentrate either. I'd no idea how I should act around him.

I knew Jack was driving so they were right on time. I answered the door and my Mum followed me out into the hall. I gave Sean a hug, which was highly unusual, and told him I was sorry to hear about his father. My Mum said hello to them both and took Sean into the living room to see my Dad. I was left with Jack. I didn't know how to greet him as I'd never even shaken his hand before. He leaned forward and kissed my cheek. I blushed and so did he.

I showed him into the living room and he went over to my father and shook his hand, "Good to see you again Mr O'Donnell." My Dad patted Jack's shoulder as he sat back down in his armchair, he was in good spirits and smiled. "Call me Hugh."

Before Jack sat down next to Sean, he turned to my Mum, "Thank you for inviting me Mrs O'Donnell." She was pleased, she'd have been annoyed if he hadn't made that greeting. I was sure that Sean hadn't given the same, "Ah now, you're very welcome." I offered them tea but my Dad was leaning forward in his chair, "Nothing for us Molly, we'll be popping over the road for an hour or so."

I hoped the disappointment didn't show on my face at their quick departure. Jack interjected, "Hugh, I'd been hoping that Molly would be able to show me Greenwich. I would really like to see the architecture there. I need to pick a building for a project on my course." He turned to me then raising his eyebrows in question and I agreed eagerly.

My Dad was perplexed at this turn of events, "well, next time then Jack. Come on now Sean, Vincent will be waiting for us." They left and my Mum was already sitting back in her chair to watch the TV as she didn't normally get the chance. "Dinner will be around 3pm so be back by then. Have fun."

As we left the house, I picked up a plastic bag by the door. Jack pointed to the car nearest the gate. "I'm parked just outside." I followed him to the car. I was impressed that his Dad had bought it for him for getting into university. He was telling me that sometimes it was good to be an only child. We talked about the journey over and the weather. It sounded like the crossing was no better that usual and it didn't look like he enjoyed it.

When I sat next to him in the front seat, I handed him the plastic bag. I was pleased that I could talk so easily with him. I'd known him a while but hadn't really spent that much time alone with him. Most of our conversations had been whispered when our cousins were out of range.

"It's a promotional item. My friend works in a record shop and when I'd told her that you love their music, she was happy to pass it on. I hope it's ok." I was embarrassed that I'd been talking about him but Jack didn't seem to mind about that. He was so enthusiastic; he'd probably like the present whatever it was.

He took out the record bag for U2s new album and he smiled and as I was saying "It's for ....." he kissed me before I could finish saying. He was really pleased. "I love it Molly. Thank you so much." I was glad that he liked it and so shocked that he had kissed me. It had been so natural, there had been no awkwardness as I'd expected.

He knew what I'd been trying to say, "I will use it for university. It's a perfect size for my notebooks." He continued to chat; he was not flustered like me. I was red in the face and glad when he leaned forward and took a paper bag from the glove compartment and gave it to me.

He was self-conscious now. "I'm sorry, it's nothing in comparison to this, looking at the black bag in his lap." I took out the keyring and I smiled. "No, it's great, thank you," I was at ease when hugged I him. I was so happy to be there, and that both gifts were though of no financial significance were so meaningful.

I directed him to Greenwich and as I did, he told me about his uncle, Sean's father. Then we were laughing about Sean's decision to move to London and neither of us could work it out.

He apologised for not going out with my Dad and I wondered if it was a bit of an excuse not to go to the club. Obviously, he was driving so he wouldn't be able to drink. More than that I didn't think he would have enjoyed the conversation as it was so often about *The Cause*. Which he never joined in with. What he did say was "I can't believe we are finally alone, there's no chance of either of them popping up at Greenwich Park!"

I knew he meant Sean and Saoirse. We always knew they were not far away whenever we stayed with them in Ireland. They could find us at any time. It had only been a problem before when we would be hatching a plan for me to meet Mary. I smiled with relief too, very strange but definitely good.

He was telling me about his course and explained, "I've picked a building in London to research and analyse. It means that I need to come over in my reading week in October. We could meet up then, if you are around?" I was surprised and happy. "It will be great to see you." He smiled too and laughed, "I love it when a plan comes together!" We were at the traffic lights so he was able to rub his hands together as he spoke.

We were parking in Greenwich Park as I knew it was difficult in Greenwich itself. He told me about the observatory and why the building fascinated him. I suggested that the best view would be to look up from the bottom of the hill. l had been to this park so many times before either to go on the swings, in the boating lake or to play tennis, never before noticing the architecture.

The path was steep so I knew it was always better to walk down slowly. A bike thundered past me from behind, Jack grabbed my hand to get me out of the way. He didn't let it go afterwards. We were walking close together now but not talking, our silences were always comfortable. I led him to a bench past the playground to look up at the building. He nodded when I recommended that he look at the view from the riverfront after aswell

I didn't speak and left him to do what he needed to do. He took a camera out of his jacket pocket and took a few snaps. He also had a notebook which he used to do a quick sketch. I was impressed, I'd never seen him do anything like this before. He was really focussed on his work and his enjoyment was clear to see.

I was enjoying the autumn sunshine and I thought of my own college and what I wanted to do next. It was not far from here and I passed the park every day to get there. I didn't enjoy any subject as much as Jack obviously did. Even if I'd, I knew that we didn't have the money for me to carry on my studies anyway. My sisters had gone straight to work after secondary school and they were both doing well in their jobs.

After we had been to the river front and were walking back up the hill to the car, he asked me if we could come back on Wednesday. He explained that he really would like to go inside the observatory. I agreed as I'd wanted to go myself but no one else had. He was apologetic, "I will be more attentive when we meet next."

I laughed, "you really put me to shame, I really need to think what I will do next year. I'veno plan for the future." He was eager to help. "I'm the king of plans as you well know. So, we will work it out together. How will Molly O'Donnell make good?" I smiled surprised he remembered the film I was named after.

Before we got to the car, he took out his camera again. "I need to take a photo of the view. Then afterwards, can I take one of you?" I smiled and hoped it would be a good one. I probably would never know as he would get the film developed in Ireland. We got in the car but he didn't start the engine. I checked the clock and we had plenty of time to get back for dinner.

He was serious now, "Thinking of plans and by that, I mean the Elliott's, what did happen between you and Robert?" I didn't really want to explain how I'd probably been the cause of the problems. He was smiling encouragingly, "Just tell me from the beginning. I can judge if it's all your own fault as you believe. I know it has you worried."

I took a fortifying breath, "Well when I was ten, it was on my second visit to Ireland that I." He interrupted showing surprise, "You only came to Ireland from the age of nine? Why? sorry, I will hear that another time, carry on."

"The first time I met Mary and Robert was on the beach. Sean and Saoirse weren't happy but back then I didn't really understand why. Near the end of my holiday, I bumped into Mary in the bookshop. She asked if she could write to me. I didn't think much of it as I'd lots of pen pals.

It wasn't until a couple of summers later that I saw them again. I knew by then that my friendship with Mary was wrong. She saw me at a disco and she pulled me to dance. Well, you can imagine Saoirse and Sean weren't dancing themselves." He raised his eyebrows at the mention of his cousin and looked heavenward in answer.

"I was having fun but Saoirse was not happy. Later she was livid when Robert asked me to dance with him." Jack looked shocked himself. "I didn't want to dance with him but I didn't want to upset Mary either. I'd never been asked to dance by a boy before so I said yes."

Jack was smiling, "so was it your politeness or were you lured by him?" I was not happy. "No! That makes it sound that I liked him! Lured by the dance, maybe." I was indignant. "Well when you meet Maria, she will tell you what I thought of him." He was laughing so I knew that he was just teasing me.

I continued with my chronology. "Then there was the year that we saw the Drifters, which was one of your ideas! I wanted a photo of Mary and me. He just appeared from nowhere to take it." I needed Jack to understand. "I don't want to sound rude but he has always given me the creeps?" He was listening intently so I carried on, unsure of his opinion.

"Last year I saw him in the bookshop. I was looking at cards. He said that he was running errands for his father. I thought it was suspicious particularly as I'd just spoken to Mary on the phone. At the time I'd wondered if Mary had told him I was in town. I'd rung her not long before."

Jack nodded, "And if anyone knows you at all, they would know to find you there. Seems like she was playing matchmaker, the same as me. I laughed that he was comparing his own plans with hers, but then my stomach turned at the thought of it.

"He asked me to go for a drink. I really didn't want to go but I didn't have an excuse, you know how crap I'm at that." He seemed to get more amused as I got more anxious. "So, you went to the diner? Saoirse must have been working at the bakery then?" I nodded, "I couldn't wait to get away from him. I left as soon as I could.

Then he turned up when I'd lunch with Mary. I was not happy and I left as soon as I could, without being rude. He was always so formal and eager to see me. I was not pleased to see him but I tried not to show it." Jack was shaking his head, "Molly, it seems that it worked too well. I would have thought that you liked me too, if you had been the same way with me."

I was embarrassed, I couldn't look at him. "I know, it was the wrong way round. I probably was doing the opposite to you. So that you didn't guess that I liked you. What an eejit!" He sounded surprised, "Are you saying that you liked me then?" Before I'd to explain myself, he apologised, "ok, we will talk about that in a minute."

I wanted to finish my story which seemed to take longer than I could have ever imagined. On the telling, it seemed worse than I'd previously thought. I was also glad not to have to answer his question.

I was blushing and taking a great interest in my fingers that were laid in my lap. "if you think that's bad. I don't think you will be impressed with what happened next. Not surprised though I should imagine." Jack prepared himself for more, "hit me with it."

"Do you remember that night we went to the club and Saoirse's boyfriend dropped us off?" Jack nodded. "Saoirse said we would get a lift back home easily but I'd worried about it." Jack looked amused again as I did worry about most things. "Robert saw me when I was standing on my own. He came over and we chatted about Mary and my holidays. I got away as quickly as I could. I only spoke to him so that I would not offend Mary."

Jack was shaking his head but smiling at me at the same time. "I really wished you had come because at the end of the night we had no lift. When Saoirse saw Robert, she stood for a moment contemplating something.

She admitted that she had seen us talking earlier. She was annoyed but given the circumstances, she let it go. We were really far from home and were desperate for a lift. He agreed readily. Saoirse rushed to the back seat of the car as not to be seen, I'd supposed. Not that there were many people left. I sat at the front so it didn't look like a cab. I didn't want to but it's a bit rude otherwise."

Jack murmured, "Yes, I'm definitely seeing a pattern here." He didn't look annoyed, which made me able to continue. "He dropped off Saoirse first. She had sent me a look of warning which had made me feel apprehensive but at the time I couldn't understand why.

He drove me down the lane to my Grannies. He parked and got out, then walked me to the front door. I didn't know what to do. I just wanted to get to the back door but before I could, he went to kiss me. I turned my head and he kissed my cheek instead. I thanked him for the lift and rushed around the side of the house and inside."

There was a pause as Jack thought about this, "and last year you saw him at the disco. And anything else?" I took a deep breath. "He said he liked me as he walked away. I didn't say anything as I'd decided not to talk to Mary again." I was looking at him now trying to persuade him it was all unintentional and hoping for reassurance, "That's it, it sounds worse than it really is."

Jack was shaking his head, "Oh Molly, what will I do with you? Ok, it is bad. I can understand why he would misjudge the signs. Do you want or did you ever want something to happen with him?" I shook my head and groaned "never." He exhaled, "He may contact you again you know." I muttered, "That's what I was scared of. I need to be honest with him if I see him again, don't I?"

Jack looked at me as if it was an impossible task. "Practise on me, how do you feel about me?" My stomach turned and I didn't know what to say. My mouth was clamped shut and I couldn't speak. "I know it's hard for you and I can hardly talk myself. I didn't tell you that I liked you for four years!"

I raised my eyebrows and laughed remembering the first summer we met. The bike ride, the song and the beach. "When you fell off your bike, you were so cute." It was his turn to be embarrassed now but I didn't want to make it worse. "I'd been relieved when you stopped to help me. I was so pleased to know that you were nothing like your cousin!" I hoped that explained my feelings as I didn't want to say anything more.

After a pause, his jovial voice returned. "Right, we need to go or we will be late but we do need a plan about Robert." He was driving off, I was crestfallen. "Really? there's no reason that I should see him again." He explained, "He is smitten. I think that he will try to contact you." I worried that Jack would think it was reciprocated as he hadn't known the full story when he had previously asked.

He must have seen the alarm on my face. "Don't worry, I don't believe that you like him, if that's what you're thinking." I was pleased. "It was and to be honest.... I like that you know what I'm thinking, it shows that you know me." I let out a breath and looked at him. "Very good, we are getting somewhere." He was pleased too. "it is a long road for you, Molly Malone. It doesn't mean you have to tell everyone everything, just the very important things."

We got home just before Sean and my Dad. My Uncle Vincent was with them. We had our roast beef and the chat was about the club and who Sean had

297

met. Not long after dinner Jack stated, "We should be going now." Sean was getting louder and louder. Obviously, he would not be able to hold his drink aswell as my Dad and uncle could.

My Mum seemed appreciative of Jacks decision. Everyone said their goodbyes. I walked them both to the door. Sean was saying, "I've always liked you Molly, you are my best friend!" As neither statement was true, Jack and I laughed.

As he led his cousin to his car, Jack confirmed the details of our next meeting, "Cannon Street at 11am on Tuesday." He was watching Sean, checking that he was able to get into the car without help. When he had, Jack waved "Take care." I watched them drive off, then I ran to call Maria to tell her everything. I told her advice was crap and laughed embracing the moment, "I'm just being honest."

I got to Cannon Street at 10.50am as the interview was 11.30am. I hoped they would be on time though I was sure Jack would get him there. I wondered if Sean even deserved all the attention that he was getting, thinking about the way he had treated us both over the years. I felt bad then as Sean had probably been grumpy having to work on the farm and having older parents who needed more help than any of ours.

At five past eleven, I was getting worried but then I saw them get off the train. I was very relieved. I looked at Sean and I was impressed by his new suit which I knew he had been planning to buy yesterday. I told him he looked very smart. I threw a quick smile at Jack which he returned knowing that Sean would not appreciate any other show of affection.

I questioned Sean about the newspaper. He had done his research and was knowledgeable about the company. He didn't seem nervous which was good. I told him to tell me his strengths. He stated that he was knowledgeable about public affairs. Confident when talking to people. Able to complete research from his doing his leaving certificate. He needed no prompting, "I'm hard working from being a farmer and the cows have to be milked at the same time each day so I know how to keep to a deadline." He was confident talking about himself. I agreed with everything that he said.

We walked him to the door of the tall building and we both wished him good luck. We had already discussed where we would meet him afterwards. I watched him enter the building, he seemed self-assured, I shrugged my shoulders, "I don't know why he wanted me here, you got him across London fine and I didn't do anything." Jack disagreed "You found the building much quicker than we would have. He knew you would bolster his confidence and remind him what to say, which you did. He would hardly listen to me, now would he?" I nodded as I knew this was very true.

I realised that Jack hadn't joined in my conversation with Sean. I was intrigued to know how he was coping. I took my opportunity as we waited for our coffees in the café nearby, "How has it been between the two of you? I know you aren't the best of friends, to put it politely." Jack laughed "Molly, what did we discuss about politeness." I decided to be very honest. "well ok, you are not just incompatible, you hate each other." I raised my eyebrows to check that was the case. I'd surprised Jack with the conviction I showed.

"I don't hate him but he isn't easy to like. I think you would agree with that. Would you have been his friend if he wasn't Saoirse's?" I considered his question for a moment and slowly shook my head. "He is entwined with most of my memories of Ireland but I doubt we would be friends. I'm sure he would feel the same but maybe not admit to it."

His question had changed the tone of the conversation, "What about Saoirse, would you be friends with her?" If it was anyone else, I would not have said, "Probably not. We don't have much in common, do we?" It was sad to say that but it was true. "Saoirse certainly feels I'm not brave enough to do the things she does. She thinks that I should take more risks. I think she takes too many. Over the years we have laughed a lot. I do enjoy her letters. I've really loved my times in Ireland. Some more than others!" We both laughed wanting to take the tension out of the air.

Jack nodded "That's about right. For me it's Sean's opinions. He is the only one that is ever right, even if you agree with him! His beliefs and principles concern me. His boasting could get him into trouble. Especially if he meets the wrong sort of people. I think he may already have. Do you understand what I'm saying Molly?" I replied "I do, it has worried me in the past. Who has he been with, that concerns you?" His brow was furrowed again, "Do you remember the pub that your Dad took us to at the seaside, with the tricolour flags outside?" I nodded "Sean has been back since."

He paused looking at me intently. "Do you know what the tricolour represents?" From his question it seemed that it was more than I'd originally thought. Jack answered for me, "sometimes for republicans, sometimes for the IRA." I exclaimed as I was shocked that it would be so openly displayed but not as much as I should have been. I asked him for his opinion. "I was always worried that they would drag you into it. I tried to be there to prevent it."

I decided to be brave as I was scared of the answer, "What do you think about Saoirse?" His reply was delayed, he was biting his lip before speaking more slowly, "her family are known sympathisers. I don't know if it goes further than that. My Mum knew it and didn't like it, even all that time ago. That's why she moved to Dublin to get away from it. I do understand why their feelings are heightened, with them living so close to the north as they do."

I didn't want to know much more so I veered off the subject. "I didn't know your Mum was from the same place. I thought it was just your Dad." Jack seemed pleased with the new direction of our conversation. "Yes, she's great friends with your Aunt Geraldine. They went to school together. How else do you think I knew when you would be on your holidays?"

I was surprised, "you checked up on me!" I expressed fake annoyance. He was pouting, pretending to be upset. "Didn't you check up on me?" I laughed at the thought of it, "The only person who I could ask was your cousin. "One," counting on my fingers "he wouldn't tell me. Two, he wouldn't know. And three, it would just make him grumpier. Not that I'm sure he could be grumpier than he often was."

I conceded "Apart from the storytelling, there were fun times too though I can't deny that!" Jack was smiling, "Yes there were. Who'd of thought Molly Malone would go skinny dipping, now that's taking a risk." I was affronted, "I didn't go skinny dipping in the river." He laughed "You didn't, oh no, I did! I wasn't sure whether to believe him or not.

I changed the subject again "next time you come over; you can see if my golfing prowess has improved." He said "Now that was a funny day. The only way that you could have improved, is if you have been practising night and day since." I shook my head as I hadn't even been once so I knew I would be still terrible. Suitably embarrassed, I lowered my head in mock shame and then we both laughed.

I was surprised that Sean's interview was so long. I'd only been to ones in shops so I thought it must be different. Jack had only worked with his Dad so he had no interview experience either. Sean came into the cafe an hour after he went in. He was singing U2s song, *Stranger, stranger in a strange land*. He seemed very confident and his smile was wide. He told us it went well. "We were chatting for about half an hour after the interview ended!"

He hadn't sat down. I asked if he wanted a coffee. He shook his head "forget that, let's have a pint." I suggested that we walk over London bridge as it was a nice day and go to a pub nearer the station, so we could enjoy the Autumn sun. I took then to an olde worldly pub, with cobbles in an enclosed courtyard. There were picnic tables mostly full but we were able to get one for just us. We all had our jackets on but it was nice because of that.

Jack asked us what we wanted to drink and he went inside to the bar. He carried out a pint of Guinness, two bottles of lager with lime and he also had bags of crisps in his teeth. Sean told us all about the interview. He liked the owner and would like to work there. They were seeing other people but they would let him know next week.

Sean was going to his Aunt's house in the morning, she lived in west London. When he'd heard we were going to the observatory, he'd laughed in disgust, "Thank the lord that I'm not going so." They were both going home on Thursday. ack was starting university next week. Sean would wait at home to hear if he got the job.

We spoke about the future. Jack about UCD, me about my college and Sean's contribution was to say that the cows would've missed him. We all laughed. "But they really will have" and he meant it. I was wondering how they would feel if he left altogether.

We had a few more drinks then went to McDonalds for food before we parted. As I wouldn't see him before he went home. I smiled encouragingly "I really think you will get this job. I hope your father is not suffering at all. Write and let me know your news." I felt like saying I was asking after him as would be expected but I couldn't, Jack caught my eye.

I'd to look away to cover my amusement so I changed the subject to one we could laugh at. "I'm so looking forward to you becoming an Englishman. You are where you live, aren't you Sean?" Repeating what he had said to me many times in the past.

He laughed and didn't disagree as he was in such a good mood. Jack was surprised by his cousin's response and had raised his eyebrows and then said to me "I will come and get you at 10am, if that's ok?" I nodded and smiled. I checked my watch and realised that I'd to run for my train. I just called bye to them as I turned. I was glad that there were no awkward farewells, with either of them.

We had a lovely day at the observatory. We had good weather so after we came out, we sat looking at the building for a long time while Jack explained the features that I hadn't seen before or been aware of. When we walked around the park, I showed him where I played tennis. Then down to the boating lake where I'd many unsuccessful attempts to even go in a straight line, which didn't surprise him at all.

He didn't suggest we hire a boat which I was pleased about and I pointed out the swings that I used to love and spend hours on! After we got in his car, Jack turned to me looking very serious. "so, is this just a holiday romance?" I tried not to giggle as I always did when I was flustered, "No, I think we have known each other too long for that." He continued "so you are my girlfriend now then?" I smiled, my heart leapt, "Yes."

I was watching his driving and he was a lot better than Sean. I suspected he had had proper lessons. He became serious now, "I'm not saying this to be a jealous boyfriend," which made us both blush "but please, if you do see Robert, be honest with him. I know it will be hard for you but I really think he does like you." He paused for a moment to ensure I understood. "Also, when Sean gets this job, take him out with you but be careful of any new friends that he meets. Is that ok?"

He seemed troubled so I nodded. I knew he was genuinely worried about these two things and that he wanted to protect me. After what had happened with Mary, I knew I should take him seriously. I hoped that I wouldn't see Robert again.

I knew I would be wary of Sean's new friends anyway. He saw that I understood him. "I'd a lovely time today" and I replied "It's been really great seeing you this last couple of days, on our own!" He nodded in agreement looking more handsome than ever. "I will write to you and hopefully I will see you in October."

I hugged him, "good luck at Uni. I can't wait to hear all about it," as I got out of the car, I watched him as he pulled away and I stood for a few moments on the pavement before I went into my house thinking about what he had said.

#

On the Monday after Sean went back home from London, his father died. It was good that he had been with him at the end. Sean had also got the news on the same day, that he'd got the job and that he would need to come to England straight after the funeral. I'd three letters to say the same things.

They all went to the funeral and they all said it was well attended. Sean's father's life was remembered by his family, neighbours and friends. Lots of potcheen was drunk, stories were told and rebels songs sang, for both Sean's father, and Sean himself.

Saoirse told me in her letter, that they sang songs for Sean too as they used to do this in days of old, when they had wakes for those immigrating to America and New Zealand. In them days, they were unlikely to ever return. I was sure that Sean wouldn't last long in England and that he'd be back home within a year but I only told Jack that. Sean's father was buried within three days as was the norm in Ireland.

His mother was matter of fact about it all as Irish women generally are. She was more upset about her youngest son leaving home to go to London. Sean had written to me with the date he was coming over. He also told me that even though her oldest son lived in Birmingham; she'd pronounced, "London was a different kettle of fish altogether."

Sean's departure was quickly arranged. Saoirse's boyfriend was driving over to England anyway so he would get a lift with him. My Dad arranged some digs at Jacinta's house. I could see him whenever I wanted, if I wanted too. I chuckled to myself but knew I would make him very welcome and help in any way I could.

He arrived on the Wednesday before the new job started and he was getting settled into his new home. He came for dinner on the Thursday night. He seemed a little nervous about the job so my Dad offered to take him to the club for a drink. He told him that my Uncle Vincent and a few of the lads including Saoirse's boyfriend would be there too.

I wished him good luck, checked that he knew how to get there on Monday and asked him what he was wearing. He seemed all set so I told him to have a good night and we agreed that we would catch up next week to see how he was getting on.

Saoirse's boyfriend was also staying there. I remembered that I hadn't really liked him the one time that we had met but he had just driven across the country to pick us up, so he may not have been in the best of moods. It was actually two countries as he came over the border from the North, where he lived.

My Mum had gone to the bingo straight after dinner so I was able to use the phone when they had all left. The phone was a real luxury in our house and often had the lock on it, especially when the bill was high. Glad that we were friends again, I rang Jacinta for her opinion of them all, especially Cillian. She spoke very favourably of them all.

I was not sure that I could take her word for it as they were living in her house. As one of them was my uncle, she probably didn't want anyone to hear that she was talking badly about any of them.

I told her about our plan to go out the next Saturday night and checked if She'd be there as normal. She told me that she was busy at home with all the visitors staying. She'd said She'd definitely come next time.

Maria was coming as she wanted to meet Sean. God knows why, after me telling her about the lectures that he had given me in the past, but I'd told her that there had been lots of fun times too. It made me smile, remembering them now. Jacinta's house was walking distance from the club so Sean would go straight to his new home at the end of the night.

#

I thought alot about Sean starting his new job. I wouldn't be seeing him before he started work. He was visiting his Aunt and I was sure he was having a great time there as he had had the last time. It had been my last full week at work. I was working on Saturday too. I needed to get up really early for work in the morning. It was a very long day at the shop but it paid well. That's why I didn't see any news until I got back from work on the Saturday evening.

My Mum was watching the TV when I got in. The newscaster said "eleven British Royal Marines have been killed and many more soldiers injured. The IRA have claimed responsibility for the bomb in the army barracks in Deal." My Mum looked upset as she always did when news like this was on the TV or in the newspaper.

I asked her where Deal was as I'd never been there. She explained, "It's a little further on from where Dads side of the family live." I remembered Sean's story, long ago about an IRA boat taking weapons to Ireland so I needed to know, "is that by the sea?"

She looked at me and knew what I was asking. "No, it's not very close. Deal is in the middle of Kent. ... more likely they drove over from Ireland. There are not many checks travelling on the boat. Definitely not enough." I wondered why she looked so concerned, it was such a terrible thing to happen but it just seemed more than that. I didn't know what it could be and I didn't want to ask her.

Part 3: Chapter 18 - Jack

When Sean did ring me, he was in the best mood that I'd ever heard. He was

brimming over with excitement about his new job. "Of course, it is admin work at

first but it could lead to writing articles later on." He told me that it was a small team

but they had been welcoming. He missed the cows but not the morning and nightly

milking.

He could get up so late, which probably meant about seven for him. He had

worn his suit on the first day but they said trousers with a shirt or jumper in the

winter where okay. There were no ties either which he said he didn't miss from

school. He told me that he was loving London and the people that lived here, but I

suspected he only meant the Irish and second generation Irish as I doubted that

he'd met anyone else in a week.

I'd written to Jack to update him on Sean's move to London. I also told him

that as part of my English A level, I was studying *A much ado about nothing*. I was

playing Beatrice in a play that we were doing to accompany the book. I told him

with ease that *here was a star danced, and under that was I born*. Especially as my

name meant I was a star. Which I'm sure made him laugh.

I didn't want to use any other quotes as they were all about love. I was

having great fun learning the words and it really helped my understanding of the play. I was anxious about the performance at the end of it, which made me practise more.

I was hearing *New Years Day* on the radio constantly which was weird as it was so old now. It always reminded me of Jack. As it made me more aware of my heart as my feelings were definitely radiating from there. *I will be with you again.....*

I told him that I was looking forward to Maria meeting Sean. She'd heard so much about him over the years. I felt that he'd changed so much since he left Ireland that She wouldn't recognise my version of him. Which was great for Sean but not for me. I very much doubted he would back me up. I thought it was ironic that he was happier in England than Ireland. She probably wouldn't believe my descriptions of Jack if Sean carried on as his new self, though he really was much more fun than ever before.

Jack told me that he was loving university. He was excited about meeting other people that liked buildings as much as he did. He said that he had been using his record bag and that it was a perfect size for his sketch pad and notebooks. They were looking at Dublin's landmarks at the moment.

He saw Kilmainham Gaol in a totally different light, and said I should tell Sean about it. Sean and Jack had no plans to write to each other so they expected all news to come via Saoirse and me. I told Jack I would let him know how the night out at The Clifton went.

On Saturday night, Sean walked over to my house and we were meeting Maria in the pub across the road from the club. We got the bus down and Sean was very impressed with the public transport in London and he acknowledged that he didn't even need a car here, but that he might get one so he could go home to see his mother. I told him not to bother as his sense of direction and parking weren't great.

We laughed as it was Saoirse's favourite come back to him, when she hadn't anything else to say.

Sean was happy at Jacinta's house and he said he liked her. I was very curious about that and he was very specific to say "as friends" and his tone suggested the same. I tried to squeeze some information about him as he was being so chatty, "not the same as Saoirse then." He didn't respond and I could see that it made him uncomfortable so I moved swiftly on with our conversation.

Saoirse was still going out with Cillian. My opinion of Cillian hadn't altered. Not that I knew him well enough to make a real judgement. I doubted Sean liked him either. Even if Saoirse split up with Cillian, Saoirse would not go out with Sean. She viewed Sean as her best friend.

If she split up with Cillian that She'd go out with someone much older than Sean again anyway. She seemed to like a more mature serious man. When I told Jack, about Sean and Saoirse, he had agreed that was probably the situation. He always responded to my questions about them but he never mentioned them himself.

Maria was already in the pub talking with her brother. When she saw us, she came straight to the bar to meet us. I introduced Maria to Sean and she was asking how he was liking England and his new job. He answered her questions but didn't ask her anything. I thought he was more nervous than he was letting on. He paid for the drinks with his first week's wages.

When he handed me my drink, he looked at me oddly, "Why have you got makeup on? I've never seen ye wear makeup before." I reminded him that we weren't eighteen yet so we needed false ID to get into the club. My sisters and Maria's next-door neighbours driving licence were at least three years older than we were. I explained that I'd more trouble than Maria as I was often turned away. He was surprised, "but you get in no bother in Ireland." I agreed, "there seems to be no minimum age in any pub in Ireland."

He was interested to carry on the chat, "It's just weird that's all. What would you do if ye don't get in tonight?" Looking glum and worried that might happen again. "go home!" He seemed genuinely concerned which definitely would go against everything I'd told Maria about him.

"What if only one of ye get in?" My being realistic was making him shake his head, "You go in, if you get the chance. The one that doesn't get in, goes home and that's usually me. We know enough people inside for it not to matter if you are on your own. I hope it doesn't happen tonight. Though with you being here, I'm sure that you'll bring me the luck of the Irish so I'll get in no bother."

We all got in okay. Maria and I went to dance immediately as the disco would end when the band came on. When the band were setting up, we met Sean at the bar and I bought a round of drinks. Lots of people from my college were there as usual and when the band turned out not to be great, we all went to the top bar. I introduced Sean to a few people and he got chatting to them while we were dancing to our favourite ABBA song. *I'm the Dancing queen, young and sweet, only 17.*"

#

Sean was coming out on Saturday nights with us. He was being very social going out with people from work too. Jacinta had told Maria that he had been out with the other lads in the house aswell. There were lots of eighteenth birthday parties coming up and Sean was being invited to them aswell. We often only saw him for a few minutes at The Clifton as time went on.

Maria was disappointed as she knew he had been grumpy and now that he was a changed man, she liked him. So, we were considering her other options for perspective boyfriends now that she was single again. I'd no concerns to report back to Jack. I hadn't met any of Sean's friends, that were of any concern to me. Also, more importantly, that I'd not heard from Mary.

#

Jack wrote to tell me the dates of his reading week. They matched my half term. When I'd asked him what days he needed to go to the observatory to do his project work, he told me that he didn't need to go. He had finished his project already but there was no need to mention that to anyone else, especially as it was the reason that he was meant to be here. That made me especially happy. So apart from Sunday lunch with his Aunt, he was around all week. He was also coming on Saturday so he could go to The Clifton.

He was looking forward to meeting Maria. I'd instructed her not to mention River Phoenix when she saw him. She still talked about the poster that I used to have of him. She had thought Jack was the spitting image of my favourite actor and always said that I'd put it up for that reason. It had been unintentional but Maria had never believed me. She didn't agree to keep quiet about it. She laughed every time I asked her not to mention it, "Wouldn't it be funny though?" I didn't agree.

I'd performed in the play at the end of half term. I'd remembered all my lines and everyone seemed to enjoy the wit in the play. Benedict's girlfriend hadn't been happy. Thankfully, we could cover our pretend kisses with my long hair. She was watching closely from the front row and made it awkward for him. She didn't seem to realise that I was uncomfortable too.

I'd made so many plans for half term. We were going bowling with Sean and Maria one evening as he was working and she was working in the holidays too. I'd not booked any overtime. I'd even taken a day's holiday on the Saturday. Normally my Mum would expect me to work all week and would have alot to say if I didn't but she didn't mention it this time. She liked Jack and his mother too, which was a bonus.

#

Uncle Emmett had gotten engaged. My Mum was happy as his fiancé was lovely. She said that She'd only have to worry about Uncle Vincent now. We'd all gone to the club to celebrate. He'd asked me to be a bridesmaid which was lovely. When I'd agreed, he gave me £50 as a thank you. I was under strict instructions not to tell my mother and I was happy to keep this secret.

I was sure that my Mum had told him that I wasn't working that week. I wouldn't have made that much on overtime shifts at work. I was able to go shopping with Maria for new clothes again just because of him. It was strange that I saw less of him than Uncle Vincent but we got on so well. I felt that I didn't know my Uncle Vincent at all.

Sean usually came for Sunday dinner after meeting my Dad at the club. My Dad liked him as he was good craic and a great story teller. I hoped that he wasn't telling any stories about me but there really wasn't much to say anyway.

Jack wanted to go to the catholic club and stay at the digs. I'd to ask Sean for him. There still had been no communication between them. As my Uncle Vincent was working away, Jack could stay there, when he was visiting.

#

Considering Jack hadn't had any pen pals in the past, he was a good letter writer. He had great stories to tell. I was glad as I did miss Mary's letters. They were more personal. I still had Saoirse's letters. She could always make me laugh. She was keeping me up to date on the gossip. She was eager for news on Sean, and Jack too so she was writing weekly for a change. I was sure she was missing Sean but she didn't say it.

Unusually I was staying up late on a Friday night because I didn't have to get up for work. My Mum and I were the only people in the house. We were watching the news, when there was a knock at the door. My Mum and I looked at each other thinking who could come around so late. I'd my pjs on so my Mum went to the door. I heard her speaking to someone and then invite them in.

I hoped that it was not anyone that I didn't know well as I would have to get dressed. I couldn't believe that it was Robert who walked into the living room. He said "Hello" to me. I stood up. I was so shocked that I couldn't make any attempt at a greeting. It wouldn't have been a positive one anyhow. My Mum told him to take a seat. "Get ye away upstairs and get dressed. It's no way to greet a visitor. I'll make some tea."

I was taking longer than it was necessary to change. I didn't want to go back downstairs. I'd to force myself to do it. I knew that I'd to be brave, like Saoirse would tell me, and honest, like Jack had said. It made me think about Jack's prophetic speech about seeing Robert again. Worse it made me think of what Saoirse and Sean's reaction would be to what was going on. Especially when I'd thought the whole sorry mess was over.

When I went back into the living room, he was drinking tea with my Mum. She looked up at me concerned, "I didn't make you anything Molly. Do you want

314

something?" I shook my head. "I will make Robert a sandwich. He has been travelling all day." She left the room obviously not wanting to be a distraction to what would be an awkward conversation. I sat on the armchair furthest from the sofa where he was sitting. I didn't speak.

He cleared his throat, "I'm sorry to drop in on you like this Molly but I only had your address with me." I was furious, he shouldn't even have that. I was very angry with Mary for giving it to him. I didn't even try to disguise what I was feeling. I hoped my face did say it all. He continued "I really needed to see you." I didn't know what to say. I was incredulous to why he would think that this was the right thing to do.

I almost shouted, "Why the hell are you here?" I sounded rude and I knew if my Mum heard she'd be annoyed with me. He was shocked, "I didn't expect you to be this way." I realised that he had never known my true opinion of him.

I attached my feelings to something else. "Do you not remember the last conversation we had. You suggested that my family are more than sympathisers. That they were involved in some way, in a murder. That it could put Mary and me at risk, just by being friends." He looked embarrassed, "I never said those words."

I wanted to place the blame of my reaction on this issue, which was part of it so I was not lying. "But that's what you meant." I stared at him to show that my distress had turned in to anger as I knew there was no argument about that.

The frustration that was building inside of me must not come out, even if he had come uninvited to my house. He was reminding me of the Elliottt's opinion of my family. "Molly, I know now that you are not involved in anything like that. I'vethought about it and it should not stop us from being together." My eyes were wide with astonishment at his suggestion. I felt like laughing at the absurd idea.

Then, felt sick reminding me of Jacks warning. Why didn't he get it? I'd to be
totally honest with him.

I sat up in my seat and took a fortifying breath. "I'm sorry if I ever gave you
the wrong impression. That...."I swallowed" I wanted to go out with you. I was
polite to you as you were my friends' brother. I do not understand what gave you
the idea that I would want us to be together. I never said that. And now. After the
way you have spoken about my family. Knowing your opinions. It would mean that
I would be putting you, before my family. I would never lose my family because of
you."

Robert's face was showing disappointment. "I'm sorry that I said words to
you that made you feel distressed and torn." I didn't feel torn. I was very clear in my
thinking. I didn't like his gentle and caring tone. "I was explaining Mary's beliefs not
mine. I know that I mentioned Noraid and that was irrelevant. I should never have
said it. Especially if I'd known how it would affect you so much." I shook my head "I
don't care about Noraid."

I didn't seem to be explaining myself correctly. Although my family's political
beliefs had come into question, this was an aside to what I wanted to express to
him. I wanted to make it very clear without referring to my family or politics that I
didn't like him.

I took a deep breath. "Robert, the main reason that we will not be together, is
that I just do not feel the same way about you as you do for me. You feel you know
me through your sister. That is the only way that I know you too. In reality we do
not know each other at all. What I do know is that we do not have anything in
common. This would be the same even if I didn't have a boyfriend but I do."

Robert had been looking at me in a dejected way but now he was annoyed. "Who are you going out with?" it was in an accusatory way, seeming to suggest that I was betraying him. I didn't think he needed to know my personal business but I thought that it might make it more real to tell him. "Jack, Sean's cousin."

He spat out the words in disgust "What. Why are you involving yourself in the McDermott's?" I lowered my own voice as I was trying to calm down the situation that was escalating. "Because I like him. Again, this is another insinuation that you are making that I do not like.

I dread to think what your opinions are of that family, after what you thought it was acceptable to say about mine. Even though you tell me that you were just repeating what Mary said. I can see it in your eyes, that you believe them too. So do not lie to me."

He was really angry now and was leaning towards me. The look in his eyes scared me. I was getting very concerned of what he might do. Even though he was a couple of feet away from me. I was shocked at his reaction. I didn't know how he would react but definitely not like this. He spat "I can tell you about that family..." I stopped him by saying "I do not care what you think about Jack's family. I do not want to hear what you have heard or what you believe."

I felt as if he was telling me off, talking down to me. "Molly, you are being naive, you need to listen to me. I need to make you understand. I need to tell you about Brompton. You are too trusting of them all." I couldn't maintain my attempt of being calm, I was angry again. "No, I do not need to hear you. I need you to leave my house now. It is much better for you, to do that before my Dad returns."

He carried on as if he was speaking to a child, "Molly, you were not born there, you have not lived there. You cannot see what is going on. They hide things

317

from you. They do not say or do things in front of you. Things that may scare or upset you. You have been taken in by them."

He was pointing at his chest to impress upon me his feelings "and I will not let that happen." Any pretence of politeness was long gone when I shouted "You are delusional. You have no right to be telling me what to do. Or even voicing such dangerous opinions about me, my family or friends, especially in my own home."

My Mum ran through the living room door, I thought she was going to tell me off for my rudeness. She stopped in front of the fire place. Half way between us both. She was angry herself. She tried not to show it. She was speaking slowly to reduce the tension in the air. "Robert, it is very clear that Molly wants you to leave. I suggest you go now."

Robert stood up but he was not moving. He turned to look directly at my Mum. "Please, Mrs O'Donnell, it has been clear from the start that you find your husband's family worthy of suspicion at best and reprehensible at worse. You need to tell Molly the truth. You need to separate her from them. You need to stop her becoming like them." He was becoming louder and louder.

My Mum said "You do not know anything about me or my family. But if your beliefs were true about them, then you should be worried about being involved with Molly yourself. Your behaviour is unacceptable and it would stop Molly liking you now anyway. Think about that…"

My Mum turned to me and said in a soft voice "the truth is Molly, that the only mistake that you made was being Mary's pen pal. I'd a hand in that myself. It is right to keep away from her especially as this is the way her family are treating you." I was glad that she knew that Robert was irrelevant to me by not including him in that statement.

When she turned back to him, it was in disbelief that he remained in her house. "Leave now. Get out of my house and never come back!" She was screaming in a fury at him now. She pointed to the door. Robert was walking to the living room door. He turned with a look that I thought meant, this wasn't over.

My Mum followed him out of the living room to the front door. I heard her shut it behind him. When she returned, she must've seen in my face that I was more scared than angry now. "O my god, Molly, are you okay?"

The next day when I saw Jack, he repeated the same thing to me as my Mum had. When he hugged me, I felt relieved. I'd not slept a wink as I was upset and confused. I was a mess and crying, when I told Jack how Robert had scared me.

It was not the welcome that I'd wanted him to have. We were sat in Jack's car as there had been nowhere in my house to tell him this tale in private. He'd a long journey over and I was sorry that he had to contend with this situation straight away.

He looked guilty. "I'm just so sorry, that I helped you stay friends with Mary. I knew it was wrong but not how wrong. I'd just wanted to spend time with you. I thought that it was a good opportunity." He hung his head and was apologetic.

He was shaking his head, "Even I didn't see this coming. Even after I'd warned you. It is so ridiculously out of control. If Saoirse and Sean shouldn't have known about Robert before, then they definitely cannot know now." Neither of us mentioned Brompton again. I definitely didn't want to consider what that meant.

We were meeting Sean and Maria later so I needed to try and forget about last night. I didn't want either of them to suspect anything. I never wanted the secret to come out, especially to Sean. I also was scared that if Maria knew what

Robert said, she'd not feel able to be around me. Jack smiled encouragingly. "We do need another plan. We will think about it tomorrow."

He changed the mood by saying "So, less of, *much ado about nothing* but more a much ado about something?" I nodded. His eyes danced which was a very easy way to cheer me up. "If I say '*I will stop you mouth*' will you be offended?* I was surprised and pleased. I said "Do you know that play then?" His colour changed in his face, "well, I read it when you said you were performing it. I'd to see how much kissing there was. I've heard what these Shakespeare tragicomedies are like."

I laughed remembering the day. "Benedicks' girlfriend was glowering at us throughout the whole play from the front row. I don't know how we got through it. Luckily, I didn't have to kiss him at all. When his girlfriend heard that there were two kisses, she had wanted him to pull out of the play. Our teacher had to persuade her to let him do it."

"So" I continued" it's a good thing that I've long hair. I just kept my hair down to hide what we weren't doing! There were no kisses for me." I smiled "Were you worried then?" He was playful, "Just a little bit. More that it should be me, don't you think?" He laughed and I nodded thinking that long distance relationships were as hard as I'd expected. I felt happy then. I was really appreciative that Jack still wanted to go out with me, after everything that I'd told him.

We all met at the pub before we went into The Clifton. The first thing Maria said to Jack was about River Phoenix. I could have killed her. Jack laughed, "Do you still have the poster?" Maria replied for me, "No, just a photo of you by her bed." Jack was being facetious, "I should hope so too. I've a poster size photo of Molly myself."

Maria looked disgusted, "that's gross." She didn't know whether to believe him of not. I just laughed at the weirdness of it. Even though I'd not seen his bedroom I knew this was a joke and was pleased he took it so well. I shook my head smiling in relief, "I told you not to bring it up."

She had to agree it was not the best introduction that she had been involved in. We all laughed. Sean said to Jack "So what do ye think of Molly, with all that makeup on?" Jack laughed as I'd told him what Sean had said before. "What are you, her Dad?" It was only then that Sean knew, it was a weird thing to say.

Thankfully, we all got into the club. I was looking forward to using my own ID after Christmas. When Paradise City by Guns N' Roses came on as usual Sean had dragged us all to the dance floor. We all danced and he sang loudly *Take me down to the Paradise City where the grass is green...* and we knew he meant it. It made it hard to dance as we were all laughing so much.

Maria had interrogated Jack throughout the night. She gave me the all clear on him, even with the poster comment. Jack spent some time chatting to Sean which was a new phenomenon. Sean had changed alot in the few weeks, that he had been here. Jack also noticed the change in Sean and he commented about it to me.

Jack seemed more comfortable about staying at the digs for the night considering his previous concerns. I wondered what he would think about Jacinta as they had never met before either. I was sure that Jacinta would tell Maria her impression of him. Jacinta seemed to be back to her old self but I'd not seen her in the club that night.

It had been a really good night out. I was pleased that Maria liked Jack. Jack liked Maria too. It would make bowling more fun. Jack was going to the catholic club to see my Dad the next day. Then he would go straight to his Aunts from there. He hadn't seen her yet and would be spending the rest of the week there.

I was looking forward to hearing Jack's thoughts on Sean's digs and the catholic club but he didn't have much to say. We went to crazy golf and Jack spent the whole time standing around, waiting for me. He was laughing so much at my terrible attempts to hit the golf ball. I think he suspected that my bowling ability would be the same.

Maria and I'd gone regularly to the bowling alley when we were younger. We were both pretty good. We made a bet with them. The losers had to buy the drinks. Sean and Jack were surprised at how good we were. We got strike after strike. They had to buy the drinks as they had lost so badly.

We told them after we had won the bet that we used to come all the time as they did a special rate for under 16s. They called us hustlers which we thought was hilarious. I'd certainly not been accused of that before. Luckily, they both took it in the right spirit and bought the drinks with good grace. I was glad that I was better at them at bowling even if it was just one thing. I looked forward to telling Saoirse too!

Jack wanted to go sightseeing but I didn't think I was the best person for the job. So, we went on the bus around London instead. Jack laughed at me for not knowing my own city. He told me that he knew all of Dublin. He would show me when I went to see him. I didn't know when that would be but I was looking forward to it. I suspected that Dublin was alot smaller than London and when I said that he just smiled

He started to sing *In Dublin's fair city, where the girls are so pretty, I first set my eyes on sweet Molly Malone, As she wheeled her wheel-barrow, Through streets broad and narrow, Crying, "Cockles and mussels, alive, alive, oh!* I will take you to the new Molly Malone statue on Grafton Street."

I showed mock distain, "I would much prefer you referring to me as my actual namesake in the silent film." He was laughing. "Molly, you being silent, I can't see it myself!

Jack was going home on Friday morning so on Thursday night we went out for a pizza. He seemed more serious and was very thoughtful. We ordered our food and I asked him what was wrong. He looked concerned. "We need to discuss Robert. I've been thinking that's not the last you will see of him. I don't think he got the really big hint to go away and stay away. I don't know what more you can say to convince him, without contacting him again to confirm what you said. How do you feel about it all?"

I was hesitant. I didn't want Jack to worry about me as he would be far away but I thought I should tell him the truth. "To be honest. I'm worried. I don't like to say that to you, because you won't be around to help in any way. I can't predict what he will do next. I can't believe he came to my home. He was really angry at the thought of you. As if I was two timing him or something. Obviously, there's the other issue about your family too." I pulled a face and he nodded his head.

I tried to be optimistic, "His reading week must be over too so he is hopefully at home now." Jack was thoughtful. "Molly, do you want to know what I know? What I've heard and perhaps what Robert heard?" I asked "Does it involve you in any way?" I was searching his face, there were no flickers in his eyes to concern me. He shook his head. "Will it help me to know anything?" Jack was uncertain, "I don't think so. More importantly the less you know the better."

I wondered if I was just putting my head in the sand. "Am I still being naïve to think like this?" He replied "Molly, you are still a bit too trusting but that makes you, you." I paused then took a deep breath. "So *Let me be that I'm and seek not to alter me,* is true?" Jack was amused. "That's definitely correct and very well remembered too. I wish that I'd seen you in that play."

Then he sighed. "I can see that it is a constant worry to you, thinking that you are naïve." I pulled a face, "I do worry. But I'm not so naive to know that I should be wary. I do wonder 'who knows the real truth?' if they are not there, themselves."

I hoped this was true and Jack nodded, "You are right there. We were always worried about Sean's boasts so maybe that's what they are. He is certainly a changed man now. Not a mention of *The Cause* at his digs or at the catholic club. I hope the way he expresses his beliefs has changed." I was agreeing with him. "I know that you are definitely not naive about Robert and that you will be careful of him. Please contact me if you hear from him." I nodded my agreement.

He changed the subject saying "But try to forget about him and have a great time at The Broadway on Saturday, I'm sorry to miss it. I'm glad that Sean will be with you. Write and tell me all about it. I will go next time, if I do come after Christmas. I really do want to spend New Year's Day here." He made me smile and this had calmed me down just by reminding me that he was coming back. I said "I just knew that you would mention U2, when you said you were coming over for New Year's Eve."

I carried on smiling. I knew that I would miss him. Not seeing him or speaking to him for two months would be hard. The letters were great and more frequent than I could have ever hoped for but long distances relationships are difficult.

"I hope that an uncomplicated girl, doesn't catch your eye before then." He laughed and said smiling "Uncomplicated just means boring. There's never a dull moment with you, Molly." I wished there was some dull moments where Robert was concerned but I laughed and tried not show my concern.

Part 3: Chapter 19 - The Secrets

On Saturday night we were all excited to be going to the Broadway. We didn't normally get to go as it's such a long way away. Maria's brother was taking us with him. It was heaving as it had been the other times, we had been but it had a great atmosphere and music. Strangely enough we got somewhere to sit.

Sean went to the bar as I was scared that I wouldn't get served. Maria had gone to the toilet. Maria's brother had met his friends. I couldn't see him around. I could see the queue for the bar and also the queue to the toilet from where I was sitting. I thought they would both be a while and I was protecting their seats with our coats.

Then someone said "Hello." I looked up thinking they were after a chair so I was smiling ready to say no but my heart sank, it was Robert. He sat down in front of me. I felt both contempt and fear at his persistence. I looked for Sean or Maria but neither was coming.

When he spoke, I could hear the anger in his voice, when he said "I know who you are here with?" I said "So" Both wanting Sean to come over to get rid of him but at the same time not wanting him to see Robert either. I was angry too "why are you even talking to me. I thought I made feelings clear, please go." He banged the table with his fist. I wanted to get away but I was blocked in between the wall and the table and him. "You will listen to me. If you leave, I will find you again."

I was confused and I didn't like what he was saying and he continued "the Irish community talk here, just like they do in Ireland. You can find anyone, if you want too." I was scared now and tried another tactic. "Please Robert, you are scaring me." When he didn't answer I said "I don't understand, why am I so important to you? Just look around, there's plenty of girls here. You might like them, if you weren't talking to me."

He was not mollified, "I need you to know, that you are in danger." I thought that the only person that I was in danger from, at the moment, was him but I didn't want to say that. "What do you want to say then" thinking if I let him speak, he would go away. He calmed slightly, "I know Sean is in England for something other than this new job. He's done one 'job' already and they are planning another. In Brompton. He got away with the first one but I can't let him get away with it again. I haven't told the police yet because of you, but I will have too."

I couldn't believe what he was saying. I stood up and he was pushing me down. He stood up too so I couldn't move at all. My head was spinning. Robert obviously wasn't right in the head but I also I wondered if what he was saying could be true. I was crying and trying to get past Robert. I looked around for help. I saw Sean coming with drinks and then Maria from the toilets. When Maria saw me, she pushed through the crowd to get to me, knocking a few drinks over on her way. She didn't even respond to the people who called out to her. She got to me but Robert hadn't seen her.

She tried to push him away from me. When he turned his face towards her, I could see she recognised him from the old photos. He was tall and very strong. His years of playing rugby had made him an immovable force. Sean had put the drinks down on the table and took in the scene. He would be no match for him, if Robert continued to be aggressive. He was tall and wiry for the amount of Gaelic football he had played and I'd never seen in him a fight.

Sean said loudly over the music "Robert, what the hell do you think ye're doing, leave them girls alone. I see that Molly, wants to come out of her seat so let her pass." I didn't know what Robert would say in reply. Maria looked from me to Sean dreading what would come next. Robert said "Don't you talk about my girlfriend like that." I looked at him in disgust. I was really concerned about his well-being.

I shouted "I'm not!" Sean said "What the fuck is going on here, Molly?" I was in shock and begging, "Sean you have to believe me. He's mad." Sean replied "Why are you together?" He was his brow furrowed in confusion and he was bewildered by what he was seeing. "I didn't even you think you knew each other that well." I was beseechingly "Sean, we don't, this is crazy, he delusional." Sean was confused and he took in my body language and face. "Even if you are together, you are blocking her path so let her out." I could see Sean was thinking but concern won over confusion, for now.

Robert said "No, I won't." He looked smug, "I came to warn Molly about you so don't tell me what to do." I was leaning towards Sean across the table. "Sean please help me. I'm not his girlfriend; he is not my friend and he is scaring me."

Sean seemed to believe me "Robert, if you let Molly out, we can talk about whatever you want to say about me." Maria had been edging towards Sean all this time but was still watching me with concern. She moved behind Sean when Robert, let me past. I sat down on the chair nearest Sean at the head of the table. I was facing Sean and could see Robert sat in the corner looking at us all, in the chair that I'd left. "Robert, it's clear that Molly doesn't want you here so it's best if you leave."

Robert was self-righteous. He looked at us as if was in control of the situation which he was. None of us knew what he would say next or how we would respond.

He said "Don't threaten me just because there's a few of your mates here." He was nodding "I know it's a republican bar, its written all over the place." He was looking up at the flags on the walls in an accusatory look in eye."

Robert turned to me "Molly, this is not you. Listen to me. Stop fooling yourself. You do not believe in these people. In *The Cause*" He spat out the words and his spittle just missed my face. I recoiled from that aswell as his words. "You must know a terrorist when you see one," giving Sean a hard look. Sean just looked surprised.

Then Robert turned back to me. "You don't believe in violence, Molly." I was looking at Sean, my eyes begging him to understand and also so that I didn't have to look at look at the madness in Roberts eyes. I was slowly moving to the edge of the seat and getting in a position that I could jump away and not be caught. Sean seemed to acknowledge this. Robert continued the devastation, by saying "As I said to you last week," my head dropped and I couldn't look at Sean in the eye anymore.

I felt that everything I'd dreaded was playing out before me. "You need to come away from the O'Sheas and the McDermotts." He started to tell Sean a story about Brompton, the one he had tried to tell me. Sean was angrier that I could think was possible. I'd seen him bicker but never angry. Sean jumped up from his chair and shouted "Ye" pointing at Robert "ye will get yourself into trouble if you talk like that in here or in fact anywhere."

Then he looked at down me. I knew he would ask me a question I didn't want to answer. It was the end of everything. There was no good reason for me to see have seen Robert. Sean in concerned shock "and you, Molly, what the hell is this all about? Why did you see him last week?" I knew how this was going to sound. I

didn't know if there was anything, I could say to make this okay.

"Sean, he came to my house on Friday. He came unannounced and

uninvited. He was shouting all the same things. My Mum had to throw him out. I'm

not going out with him. You know I'm going out with Jack. I've never been out with

him. Please believe me, he is lying."

Whilst Sean was speaking Maria had put her hand on his shoulder to calm

him down, to stop and listen to her. "He has always liked Molly; he is obsessed with

her. She tried to hide that from you all this time." I shot a grateful look at Maria but

she looked away. This helped in one way as Sean was believing that there was no

relationship with Robert, but he must have also noted the word *always* as I'd.

I closed my eyes in a prayer and my fists were clenched and my thumbs

rubbing my fingers in hope, as Sean was digesting this information. "Ok I get that

but how did he come to be obsessed with you Molly? and how did he get your

address?"

I knew my world was about to tumble down. In the pause Robert jumped in

before me. "Mary gave me the address. They have been pen pals from the first

summer. When we went out only Mary knew. I know Molly hid the times we met

from you and Saoirse." He seemed very pleased with himself while Sean was getting

angrier if that was possible. Maria was scared and I was dumbstruck at how Robert

was acting. This was true but also not true. I took a deep breath then looked up,

"Sean it's not like it sounds."

I felt sick when I told him, what I'd tried to hide for so many years "Sean, I'm

so sorry I didn't tell you. It's true that I wrote to Mary and I did meet her. He came

again and again but he wasn't invited. You are right, I didn't really get it. The seriousness of it all but I do now. Please believe me, that I never even had a date with him. I don't like him and I would never do that to you and Saoirse." He looked at me sadly and was deflated now. "But you were happy to deceive us about Mary." The look of disappointment was turning into disgust.

Again, Maria intervened, "I'm sorry Sean, I did encourage the friendship with Mary. Molly had so many pen pals I didn't think it was important. After the thing near the church, she stopped all contact, when it became real to her."

Sean shrugged her hand off his shoulder and looked at her in disgust aswell. I'd been looking at Maria to thank her but she didn't catch my eye. Sean turned back to me and shouted in disbelief, "It only became real to you this summer! Jesus Christ Molly. You just didn't get it." Shaking his head, "You didn't understand then or now. You have put everyone in danger, especially with what he's spouting," indicating Robert with a brush of his hand but not looking at him.

Robert was irrelevant to him now; all his feelings were directed towards me. "All these accusations, they affect you as well as me. It looks like someone has been sharing information. Informing, Molly, do ye not get that?" He was incredulous. I definitely did now.

I was so sorry, I wanted to get down on my knees and beg forgiveness. I was so wrong. I was slipping down my seat. I could hardly hold myself up. I wouldn't be still upright if I'd been standing, all I could say was "I only just got that. I'm sorry to involved myself in that family. I promise that never happened. I never shared any information. I'd no information to share but I can see what it looks like to you or anyone else." Sean was in a conversation with just me, even though Maria and Robert were still there. "Molly, you must have said something. What did you hear? Who did you tell?"

I was shaking my head vigorously to show Sean, for him to hear me and believe me, "Sean, please believe when I say. I heard nothing; I saw nothing. I said nothing. This is information that he is telling us. Its Robert who has told this to me. It really is the other way around. I would never do that.

Mary and I never even talked about the troubles. We talked about Wham, Molly Ringwood and Maeve Binchy. It really was just music, films and books. Things that you and Saoirse would never understand. That's why I thought it was ok. I only met her a handful of times but she brought him with her." I indicated to Robert and shook my head in disgust, that I'd let this happen. "That was it. Sean think of how much time I spent with you and Saoirse. We could never be, what he is suggesting."

I took a deep breath as this was another sore point between us, "Look at me and Jack, even we were always with you and Saoirse." Sean seemed to be listening and considering what I was saying now, his brow furrowed again. "Jack. So does Jack know what's been going on?" I felt that this may help him believe me. "He knows everything. He believes me. He didn't even think the letters were wrong, he encouraged me too. He thought that you and Saoirse took things too seriously.

We were both wrong. You are right." Sean's face twisted in anger, "that's why I never liked him. He didn't get it either. He is worse than you, he lives in Ireland. He should understand. You are made for each other." He was revolted with both of us.

Sean turned to Robert, "I believe Molly has been stupid, naive or whatever but I don't think She'd pass information." He cast a look over me, clearly, he Couldn't be entirely sure, after everything he had heard tonight. "If you start these rumours, we could all be in trouble. Not just me or Molly's family but you and Mary too. You have left Mary alone and unprotected while you are away at university.

Also, if you were in a 'relationship' with Molly or like her at all, know that she is the most at risk from all this. It might already be too late, if you have told anyone your suspicions. Go away now and think about how your eagerness to catch me out has effected everyone else."

There was no movement on Robert's part. I didn't know if he'd taken anything in. I looked at his eyes and I saw that they were glazed over. "Leave now." Sean repeated, with more authority. He was in control now but Robert hadn't moved an inch. He was staring at Sean, maybe considering what was been said. Sean was staring directly into Roberts eyes, right in to his mind, to convince him that he should do as he was saying, "Go home, forget everything. Forget all of us. Ye know that this is the right thing to do. It's the only thing you can do or all hell could break loose. This is a warning. Not a threat. It is very real. Molly didn't get it and nor do you."

I looked at Maria. She had moved back away from Sean and was standing outside our group, looking scared and angry. Her face was chalk white and I could see her shaking. I went to put my hand towards her but she backed away further. "Do not contact Molly again and for you own sake do not tell anyone about what you said tonight. People can go to prison for what you are insinuating so it's not just 'Republicans' that should worry you. Though that is certainly bad enough. Who knows who could be listening right now."

Sean didn't look around; he kept his eyes on Robert." I did check around and I felt that the sound of the music which we had come here to hear, meant we weren't being overheard or watched, even though we were obviously arguing.

Robert made to move. I jumped out of my seat in case he would grab me or hold me back again. I was behind the seat that he had been sitting at before, to let him pass in front of me. Robert turned to look at me but said nothing. His eyes were wild and I didn't know if he had taken in anything that Sean had said. He walked slowly in the direction of the door not looking at anyone, in a complete world of his own.

I was relieved that he had gone. I felt that Sean had made things very clear about how disastrous this situation was. I knew now it was time for me to get my justifiable remonstration. Clearly though Sean thought that he had said enough and turned away from the table. He looked very fatigued by the argument.

He didn't look at me "I will never forgive you Molly." It did seem like he was distressed to be saying this to me. "I believe you when you say, you didn't mean to cause this or understand the consequences. Your naivety has won over, again and again. I don't know what Saoirse would think......." He was shaking his head and it was hanging down.

He turned and walked away in the same direction as Robert. I was crying and didn't even know it. I looked at Maria but she didn't comfort me. She said in a hard voice "I will get my brother to take us home." Her face was of complete desolation. Her brother on seeing me and hearing whatever Maria whispered in to his ear, nodded his head. He looked at me for a moment, then looked away. I couldn't discern his thinking. He didn't complain which I would have expected.

I felt the full gravity of the situation and it weighed down heavily on me. I was struggling to keep upright or even walk. My mind went blank and I couldn't think about anything other than getting home. Maria's brother gestured for Maria and me, to go before him. I saw him say his goodbyes to his friends, who must have been surprised and none too happy about his sudden departure. He walked passed us to the door. I'd to focus on each step to get to the car and I knew I deserved every difficult step that I took.

Maria never looked at me in the car and I knew she wouldn't be able to forgive me for putting her at risk. I knew she was disassociating herself from me. I couldn't blame her. This was way above what any friend should accept. I knew that She'd never speak to me again. I also knew that neither Sean, and in the near future Saoirse too, would not forgive me either. I felt sad and lonely but it was all of my own making. I'd to take responsibility and accept the consequences. I was feeling them already. The was a pain in my head and my heart.

Neither Maria or her brother responded to my thanks or goodbye as I got out or the car. I knew I was alone now. I stood outside my front door and looked at my Fido dido keyring as I put the key in the lock. I ran to my room and I wrote down immediately what had happened. I hoped and prayed that at least Jack would understand. I didn't deserve it as I'd probably ended his relationship with his cousin as well. I didn't dare to pray for Sean's forgiveness. I wondered sadly, if or more likely, when Sean would tell Saoirse.

In the morning my Mum asked why I'd got back so early and when she looked at me, I knew she could see my swollen eyes. I started to cry again. I was angry with myself for causing all this trouble. I knew my Mum would understand how this had happened and agree that the outcome was justified. Just as I did too. When I finished telling her, we realised we had missed mass. My Mum started to make some breakfast and I helped. It was just for me and my Dad. My sisters had left home already.

When the food was ready. I was scared to see my Dad. I knew he would be reading the Sunday papers and couldn't face him. My Mum said "Come back when you have given Dad his breakfast and eat here with me. While you get dressed, I will speak to him." I was scared "what are you going to tell him?" She sighed, "well I doubt Sean will be coming anymore so I have to tell him why."

When she saw my face, "Not about these IRA operations or plots. Whatever they call them. He must be making it up. Why in god's name, I don't know. Or that you're an informer." Seeing my face, she reassured me, "because you're not. You are right, Robert is delusional. He is infatuated with you. Jesus Mary and Joseph, why didn't I see that coming." Now I realised I should have. Being naive was not an excuse for any of it.

#

I sent Molly away. I knew I'd to speak to Hugh. Molly's secret was out. The truth that I'd kept from Hugh needed to be spoken. I went into the living room. I sat down on the sofa, on the edge of the seat, looking at my husband. I didn't know what to say. He must have felt my stare and lowered the Sunday World to look at me. "Are you okay Clare? Ye didn't go to Mass?"

I explained that Molly was upset. She'd had a row with Sean. I told him that it was serious and that he was never likely to talk to her again. He was shocked. He folded the newspaper and put it on the floor.

He got up and sat next to me. "What's so serious?" I started by saying Molly hadn't meant to cause any upset. Hugh had nodded his head and smiled. His youngest, his favourite daughter was always getting things wrong. He loved her all the more for it. He would forgive her anything. Would he forgive her this? I doubted it very much but I'd to say something or he would push Sean to say what happened.

That would lead to the very uncomfortable answers about sharing of information. As I knew Molly would never do that, I felt confident not to have to mention that, yet.

"You know the Elliott's? Your neighbours from home." Hugh nodded "I, I do of course." He looked intrigued. "Molly did a silly thing. She met the girl, Mary at the beach that first summer and they became pen pals. You know she loves getting her letters?" For some reason my mind jumped to "say your prayers and write your letters." A fear now radiated around my body. What if they found out? What if they thought she was an informer? I shivered. I crossed my arms around my shoulders. I knew I'd to continue along the same vein and forget my worries.

After this pause, "For god's sake, tell me she has stopped." I nodded, "yes but she never told Saoirse or Sean. It seems that Robert, the son, took a bit of a shine to Molly. He was here in his reading week and he saw her last night at the Broadway." Hugh was confused "What would he be doing there, surely he'd know it's full of Catholics?" I shrugged my shoulders, thinking the same.

I continued. "Well, he had seen Molly a couple of times with Mary. He thought she liked him. Obviously, she didn't...." Hugh digested this and knew what I meant. He nodded relieved. Then his eyes widened "Why was she meeting them at all? How?" I was careful to tell the truth, some of it. "Mostly at places that they all went. The discos, festivals, the clubs and in town." This was true though the planned element could be discussed at a later date. "No wonder Sean is angry. Keeping that from them. Well I know why. Sure, the pair of them would be livid. Haven't they always told her the way of it." He was shaking his head.

He stood up and looked down at me. Then he walked to the fire place. He looked at the wall. Then down to the fire. It wasn't on. When he turned. He looked directly at me and I felt the anger against me. "This is down to you, you know. Always telling her the other point of view. Always going against your history, your upbringing. Being grateful to be here. That didn't help you when you were abused on the estate or your children in the street. I started to say "My father, he…"

Hugh sat back down on his armchair. He looked at me, "O now you want to tell me about how he was with you. Don't bother, I've heard it from all sides. Emmett, Patrick and Vincent." I was shocked. "Why didn't you tell me you were asking questions."

He shook his head, "That's because I didn't ask questions. Sure, they thought I knew. I didn't tell them otherwise of course. I listened to what they had to say. I can see how you felt about your Father, that made sense. But to keep it from me…" He was looking down. I couldn't see his eyes but I suppose there was many feelings; disappointment, anger, understanding, relief.

I leaned forward and touched his hand. He flinched. "I'm sorry. I should've told you. I should have explained." He looked at me "I get all that and I hate that you went through it. You, your mother and Seamus." He pulled away his hand as he straightened up in the chair. "It's not that. The Cause was not to blame for that. Even Emmett and Patrick understand about The Cause. They are not involved as you know. The sympathise of course. Why do you not sympathise with the never-ending war?"

I was beseeching, "I've never thought of it as war. I always thought it about violence. I hate violence." Hugh shook his head. "But Clare, it has rubbed off on Molly. Your fear of violence has made her unaware of the truth about The Cause. You caused this thing with Sean. You have upset Molly, Sean, Saoirse and those Elliottt's."

I knew what he was saying was true. Things other people had said too. You need to pick a side... you need to believe... you need to understand the truth of it.... Remember the pain it caused." Molly's story was now forgotten. The consequences not yet considered. Not yet known. Not any if possible. Now I'd to take on my part in this. I was responsible. I wondered now if Hugh would forgive me. I couldn't look at him. I looked at my slippers. They were as tired as I felt. How could I fix this?

I called his name. He looked into my eyes. "Now, is there anything else that you want to tell me about your family. I think it's time you did, especially as I know already." When I looked at him, he was pleading for my honesty.

I knew it was about Vincent. "I don't know much. But I know why Vincent left. I don't know what happened to him... Do you?" He let out a long breath, "Finally." He raised his eyes and his hands to the ceiling. He looked like a weight lifted from him. "Yes, I do know...do you want to?" I didn't but I nodded anyway. I sat back in my seat to listen.

Part 4

1990

London

Part 4: Chapter 20 - Saoirse

Saoirse wrote asking me for details about Jack's trip. Even though it meant that

Sean hadn't told her about Mary, Robert or the accusations yet, I knew it would be

only a matter of time.

Thankfully Jack wrote a very supportive letter back to me quickly. He didn't

care about Sean. He wrote that they had never gotten on anyway and that it was no

loss to him if Sean had cut him out. He wrote that he doubted he would even notice.

He understood it was different for me and didn't dismiss my distress.

Jack agreed that Sean would feel betrayed and distrustful of me. I'd kept my

correspondence and meetings with Mary, with Robert often in attendance, a secret.

Sean would see this was the reason that led to Robert's decision to investigate both

his and my family.

He knew it was painful for me to lose two childhood friends but he

rationalised it. He told me that in reality having a pen pal and having an

unreciprocated interest by a boy, should not cause this many problems. He stated

that as I'd not felt able to tell Saoirse and Sean about Mary, it showed that there had

always been an issue in my friendships with them. I should not have been scared to

tell them. Robert's allegations though had taken it all to another level entirely. He

didn't blame me for that either.

He completely understood why Maria would feel and agreed with her decision to cut ties to me due to the seriousness of the accusations. As they included not only links to the IRA but Molly's family's possible involvement too. He knew that this didn't lessen the pain for me losing such a good friend. I'd never kept secrets from her except about Roberts visit. I should have warned her. I should have taken it more seriously. Maria had been with me since starting secondary school. We enjoyed the same music, films and books. We loved to laugh which seemed alien now. I'd already lost Mary who was the only other person that I'd a similar kind of friendship.

Jack agreed that Saoirse would find out. He suggested that I should tell her or I'd just be waiting till someone else did? He knew that there would be the same reaction, if not worse. He described them as fireworks which was an apt description. He tried to distract me with some funny stories which did make me smile for a while. He reassured me that I would always have him and that I would make new friends.

I called Maria to apologise but she wasn't interested. Jacinta was vague with me when I called her. I wondered if it had been Sean or Maria that had told her about the row. She just agreed. "Yeah, it's pretty bad." She never called me back again. I saw her at college with Maria. She didn't even catch my eye. I didn't try to approach them. I didn't go out anymore. I didn't want to see Sean, Maria or Jacinta. I didn't have anyone else to go out with now anyway.

I went to work on Saturdays and studied. I couldn't even listen to my new Wet Wet Wet tape my sister had given me to cheer me up. She didn't know what happened. Only that Maria and I were not talking. She didn't know or care about Saoirse or Sean. I was sorry that I'd put everyone in this position. Dad said "don't be thinking about it anymore" but his eyes showed concern that his encouraging words didn't.

I still listened to capital radio but had to turn it off when sweet surrender came on the tape *Hey little fella...* Maria was the only person I knew to say fella. It had always made me laugh. Now the tears had stopped but the guilt weighed heavily on my heart and mind. No amount of *Hail Mary's* could fix this. When the room was quiet, other words entered my mind. Wet Wet Wet doing it again *When the big gun starts to shooting With their bullets of deception...* It reminded me of my deceit and the terrible consequences.

I squeezed my eyes shut and sang instead *peace love and understanding* Wishing didn't help. I might have had it, if I'd never played with Mary in the first place. I could hear Saoirse voice sing *Lie, lie, lie.* Even though she never would have sung that song. Then Maria singing *Cry, cry, cry* which she did probably say to Jacinta about me, if she listened to that song again as we had done a thousand times.

My mocks were coming up and I was studying hard. Even my Mum noticed that I wasn't on the phone all the time, going out or writing as many letters. At least three had come from Saoirse that I didn't open immediately as I would normally would have done seeing Saoirse's handwriting.

She came to my room with a letter that I'd left on the mantelpiece unopened. "It seems that Sean has not told Saoirse yet. You could try and explain it from your point of you." She agreed with Jack that Saoirse would not cope well with the betrayal with Mary so the situation with Robert would probably not be forgiven.

"You should have been brave enough at the beginning to tell Saoirse about Mary though. You should not have deceived them. None of us helped" meaning

Jack, Maria and herself. "Telling you to keep up the correspondence. Maria has her part to play aswell but I can understand why She'd be scared after Sean's reaction to what Robert had to say. It is not all your fault even though you think it is. Who knew that Robert would do, what he did? Otherwise, being Mary's pen pal would have been a distant memory by now as you had already made the decision not to write to her anymore."

My Mum paused, thinking. "You still have a chance though. You must be the one to explain it to Saoirse. It would be better to tell her in person but as you can't the next best thing is the telephone." I was shocked, "But Mum, it is really expensive." Her reply was "this is important. You cannot carry on fearing her reaction. You must find out and deal with the outcome afterwards. Write to her to say that something has happened and that you need to tell her on the telephone. Give her a date and time that you will call. It's best to do it right now so you don't chicken out."

My Mum was looking at my face. She knew that I didn't want to do this but I was thankful for her that She'd help me in this way. I was scared of what would come out of it. But I did write to Saoirse telling her I needed to talk about the night out with Sean. She was surprised in her response but agreed in her swift reply. She must surely have thought something had gone on asI hadn'tanswered any of her letters. I'd to explain to her that I'd not written as I would be a hypocrite alongside everything else.

Mum told me to take as much time as I needed on the phone which made me realise that she felt this was important too. Jack had written back when I told him about my Mums idea. He thought this was a good way forward. I really needed to know how she felt, instead of making up theories. Saoirse answered on the first ring.

She was excited to hear from me. It seemed like she was expecting some sort of good news.

I'd thought hard about whether to tell her from my first meeting with Mary or work backwards from what happened at the Broadway. I decided if I started with meeting with Sean and Robert, she may not listen to the whole thing. I explained how it seemed unimportant at the time and that our letters were about things that Saoirse and I never talked about just books, music and films. Even though that argument hadn't persuaded Sean, it was the truth.

I explained that I'd never liked Robert and that I was being polite to him when we met and his presence was never wanted. I begged her to believe me, when I said that I didn't like him as a person and that it was an aside to his religion.

As I spoke, I realised how ridiculous that sounded. What was the difference between a friendship and a relationship anyway? Just a piece of paper. I could never have done one so I shouldn't have done the other. I told her that I've severed all ties with Mary on the night that we had gone swimming in the river.

Then I told her about Roberts visit to my home. About the accusations he had made. I finished with the argument between Sean, Robert and I at the pub. She didn't ask any questions, agree or disagree with anything. I was hopeful as there was no reaction. When I finished with Sean leaving the pub, there was a short pause. "I don't forgive you either," and she hung up the phone.

I was unhappy but not surprised. I'd known that this would be her response. Though I did think She'd shout, scream and abuse me as I deserved. I wrote a letter to Saoirse after the telephone call to apologise again. As expected, I didn't get a reply. I told Jack about Saoirse. He was not surprised by Saoirse's reaction, he said she was always very controlled in her emotions.

I wondered if or when She'd ask Sean about the argument. I was sure that it would be discussed at Christmas, if not before. My Dad had said that Sean had taken his holidays to go back home for two weeks. My Dad didn't say anything else which surprised me as I knew my Mum had spoken to him about it.

Robert didn't contact me nor did Mary. I'd no idea of what their reaction had been to the argument and I probably would never know. I wondered if they had or if they would tell someone about Robert's accusations. They may have heeded Sean's warnings. He certainly had made the risks clear to me. I spent a lot of time worrying, about the information that Robert had gathered. The possible outcomes and impact it would have. I tried not to think about who had been the one to tell him. The trail back was somewhere I didn't want to go.

I didn't tell Jack my fears about repercussions. I felt that I deserved my fears to atone for my betrayals. He knew that I felt guilty about my part in the whole situation. He tried to convince me that I'd done nothing wrong. My Mum had said the same. I made them feel like I believed them but I didn't.

Jack tried to comprehend how the loss of three friends, or four with Mary, was having on me. It had no real impact on him even though he had been in our little group of four. I didn't tell him though how really bad it made me feel, because it was my fault and I didn't deserve any sympathy. I was as upbeat as I could be without it seeming that I was pretending.

Mr O'Malley, my English teacher took me aside at the end of a lesson. He asked me if everything was okay as I was no longer contributing in class, like I usually did. I told him everything was fine. He didn't believe me. "Look Molly, I'm worried about you. You and Maria have fallen out that is clear. I don't see you in the hall, library, playground or wherever I used to, giggling or singing and me having to shush you. I've heard that you are not going out to The Clifton either."

I looked at him in surprise, he seemed to know alot about me. He laughed at my reaction. "I'vea pastoral care for my students too, you know." I nodded, supposing that was the point of a catholic college and therefore why it was different to the other colleges that I could have gone too.

He changed the subject, "What are your plans for next year?" I told him that I didn't know yet. He asked, "Have you thought about University." I told him about my family situation and me being the only one that had even stayed on until eighteen. I told him how well my sisters had done and that I was expected to follow in their footsteps.

He nodded telling me that he understood as that he had been in a similar situation himself. He explained that I could get the fees paid and a grant, if I wanted to go away to study or I could stay at home too. I wasn't sure that my parents would agree with that. He said he would talk to them about it at the parents evening that was coming up.

He explained, "The reason I'm saying this, is that the university down the road from here, has a degree in English and Drama. I think would suit you but obviously you need to get good grades, and for that to happen, you need to cheer up." I looked at him as if to show him it that it wasn't that simple.

He was empathetic, "I can tell from your reaction that whatever it is, it's really bad and I'm not asking you to tell me about it. But if there is something that I can help with, then I will. Ask me if you ever need to talk or me to advise you. Is that okay? Will you at least think about that?" I gave a small smile and nodded my head.

His smile was wide, "It's not just you, you know, the whole class is struggling with the Wife of Bath. It's hard going isn't?" I confirmed, "I don't like it. I wish we could study a different poet." Mr O'Malley raised an eyebrow, "So you do like some poetry then?" I agreed and he paused.

"I've an idea, well two ideas now as I'd one already, that I was going to tell you about. The one that just popped into my mind, is that in the next lesson, I will ask each of you to bring a poem that you like so we can discuss them. Whether they are limerick or sonnet or whatever else they may be." He saw my smile. "I see you already have one in mind. That's great. Don't tell me now. Surprise me.

My other idea is for you to work with 'Hero' again. I knew he was referring to our play. You worked well together then and you may be able to bring the Canterbury Tales to life, between you." I was thankful to him and it was a lovely idea but even though I was pleased, I bit my lip in worry. Would I put Hero/Sammy at risk? Seeing my hesitation, he was adamant, "and that's an order!" I appreciated having no choice.

At the next lesson, Sammy had sat down next to me. "It looks like we are working together again." She gave me a big smile. I was tentative, I thought of Maria and didn't want to put Sammy in any danger too. Then I remembered what my Mum and Jack had said. If the accusations were not true then there should not be an issue. Also, as Mr O'Malley had told me to work with Sammy it shouldn't be a risk, just to talk in class. I knew that I was trying to fool myself because the whole situation could be true. It all relied on Robert not reporting Sean and I'd no idea if he would or not.

I couldn't believe how unpredictable Robert had been. He could still be investigating Sean now. It was only then that I remembered Robert was studying to be a solicitor. Not only was research vital for his course but he must uphold the law too. He certainly had to believe in it. I knew that I couldn't voice this concern to anyone as my Mum and Jack would just tell me not to worry. I wondered if Sean was worried about this. He must know about what Robert was studying as they had been neighbour's their whole life. I pulled my mind back to my class and smiled back at Sammy.

I liked Sammy she was good fun, I decided not to tell her about Robert and Sean but if we did become friends, I would warn her. I promised myself that I would not get too involved, for her sake.

Sammy was catholic but not Irish and that was a good thing. I thought that being Irish had already gotten me into enough trouble already. I felt that my Irish heritage had been stripped from my heart and that I'd no connection with the country anymore. Which was of course not true as my family and Jack were Irish. It had been Sean and Saoirse that had immersed me in my Irish history every summer. I felt that they were the key to my love of Ireland. I made a decision then, that I should not let them take that away from me.

At the next English lesson, Mr O'Malley carried out his promise. "I need to try to reinvigorate this class, in the enjoyment of poetry. The book we are reading now certainly does not seem to be exciting most of you." He told us to bring a poem to class that we would like or had a connection to. We would then read or recite it, whatever we preferred. Some people groaned but in comparison to what we were reading, I think they all knew that it was the far better option.

Mr O'Malley asked me to read first. I knew we would discuss our choice of poem after. I wondered what they would think of mine. It was my Mums favourite poet. It was she who had led me to Yeats. Even though we agreed we didn't understand most of it! When I stood up to recite it, I knew that it would be saying

something about me and I was about to find out what;

> *Had I the heavens' embroidered cloths,*
>
> *Enwrought with golden and silver light,*
>
> *The blue and the dim and the dark cloths*
>
> *Of night and light and the half-light,*
>
> *I would spread the cloths under your feet:*
>
> *But I, being poor, have only my dreams;*
>
> *I've spread my dreams under your feet;*
>
> *Tread softly because you tread on my dreams.*

As I read it, I knew what Saoirse would say about me liking this poem. She'd

say that it explained my naivety. That I was foolish and a dreamer which had led me

to this awful situation that we were in.

As it was a really good poem, everyone had alot to say about it. No one had

heard it before. I repeated it many times, enabling me to forget what I believed

Saoirse might say about it. The class really seemed to like it too. Mr O'Malley was

smiling. I suspected that he was pleased, not only that he didn't have to lead the

class in the discussion today but also, he obviously knew the poem himself. After

class he told me that Yeats was a favourite of his too.

Mr O'Malley was right it had cheered me up. I told Jack about the poem too.

I knew he would read it and have an opinion about it. I could feel the relief in Jack's

letter to me, after I'd told him everything that had happened in a matter of a few

days. He must have felt cheered up too by the tone of the letter. It had been weeks

since I'd anything to report to him. He was relieved as all his letters had been about him. His course, his friends, his golf or where he had been out. He had been bored talking about himself.

He wrote that he had been under pressure to make fun things up to write to me. I told him that I didn't believe him as I knew the stories were all true. I said that I did love to hear all that was going good for him and that he must not feel guilty about that.

I did chide that he seemed to be having too much fun without me. He denied that vehemently. He said he was just filling up his time until he saw me on New Year's Eve. I was happy to know he still wanted to come to England and to see me after everything that had happened.

On the Sunday before Christmas my Dad returned home from the club early. I could see by his face that he was upset. He said Sean had come to the club before he went home for Christmas and told him about Robert.

He didn't sit down. He stood over me on the armchair. He was apprehensive when he asked me if I told the Elliottt's anything. I looked up at him. I was firm, "No I didn't and I'd nothing to tell them anyway." I hoped that by being clear and definite it would persuade him.

"Dad, it really wasn't like that at all. It was just a normal friendship with Mary. The only time *The Cause* was discussed in Ireland was with Saoirse and Sean. Here it was whatever I'd heard at home or in the club."

He was quick to ask "What have you heard at the club?" I responded "well nothing recently of course as I don't go there much anymore, just talk about the fighting in the North and attacks in England." He was considering what I was saying, "This Brompton thing, did you know about this before Robert told you? Did you tell him anything like that"? I reiterated my position "No Dad, honestly I didn't know before. Just as I didn't know anything, I couldn't tell him anything either." I needed for him to believe me because if he didn't, who would?

My Dad's mouth set in a line as he thought. Then his face turned into concern for me. He sighed, "Do you know how serious this could be, if it got out." I nodded showing my understanding of the enormity of the situation. "I hope you do as I couldn't help you, if it does. You know that, don't you?" He was staring at me.

My Mum intervened, "Hugh, look at her face, why are you scaring her. You know in your heart that she hasn't done anything wrong. Like me she doesn't agree with the violence but she understands the history and how the Irish have suffered both then and now. Isn't that right Molly?" I agreed as it wasn't right what was going on in Ireland, Dad rubbed his cheek with his hand, "Sean may come around in time. He knows that you didn't mean to cause any trouble but he is worried about any consequences. To be fair he's right to be worried."

His face was grim. "What has Saoirse said? Does she know?" I was surprised that Sean hadn't told him this. Maybe he hadn't discussed it with Saoirse. Though I doubt it couldn't be done in a letter, even if he did write to her. I realised the cost of a call in the telephone box wouldn't give him the time to tell her everything.

I explained to my Dad how I'd told Saoirse. He was nodding and grateful for my honesty. Then he shook his head, "Robert is a problem though. I need to think about this." It was only afterwards that I remembered the last conversation I'd with Robert in Ireland and wondered if I needed to mention that.

My parents discussed whether I should contact Robert to find out what his plans were. I was the one to say no because he had been told emphatically by Sean already not to report it. He was aware of the consequences of my being an informer and also potential criminal proceedings. If that hadn't worked, then me contacting

him might only confuse things.

I was worried that he might think I'd changed my mind about him. Which I

definitely hadn't, except that I disliked him even more. My Dad was hopeful, "We'll

just have to wait and see, maybe say a few prayers." I didn't think lighting a candle

at mass was the right thing to do about this. My prayers at night and at mass were

always for this 'private intention.'

I'd heard that something had happened in Brompton but I didn't discuss that

with anyone as it could be something different entirely. I knew that Sean was not

involved as I'd seen him at the club that day. My Uncle Emmett had come to talk

about the wedding and the whole family had gone there for a drink to discuss the

plans. Just because Robert had heard something didn't mean it was linked to my

family or Jacks. I thought it best that I didn't mention it to Jack in a letter but I did

think that we should discuss it when he came over to see me.

I was watching the news more closely than before. I was paranoid that

something could be linked to Sean and this was all Roberts fault. I tried to blame

him but I knew if he hadn't met me, he wouldn't have been investigating his

neighbours. So, before Christmas when two IRA members were arrested, I was

relieved that there was no link to us. It made me think that the accusations had been

wrongly directed and I hoped that Robert was watching the news too. I wondered if

Saoirse was and if her thoughts about me had changed at all.

Two days before New Year's Eve, Jack arrived as planned. I was really

looking forward to seeing him. This time I was not a blubbering mess when I met

him. Thankfully I could confirm that there had been no contact from the Elliott's.

My other news was that I'd had no contact with Saoirse or Sean either.

I was torn, I didn't know whether to tell him about Brompton. When I did, he listened and he agreed that Robert had got the wrong person but he didn't look entirely sure. We both seemed to silently agree not to talk about it anymore than that.

It would be strange that Sean would not be around for the few days with Jack. They had no contact since the Broadway either not that I would have expected them too. I knew that it was for the best that Sean had driven off to Ireland in his new car.

I'd written to Jack to see if he'd wanted to look at any particular buildings that would help in his course while he was here. At first, he was reluctant as he thought I might not enjoy it. I reassured him that I would as his enthusiasm and passion was catching.

He chose something that he thought that I might like to see too so he had come up with the Globe theatre. He'd heard about it when he read *Much ado about nothing* and he knew how much I'd enjoyed doing the play. I was so impressed that he had read a book that some English students wouldn't even want to. He made some sketches outside and inside of the Globe. I loved the atmosphere and he loved the building which worked out well.

We went to the cinema to see the *Field of dreams* as it wasn't out in Ireland yet. It reminded me of my favourite poem even though they were really not the same.

I decided to go to The Clifton with Jack on New Year's Eve. I hadn't been since before the night at the Broadway. Sammy and her boyfriend were there too. We had a great night with them. I'd looked around but didn't see Maria. I wondered if She'd ever speak to me again. I doubted it and any thought of Maria led me straight back to Saoirse. I put it out of my head as Jack was going home on the Tuesday.

After New Year's Day lunch, we went for a walk. Jack had his Walkman and we climbed the hill in the park and we sang U2 loudly *New Year's Day* When we heard *I want to be with you.* Our voices were lowered but smiled tentatively at each other.

And then he was gone again. We had talked about me going to Dublin after my exams. I hoped that my Mum would let me stay at Jack's house. Jack said his Mum would sort it out with my Mum out so I was really excited. He planned to come to England and take me back to keep the cost down. Jack also promised that he would be over at Easter for a couple of days but he didn't want to interrupt my revision.

Mr O'Malley had helped me to fill out the UCAS form, my parents were not convinced about me going to university but Mr O'Malley said it would be good to have this option, if I wanted too. I would need to work for the summer after my exams so it would be a short trip to Ireland. It would be weird going to Ireland and not seeing Saoirse as I'd every other summer since I was eight. This was the way it would be from now on so I needed to get used to it.

#

I was shocked to see Mary walking purposely towards me. We were at the same school but not in the same year. I'd never had a reason to meet her. I stared at her in disbelief. Mary faltered for a moment and then steeled herself to have this conversation. When she stopped in front of me, I could see that she had been crying. "Saoirse, I need to speak to you." I eyed her suspiciously but before I could reply, words were tumbling out of her mouth "My brother has gone."

I was confused. My mind was going over scenarios in my head. Had he gone to London to act on the information he had? Mary continued speaking, large teardrops were falling from her eyes. "Robert is dead." My mind was working overtime again, more questions, different questions, how? Words were jumping around my mind was he murdered? In an accident? had an illness? or Suicide? Mary answered my unasked question saying "he killed himself. I found him this morning... hanged."

The silence between us was overwhelming. The noise from the corridor and classrooms had disappeared. I knew I'd to speak but I felt nothing for the boy that had caused so much trouble. I'd discussed it at length with Sean at Christmas. We had seen that his part was much worse than Molly's. Everything that he had done was intentional. Molly had just been Molly, so like fido dido. My own words popped into my mind "Molly is for Molly; Molly is against no one." I tried not to smile. I was still too angry with Molly for that and it really wasn't the time to laugh.

I dragged my thoughts back to the girl in front of me. I swallowed, "I'm sorry for your loss." Which is the stock response to this news. Mary nodded she understood there was no sincerity in my words and hadn't expected any either. I wanted to know what Mary knew. She must know something to come and find me on the day of her brother's death.

Mary again answered an unspoken question. "I know about London. I know Robert went to Molly's home. I know what Robert said about Sean. I know about the warning from Sean. I know how he behaved with Molly. He didn't say where he got or who gave him the information. I won't tell anyone as I know I would put Molly at risk.

Robert had been torn, he was studying law you know. He knew he should tell what he'd found out. Once the information was out there it was dangerous to people he cared about. He knew more than he wanted to know. If he knew this information and it was just about Sean, there might have been a different outcome."

I was staring at Mary wanting to rage at her but I couldn't as this girl's brother was dead. It seemed like the threat was over but I knew that Mary may now struggle with that information herself.

I lied, "I blame Molly for it. This was not Robert's fault; it would never have happened without her." Mary was upset by this statement. It was obvious that Mary didn't blame Molly. "No, it's not her fault. Molly didn't know when I asked her to write to me that it would cause a problem. I know she struggled with her decision to carry on writing. She never said this but I know that she found it hard to take a side. She lived in a community that hated Irish people. She didn't understand or want to treat other people like that. In my case, for my religion. Just as she was considered a terrorist for being Irish in England. She didn't want to do the same to others.

As I was not doing anything bad to her, she looked at me as a person not a religion. She wasn't brought up here, she couldn't feel the anger or hear it, in person. She listened to what she was told had happened. She cared about her family history. She was very affected by seeing the army on the streets of the North and how she was treated at home. She wanted to be treated as an individual and treat others the same. Please don't be hard on her."

I was listening but not showing any reaction. It felt like she was begging me but I didn't trust her. Mary was waiting for some type of response. "Molly deceived me by not telling me about you. I cannot trust her. I cannot trust it when she says that she didn't have a relationship with Robert either." Mary was sad hearing her brother's name but soldiered on, "That's my fault, I loved my brother and had childish dreams that they could be together." She faltered and closed her eyes. Her tears were flowing again when she used the past tense.

"I loved Molly too. She was fun. Her letters were a joy to receive. We liked the same things. I wanted her to be my sister. I know now that she was only being polite to Robert. I didn't want to see that she didn't like him. Robert liked her and he wanted to come when we met up. I let him come."

I was curious as to how these meetings had occurred, "where did you meet and how many times?" Mary took deep breaths and the tears stopped. "Not many. We bumped into each other on the beach, in the bookshop, then at that disco and the community day. The only planned meetings were once at the drifters and for lunch twice. That's it, in eight years."

I was considering what Mary had said. I tried hard not to show any emotion. These were excuses not acceptable reasons. "What about Robert, when did she see him? all those times?"

Mary shook her head, she seemed to be struggling with all these questions about her brother, but I needed to know and wouldn't get the same chance again. "not at the community day or our second lunch but I did tell him to look for her at the bookshop one day. He took her for a drink at the diner. From what he said, she was desperate to get away but he took it that it was because he was a protestant not that she didn't like him. I should have tried to explain even then, that was probably not the case."

"When he got the opportunity to drive you both home that night. He was in a great mood about it. Molly never mentioned it to me so I should have known that she didn't like him.

She was writing more and more about Jack. I knew it was Jack she liked really. She had run away from my house when I'd explained my link with the murder near the church. Robert followed you when you went to the club. He knew where She'd be on her last night out in Ireland. He tried to explain to her why I was worried. He made things worse saying you and Sean's family were more than sympathizers and about Noraid.

I sneered at that but Mary continued "Molly cut all ties with me. She put her family over mine. There was no doubt that would happen once she knew. Robert was convinced that it was you and Sean who were stopping them being together. He was obsessed with her. He started to talk to people and ask questions. Questions that he shouldn't have asked. When he found the answers, he didn't like them."

"He decided that Molly was in danger and that he should protect her. I tried to stop him going to England. I tried to tell him without hurting him. I knew that Molly would not listen to him, whatever evidence he may have. I knew Molly would never go against you and she never did. Molly didn't listen to his beliefs about you and Sean.

When he came back from England, he was so angry with himself. For going to Molly's house and following her to the pub. He knew that how he'd behaved was unacceptable. He Couldn't forgive himself nor did he think Molly would be able to either."

"He was in anguish for months after that night. He asked if he could stay here and work in our Dad's office for the rest of the year. Then go back to university next year. I tried to talk to him but he wouldn't listen. He was depressed but I didn't know how depressed until today."

I was glad that he knew he had been wrong and had listened to Sean. He had suffered the consequences of his actions but rather him than them. I knew my face was hard and I'd no empathy or sympathy to show.

"I can understand you and Molly would be friends. Molly told me that you had alot in common. Not just books, films and music but you both didn't see what was going on in front of your eyes. You are both naïve. Molly's naivety has led to this. So, she has to suffer the consequences of her actions as have you. Sean and I've had to cut her out of our lives and her friend Maria have done the same. Luckily, you had already been cut out." Mary was crying again, "so she has no one now?" I shook my head. "Well, she has her family for now and Jack, but he is in Dublin which is no good for her."

Mary was shocked by my attitude. "Please forgive Molly. As soon as there was something that made her have to choose. She chose you. She stopped writing to me and I understood that but I missed her. She didn't do anything on purpose. In trying to be nice, she has been left with nothing." I said "Molly tried hard to understand but she didn't get it, didn't get the seriousness of how life is for some people but she knows now."

Mary was distressed more than just about her brother but she knew that there was no changing my mind. I would never forgive Molly. Mary recovered herself. "I actually didn't even want to speak to you today but I'd too. There was no note from Robert but a letter to Molly." Mary took an envelope out of her pocket "Can you get it to her for me please."

I was surprised and suspicious, "Have you read it?" Mary shook her head "No, it's for Molly and I don't think I want to know what is says. I loved him so much. He could do everything he tried. He was so clever. So kind. So protective. I don't know how I will live without him."

Mary was so pale and her eyes were red. The tears had stopped but her face was stained with them. Mary looked small and frail. Her red hair seemed brighter than ever. Her face was whiter than normal so her freckles were really pronounced. I looked at her and nodded, acknowledging her pain

Even though she was a protestant, I felt sad for her. "I will go to London tomorrow. I will tell Molly about your brother. I will tell her what she has done. Please don't contact her, for the same reasons as before. I know Molly will want to write to you but she can't. It's too difficult at the moment but I know Molly, she will be devastated for you especially as you were friends for that long. Again, my condolences."

This was the most I could say. I turned and walked away. I was grateful that from today, I was off school for Easter. I could visit London to hand deliver this letter. It would be easy to arrange; Cillian was going over this weekend anyway so he could take me there and back. I turned the letter from Robert to Molly over in my hand and wondered what it said inside.

Part 4: Chapter 21 - The Letter

I walked up from the bus stop to my house. I felt really tired today. Ryan at work was off sick and the delivery still had to be put out. I was glad that I didn't have to work this Easter holidays. I knew that my revision needed to really pick up now. As promised Jack was coming over tomorrow. I was looking forward to seeing him but my exams were at the front of my mind all the time. Even stacking the shelves at work hadn't made me forget about them, which normally did work.

I saw a car parked outside my house with two people in it. I didn't know the car and I couldn't see the people so I let myself into the house. I'd planned to do a couple of hours revision but I would have to have an early night instead. Most Saturdays had been early for me anyway for quite a while now. My Fido dido keyring brought me no joy today either. I took off my jacket and put it on the end of the bannister. I knew that I should put it away in the cupboard but I just wanted to sit down for a few minutes.

I was facing away from the door when there was a knock. I turned quickly to see who it was. I was drained already but even more so when I realised who it was. I shouted out, "I'll get it" but I was not even sure who was in the house. The living room and kitchen doors were shut and I'd no idea if anyone was upstairs.

Saoirse was looking at me through the glass. She looked agitated. I opened the door. Saoirse walked in with no greeting at all. When the door was shut, she turned to face me. There was no preamble. I'd my back to the living room door and she was in front of the telephone table. It was only a small space behind the front door but I tried to create a gap between us. I'd had no contact with her since our telephone call. There really was no reason for her to be here unless something terrible had happened.

"He's dead." She was calm. I was confused, "What? Who?" My first thought was Sean. Then I realised that she hadn't come to England to tell me that as my dad would've known. I thought that it couldn't possibly be Jack either. Surely, I would have heard that in the time that it would have taken her to get here.

She saw my mind working and a sneer played on her lips. She was so much taller than me now. Over six foot so she looked down upon me. She was athletic in build which was to be expected given all the sport that she played now. Her long black hair was down and as usual she wore no makeup. Her face was no longer beautiful It seemed to me ugly and cold. It was like I didn't know her at all.

I thought I must look terrified and tried to conceal my feelings. I knew it was too late. Her eyes danced in enjoyment; at the affect she was having on me. She seemed to take pleasure out of the answer, "Robert." Questions jumped into my head; things Saoirse must have thought about herself but she has had enough time to compose herself. My mouth was suddenly very dry. I croaked the words "What?.. Why?... How?..." She waited, in pausing she knew it would make me more anxious. My heart was beating loudly. I hoped that she Couldn't hear it too. I tried not to but I was looking at her imploringly. I needed her to tell me what had happened. Finally, she spoke with contempt, "Suicide."

The power of that one word made me lose sight of my mind, body and surroundings. I was drawn into a void. A total emptiness. As if I was where he might be. It was only when I heard a noise from Saoirse that I was pulled back to reality. In that small sound I could feel her lack of compassion. I didn't respond to her. I was aware of my body again. My stomach churned. What little energy that I'd left from the day, had drained away completely.

I noticed her eyes; they were blacker than I'd ever seen. I turned away but I knew she had already seen the damage she had inflicted. I knew torment must show in my face. There was no expression on Saoirse's face for me to guess how she felt about this news. Her total lack of empathy confirmed that her feelings towards me were unchanged.

I was sad. I wanted to say how terrible it was. In despite of my dislike of him. Any suggestion now of sympathy from me, might indicate a relationship. Which I'd repeatedly and truthfully, denied. I knew that Sean and Saoirse would never believe me anyway. The real truth could never be established now. I was overwhelmed with sorrow for Mary. She was devoted to her brother and he to her. I thought She'd need to be very strong to live without him.

As I turned back towards Saoirse. I willed my face to mirror hers. "Why are you telling me this in person? You have never even been to England before." Her eyes darkened, "I've come to warn you." I knew it was not out of concern for me. From her tone, I took this as a threat. I felt intimidated by her as she intended me to be.

She was in control. I decided that I would not let that happen. She was no longer my friend and she was in my house. "What about?" She saw my demeanour had changed. She looked slightly surprised that I was not reacting as she expected. Internally I felt the menace in her voice but I changed my stance to suggest that I'd not.

She spoke to me as if I was a child. "This is how serious this situation is. The situation that you created. By your deception." My mind rushed back to Mary as a child. She was standing in the book shop asking for my address. Then back to before that, to the beach. Playing catch with her and Robert. With these pictures flashing in my mind, I heard her continue "This is all your fault. You are responsible."

My mind was fast forwarding to dancing with Robert at the disco. Then him getting out of his car at my granny's house. I didn't want to think about it. I tried to close my mind. I focused myself on what she was saying. Saoirse's contempt showed starkly on her face, "I wanted to tell you myself. I want you to understand what you caused."

I didn't speak. I couldn't as my mind was whirling out of control. I then remembered the nite club in Ireland, less than a year ago. He was warning me. He had tried to explain the danger. His concern had been for me but it was him that had succumbed to the pressure. She didn't need to persuade me it was my fault. I would not argue with her.

She was annoyed, she wanted me to respond. "My first thought was that he had been killed by the IRA. That they had found out that he was passing false information. Lies.... It's what he deserved." This was her warning to me. That this could still be my fate. She watched me as I digested this.

I'd thought about it before. It terrified me. Not just now but every day since I'd gone to Mary's house. I tried to block it out. This consequence of my actions was worse than losing friendships. The fear would probably never go away. Saoirse was surprised at my reaction. Maybe my acceptance seemed that I was not concerned.

She was pushing me for a reaction. "But Mary said that he didn't tell anyone else." Which meant Mary knew. Of course, she knew. She'd have made him tell her. He could never say no to her. I wondered if his accusations were true. Everyone's feelings were too pronounced surely, for them to be not.

I questioned the allegations again. I'd no allegiances to them now. I didn't need to care about their feelings anymore. They had made their attitude towards me very clear. They may have been the ones to cut me out but I was grateful that they had.

"What made him think I was more than a sympathiser? Was it you?" I shook my head. The murder at the church came into my mind. Then Roberts pronouncement about Noraid. Which I still didn't understand as I'd never heard of it since.

"Mary said something about Noraid when we spoke." I nodded and shrugged. Her hollow laugh made me fear for Mary. I felt a pain in my chest knowing how Saoirse must have treated her when they met. On top of her having to hear that most terrible news. I was so sad for Mary that I hardly heard the angry words falling from Saoirse's mouth. "Noraid. Noraid if that's what he had on me." She was mocking the idea that this could be everything. "I did an essay at school. You know I want to be a teacher. I'm a republican too so I wanted to research this charity." I agreed that seemed reasonable by lifting my chin.

She was taking my silence as an opportunity to justify herself. "I would not have denied to anyone that I'm republican, especially him. If I'd talked to him, I would have told him that. I would've said, good luck to ye, if that's all he had. Well, he certainly didn't get any luck after his carry-on." She laughed in relief.

Hatred washed over her face again. "He's the one lying dead……. because of ye. But it could still be you…. or the rest of us that ye put at risk." She reverted back to the threats that she so wanted to reinforce to me about the realism of the situation. "You were so naive to believe him."

When I did speak, I could only stammer, "I didn't." It was true but I didn't want her to think I still cared about her or her opinions. I took a deep breath to fortify myself. "I didn't then but hearing you say it now, makes me wonder."

She was talking now more to herself than to me, "Someone must have whispered in his ears though…. *Say your prayers and write your letters*…. as he wrote a letter to you. How very strange that he would do that when you hardly knew each other." She stared into my eyes to let me know that she didn't believe anything that I'd said.

She held out her hand. I realised that a letter had been there the whole time. I went to take the letter but she held it back for a moment. Then she made a throw away action with the letter. When I'd taken it from her. She looked at her empty hand as if it had been contaminated.

Saoirse's mouth was curled in anger, "I don't believe your lies and I will never forgive you." I knew that anyway. She had done what she had come for. To place blame and issue her warning in the guise of hand delivering a letter.

"Leave now." My voice was small. I heard arrogance in hers. I don't want to keep Cillian waiting. He needs to get somewhere." She looked out of the window in the front door and so did I. It was odd for her to tell me her plans after the conversation that we had just had. I felt this was a warning too. I wondered if she knew that her boyfriend scared me. I guessed that she did.

Cillian was looking in our direction. I didn't want to catch his eye. I didn't

want to see his reaction. Saoirse would have told him everything. I dreaded his

opinion on this situation. I felt scared so I looked away. I felt like I was falling. I

opened the door for her but I was only really using it to help keep me standing up.

As I was more stable now, I repeated, with more authority, "Please leave."

She smiled. "I'm going. Do not contact Mary. It is still dangerous. Robert may have

been contacted by the IRA. What a fool that he was, asking those questions. Be very

careful of what you say and who you say it too." I knew she was protecting herself. I

didn't need to listen to her anymore, "Just go." I didn't have the energy to express

the anger she was making me feel.

I shut the door behind her. I suddenly had a blinding headache. I wanted to

be sick. I ran up the stairs into the toilet. I threw up until my body was empty. My

eyes were watering but not from crying. I was kneeling and holding onto the sides

of the toilet. I knew that I wouldn't be sick again. I waited for my breathing to slow

down. I realised I'd been gasping for air.

I wiped my face with toilet tissue. I turned and slowly got up and used the

walls for support. I closed the seat as I flushed and sat on top of it. I held my head

up with my hands under my chin. To help reduce the pain in my head by keeping it

still. I needed to be able to think to make sense of my reaction.

I realised that I'd not even shut the toilet door but no one had seemed to

have heard me getting sick or that we'd even had a visitor. I looked at the letter that

I'd dropped on the floor. I bent over to pick it up. In unfamiliar writing was just one

word, Molly.

I went into the bathroom to wash my face. I looked in the mirror. I was

white and I'd red eyes. I must have cried but I couldn't remember that. I looked tired and drawn, all my energy had gone. Not just from my day at work but in my mind too. I left the letter on the side of the bath; my name was staring at me. I washed my face but my eyes were still red and my skin pale.

I looked at the letter again. It was the same small type of envelope that Mary had used to write to me. It had been folded into two and the sides were curling up. It was very crumpled as if it was an insignificant piece of rubbish. I knew that it must contain something important as Robert had taken time to write it. I didn't want to read it.

Eventually I picked it up to take it into my room. The house was silent or I was deaf to the sounds around me. It was normally a very noisy house. I made my way across the short hallway holding the bannister as I needed support to get there. I shut the door and sat on my bed.

I looked around. I knew I was procrastinating. When I'm stressed, I tidy up but the room was already tidy and clean. My mum would not have let me keep it any other way. I wondered if I could just throw the letter away and not have to see what had been written. Even if I did, I would probably wonder forever. I knew I'd to read it now. Even though my decision was made, I didn't open it.

I laid the envelope onto my knees and smoothed it out flat. I looked at my name again. I noticed that the handwriting was tidy and unrushed. That surprised me considering how he had died. Finally, I turned it over and looked at the back. It was sealed so I didn't think it had been opened by anyone else.

I opened it carefully not to tear the envelope, though I didn't know why. I unfolded one sheet of paper that was inside. The writing was clear, concise and controlled not frenzied as I think I'd feared. The handwriting showed no signs of distress or haste. I remembered that he had wanted to be a solicitor and must have taken time over his work.

I was sad again at the loss of life, not for him as a person. I found it hard to dislike him now, but I did know that he could hurt me again by any actions that he might've already taken. I was looking at the words on the paper in my lap but yet not able to focus on what they were.

I wondered if things should be black and white, like Saoirse and Sean felt. Should I be feeling sorry for Robert? Should I've been more considerate of the ideas of English or Irish and Catholic or Protestant. Were there any grey areas? I'd thought there was and this had led to Robert's death.

I was distraught to think of my involvement in his life and death. I hadn't liked him but more so that I hated that, he liked me. I didn't know him at all. The fact that he was writing to me meant I must have played a large part of his thought processes as he prepared to kill himself.

A young man, who had only been striving to do the right thing. I was overcome with guilt. Not just my normal expected roman catholic guilt. The knowledge that I'd caused this to happen.

I thought of his mother and her welcoming smile. I knew She'd hate me. She'd blame me. If I was her, I would probably feel the same. I'd never met Mary's father. I'd only seen a photo of the four of them smiling. A happy family. Now there were only three, could they be happy again.

He is...was a serious person. He had smiled when I saw him at the Drifters and in the restaurant. All that I'd felt was dislike. I wished that I'd not been so polite. That was another mistake I made. I thought about Mr O'Malley. He said I was a good actress and I should study that at uni. Had I been too good of an actress? Enough for him to think I liked him?

Had he done this because of Sean's warning? He had told him not to tell anyone what he had found out. I suspected it was true. I came back to the same question, was it the truth? Had Robert been right about Sean.

I knew I'd to read the letter even if I would not like the words. I prepared myself to be sad or angry or ashamed. I saw my mum throwing him out of this house. Remembering Sean's surprise at seeing us together in the pub. Then I did cry as I saw Mary standing beside him. Petite, pale skinned and red haired next to him broad, tall and brown haired. They were so different physically. Poor sweet Mary loving her brother so much. I was sure that her tears would never stop.

I'd to read his words. He had put so much thought into them. I took a deep breath. It was a very short letter. It didn't have a date or address but his name was at the bottom. I realised that Saoirse hadn't told me any details of how or when he had died. The letter was undoubtedly going to tell me why. The most difficult part was to let my eyes see what was in front of them. His words would never be unseen;

Dear Molly

This is not your fault. Please do not blame yourself. I don't blame you. Mary won't either. I know that you will want to comfort Mary but please do not contact her. This is very important for you both. She will understand and will know that you will be thinking of her. I'm sure that Saoirse will say the same but for different reasons.

I was right about Sean but I decided not to tell anyone. I couldn't live not telling and I couldn't live telling. I know you don't want to believe it but it is the truth. You will always be in danger, be very careful. You are not naive; you are a kind and caring person. They are very rare traits, never stop being you.

I'm sorry that I scared you.

Love…. always

Robert

The only word that he'd faltered at was love. As if he had been unsure whether to write it or not. It was hard to read. I felt sick again but I knew I couldn't be as my inside were empty. I turned paper over as I couldn't look at it anymore. I never wanted to look at it again. I wanted to destroy it but didn't have the energy. I left it on the floor where I'd been sitting. I laid down on my bed, still in my work clothes. My mind was blank now. I didn't expect to but I slept.

#

My mum woke me to the news of Robert. I explained that I knew. I told her that he had left me a letter. I pointed to it. I made to show it to her. She shook her head and said it was private. She asked whether he blamed me. I shook my head in response. My mum sighed. "I'm glad because you are not to blame. I don't want you to feel guilty about his death. You will though. I know what you are like. Please don't. But it is ok to be sad."

She explained what she had been told about Robert's death. I don't know by who. I supposed Aunt Geraldine. I wondered where Saoirse was and if she was thinking about the letter. I picked it up and put it in the envelope. I sat up and felt for the box under my bed to put it in.

I explained that both Saoirse and Robert told me not to contact Mary. I expressed my sadness for her. My mum agreed that contacting Mary now would be like opening an old wound.

She said "Come on now, it's Palm Sunday. We need to get to mass. I checked on you about 8pm. I couldn't believe that you were asleep, still in your work clothes. You slept for hours and now I know why.

Jack will be here soon too. You need to get ready." She left me. I wondered what Jack would say and whether I should show him the letter. I pondered this whilst I got ready. I looked a mess again and remembered last year when I'd been in a similar state. Robert had been still alive then. I put the letter in the back pocket of my jeans. I would decide what to do with it later. Jack might not want to read it anyway.

I got to mass to do the normal possession on Palm Sunday. We walked into the church waving our palms. I let the holy water wash over me. We got our normal seat at the back of the church, which was lucky. On days like this it's easy to lose your seat. My mum would not like to have to sit nearer the front. For a reason She'd not explain nor I could fathom.

It was a good seat to see everyone and what was going on. My mum usually whispered things to me but today she looked solemn. I was sure I looked the same. I was still pale and had dark circles under my eyes. We haven't discussed it but we would of course be lighting a candle after mass for Robert. We would also request a mass to be said for the repose of his soul. Protestants are still Christians even though it didn't feel like that sometimes.

After mass my mum spoke to the priest when she shook his hand. He was very busy but leaned in to listen. He nodded his head and looked at me. My mum came to stand by me. It was unusual as we were usually the first out. When most of the congregation had left, my mum led me inside towards the confessional box. I was distressed and actually thought that speaking to the priest might help. Robert had committed a mortal sin in the eyes of the catholic church. But he wasn't catholic so I didn't know if it was the same. I didn't want him to go to hell.

I knew that the priest would not come out for a while. I lit a candle for Robert and one for his family to ease their suffering. How that would be possible I couldn't comprehend. I never personally knew someone so young to die. I'd been to a lot of funerals of family and family friends. They had all been older and had had a life. I went back to the seat and knelt down.

I looked at the gospel that we had read at mass. I wanted to see again what it had said about Judas's suicide. I definitely didn't think that it was the same as Robert's death. I was unsure what the priest could say to make things any better. He might make me feel worse. God knew my involvement so it was better to find out now. We waited some time for the priest. I knew it was the busiest time of the year for priests with extra masses, stations of the cross and washing of feet.

I stayed kneeling all the time we waited, just thinking. The only prayer I could think of was *"Eternal rest grant unto them, O Lord, and let perpetual light shine upon them. May they rest in peace. Amen."* I could only say it so many times. My mum walked to meet Father Tom, when he came towards us. He had already changed back to his normal clothes. My mum had the money in her hand to pay for a mass to be said for Robert. I heard her explain that we didn't need a mass card. He took the money. He told her that he would call into the house with the details of the mass for Robert.

Father Tom indicated that I should go into the confessional box. I went inside and closed the door. I knelt in front of the opening to speak. I knew that the priest Couldn't repeat anything I said to anyone. I did the sign of the cross. I murmured the necessary words *"Bless me father for I've sinned, it has been one month since my last confession and these are my sins..."* I started from Mary to yesterday.

I paused, then a question left my lips not observing the rules I always followed in this sacrament, "Did Robert commit a mortal sin?" The priest was silent and didn't answer immediately. I was scared about what he would say. "John said.. *he walks in the darkness, does not know where he is going....* and.... *The greatest love a person can show is to die for his friends.* The church believes that suicide is distinguished from the sacrifice of one's life for God or another. As in the cases of martyrdom; the offering of one's life or risking it to save another person." He said nothing else so I ended my confession with an *Act of contrition.*

I was shocked and remained on my knees. Surely, he would explain himself further than the words of the gospel. "Your sin was in deceiving your friends for which your penance will be a decade of the rosary. You need to ask them again for forgiveness. You should also pray for Roberts family." He followed up the prayer of absolution.

I swallowed because I didn't want to see Saoirse again and wondered whether I would be able to carry out my penance. I was really appreciative of his time, "Thank you Father" and I left to start my penance which I didn't deserve after the way I'd behaved.

I was glad that Jack wouldn't be arriving until early evening. I was helping my mum prepare the dinner. We didn't speak. I thought about what the priest had said. I'd been forgiven by god but I doubted I would be by Saoirse after her visit yesterday. My Dad believed that Sean would come around but I didn't.

There was a loud and impatient knock on the front door. I knew it was Jack. He was flustered when he came in. He kissed then hugged me. He was explaining that after his mam had told him this morning about Robert, he had driven as quickly as possible to get here. He whispered in my ear "should I've called you before I left? It was early and I only really wanted to speak to you in person about it." I shook my head. I told him I'd slept for over twelve hours and that my mum had to get me up for mass. He continued to hug me, he didn't say anything. I could feel his concern in his arms that he had wrapped tightly around me. I was glad for his presence.

After a while he stepped away from me and looked at my face. It was calm but sad. I didn't cry for Robert and was grateful to have Jack here to talk to about it. We went into the living room and sat on the sofa, just looking at each other, not knowing where to start. My mum came into the living room. He stood up to greet her. He put out his hand and she shook it in return. "How are you, Mrs O'Donnell. My mam told me the news. It's so shocking."

My mum was shaking her head, "Jesus Mary and Joseph.... Ar the poor craythur, what agony must he have gone through. Sure, hasn't Molly been devastated for her part in it all. We have been up at the church. It did seem to help. Look at her now, you should have seen the state of her before."

Jack and I looked at each other at that comment and tried not to laugh. "She went to confession and has taken her penance. Which of course we can't discuss though it seems acceptable to her. Father Tom was brilliant so he was."

I could have laughed again as my mum's Irish accent was always more pronounced on occasions like this. Just meeting another Irish person especially when they were discussing death. Which is a favourite topic of conversation of most Irish people.

I remembered Saoirse and Sean teaching me the Irish sayings. When we returned from our school holidays. Maria and I would use them at school, until we forgot them again. I wondered if Saoirse was with Sean and what they were saying. About Robert and Mary. About me. My smile was gone and brow was furrowed as usual when I was worried.

Jack thanked my mum for asking him for dinner. "Your very welcome Jack, but it will be a while yet. Sure, we were up at the church for far longer than I expected. There's no sign of Molly's dad either." He was formal, "Can we go out for a little while before its ready then?" She agreed and told us it would be about an hour." She smiled at me to show me comfort and left the room.

He turned to me as she left, "Is that ok?" I nodded. I got up and as I left, called goodbye to my mum. I'd no idea of our destination but I didn't care. Jack was taking charge, "We can go to my aunt's. She will be out but she has left the key under the mat for me, in case I got back before they did." We didn't speak in the car but Jack was watching me checking I was okay. I smiled at him at intervals.

I looked out of the window trying not to think about Robert. I thought about Father Tom. I was glad that Robert hadn't committed a mortal sin. Which meant I'd not either. The penance I received was for lying and the actions to pray were

377

necessary. Sean and Saoirse felt this deception was much more than a misdemeanour of lying. The further requests for forgiveness would be difficult, if not impossible.

Their concern about Mary would be purely selfish. I sincerely hoped that Robert wouldn't have told her who passed on the information to him. Therefore, no further contact should be able to be made. I knew Robert would never have put Mary in danger by introducing her to informers. Anything else would-be hearsay to the police.

The real threat was from the IRA. They were a faceless organisation. I couldn't find out if they knew or not. I wouldn't even attempt to ask anyone, any questions. Now it didn't matter if Sean or Saoirse were involved. It was the passing of information that could be the issue. It was me; I could still be seen as some sort of informer.

Which reminded me of Mary again. I remembered the last time that I saw her, standing by the stairs in her house so scared and distressed about our conversation. I started the decade of the rosary sitting in the car. If Saoirse heard me, she'd probably say that prayer won't save ye.

We settled in Jack's Aunts living room. For me to talk and Jack to listen. I'd to try again to explain the consequences of my actions. He agreed and disagreed at some parts. He had a few choice words for Saoirse, which I could understand. He was shocked by how she had delivered the news. He agreed that contacting Mary was a bad idea. He was relieved when I told him that I wouldn't.

I told him about the letter and then the priest. He'd chuckled when I'd started to share my confession, "as long as you don't tell me your penance otherwise, we'll be in a whole heap of trouble." He was surprised by the priest's take on the situation. He was sure that his own priest would probably say something completely different. Father Tom didn't need to say what he did. I'm sure this was not the catholic church's standard view on suicide. I'd certainly never heard it before.

Jack was hesitant about whether to read the letter but I gave him the option. After a long deliberation, I could see in his eyes that he wanted to and he nodded. I took the letter out of my pocket and out of the envelope. I passed the letter to him. He was apprehensive, "I do feel very uneasy. It's personal for him and you." He looked at the letter again and closed his eyes as if in divine inspiration on how he should react.

Jack was looking down for a long time. He must have read the short letter five or six times, before he spoke. I knew he needed to compose himself. He was relieved that Robert didn't blame me. He knew that Mary wouldn't either. He was sad for her and for me not being able to try to comfort her as She'd need. We both knew if I did, more people could get hurt.

He was troubled about Robert's conviction about Sean. He was thankful that he had decided not to tell anyone. It was concerning that he believed to the end that Sean was involved in and responsible for some kind of IRA activities. He recited '*I couldn't live not telling and I couldn't live telling.* It is agony to read, the torment that Robert must have felt was unimaginable."

I agreed and he put the letter between us. We held hands as if in prayer but no words were spoken. Both our heads were bowed. We didn't look at each other. I wondered if things could have been done differently. What could have been done to prevent this.

I was racked with guilt that I didn't contact him. Which I said out loud aswell. Jack squeezed my hand and I looked up and met his gaze. "You couldn't have and it probably would have made things worse. Robert may have taken it as sign of interest. Worse, acceptance of his investigations and your agreement in the accusations. It could have looked like a new opportunity to share information, if anyone had been watching."

Our intakes of breath showed that we were both concerned but didn't want to admit it. It would open a can of worms, if we discussed how we viewed our cousins. Jack continued in his view of the letter. He was concerned that Robert had continued to fear danger for me. He agreed Robert had made the ultimate sacrifice to stop it. "Molly you must be very careful as he says. You must do that for him as it is his last plea in life."

I wondered how that matched with my penance from confession. I was required to contact Sean and Saoirse. Even though I already knew they would not forgive me. If we did believe Robert even being in contact with them at all, could put us at risk.

I didn't have to tell Jack what my penance would be. Jack would have used lying as a sin at confession too. Everyone did. So, he knew that I would need to say sorry. He was adamant and imploring, "this is a penance you cannot keep. You will just have to confess why next time you go." I knew he was right.

We discussed whether mine was a mortal sin. I'd kept a secret from my cousin. I knew it was wrong to lie, being fully aware that it could upset someone and I continued to do it for a long time. In reality it was not a grave matter so therefore I could be forgiven.

We knew that there was more to discuss but time was ticking on. We were already too late to get back in time for dinner. Jack suggested that I ring my mum to tell her. She was okay about it, she'd leave our plates in the oven for when we got back.

We went to the kitchen. He was hungry after his long journey. I remembered that I hadn't eaten since lunchtime yesterday. I'd been sick aswell so I knew I should eat something. Jack made us some sandwiches.

We sat in the kitchen to eat. We were laughing as neither of us could remember when we had spoken so much about religion. Even in lessons or at mass. We were impressed with ourselves. We must have listened when they taught us about confession. Considering how much we knew about types of sins and their level of importance.

When we got back into the living room. Jack picked up the letter again. He reread what we had discussed before. He wanted to ensure that we had covered everything. He smiled "I agree with Robert that you are a 'kind and caring person'. Not naive as Sean and Saoirse always said. They were always trying to change you. You didn't think it but you didn't always agree with them. You do make your own decisions. You can trust your own beliefs."

"I think that you do support *The Cause* in your own way. How could we not. Hearing what we do from family and friends. We both agree there have been terrible and shocking experiences. You live in a small Irish community here in England and have experienced abuse. We have chosen not to be involved in the war. I know we would both want a way to change things other than by violence. We have tried to see both sides." I nodded in response. I didn't want to say, that it was the cause of all this. As we would be going back to the beginning again.

"I'm glad that he apologised to you for his behaviour as he did scare you. I think that's a part of why you stopped going out. The fear he might turn up. Not just the thought of meeting Marie or Sean." I didn't realise that but it probably was true. "Well he never will follow you again. Just before your exams, take a night off revision and go out. You need to go out as often as possible afterwards too. You can go with Sammy and all the other people at college that you talk too. You don't have to rely on one friend anymore. You have more friends that you know. I saw you chatting to everyone at The Clifton. The *craic is mighty* with you. Whether you are trying to play golf, beating me at bowling or dancing and singing."

His tone changed and became more serious. "Now to '*Love.... Always*'. I know it's wrong to be... And I only say this word as I cannot think of another to describe it. I do feel jealous that someone else loved you. Even though I know he is not around. I'm so sorry that's what I'm thinking." He looked concerned.

I was confused, "Do you now think or did you always believe that I did like Robert?" He was shaking his head "No, no. I've never doubted that. I'm lucky you chose me. It could have been him. I might have been in his position if you had chosen Sean and Saoirse over me. Just because they didn't like me. I might have investigated them myself. To protect you. I might have been the one to warn you against them. Robert or someone else could be sitting here now."

We sat in silence taking this in. "Sean could have easily made the same threats to me. He would have no qualms about doing that. Even though I'm his cousin." He made it sound as if it was possible that Roberts reaction was normal. That it could easily be something someone else would have to wrestle with.

"If it had been me. I would know that I would have had to take the consequences of my own actions. That shows it's not your fault. He made his own decisions." His understanding of Roberts mind was convincing me. We both had suspicions about Sean so we could have investigated them ourselves.

Jack's mind was somewhere else for a moment or two. Then he turned and smiled at me "I want you to know. The way I end my letters says how I feel about you too."

Part 4: Chapter 22 - The Questions

As Jack suggested, I went out on Saturday night. It seemed to be the party that everyone needed before the revision started in earnest. Everyone from college was out. We had such a great time. We laughed, danced, sung and drank a lot. People would be going off on holidays after the exams or to university so we'd never be all together again. It wasn't said but it was subconscious. We didn't say it as it would have made us sad.

Maria and Jacinta were there but it was so packed I wouldn't have been able to speak to them, even if I wanted too. I wondered if Maria knew about Robert. I hated the way his death popped into my mind. I felt many emotions when I did. So guilty that his death had been my fault. Sad that Mary had lost a brother and her parents, a son.

I was scared that Mary wouldn't have forgiven me. I hoped that She'd understand why I hadn't written to her. I was so sorry for dragging Maria into something so serious. I constantly worried that I was getting what I deserved for my actions.

I thought about Saoirse and Sean. I didn't contact them as my penance required. I went to confession the week after and explained this to Father Tom. He told me that I still must do it. That I would know when the time was right.

He was very understanding and knowing. I thought someone else had confessed their sins to him. I'd no idea who that could be but the priest knew alot of people within the Irish catholic community. The ones that came to church and ones that should. If they were in his parish, he would know them whether they came or not.

#

My mum was constantly worried about me. I saw her whispering to my Dad, surely more than ever before. Both my sisters had left home so it was alot quieter about the place now. There were lots of young people over from Ireland looking for work. Some from families I knew and some I didn't. They came and went but they never stayed with us. Even though we had the room now.

I gathered from my dad that Sean had moved on. I didn't know if that meant a new home, new job or both. I'd no one to discuss what was happening. Jack never mentioned Sean at all. I didn't want Jack to be burdened. He had heard my thoughts a thousand times. He wanted to fix it but he couldn't so I kept them to myself. I was surprised my revision was going so well. It was helping me to block out my worries

I was even happy to go to work on a Saturday now. Most of the revision was at home not at college anymore. I did meet Sammy in the library from time to time to revise English. I never invited her to my home, just in case. I never accepted an invite from her. She always nodded and smiled. I guessed that she had heard something. There were no secrets in this college. She was happy to be friends anyway.

One day she was reading an English text and mused, "Do you think you will ever be friends with Maria again?" I shook my head, "It's all my fault. I completely

385

understand why she can't forgive me." I wondered why she asked now. I looked at her quizzically "What have you heard?" She replied "Everyone seems to know and it doesn't bother them or surprise most people."

I was so shocked, I wondered who had let this slip; Maria, Jacinta or Sean or all of them. "The Irish families say that there are always rumours. I heard someone say to her "Catch yourself on Maria! I love that saying" I said "me too." We were giggling. It felt good to laugh. "I would love to say it but people might think I was taking the mickey." I said "I know what you mean. Even me, second generation Irish, saying that can sound weird."

The stress of the revision meant that we needed a good laugh. I tried not to think about the whole college knowing my business. I was surprised no one had spoken to me about this. I told Sammy this. "Catch yourself on."

We were laughing so much when I heard my name being shouted across the library. Mr O'Malley was gruff, "I think you and Sammy need a break." He indicated that he should leave the library as we were disturbing the other students. He was smiling so I knew he wasn't angry with us.

I told Jack about the library. I speculated on what had been said. He was glad that no one seemed to care. He'd laughed at Sammy's comment too. He was glad I was more upbeat. He told me to stop apologising, "you never saw me doing my leaving. I was like a devil so I was."

That made me laugh so we were using Irish phrases all the time. Jack's accent was not strong like Sean or Saoirse's. Them both being from the country. He hardly ever used the Irish sayings but now we were using them all the time. So much so that I'd to make sure that I didn't say them in day-to-day life.

#

It was my last exam. I was relieved that by the end of the day there'd be no more revision. Mr O'Malley wished me good luck before it. He approached me, "You're my star student so I need you to do well. It makes me look good you know." I knew that he probably said this to all the students but it did boost my confidence. He spoke to Sammy too and she smiled at me from across the hall. I heard "Open your papers."

When I checked the clock, I saw that time was running out. I'd finished but I was rereading it and was seeing all the spelling mistakes and grammatical errors. My writing wasn't as good as usual but I hoped it could be understood. I heard loud talking from the lobby which was in front of the hall's doors. So did a few other people including Sammy. Some of us sat up and turned to look.

The teacher who was in charge noticed too, "Eyes down now, there's only fifteen minutes left." The voices were getting louder. Then I heard "Will you not let her finish the exam. There are only a few minutes to go. You will disturb the rest of them aswell." There was a response but I couldn't make it out. I closed my ears and looked down. I just wanted to get this done.

Then the teacher called, "Pens down. Leave your exam papers on the desk. You can take the exam questions if you wish." The doors opened. Three policemen came in. Two big men and the smaller one was a woman. Mr O'Malley was coming in behind them. "Hurry up now, nothing to see here. Move along. Haven't ye a pub to go too." Lots of people laughed but didn't speed up as this was too interesting to miss.

I was headed towards the side doors to get my stuff and go home to sleep. I was tired. I was up all-night revising. I would be meeting my English class later in the pub. One of the policemen was looking around and called loudly, "Molly O'Donnell" and then repeated it.

All the other students were looking around to find me. Sammy and Mr O'Malley saw me first. Both of them looked worried. Mr O'Malley seemed angry too. Mr O'Malley was striding towards me. Sammy had turned to look at me. He caught Sammy's eye and shook his head. He probably thought as I did, that She'd try to come over.

Mr O'Malley shouted again firmer now, "Come on. Off you go. I mean it. There's another exam later. We need to set up for that." I could see that everyone doubted that was true but people started to move slowly. Mr O'Malley stopped by me. He indicated for the policemen to come to him to prevent a scene in the hall. I was standing still. I couldn't move. I didn't understand what was going on. There was a niggle in my mind that it had something to do with Sean.

The policeman spoke loudly from where he was, "Molly O'Donnell, we'd like you to accompany us to the station to answer a few questions regarding your involvement in... "but he was cut off by Mr O'Malley saying loudly "let's go to the office," As he passed the policeman, he spoke in an angry undertone, "Now that you have had your fun." Mr O'Malley was reassuring, "Come on now Molly, best to see what this is all about."

The look in his eye said he knew this was the "something really bad" that we had discussed last year. There was no crossness in his eyes. The look that teachers sometimes have when they know you have done something wrong. I just felt solidarity from him.

I walked with heavy legs towards the policemen. We all followed Mr O'Malley into the office. There was alot of talking some directed at me and some with Mr O'Malley. He was asking the questions that I should have. I understood I was going to the police station. There was mention of the IRA and my heart sank. Alongside the guilt over Roberts death, this is what I'd been worried about. The police arresting me. Both things were entangled in my thoughts.

Robert had tried to stop this happening and it hadn't worked. He was dead. There was no point to it all. I was crying not for me but for Robert. Mr O'Malley was asking if I was being arrested. The police woman replied, "No, not yet but it's better all-around if she comes with us now." Mr O'Malley asked to come with me. They explained that as I was eighteen, I didn't need to be accompanied.

The policewoman took me by the right arm and the policeman who hadn't spoken yet took my left arm. They turned me towards the door. Mr O'Malley was supportive, "Molly, I've called your mum. She will meet you there." I didn't know where that was but I knew it was a police station. The only time I'd been to one before was when we reported our dog missing.

When I got back into the big lobby there was a crowd of people. I looked down. I was so ashamed of myself. Everyone would believe that I was guilty of something. Especially after Sammy told me that there had been rumours about me.

Someone shouted out "There's no way Molly has done anything wrong." I looked up. It was Ryan. He was in my English class and he worked with me on Saturdays too. I was grateful for his support. I was surprised not to see mocking looks from the other students. Just disbelief.

I saw Sammy too she was smiling in an encouraging way but there was fear in her eyes. It was good to have her support too. I swallowed and attempted a smile but I couldn't muster one. Anyway, what did I'veto smile about.

I thought of the Birmingham six, they were still in prison even though everyone knew they were innocent. The Guildford four had only been let out last year. They had spent years in prison aswell for crimes they didn't commit. Just because they were Irish.

I wondered if police interviews were the same now and this terrified me. Who knew how long I would be questioned for? When it came to terrorist activity, I was sure the police still needed to make arrests. To appease the English people after their suffering and fear of the IRA.

As I sat in the police car, the words of my favourite song Hold on by Wilson Phillips came in my head. *no one to blame for your unhappiness....your own mess...*

I was dreading what they would ask me and if the truth would harm anyone. By answering the truth, would that make me some kind of informer? I reminded myself that I didn't know anything. I was so scared. I thought they might put me in a cell.

I asked if my mum was there. They told me they would find out. "If not, can I ring her?" The largest policeman who was driving replied, "It's not like the TV." Which must have meant there was no phone call allowed. I thought the TV was bad but I wondered was this going to be worse?

When I got there. I was looking at the floor as if people would not see me. I felt like a small child again. I was terrified, "Do I needed a solicitor?" The policewoman that brought me in was condescending, "Why would you need one?" I stammered, "Because I don't know what's going on."

The older policeman was intimidating, "You won't want to go in a cell so let's get on with it." They led me to the interview room. I sat opposite the older policeman. A different police woman said they would tape the interview. They asked if I minded. I did mind but I couldn't see a reason to say no.

The new policewoman was in plain clothes. They said their names and rank for the tape. I immediately forgot them. I didn't know where I was and I didn't know who I was with. The terror was seeping through my mind. I so wanted to go home. I needed to go to sleep as I'd planned after the exam. I knew I was not able to answer their questions. I looked around the walls of the small room, they were dirty. The window was high up. It wasn't open. The table between us was metal. The chair was more uncomfortable than one that I'd sat in for my exam.

They asked to confirm my name for the tape I gave them my full name. She asked me the name of my college, even though already knew. Then about my Saturday job which they just nodded at the answer. The policewoman opened a file and was moving around papers. There was alot of pages. She started asking questions. I didn't have time to think as they were firing them at me. I just answered them as concisely as I could.

PW (Police woman) - Molly, are you a member of the IRA?

MOD (Molly) - No

PW - Ok, do you know any members of the IRA?

MOD - No

PW - Are you Irish, Molly?

MOD - I'm second generation

PW - What does that mean?

MOD - That I was born in England, live in England but my parents are Irish

PW - How do other people, non-Irish people, view you?

MOD - As Irish

PW - Ok and have you or your family suffered any abuse from that?

MOD - Yes, some

PW - did that make you angry?

MOD - not angry

PW - what then?

MOD - upset

PW - How did you respond to this abuse?

MOD - I didn't

PW - why not?

MOD - I was too scared

PW - Why? Didn't you think it was wrong?

MOD - Yes. It was wrong

PW - Why not tell them that then?

MOD - We didn't want any trouble

PW - Is it because you are members of the IRA and thought that you deserved it?

MOD – No. We are not members of the IRA and we didn't deserve it

PW - Why did or do you accept it?

MOD - We are Irish, it happens

PW - so you expect it?

MOD - It happens

PW - A lot it seems.

The policewoman stopped and picked up a piece of paper. I couldn't see what it said. She seemed to be rereading it. She put the paper face down so I couldn't see it.

PW - What about on the estate where you were born, were there problems there?

MOD - I don't know

PW - why don't you know Molly?

MOD - I was only three when I left

PW - But what have you heard about that estate since?

MOD - Not alot except that some people weren't very nice

PW - who? English people?

MOD - I don't know, maybe

PW - Did they shout abuse at your mum

MOD - I don't know, maybe

PW - Was the abuse because you were Irish

MOD - Maybe, I don't remember it

PW - Was it because your parents were members of the IRA?

MOD - They aren't

PW - But Molly, people thought they were?

MOD - I don't know what they were thinking

PW - Are your parents' members of the IRA?

MOD - No

PW - Why are you so sure?

MOD - Because I'm

PW - That is not an answer Molly. I'll ask you again why are you so sure?

MOD - I don't know. They never said they were. I didn't see anything that made me concerned

PW - Are you sure about that? Let's come back to that

The policewoman paused. I was so confused about how they knew so much about me. Where I lived. Probably where I was born too. She picked up the page and returned it to the folder. She took out a different page. She read it too. The policeman still hadn't said anything. He didn't look at the paper. He just stared at me. I looked down. His eyes showed disgust. She did the same again, putting the new page face done on top of the file.

PW - So when you left the estate you moved to the house that you live in now with your parents?

MOD - Yes

PW - What happened there, were there any problems there?

MOD - Not much

PW - Are you sure? Do you have friends on the street?

MOD - I did when I was a child

PW - Not now, why?

MOD - I went to secondary school and they didn't

PW - But Molly that is not true, is it? they stopped talking to you before that. Do you remember why?

MOD - Maybe, things on the news as well

PW - what things on the news?

MOD - About fighting in Ireland and attacks in England

PW - So about the IRA

MOD - Not always. About Irish people protesting too

PW - so Irish people, not the IRA?

MOD - some people can't see the difference

PW - mmm we will come back to that.

The policewoman looked at the policeman and shook her head as if in disbelief.

PW - What about your next-door neighbour. Did he like you?

MOD - No

PW - Why because you were Irish?

MOD - Maybe

PW - Why else?

MOD - I don't know

PW - He was in the English army and fought in Northern Ireland. Did you know that?

MOD – Yes. I know that

PW - Did he say anything to you?

MOD - sometimes

PW - What exactly?

MOD - He shouted alot of things. He was an angry man

PW - Did he ever say that he thought your father was in the IRA

MOD - I think so

PW - You think so, would you not remember that

MOD - Probably, some people can't tell the difference

The policewoman lifted the sheet again and scanned what was written there.

PW - Did anyone else in your street think that?

MOD - Maybe

PW - Surely, it's definitely Molly. What about the man who lived at the top of the road? He frightened you didn't he

MOD - Yes

PW - Because you were Irish

MOD - Yes

   PW - Do you remember why?

MOD - He was drunk

PW - Yes, I believe he was. Was it about anything specific?

MOD - The Hunger strikes

PW - Yes that's right. It seems alot of people thought you were members of the IRA

MOD - No

PW - No, what? That there were not a lot of people or that you were not members of the IRA?

MOD - Both

   PW - I think that's alot of people, don't you Phil?

PM (policeman) - Yes that's a hell of a lot of abuse Sandra. I'm sorry that you went through that Molly. Does that haunt you?

I was surprised that he had started talking. His tone had changed as if he cared. I knew he didn't.

MOD - Not really

PM - Not really. It would upset me.

MOD - It wasn't nice but it happened to us and other people we knew.

PM - That must have made them angry?

MOD - I don't know

   PM - So back to your family. Is your mum a member of the IRA?

MOD - Definitely not

PM - so everyone else was No but your mum is definitely not, why is she different?

MOD - It upsets her

PM - It upsets her, why?

MOD - I don't know really, she hates any sort of violence and she appreciates being able to live in England.

PM - What about your Dad. He likes the violence and does not appreciate being in England

MOD - That's not what I said.

PM - I think it was.

MOD - No it's just that my Dad would rather be in Ireland and he cannot be there due to the War

PM - I'm confused, what war?

MOD - Between Ireland and England

PM - There's no war Molly. Do you believe that there is a war?

MOD - I know that the army are in Northern Ireland and bombs going off there.

PM - That's called terrorism, Molly. I thought you would understand that. You just finished your A level examinations today. Do you not understand that it is terrorism?

MOD - I think violence is wrong. Whether it is terrorism or war.

PM - Molly, some people would think that you were a sympathiser saying that. Are you a sympathiser?

MOD - No, I would not call myself that

PM - Why not, that's what you doing sympathising, is it not? It's simple

MOD - It is not simple

PM - Why not? It sounds simple to me

MOD - Lots of Irish people want the Island of Ireland to be a republic.

PM - Is that just Catholics though, Molly? The ones rioting in the streets of Northern Ireland and killing civilians

MOD - I don't know

PM - Molly, you seem to be getting upset. Why is that? You are just helping with are inquiries.

MOD - I'm tired, I was up all-night revising. Can I come back tomorrow and help?

PM - No No No Molly. We need your help now

MOD - Why? I don't even know why I'm here. How can I be helping you?

PM - Oh but you are. More helpful that some of your friends

MOD - What friends?

PM - We will get to that but some others were very happy to help. They told us what we asked. You have confirmed that most of it is true. So, you Molly you have been very helpful too. You have given us a full background on your history. That's very helpful in our enquiries

MOD - That's not a full history. It's a handful of incidents that could have happened to anyone. What are you enquiring about?

The policewoman was looking at the file again and took out another piece of paper

PW - Molly, you said before that you are not in the IRA. Is that correct?

MOD - Yes, that's right. I'm not in the IRA

PW - You also said that you don't know anyone in the IRA

MOD - Yes that's right. I don't know anyone in the IRA

PW - Are you sure? Take your time and think about that.

MOD - Yes, I'm sure

PW - Ok then, let's try this, do you go to the Catholic Club near your house?

MOD - Not as much as I used too

PW - Is that a yes or no

MOD - Yes

> PW - Do you know when the last time was

MOD - Christmas Day

PW - Is that unusual, to leave it so long

MOD - I'vebeen revising

> PW - Ok but you have been going there for many years

MOD - Yes

PW - So it would be okay to check a few names with you

MOD – Yes

> PW - Michael McCann

MOD - Maybe, I don't remember

> PW - Tom Magee

MOD - Yes, I think so

> PW - Paul Murphy

PMOD - Yes, I think so

> PW - Brendan Horan

MOD - Maybe, I think so

> PW - Why only you think so?

MOD - There so many different people that have gone there over the years. Some

have similar names. Some men are called by the county they are from. And some

use different names

PW - Why do you think they changed their names?

MOD - I heard it was work

PW - For work? What type of work?

MOD - The buildings

PW - Would it surprise you that these men are all members of the IRA and have frequented the catholic club

MOD - Yes, I'm surprised that they are members of the IRA.

PW - So when you said you didn't know any IRA members that was not true Molly?

MOD - I may know of these people but not personally

PW - so are you saying that you've never spoken to them

MOD - Not that I know of

PW - Not that you know of, strange that you don't remember, isn't it?

MOD - No I'd say most Irish people in London had been there and maybe from around the country. It's well known for the bands

PW - You are right Molly. It is well known but not for the bands. No, I would say it's well known for sympathisers to The Cause or Republicans or IRA. What do you call them?

MOD - Irish people

PW - Irish Catholics?

MOD - no you don't have to be catholic. I think there have been protestant people there.

PW - Could you name some

MOD - No

PW - Does your Dad know them

MOD - Who the protestants?

PW - No the IRA members?

MOD - He might know those men, if they went there

PW - Are they his friends

MOD - not that I know of

    PW - Its known to be an IRA club isn't it

MOD - No

PW - O but it is Molly, very well known

MOD - Not to me, it's a catholic club. It's run by our church

    PW - Ok, what do you know about The Cause

MOD - It is wanting the whole country of Ireland to be Irish

PW - Now Molly, you know it's more than that. Do they sing rebel songs there?

MOD - They sing old Irish ballads and some country songs too

PW - Molly, come on now. Don't tell me that you don't know that the rebel songs

are about the IRA? And that a sympathiser is another word for an IRA volunteer?

MOD - Some songs are about the history in Ireland and some people are

republicans

    PW - Molly, you have been well taught. Indoctrinated some might say.

Unaware that you are part of the problem

MOD - What problem?

PW - The terrorist attacks. The death of innocent people. Injuries that people don't

recover from. You're helping IRA members? You are not that naive surely

MOD - No I'm not part of that

PW - O but you are. You would have to be extremely naive to think otherwise

    She opened the file. Put in the paper she had been looking at and slid the

folder sideways to the policeman. He fished through some pages then removed one.

He glanced at it briefly.

    PM - Lets go over a few more people. Do you know Finola Alcorn?

MOD - Jacinta's mum?

PM - Yes that's right. Have you been to her house?

MOD - yes. Not for a while though

PM - Why's that?

MOD - She's being letting out rooms since Jacinta's dad died.

PM - Her Mum's brother, Jacinta's uncle, died too recently. Did you know him?

MOD - No

PM - do you know what happened to him.

MOD - Not really.

PM - I thought you were friends with Jacinta?

MOD - Yes but we are but we didn't talk about that

PM - I'm not sure that I agree with that. Let's talk about Jacinta's home a bit more. Was it a digs for Irish people?

MOD - Yes

PM - I believe your Uncle Vincent stayed there?

MOD - Yes

PM - did you see him there?

MOD - No

PM - where did you see him then?

MOD - at home

PM - and your friend, Sean McDermott he lived at Jacinta's house too?

MOD – Yes

PM - Do you know who set that up

MOD - I think it was my dad

PM - Yes, your Dad, he was very helpful to alot of the Irish that immigrated to England for work. Did your Dad help other people?

MOD - I think so

PM - That's good, thanks for clarifying that.

PM - Who else did you know?

MOD - No one else really

PM - Not your boyfriend Jack

MOD - I think he spent a night or two there maybe

PM - Is Jack a member of the IRA?

MOD - No

PM - You are sure?

MOD - Yes.

PM - We are pretty sure about that aswell. From our own investigations

They wanted me to know how thorough their investigations were and therefore already had made their minds up. I wasn't giving a good account of myself but I didn't know how else I could've answered their questions. He made a show of taking a piece of paper and putting it into a pocket of the folder. He took another sheet from the top of the pile and he looked pleased with himself.

PM - What about Sean, is he a member of the IRA?

I paused and swallowed. I knew this was just the start.

MOD - No

PM - You don't seem so sure about Sean

MOD - I'm sure but I don't know him as well as Jack

PM - but you have known Sean since.....

He made a show of checking dates. Tracing his fingers along a line of the paper.

PM – 1981......... and you have only known Jack since 1985, isn't that correct?

MOD - I don't know anyone from the IRA so no I don't think Sean is in the IRA

PM - We will come back to Sean.

PM - What about your grandfather was he a member of the IRA?

MOD - I'venever met either my mum or my dad's fathers

PM - Your mother's father was a member of the Irish Republican Army

MOD – That would have been a long time ago

PM – Does that matter?

MOD – It's not the IRA as it was the name of an army in the civil war

PM - You think there's a difference, that's interesting.

PM - Why do you think you never met?

He checked the file again.

PM – I know your dad's dad died before you were born but you never met your mother's father, James O'Callaghan. He died in 1979 after you were born.

MOD - I don't think he was a nice man

PM - Your right he was a very violent man, how do you know that?

MOD - He beat his wife and his children

PM - Yes, he did. He was violent to protestants and the English too. Do you think that is okay?

MOD - No, I don't believe in violence

PM - He left money to The Cause in his will, did you know that?

MOD - No I didn't

PM - Your mum didn't tell you?

MOD - No

PM - What about your Uncle Vincent, did you know he was in prison?

MOD - No I didn't

PM - Yes, you do look very shocked. Did your mum know?

MOD - I'm. I don't know, if she did, she never told me

PM - do you think She'd hide it?

MOD - I don't know but she didn't see him for many years. She thought he might be dead

PM - No, she knew he'd taken the oath. Did she tell you that?

MOD - No, what oath

PM – tut tut Molly you know full well it's the oath to join the IRA. Have you taken it?

MOD - No

PM - What about your Dad?

MOD - No

PM - How can you be sure?

MOD - He is not a member of the IRA

PM - He is a Republican or sympathiser

MOD - Yes, he is a republican, that's different

PM - I don't think it is. What about your mum has she taken the oath?

MOD - No

PM – Really? Her father and brother were members of the IRA and the rest of the O'Callaghan's are republicans, maybe volunteers or members too, so why do you think that?

MOD - I don't know that.

PM - You have met them. You must know?

MOD - Only a couple of times I don't know them really except Uncle Emmet

PM - Do you think he has taken the oath?

MOD - No

PM - No I agree, we don't think he has either

      PM - We know who are members. The O'Sheas. Your dad's sister, her husband and your cousins. Did you know that they are members of the IRA?

MOD - No

PM - are you sure?

MOD - Yes, I'm sure

PM - You know them very well, don't you Molly? You stayed there for the last ten summers? Surely you know that they believe in The Cause

      They knew my whole history. I was scared why would they investigate me like this. They didn't care if I'd passed information from gossip. This was so much worse. They thought I was a member of the IRA. I put my head in my hands. Then I held up my chin with my elbows leaning on the table. I could hardly keep my eyes open but I'd to persuade them that I wasn't. The fear inside me was growing. He called my name to answer his question.

      MOD - They are republicans

PM - You know that is the same as the IRA.

MOD - It isn't. Please let me go home. I'm telling the truth. You are asking me all these questions and not believing my answers.

PM – You're right, we don't believe you. We know that you're a good liar Molly. So, let's talk about that. Let's talk about Mary....

Part 4: Chapter 23 - The Answers

My heart sank. I looked down. I couldn't help myself. I knew that it would make me look guilty. I did feel guilty but not for any crime. For the affect that I, we. Of Mary and I being pen pals. This just Couldn't be happening. I closed my eyes. I was free falling again. Everything was plummeting around me. I seemed to be still and pictures, which were solid, were dropping past me at speed. I didn't know if they were feelings, memories or things.

The exam seemed like days ago but my tiredness hadn't gone. I felt sapped, empty and weary. I needed to sleep. I asked again to leave. Which they shook their heads at. I said I needed a break. They said I could have one soon.

PW - Now Molly as I said we need to talk about Mary. How long have you known Mary Elliott?

MOD - About nine years

PW - How did you meet?

MOD - on the beach

PW - You were pen pals?

MOD - yes

PW - I'm glad you said that as we have the letters. Yes Molly, don't looked shocked. We have been at your home while you were at college and while your Dad was at work. But we will talk about that later. Now your family and friends in

Ireland, they didn't mind you writing to a protestant?

MOD - They didn't know

PW - So does that mean that they would have minded?

MOD - They may have

PW - you don't know? you lied to them for nine years, didn't you? Why?

MOD - Once I kept it a secret it was harder to tell them.

     PW - Are you still friends with Mary?

MOD - No

PW - That's a shame. Why's that then Molly?

MOD - We thought that it was for the best to stop writing

PW - was it anything to do with her cousin witnessing a murder

MOD - Mary was worried so we decided to stop writing

     How could they possibly know so much? Who would have told them? Only a

handful of people knew. Mary, Jack, my Mum and Maria. Robert knew but he was

dead. Sean and Saoirse knew somethings but not all. I was confused. I didn't know

who knew what anymore.

     PW - Why was she worried? Did she think you knew something about it?

MOD - No

PW - Then why?

MOD - I don't really know, she heard rumours and she was worried.

PW - What were the rumours?

MOD - She didn't really say. I think there was alot of tension between catholic and

protestants so it was for the best to end our contact. I didn't really realise until then

how it could be an issue. It's not like that here in England

PW - It was good for you too, got you out of a hole. You didn't have to lie anymore.

MOD - Yes

PM - Now about Mary's brother, Robert. How long did you go out with him for?

MOD - I didn't go out with him

PW - You didn't, are you sure?

MOD - Yes

PW - But you met him a few times?

MOD - I saw him a few times

PW - You talked each time, didn't you?

MOD - Yes but I've spoken to lots of people a handful of times but I didn't go out with them

PW - Molly, this seems to be distressing you, the idea of going out with him, why?

MOD - Because I didn't

PW - What did your boyfriend Jack say about your relationship with Robert?

MOD - He knew that I didn't have a relationship

PW - But Robert came to see you during his reading week

MOD - Yes but I didn't invite him

PW - and you asked him to leave, why was that?

MOD - because I didn't like him

PW - Molly, Molly you need to tell us the truth as we know it already

MOD - I didn't like him. He thought that Saoirse and Sean were stopping us having a relationship. That wasn't true. I told him that. He said that he had to warn me about them but I didn't listen to his lies

PW - perhaps you didn't want to believe him

MOD - I didn't believe him

My voice was raising in desperation. I didn't understand how they could know, only my Mum and Jack knew about this meeting. I prayed they hadn't been the ones to tell but I could understand if they did. The questioning was agonizing and they knew the answers. Some of them anyway. Robert knew. Did he tell anyone?

PW - He met you at the Broadway at the end of that week, didn't he?

MOD - Yes. I didn't invite him then either

PW - Who were you with?

MOD - Maria and Sean.

PW - Was Jacinta not there?

MOD - No

PW - That's interesting. Why did you think that was?

MOD - I don't know, I guess she was busy

PW - to miss a big night like that, it must have been important?

MOD - I don't know, Maria told her about it. Maria didn't tell me why

PW - Maria told us why and we are waiting for Jacinta to confirm it. It's unfortunate that you can't confirm it for her.

PW - Yes Molly, we aren't just talking to you, the whole circle or group or as we like to call it, a cell

MOD - What?

PW - I can see that upsets you. You know what that means. Are you frightened that we have found out?

MOD - No, there is nothing to find out. I'm scared that you are making things up. What you are saying is not true. I feel like the information and questions you are asking me do not equal what you are suggesting. It's happened before, just because people are Irish

PW - Molly, why are you crying? if you have done nothing wrong, then you don't need to worry, do you?

MOD - These things you are saying don't make me a terrorist.

PW - Molly calm down, you will hyperventilate if you carry on and none of us want that. We will have a break soon after we have finished talking about Robert

PW - Robert told Sean about your relationship, didn't he?

MOD - Yes, he lied to Sean and said I was his girlfriend. He was delusional. There was no relationship

PW - Was Robert really lying?

MOD - Yes he lied

PW - Ok we will talk about that later. There was an argument, what was it about?

MOD - Robert told Sean that he said he was my boyfriend which wasn't true and about me writing to Mary

PW - What else?

MOD - He said he wanted to warn me about Sean

PW - What did he say?

MOD - He said that he was doing jobs for the republicans

PW - You mean the IRA?

MOD - He may have meant that

PW - Why didn't you believe what he had to say?

MOD - He was being crazy. He thought I was having a relationship with him. He came to my house and scared me. He followed me to the pub and he stopped me from leaving

PW - so you're telling me that you didn't believe what he said

MOD - I didn't believe what he said

PW - He told you about a terrorist attack that did happen and you didn't believe Robert still

MOD – It didn't happen. Not the way he said.

PW - Are you sure that he was wrong?

MOD - Yes

PW - Why?

MOD – Because nothing happened. I saw Sean that day at the catholic club

PW – Are you sure it was the same day. What date are you talking about?

MOD – I'd have to check. It was after the reading week. In November.

PW - Who else did you see that day? Your Dad and your Uncle Vincent?

MOD - Yes

PW - All three of them together. That was lucky for them. Why were you there?

MOD - We all met my Uncle Emmet to talk about his wedding

PW - I know. That was nice, that your whole family were there that day. How often did that happen?

MOD - It was the first time

PW - Did you think it was strange?

MOD - No, we only met my mum's family after my Aunt Anne died. I never even met her

PW - An alibi like that, that was helpful. Although we know that the prep for this was done in advance. Where were your Dad, Your Uncle Vincent and Sean before that?

MOD - I don't know

PW – Did you know that they decided not to do anything that day because Robert had been spreading rumours

MOD – I only know what was on the news

PW – They had their alibi in place. The prep was done in advance but you know that. You arranged the meeting.

MOD – No that's not true.

PW - Was Jacinta there?

MOD - No, she didn't go to the club any more. She stopped after her dad died

PW - Yes, we know that

PW - so back to the night in the Broadway, for now. Sean and you argued. Did he not believe you?

MOD - I think he did believe me because Robert was acting crazy, telling lies

PW - Are you talking again?

MOD - No

PW - Why not?

MOD - He was angry about my being friends with Mary

PW - Is that it, really? He says he won't forgive you just for that. Don't worry we know everything. We just want you to confirm that you're telling us the truth. O yes, Molly, Maria has been very helpful. Surely being someone's pen pal should not cause that sort of reaction

MOD - but it did

PW - Do you agree with Sean's decision?

MOD - Not really but it's how it makes him feel that is important. I can only say sorry. I can't change what I did.

PW - Was there also an allegation of you being an informant

MOD - It was discussed. Sean said if Robert reported the lies it would make me look guilty of informing. Especially as I was a friend of a protestant for so long

PW - Yes and that would put Sean at risk too. I can see that all parties could be affected. All because you had two friends who were protestants. Well that does put another spin on it. It's not exactly as you told it. Did you forget or were you lying to protect yourself?

MOD - I wasn't lying to you. By not telling Sean and Saoirse about the letters they thought I was deceiving them. They knew there would be a consequence. I thought that I'd done nothing wrong. I felt that it was over dramatic. Sean can be like that sometimes

PW - I agree, I've seen that side of him too. What about your cousin Saoirse O'Shea, didn't she react in the same way?

MOD - Yes

PW - was she normally over dramatic?

MOD – No. She thought I was being disloyal. She expects her friends to be honest. People she can trust. I suppose she doesn't trust me anymore

PW - So you still think that this is all about you hiding a pen pal from them? That's the fact you deceived them, is the reason that they haven't forgiven you yet?

MOD - Yes

PW - Molly, are you naive, stupid or lying? Anyone would know that's over the top. Could it really be more to do with the fact that they thought it was you that was passing the information about Brompton to Robert

MOD - I didn't tell Robert anything. I didn't know anything about Brompton. Robert told me. Nothing happened at Brompton

PW - But do Sean and Saoirse think you are an informer

MOD - No, not really but they just don't trust me anymore.

PW - Do they really believe you though? They must be concerned that you know something, don't you think?

MOD - They know, I don't know about anything. Robert confused them with his lies

PW - Maybe they think you are a member of the IRA and they are scared of you

MOD - No that's not true

I nearly laughed the thought of that being true was farcical. But it wasn't a joke. It wasn't even a nightmare it was real. So very real.

PW - Didn't you, Sean and Saoirse talk about the IRA alot?

MOD - No

PW - No are you sure?

MOD - we talked about Irish history alot

PW - Isn't that the same thing?

MOD - No

MOD - Can I go to the toilet please

PM - okay let's stop for a break, we still have alot to discuss.

When I got to the toilet. I sat on the seat and cried. I took deep breaths that just made me feel light headed. I didn't understand what was going on. Where did they get all that information? It could've only been Maria. Did they ask her or did she tell them? She was the only one that knew all those stories. Why would she do this. She must believe it all. She must think I'm involved.

They were twisting things around so much. Am I not being as honest with them? Am I even being honest with myself? Was I protecting people more than myself? I know what Jack would say. Just tell the truth. Don't worry about anyone else. But they kept asking about my Dad. What the hell was going on with Uncle Vincent. My hands raised to my head. My fingers were outstretched. I pushed my hands through my hair. I stared at the toilet door. I went blank. I sat for a long time.

Then I realised I only had a little bit of time. I needed to get my head together. I asked myself some questions. Why didn't I just say I've concerns about Sean. Because I'd no evidence. Just because he was a fantasist when he was younger. Hearsay from Robert does not make it true. I've been so upset that Robert had killed himself to protect me. It might have been to protect himself. He could have made up lies for me. To distance me from Sean and Saoirse. He had no need to tell them about Mary.

I was getting more confused. It was all rubbish, surely no one could go to prison for what questions they'd been asking. My mind kept jumping to a picture of the Birmingham six. Something they said made me think that they weren't just interviewing me as a witness. Yes, they said I was backing up their stories. Who else could it be? It must be my dad, Uncle Vincent and Sean but they were also mentioning Saoirse too. I wondered what else they could possibly ask. There was a bang on the door. I went out and washed my hands and face.

I didn't want to go back to the room but I'd no choice. The dread was dragging me down. I couldn't even remember when I slept last. My eye caught the clock on the wall. It was not working but I knew my English class would be in the pub now. They would talk about the exam. They would discuss their holidays. They would speculate about me aswell. I wondered if Sammy was there. What would she be saying? They were recommencing the interview so my mind was dragged back to the here and now.

MOD - Please can I have a solicitor. The things you are saying are not true. I need someone with me

PM - We can arrange one but we can be out of here long before one gets here. I suggest that we continue. I don't want to have to arrest you and put you in a cell while we wait for a solicitor

MOD - What would you arrest me for? This is ridiculous, crazy...... it's all wrong. You are making something out of nothing. I will carry on but please ask for a solicitor. I think you are planning to arrest me, whatever I say.

PM - Ok Molly we will arrange that. It was good timing to have a break. We were able to consult the other police officers in this case, about their witnesses. We knew at any given time they could be become more than that. We are hoping for a few arrests today. Definitely we will be charging some people, There's no doubt about that. Do you know what happens then Molly?

MOD - No

PM - If it was you, you could be charged. Put in a cell while you wait to go to court. Then you are remanded into custody to await trial. These are very serious charges. If you don't tell the truth, you will go to prison. We are gathering evidence today from a number of people. We have done alot of work to get to this point.

Surveillance and crime scene investigations. There is alot of work still that will need to be done. At least six months at a prison, on remand. I think that you would find it very hard, don't you Molly?

MOD - yes but I haven't done anything wrong, so you can't do that. I really haven't done anything wrong

PM - let's see about that. Let's talk about Sean again. I believe you said he was very interested in teaching you Irish history.

MOD - Yes

PM - Did you enjoy that

MOD - Sometimes

PM - Did you enjoy what you learnt

MOD - sometimes

PM - Which bits didn't you enjoy

MOD - I don't remember

PM - Did Sean ever talk about the IRA

MOD - Yes

PM - Why?

MOD - It was on the news all the time

PM - Did Sean ever mention Clogga Strand?

MOD - Yes

PM - What did he tell you?

MOD - He was young, he talked a load of rubbish, saying his family were involved in someway

PM - You didn't believe him?

MOD - No he was talking for effect, to scare me probably

PM - did you know he had family in Clogga Strand?

MOD - No

PM - Well he does. They were involved, they are in the IRA. They are in prison for that incident. Did he tell you that?

MOD - No

PM – Okay. That's strange.

PM - Do you still think Sean isn't in the IRA?

MOD - I don't know anything that would make me think that he was in the IRA

PM - Molly, you surprise me with your naivety.

He was shaking his head at me as if I was stupid. I couldn't believe this was happening. It was so extreme. My insides were contracting. As if I could feel each organ moving.

PM - So let's talk about your relationship with Robert again. You danced at a disco. Is that when your relationship started? Did you know it was wrong?

MOD - I was twelve years old. I just wanted to be asked to dance. There was never a relationship

PM - So you would say he was obsessed with you

MOD - I don't think he knew, that I didn't like him. I gave him no indication that I did.

PM - but you met him on a number of occasions at the beach and in the town

MOD - Mostly with Mary, he was uninvited on those occasions

PM - All the time except when he took you for a drink or drove you back from the disco when you were sixteen

MOD - Once I saw him in the bookshop and I went for a coke with him. I didn't want to be rude. Once we had no lift home so Saoirse asked me to ask him to take us

PM - On what occasion did you say you didn't like the violence in the North and England. For him to know that you wanted to start passing information. To stop the terrorist attacks.

MOD - Never. We never spoke about that and I never passed any information

PM - What about Mary did you pass information to her?

MOD - No. We didn't talk about that. She never asked me and I never asked her

PM - We are reviewing the letters from her. We have asked the Gardai to obtain your letters from Mary. They have not been forthcoming at this time but we will get them. In the meantime, please tell us about the letters

MOD - That's good because then you will see that we just talked about books, films and music. Just like normal teenage girls

PM - You saw her on the beach, what happened then?

MOD - we arranged to meet for lunch

PM - You really wanted to see Robert, didn't you?

MOD - No

PM - You seem to get upset when we talk about Robert. Are you still grieving over his death?

MOD - No I'm not grieving

PM - Do you miss him?

MOD - No

PM - It's interesting that he wrote to you before he died, don't you think?

MOD - He said sorry for his behaviour and he still believed that my situation was dangerous

PM - We know that we saw the letter. Why was he warning you again?

MOD - I don't know. I don't think he was well

PM - Because he was obsessed with you or that you would get caught for passing information

MOD - Coming to my house. Finding out where I was going, was not normal behaviour

PM - Okay so you will not admit that you were passing information to Robert and Mary

MOD - No because I wasn't.

MOD - When is the solicitor going to be here? You are accusing me of very serious things that are not true

PM - That is a matter of opinion. This is the least of your worries. We are establishing that if you are an informer. Then that you are a member of the IRA. As a member of this London cell. That you are responsible for the recent attacks in Ireland and in England

MOD - No the truth is the truth. I should not have had Mary as a pen pal. I know that now. I should not have kept my friendship with Mary a secret from Saoirse and Sean. That is what I have done wrong. Nothing criminal that needs to be investigated.

PM - I disagree and you will see why

PM - Do you remember going to the open-air cinema in Ireland when you were on your holidays? What did you see?

MOD - Top Gun

PM - Do you know where the cinema was?

MOD - No

PM - It was in the north. Do you remember crossing the border?

MOD - No. I didn't realise we had

PM - No you wouldn't as Sean's brother didn't go through the checkpoint. Which brother was it that brought you there? It was Sean's brother wasn't it, which one?

MOD - Yes it was Sean's brother but he didn't introduce himself

PM - So it might not have been Sean's brother at all, have you seen him since?

MOD - I don't think so

PM - it was very generous for him to take you don't you think?

MOD - Yes

PM - it's a good cover taking kids to the cinema, in case someone asks

MOD - I don't know what you mean

PM - I mean we were watching that car and it did many trips to the north. Why do you think we were watching it?

MOD - I don't know

PM - We arrested a man with weapons in that car. He was transporting guns. Did you know that?

MOD - No

PM - so you didn't know an IRA man when you meet one

MOD - I didn't know that he was a member of the IRA

I was so scared. Could this be true. Could they be making this up. Surely it was not Sean's brother. Jack would have said otherwise. Jack would not have gone in the car if he was suspicious. This really was getting serious.

PM - Do you remember going to the Mary of Dungloe festival

MOD - Yes

PM - Who did you go with

MOD - my family, Sean and Jack

PM - and you met Mary and Robert in the interval of the Drifters

MOD - Yes

PM - was this planned

MOD - Yes

PM - You didn't get much time to see Robert

MOD - I was there to see Mary. He was not invited

PM - But you knew he would be there. She wouldn't have gone all that way alone

MOD - I didn't think about that

PM - Ok did you think about telling Saoirse or Sean or Jack

MOD - Jack knew

PM - Jack helped you meet your boyfriend?

MOD - No he helped me to meet Mary

PM - Jack wasn't your boyfriend then

MOD - No but I liked him

PM - when you were going out with Robert?

MOD - I didn't go out with Robert

PM - You kept arranging to meet Robert though when you say you liked Jack

MOD - I saw him but that was only because he was Mary's brother

PM - You also kept meeting Robert a secret from Saoirse and Sean

MOD - Yes, I did keep my meeting with Mary a secret. I didn't arrange to meet Robert. He was just my friends' brother so I didn't want to be rude to him

PM - So you led him on

MOD - No

PM - Did you not like him because he was a protestant

MOD - No I didn't like him because he was too intense

PM - So Robert warned you off Saoirse

MOD - Yes

PM - He warned you off Sean

MOD - Yes

PM – Why? Was it because they were in the IRA?

MOD - No they weren't

PM - Did he ask you questions?

MOD - No

PM - Why do you think he started asking questions when he started university?

MOD - I don't know

PM - Did you tell him information

MOD - No

PM - Poor Robert, you rejected him. You started going out with Jack. Robert didn't like that did he?

MOD - He didn't like my or Jack's family

PM - Why? If it's not because they were in the IRA

MOD - I don't know

PM - so you were not passing information to the IRA or Robert

MOD - No

PM - you were not an informant to the Unionists, the police or the IRA

MOD - No

PM - why did Sean think that was happening then

MOD - He didn't really. He knew Robert was being crazy

PM - Was he crazy as you had stopped going out with him

MOD - I never went out with him

PM - Did he kill himself because you didn't love him anymore

MOD - No. I never loved him

PM - Why did he say "Love always" in his letter

MOD - I don't know

PM - Sean warned him off you

MOD - Yes because Robert was telling lies

PM - But Sean still will not talk to you. So, he believed Robert, that you went out together and was an informer?

MOD - No because I didn't go out with him. I didn't tell anyone anything about any terrorist attacks

PM – You are like a double agent. Passing information one way then the other

MOD – No That never happened, please believe me

PM - Why are you getting so upset, if it's not true

MOD - Because you don't believe me

PM - Well Sean doesn't believe you either, does he?

MOD - He does in his heart

PM - Maria doesn't believe you, does she?

MOD - She knows that I didn't go out with Robert. She is scared. If people think I'm an informer, then she could get mixed up in it all. She knows that I'm not an informer

PM - That is not exactly what she told us. Are you lying or fooling yourself?

MOD - No she knows that

MOD - Please can I have another break

PM - No not yet Molly.

PM - What about Sean driving you to the disco for the first time. Do you really think he got lost?

MOD - Yes

PM - Whose idea was it to go into the pub to get directions?

MOD – Saoirse's. Or Sean's I don't remember.

PM - Did you see Sean carrying a package?

MOD - No

PM - Are you sure that you didn't see a very large envelope of cash

MOD - No I didn't

PM - He was in and out quick, wasn't he?

MOD - Yes

PM - and he didn't even ask where you were? That's why he was there. He was happy to be away.

MOD – No. We were just laughing about what happened

PM - No he was relieved that his first drop off went well. Are you sure that you we not part of that delivery?

MOD - No I wasn't. I don't believe it happened

PM - You were there but you didn't see anything? Are you lying to protect Saoirse and Sean? Are you lying to protect yourself? Do you think Saoirse knew?

MOD – No. I didn't see anything. I'm not lying to protect anyone. I don't think Saoirse was involved with what you are suggesting.

PM - What about when you went to 'John's' house? Do you really think that his name was John?

MOD - Yes

PM - Do you know where that house was?

MOD - No

PM - Molly, this seems to be a problem. You should always know where you are. It was in the north, again

MOD - I didn't know that

PM - Did you know what was in the car boot?

MOD - No

PM - You didn't look? You didn't ask? They didn't tell you?

MOD - No I didn't look or ask

PM - Did anything significant happen that night

MOD - Sean's car didn't have the hand brake on fully and it hit the wall of the house with a bang

PM - Did you think that was funny

MOD - Yes

PM - Was Sean upset?

MOD - A bit but he found it funny afterwards when the car was okay

PM - Was he relieved that the car was ok?

MOD - Yes

PM - or was he relieved that the guns from the boot had been removed?

MOD - I can't believe that there were guns in the boot of the car

PM - so you didn't see the guns? Or know that they were there?

MOD - No

PM - Why are you getting agitated Molly

MOD - This is all crazy. This cannot be true. Please get me a solicitor. This is ridiculous. I don't believe any of this is true

PM - Are you sure?

MOD - I didn't hear or see anything that could make this true

PM - Was Jack with you on any of these occasions?

MOD - No

PM - He was lucky wasn't he or did Sean and Saoirse think he was not as gullible as you? I can't work out if you are lying or stupid.

MOD - I'm not lying

PM - Did you tell Maria about the excursions that you had with Sean and Saoirse

MOD – Yes. We laughed about them.

PM - Yes, she told us the stories just like you did.

MOD - They are not stories, they are the truth

PM - You can't say it didn't happen, just because you didn't see them. That means we have to work out if you didn't know or you are lying. The problem for you is that you are a good liar. You lied to your cousin for nine years. No wonder she was upset but more importantly it shows us your character. Do you think you are a good liar Molly?

MOD - I'm not lying

The police man looked at the file again. He took a sheet of paper out and laid it on top of the file.

PM - You have applied to university, haven't you? To do a degree. What's that in?

MOD - English and Drama

PM - English and Drama. So you are a good actress then

MOD - Not how you are suggesting

PM - Ok let's talk about Galway. Did you go to see the Saw Doctors?

MOD - Yes

PM - Who with, Sean and Saoirse?

MOD - Yes

PM - No Jack?

MOD - He had to milk the cows

PM - So what do you think you collected this time?

MOD - I didn't see anything.

PM - What about clothes, you must have brought things with you.

MOD - I'd a bag with me in the back seat.

PM - You didn't put the bag in the boot of the car.

MOD - No

PM - That's lucky for you. Did you know that there were guns in the boot and that you brought them back to your cousin's house with you?

MOD - I didn't see any guns.

PM - Though they were probably well hidden. You stayed at Sean's Aunt's house. Had you met her before?

MOD - No

PM - But your father has, he knows the family well, I believe?

MOD - I didn't know that but that's what she said

PM - Did she tell you she's a member of the IRA

MOD - No she didn't.

PM - Did you know that she was?

MOD - No

PM - Had you met her sons before or since

MOD - No

PM - Did you know they are members of the IRA

PM – Molly?

PM – Molly? For the tape. Does your shaking of your head mean you knew they were members and you are upset that we have found out

PM – Your tears make you seem guilty don't you think?

MOD – no no no

PM - To clarify you didn't know that they were IRA members or that there were guns in the car?

MOD - No I didn't

PM - Did you know that Sean's cousins were living in England and were only home for their holidays. Apparently, they drove over in a new car. Did you know that?

MOD - No

PM - Do you know who bought their new car, Molly

MOD - No I'veno idea

PM - Even after what I'm telling you? You know it's the IRA, don't you?

PM - No

My face was sore from rubbing it. The questions were so ridiculous. I couldn't believe I'd to respond to them.

PM - Did you know where Sean's cousins lived in England?

MOD - No

PM – The digs. At Jacinta's house. Do you know who would have arranged that?

MOD - They said it was my Dad

PM - So your dad was finding known IRA members places to stay. Often these places are called Safe houses but I'm sure you knew that. So that would make Jacinta's house a safe house, would it not?

MOD - What! No! That can't be right

PM – Ok sorry back to Saoirse. I got side tracked for a second. She used to write about terrorist attacks though when she wrote, didn't she?

MOD - Yes

PM - that's weird, don't you think? That she did that

MOD – No. She was interested in politics

PM - I know. I've seen the letters. It's not there but did she talk to you about Noraid

MOD - She said she researched it for a school project

PM - and you believed her? You know what that is, don't you?

MOD - a charity

PM - Come on Molly it's not a charity it is another way of collecting for the cause. How do you think she was involved?

MOD - I didn't think she was involved

PM - Ok. Back to your father now. On your last visit to Ireland, you went to a well-known IRA pub, yes?

MOD - we went to a republican bar at the seaside

PM - Come on Molly your dad went there looking for new recruits

MOD - No

PM - Why not?

MOD - He is not in the IRA.

PM - you sound like a child. You see nothing, you hear nothing and know nothing

MOD - There is nothing to know. It's just normal things that have happened to my family and friends

PM - Let's recap. This is what has happened;

- You were in the car, that was taking drugs to the north for the IRA.

- You were in the car, when cash was taken to the north for the IRA.

- You were in the car, when guns were taken from Galway.

- You were with your Dad, when he was recruiting young Irish men to the IRA.

- You knew that your Uncle Vincent is a known member of the IRA who could make bombs.

- You were in the car, when guns were delivered to an IRA members house.

- You knew where Mary's cousin would be and this led to a death of a protestant.

- You knew Sean was in England to work for the IRA.

- You knew about the Deal bombing in advance.

MOD - No I didn't know about any of that. I don't know about any deliveries. I don't know about any attacks in England. I don't know anything, please stop saying these things. They are not true. Please stop.

PM – You need to admit to this and recognise the pain and suffering that you caused by being involved.

He shut the file and lifted it as if he was going to hand it to me. I didn't want to see it now. He didn't give it to me. He held it out.

PM – There's pictures in here. I think you need to see. The damage that this cell has inflicted in the name of the Cause. In the name of a united Ireland.

MOD – Please, none of this is true. Please let me go home.

I was crying. I couldn't catch my breath. I wiped the tears from my face with the back of my hands. I wiped my nose on my sleeve. My hands were wet. I put them into my hair. My hair was damp. It must be getting warmer in the room. I felt

like I was red in the face. I was sweating too. Not just under my arms but

everywhere. I loosened my tee-shirt from the front. I sat forward to get air to my

back.

PM - No Molly, that's not going to happen. We need to know everything.

The information that was passed. The deliveries that were made. The alibi's that

were arranged. Who helped to plan and implement the IRA attacks? Who are the

others in this London cell? We need to get to the truth

Part 4: Chapter 24 – Hugh

I was glad to be out of the cell. They had kept me waiting. They said they were with Molly. They knew this would rile me.

 The policeman was asking my name for the tape. They said who they were. As expected, they had said a solicitor was on their way. I'd heard about that before. He wasn't coming. I knew to let them talk for as long as possible. They would tell me why I was here. The policemen seemed very confident. They were sharing smiles between themselves. The younger policeman was holding their thick file with my name. He handled it like it was a baby. Gently and with pride.

 As I'd once held Molly. I couldn't believe they had taken her in. I was worried about what she might say. She could easily get in a pickle. They would confuse her. I didn't know what she knew. She said she knew nothing. She hadn't been around the lads at the club. Sean of course but not so much Cillian. They never seemed to have gotten along. Molly was suspicious of him.

 I wondered if she had ever asked around about him. Molly didn't like Sean much but she loved him like a brother. If anyone asked about him surely, She'dn't say anything. Sean had been so loud about his opinions in the past. It had gotten him into trouble but that was all sorted now. He'd laid off the drink and didn't talk about that stuff anymore. Sean and Molly had though had that argument. He'd kept that quiet from me. Luckily that little Jacinta had let it slip so I could sort it out.

That had been a hard one to stifle but Molly was well known in the community. No other Molly's around. We had quashed any rumours especially to visitors to the club. I'd not told Molly. I didn't want her getting mixed up with anything else. I felt bad for scaring her but it was better for her to be on her guard. Getting away from those Elliott's had been the first step. Thankfully Jack was of the same opinion. He had reinforced that to the child. It was good that Jack was away from it all. It kept Molly out of it aswell.

I didn't know whether to say no comment or not. It was the standard response everyone knew to say but it made you sound guilty straight away. To immediately say you're a political prisoner and refuse to speak. I took in a slow intake of breath. I needed a cigarette. I hope they offered it.

I was worried about Molly again. She'd never heard the stories of your ones that had been picked up. Clare had made sure of that. Now that Molly was in trouble, she had nothing to help her. Right now, I'd to protect my baby. I'd have to deal with the rest later. I would be very careful of what I said.

I knew the first questions would be standard; place of employment, occupation, education. They sneered at that. I knew they would. Not one of my family had got into secondary school. How would they had afforded it. We were young men by ten years old and never considered going anyway.

PM – Now Hugh. How long have you been in England now? Nigh on 30 years I believe.

I nodded.

PM – You consider yourself British now

I shook my head

PM – Why not?

I knew this was the start of the political conversation. I shrugged.

PM - is it that you want to go home? Why not go home then?

He knew the answer. So, I raised my eyebrows.

PM – For the tape you need to answer my questions. Shrugging like that won't help you.

He meant it won't help him. I looked evenly at him. I knew this was just the start and I needed to keep calm

PM – Hugh, are you a republican

I smiled this time, in acknowledgement.

PM – Do you believe in the cause?

I continued to look at him. I knew he would get me talking soon enough as soon as Molly's name was mentioned but I knew I'd to go through the standard questions.

The police gave me name after name. I knew them all. Of course, I knew them, they all went to the catholic club.

PM – Did you know they were in the IRA?

Again, I shook my head. I didn't mean to wind him up but I was. I'd to say as little as possible.

PM – Are you a member of the IRA?

I should say no comment. I never responded. They knew the game.

PM – Do you know why the men I mentioned go to the club?

I shrugged. Off course I did.

PM – Your daughter Molly. She confirmed that you might know those men

There it was, the threat. I knew She'd. Why wouldn't she. It was the truth

PM - Do you know why Molly would know them?

We went to the catholic club since it opened. The policeman knew that well. He had the big file; it would all be in there.

   PM – Molly said that Irish people went there for the bands.

That was true. I nodded. The policemen wouldn't believe that though

PM – There were all republicans, sympathisers, rebels, weren't they? They were members of the IRA.

I couldn't agree with that statement.

   PM – Molly doesn't think so either but she's young for her age don't you think? She is naive. Don't you agree?

I totally agreed with him. An idealist. A lover of poetry. Quoting Shakespeare and Yeats at home.

   PM – Is Molly a member of the IRA

I choked to stop myself laughing

PM – She is a republican and believes in the Cause

I shook my head. She wanted the violence to stop but like her mother didn't have a clue how

PM – hmm Molly said she wanted a united Ireland.

I bet she did. Well, it was hardly the same. I stopped myself giving a wry smile.

   PM – Well she was friends with IRA members

I knew what was coming next.

PM – Sean McDermott

I shook my head

PM – Saoirse O'Shea

I shook my head

PM – Cillian Cullen

He definitely wasn't a friend.

PM – Did you know what she got up to on her visits to Ireland

Not much I imagined. The disco. The cinema. To see the bands. Just like she did here.

PM – We know she was present during IRA activities

I doubted that

PM – Deliveries. Can you imagine what that was?

I knew what they were saying. I shook my head vigorously. I couldn't stop myself

HOD - No

PM – That seems to shock you

It didn't shock me. I knew it wasn't true.

PM – You say Sean was not a member of the IRA but who bought that car he drove at home in Ireland

I shook my head. He was just a child then. Who knew what he would be at?

PM – You took a shine to Sean, didn't you? You liked his passion? You thought he would fit in. Is that why you took him to that IRA pub by the seaside

Jesus if this is what they had.

PM – Did you like Molly's boyfriend

What was he at now? Then it dawned on me. That bloody Elliott family again. What a fool she had been.

PM – I take it from that look on your face that you knew Robert

O I, I did. Stupid boy asking questions

PM – Did you like him?

HOD – She didn't go out with him.

I couldn't help myself. I needed to be more careful

The policeman was pleased with my response.

PM – Yes going out with a protestant in Ireland was more than just a big no no. Especially in your family.

I knew what he was insinuating

PM – When you found out you asked her to get information from his sister.

I took a sigh of relief. That was untrue. That little Mary would back that up. By all accounts she was a sweet girl. She wouldn't lie.

PM – When Robert found out about that, he asked her to make amends. He asked her to give him details of planned attacks. Did she ask you?

I looked down and shook my head. Someone was setting Molly up but not doing a very good job. Molly was right she didn't know anything.

PM – She told him the IRA plans. She was an informer

I looked at him. They had nothing. Who would Robert be telling? He wouldn't be going to police. He didn't have an affiliation either. Cillian told me that.

The policeman didn't like my reaction. He changed tact. He opened the file and took out some pages. It was a show, I knew all this already. You could tell because of the smug look on his face.

PM – We will come back to Molly. Now I need some details on where you were on some dates. Dates that you should know well and remember

PM2 – Where were you on 22 September 1989. It was a Friday

Hugh – I would have been working then

The second policeman seemed surprised to hear me speak. He had a glint in his eye. I'm not sure what it meant but I didn't like it.

PM2 – Are you sure?

I nodded. I couldn't place the date. I knew he would reveal it when he wanted to.

PM2 – What about 26th November 1989? It was a Sunday

I shook my head. I didn't remember anything happening that day.

PM2 – Are you so sure? Wouldn't you be at the catholic club. You do go there every week I believe.

You know it more like. My chin moved automatically in agreement.

PM2 – So you may or may not have been there. Or do you remember any other events that day.

Obviously, something else happened but for the life of me I couldn't guess what. He would tell me in his own time.

PM2 – What about 14 May 1990. It was a Monday. Just a couple of weeks ago.

I understood that this was getting serious now. I shrugged. I would have been at work.

PM2 – At work eh?

I nodded and shrugged again.

PM2 – Lastly, for now, 26th May 1990. It was a Wednesday?

I let him answer for me. I'd not taken a day off for the last five months. When you get seven days, you take it. It looked like I needed an alibi and thank god I'd have one. The new gaffer was Irish descent so there were no issues there.

PM2 – Were you in Deal on or around 22nd September 2019?

The shock must have shown in my face. This was more unbelievable than I could have ever imagined. I knew what he was suggesting. I'd to stop myself putting my head in my hands. This was big time stuff. This was the new campaign that was on the news.

The policeman's hand was opening the file. I knew there were photos inside. I'd seen pictures on the news and in the newspapers. This was another level, when blame was being placed upon you.

PM2 – Eleven young men were murdered. Young men the same ages as your daughter. Do you think that was a legitimate military target?

It didn't matter what my opinion was. I would be lying to someone. I waited for the next question. I looked at the policeman evenly. Hopefully showing no emotion.

PM2 – I know it's hard Hugh. You can't say anything that would be against the provisional IRA. You know as well as I do what happens to informers.

Now he did take a photo out of the file but it wasn't the results of the bomb. It was Lennon. I'd never seen it but I'd heard this tactic before. My eyes flicked from the photo after seeing the man lying dead in a ditch. I knew I wasn't going to be an informer. I was worried about Molly. That rumours about her would get to them now. I believed her but not many would think how she could be that naïve. I knew they were saying I was dead anyway by speaking at all but I'd had to, up until now. They were getting nothing more out of me.

PM2 – Ok. On or around 14 May 1990 then. Anywhere near Eltham.

The bomb at the palace! It was an army barracks. I shook my head.

PM2 – Not the damage you all would have wanted. The garden was just a bit messed up by the bomb. A few civilians were injured but no damage to the house. Its stood since Tudor times. A bit amateur some might say. Well, it's been awhile since the mainland was bombed. You'd have got out of the habit. Your skills are a bit rusty; I'd say. Maybe you all got lucky in Deal. Not so lucky for the young men, their family and friends.

I carried on looking at him. I'd heard it all before. Back in the day they had used these tactics. The police wanted a rise out of me. I would not react. I knew what was coming next. The sympathy.

PM2 – I get it you know. I want a United Ireland myself. Senseless all of this death. On all sides. My grandfather was Irish. He had to come here for work too. He integrated himself in to the English way of life. He lived in Wembley you know.

That's what happened on the 16th, the army recruiting centre. I got it now. I'd been told a lot of lads had been picked up. Someone would talk. Probably Molly but that would be hearsay. She may mention Brompton. That fool of a boy had talked about. Nothing had happened so he may not ask her about it

PM2 – On or around 16th May 1989. Where were you?

I knew what they were asking. That was it, that was what they were getting.

HOD – I'm not saying anything else until I've seen a solicitor. These are serious allegations. Put me in a cell now.

I needed to think. Who the fuck was setting up Molly and why?

Part 4: Chapter 25 – Clare

The policemen were leaving. I still had the warrant in my hand. They had taken a few things. Letters to Hugh from his sister. I'd read them there was nothing to concern me. I supposed it was all to do with the IRA. I cleaned the house top to bottom every week. I knew that they would find nothing. There was nothing to find. If there had been anything, I would have found it myself. There were always rumours that sympathisers houses were used to store things. That had never happened here.

There were hundreds of letters from all the pen pals Molly had over the years. America, Europe and one from Africa too. The police didn't take those. She had kept them in batches so they didn't have to mess things up to get to what they wanted. Letters to Molly from Mary. Why did she keep them?

Saoirse's letters of course. There was a lot of them too. Over the years sometimes weekly after Molly had come back or when she was planning her holidays. A couple from Sean probably about his move to London. A few from Jack. And Roberts letter. That was the real concern. I didn't know what it said but I doubted that it would help her.

During the search Molly's teacher had called. As I talked on the phone, I could see the neighbours outside watching. The shame of it all. I turned my back to the window in the front door. I needed to concentrate on what he had to say. Molly's nice Irish teacher wasn't judgemental. In fact, he was sympathetic.

I could hear the policemen joining in with my conversation over the phone. Mr O'Malley said they had kindly agreed to let Molly finish her exam but the sarcasm was clear to hear. He told me the name of the police station. He said he would meet me there. I explained that they had arrested Hugh aswell. He didn't say anything but even down the phone his sigh showed his concern and empathy.

The policemen had asked where Vincent O'Callaghan slept. I'd confirmed that he didn't live here. They said he had used this address. I didn't know that. I said no post had ever come for him. I explained that he stayed at Finola's digs when he came over to see us.

The memory of the day Vincent left home had faded since I found him. It was right at the front of my mind now. He had denied being a member of the IRA anymore. He said he'd been away from all that for years.

I'd wondered why they had let him go. I'd heard that once you're in, you're in and could never get out. I'd thought it was because he was so young. In my heart I knew it was what I'd wanted to believe. I asked and they confirmed that he had been taken in too.

They said there were others but they didn't say who. They hadn't mentioned Molly and I never thought in a million years to ask.

I thought they would interview me but they had said not at this time but not to go anyway. Where would I go? My daughter and husband were being questioned by the police. They never mentioned Emmet and I was glad. He was married to a lovely girl. I'd never had worries about him. I'd call him if I needed someone.

Jenny and Kitty didn't live at home so they wouldn't find out straight away. I would not tell them yet. Not until I knew more. I didn't want to worry them. If it got on the news, then I would have too. I prayed that it would not get on the news. I locked the door behind me and went to the bus stop. The bus took an age to get there. It was the slowest journey I'd taken. What would I find when I got there?

I worried about Molly. She'd tell the truth. What would that truth mean to her and everyone else? I'd drilled into my girls to always tell the truth I knew that at times like this, less is more. If the police didn't get her, the IRA could. I hoped I'd just listened to too much rumour and news reports. The IRA couldn't punish everyone. She hadn't passed information but she had put herself in a difficult permission. If she had heard something. It would have been in conversation.

Hugh had heard stories from the horse's mouth. Fellow Irishmen had been arrested, charged and convicted. Not all had been guilty. They must have changed the investigation techniques after the quashing of convictions. I silently prayed but thought it was wrong in some way.

Mr O'Malley was already at the police station. He was asking questions at the desk. He wasn't getting anywhere. His hands were raised, he was restless. Pacing on the spot. The reception was busy. Not enough chairs for the people reporting being a victim of crime.

I looked down. My family were thought to be the criminals. What would they think of me if they knew that? I stood by the noticeboard. I listened to what Molly's teacher was saying. The Officer was asking him to take a seat as there were a queue of people needing to be seen. He understood. He nodded and as he turned, he saw me.

He came to tell me what he knew. It wasn't much. Molly was here but Hugh was not. No details of Hugh were allowed to be given to him. I would join the queue and find out what was going on.

I'd sent Mr O'Malley home. The girls were on their way. I told them just before they left work. I didn't know if it was on tv but in case it was it was better for them to find out from me. Jenny was the first to arrive. She worked closer than her sister.

There were less people here now. There were seats next to me for her and Kitty. She asked how long I'd been there. She nodded and went to the counter. It was now free. I saw her talking to the policeman. He was nodding. He understood.

Jenny confirmed to me, "It's been four hours. She's had a break. She's not been arrested but there was no solicitor present. I asked that they come immediately. He couldn't say what it was about. Do you know?" I told her what I did know. The things I'd kept from her. About my family. About Hugh. About Sean and Robert. I knew we had all the time in the world.

Jenny was angry her lips with thin and closed. She was white with shock. I could see her processing this information. She was disappointed that it had been kept from her. Her only response was, "When Kitty gets here. I will go to the police station Dad is at and find out what is going on."

She turned away from me. She was staring ahead. I knew she didn't want to talk to me. It seemed like an age until Kitty arrived. I stood up. Jenny hugged me but in a stiff formal way. She told her sister that I'd a lot to tell her and she left by the door that Kitty had entered.

I swallowed; Kitty would not be as accommodating as her sister when she found out. We sat looking at each other as I explained. She didn't speak. I placed my hand on her knee to try to keep her calm, after seeing her sister's reaction. I told her everything that she needed to know. Not as much as Jenny.

There was no surprise in her response. She was shouting, disgusted, "this is why I don't like Ireland." Then she was ranting that she was at risk and hadn't known about it. I disagreed with her on that. I reassured her that nothing would happen to her. She wasn't placated.

I didn't understand why she wasn't concerned about her younger sister being interviewed by the police for hours. I begged her to think about Molly. "I don't care about Molly. She has brought this on herself. She's stupid not naive. Why do you all stick up for her?" Her tone was scornful. I tried to explain that they were both innocent. She jumped up and screamed down into my face, "I don't believe you".

The policeman had returned to the window. There was no one else there now. His arms were crossed. I whispered her name and touched her arm and indicated with my head that we were being watched. She shook my hand away.

She was pacing. "I suppose you are involved too." She had lowered her tone now. A look in her eyes that I'd never seen. Revulsion. I was shaking my head and my eyes pleaded with hers. She spat the words in my face. "Uncle Vincent!" She looked at me with contempt. She turned away unable to look at me. I was ashamed not only of my brother but myself bringing him into our lives.

I repeated her name. She whirled around on the spot. The policeman was still looking. She directed her response to him. "Don't worry I won't be staying. I'm not involved in any of this."

She turned back to me. "I don't believe you and I don't care. I need to think about myself. I'm so embarrassed. Don't contact me. I will tell people the truth, I'm not a part of this family anymore." She turned and left the building. Her face showed disgust that she could have been drawn into something so distasteful. I was alone again.

This was all my fault. Why had I ever gone back to Ireland. I'd not even wanted to go. I'd never wanted to see my Father alive or dead. I would never have heard the things that I'd heard from Anne and be aware of Maggie's beliefs. I should never have tried to find Vincent. I'd been so desperate for a family. I wanted what Hugh had. I was naïve to think my family had changed. Obviously in my heart I'd known. That's why I'd distanced myself from them and I'd not gone back. It would've been the right thing to have stayed away. Anne had known that. Everything I'd tried to avoid. I should've never made a choice to involve myself again.

I'd suspected that Vincent was still a member of the IRA. I'd heard rumours. Vincent had denied them. I wanted him to deny them. I didn't want to believe that he had been to prison. That he had made bombs. I thought he had changed. That he was only young then. That he had changed his mind. Why would he change.

I was a fool. I was just like Molly. Molly had been naïve to keep a relationship that she knew was wrong too. I'd encouraged that. I couldn't blame her. I was responsible for that too. My tears were undeserved, I wiped them away. How dare I feel sorry for myself.

Thank god that I'd not harboured criminals in my home. That Hugh hadn't let that happen. Jesus Christ, what about the Alcorn's what was going on there. Jenny had said they had done a raid there aswell. There had been talk about the uncle but I'd not listened. I thought it was nothing to do with us. Molly had stayed away from Jacinta, thank god. Why would Jacinta take Maria's side if she was involved? I didn't know anything anymore. I shook my head. I'd worries of my own.

The only good thing about going back to see my family had been to see Emmett. Was he involved, did I need to cut all ties again? Someone came in the door it, was Emmett. His smile was wide. It was supportive. A rush of affection for this young man came to me. I cried again when he hugged me. And I felt his understanding envelope me. I wasn't alone.

Jenny had called him. I was not to worry; her boyfriend was with her. I told him about Kitty. He was reassuring. Kitty would be back when she got over the shock. I told him it was my fault. That I'd brought the danger to the family. Jenny was right to be angry. Kitty needed to be scared. I'd caused this.

Emmett didn't agree, "it wasn't your fault. It was that man's decision to send his son to God knows where." He saw my confusion. "Patrick told me what you saw that night." I'd never told anyone. I should've told Hugh a long time ago especially when I brought Vincent into our family.

My thoughts came back to the here and now. "Where is Hugh?" Jenny had told Emmett that Hugh was in the cell waiting for a solicitor. No arrest or charges had been made against him. I knew he wanted to say yet and had stopped himself.

I knew that Hugh was a republican but he wasn't a member of the IRA. He was a sympathiser but was he a volunteer? I doubted that he would do anything to put his family at risk. I'd felt uneasy as he knew so many young one's over from Ireland.

I shook my head. Hugh was popular. Everyone liked him. He would help anyone. If it was anything, that would be what it was. I would be telling him that when he came home. How could I have the cheek to say anything at all? When it was my family, the O'Callaghan's, that had caused this to happen. I was ashamed.

Emmett had gone to the police station that Vincent was at first as it was on his way. He told them he was his next of kin. I realised that I was Vincent's next of kin in England. Emmett had known that too. He had taken that pressure away from me.

How could I have doubted him. He smiled and guessed my thoughts. "It was right for you to doubt me. Don't be worrying your head about that now. I'm not involved. I've never been involved. I heard and saw so much. I was out of there, into Uncle John's garage as soon as I left primary." I knew this was true. I was so thankful to have him at least. I'd lost everyone else.

Emmett updated me. Vincent had been charged. He wouldn't be coming out today or anytime soon. I felt no sorrow for him. Sean and Cillian had been arrested. Sean's brother had been at the station too. My heart went out to the young boy that had been to our house so many times, he'd been so susceptible to the draw of the Cause.

They were going on the no comment approach. That wouldn't be good for them. We both knew that this had been the IRA's standard response to interrogation in the past. Finola and Jacinta were still being questioned. Finola's sister was also there. They were still helping the police with their enquiries. Poor wee Jacinta. She'd suffered such a lot of loss in her life so far. To have this too, it was unspeakable.

Emmett looked ahead. He was in shock himself. He shook his head over and over. I could see he was becoming incensed. I'd never seen him look that way before. His face was tight. A shadow passed over his eyes. I knew he'd been exported somewhere else. He didn't smile or try to lighten the mood as I would have expected.

When he finally spoke, it was with hate, an emotion that I'd never seen from him before. "That man has a lot to answer for." I could see that he blamed everything on our father. I knew it was me aswell but I couldn't say, he would just disagree.

It was just about Molly now. That stupid film came into my mind. How Molly Malone made good. What will Molly O'Donnell do? I couldn't support her now. I didn't support her in the past. How could I, of all people, given her advice. All my own decisions had been wrong. This had been all about me. About me finding my family. I'd always had one. What had I done? The tears came again. The fear in my heart was growing deeper with each tear I shed. I prayed that Molly didn't have to pay for my mistakes.

As the nurse had said she had been a real fighter to get into this world. I prayed that She'd survive this aswell.

Part 4: Chapter 26 – Molly

PM – Now this London IRA cell. It was at Jacinta's house.

MOD – No. That can't be true. There is no cell

PM – You knew who stayed there though. Your Uncle Vincent, Sean, Cillian

MOD – Yes. It is a digs.

PM – You know they are all IRA members and used Jacinta's house as a safe house

MOD – No. It isn't. That can't be right

    PM – Did Jacinta say it was a safe house

MOD – No. never

PM – You knew that a known IRA member lived there before his death.

MOD – No

PM – Yes. Jacinta's uncle, Innes Kelly.

MOD – No. I didn't know him

    The police man looked at the file again as if checking details. I tried to see
what it said but it was too far away.

PM – You're saying that you didn't know about Jacinta's uncle. Your oldest friend
Jacinta. Jacinta that you know so well. Since primary school. You went to primary,
secondary school and college together. How could you not know?

MOD – I didn't know him

PM – If you didn't know, that's very sad. So, what did happen to your friendship with Jacinta? After the arguments in the Broadway, she took Maria's side, didn't she? Why?

MOD - They were on the same course at college. They were both doing a BTEC

PM – We spoken to Jacinta. She said that she didn't discuss the Broadway arguments with Maria. She has also said she was unaware of what happened.

PM – But she seems to know alot about you Molly. Your comings and goings. Your family. Your friends. Your affiliations. Yet you don't seem to know alot about her. Do you think Jacinta is in the IRA?

MOD - No

PM – Jacinta thinks you are.

PM - Do you know Cillian Cullen? He stayed at Jacinta's house too

MOD - Yes

PM - do you think he is in the IRA

MOD - No

PM - Do you remember when he drove you to the disco. He had to go from the North to the south. Then back again just to drop you and Saoirse there. Why did you think he did that?

MOD - Cillian is her boyfriend. Saoirse said she had told him about Sean's bad driving. That he had offered to give us a lift

PM - He had to come through the border twice to do that. Do you think when you go to a checkpoint, the soldiers would be likely to let you through if you say you are going to see your girlfriend.

MOD – I don't know

PM - He wasn't really Saoirse's boyfriend though. He was Jacinta's boyfriend; did you know that?

MOD – No, he's Saoirse's boyfriend.

PM - didn't you realise that he seemed to spend as much time in England as Ireland. Did you not wonder about his visits?

MOD - No not really

PM - Is that because you didn't like him

MOD - No I didn't like him

PM - They wanted it that way. They would have been expected to come out with you, wouldn't they? So, you would say that Jacinta didn't have a boyfriend then?

MOD – Yes, we would have gone out together. I didn't know she had a boyfriend

PM - and you really had no idea about Jacinta and Cillian?

MOD - No because he is Saoirse's boyfriend

PM – Saoirse has said the same. She didn't know about Jacinta. Well actually she is adamant that she didn't. We think Jacinta knew about her. We think that Cillian could travel everywhere with the excuse to see a girlfriend in the South. Otherwise what other reason would there be?

MOD - I don't know. He wanted to see Saoirse. They got on well.

PM - What did Jacinta say about your uncle and your friend staying at the house

MOD - Not much

PM - Did you think Jacinta knew about your Uncle Vincent being in prison

MOD - No

PM – Was this the safehouse they used to create a bomb. A bomb made of Semtex. Do you know what damage that could do? Did you know that?

MOD - No. I can't believe it. I can imagine a bomb could be devasting. I'veseen it on the TV.

PM - Your Uncle Vincent would need a safe house when he came out of prison, wouldn't you agree?

MOD - I don't know

PM - Do you know what was used in the last terrorist attack Molly?

MOD - I don't know. I haven't seen the news. I've been studying

PM - but you were still writing to Jack. Would he not tell you?

MOD - No he didn't

PM - Yes, I know. We have read the letters and he didn't mention it.

PM – How did you get on with your Uncle Vincent

MOD – I don't really know him. I only found out about him recently

PM – Whys that?

MOD – He didn't come to the house much

PM – Is that because he was working away?

MOD – Yes, he was away a lot.

PM – What did he do when he was away?

MOD - I don't know.

PM – You don't know. Didn't you ask?

MOD - No

PM – Really? You don't seem to like your Uncle. Why is that?

MOD – I don't know. I didn't know much about him. He didn't really speak to me.

PM – That's a bit sad. It wasn't the same with you Uncle Emmett, was it?

MOD – Uncle Emmett came to the house. He chatted to us. He was interested.

PM – He gave you money?

MOD – Yes. He is very generous

PM – How do you know they are your Uncles?

MOD – My mum told me

PM – Did you see any proof, any photos. Of them, of anyone else.

MOD – No

PM – Your mum lost contact with them for a very long time. She was just a child wasn't she.

MOD – I think so

PM – So they might not be who they say they are

I didn't speak. Could this possibly be true. That they all lied. That my mum was mistaken?

PM – Molly?

MOD – It seems improbable.

Pm – Yes it would be very clever to carry that through, don't you think?

PM – No wonder you don't have anything to say. You see your Uncle Vincent used a different surname. Would that surprise you?

MOD – No

PM – and that different surname. Was what he used when he was in prison.

PM – You look shocked Molly. It is shocking isn't it.

I nodded. This couldn't be true. My uncle Vincent must not be my uncle. He must be pretending to be.

PM – After what you have heard today. You would prefer he lied and wasn't your Uncle. Wouldn't you? Sorry to disappoint you we know differently now

He left me to ponder this thought. He was trying to confuse me. It was working.

PW – Lets go back to Mary and Robert for a moment. The IRA knew you were friends with the Elliott's?

MOD – No I don't know how they could.

PM – they asked you about their cousin. You asked Robert. He told you. Then there was the murder. They were devasted. You were sorry. That's why you told Robert about Brompton. Why? You believe in the Cause. Was it just to stop the violence?

MOD - I didn't tell Robert anything

PM - But he was your boyfriend, is that why he told you about his cousin

MOD - I don't know any of his cousins

PW - Are you sure.

MOD – Yes

PM – You told Robert about Brompton for him to stop it, didn't you? Passing on this information would make you an informer. You must know what would happen to an informer

MOD - I know what the IRA do to informers. I didn't pass any information; I don't know anyone in the IRA or to Robert

PW - You told Robert about Brompton because you loved him and you were sorry

MOD - That does not make sense. Telling Robert about Brompton would not make me or him feel better. That's if I'd passed on that information to the IRA about his cousin. Which I couldn't have done as I didn't know any members

PM – Where else could he have got this information

MOD – I don't know

PW – Why would Robert visit your home in his reading week if he was not your boyfriend

MOD - I didn't invite him. He has never been my boyfriend.

Why didn't he believe me? I couldn't keep saying the same thing over and over. I closed my eyes and thought god help me. I couldn't even think of a prayer that would help.

PW - Did he give you something or did you give him information

MOD - no he didn't give me anything

PW - not even a present or flowers

MOD - No

PW - He came all the way from Ireland to see his girlfriend and didn't buy you anything

MOD – Please believe me, he wasn't my boyfriend and I wouldn't accept anything from him

PW - Who did you tell about Roberts visit

MOD - My mum was there, Jack and Maria

PW - What about Jacinta

MOD - No

PW - Would Maria have told Jacinta about Robert

MOD - No, I hope not

PW - Is your Jack your boyfriend now?

MOD - Yes

PW - That must have upset Robert?

MOD - If it did, it wasn't because we had split up as we never went out together

PW - So Jack is your boyfriend now. Was he worried about Robert's behaviour?

MOD - Yes

PW - Did he contact Robert to tell him to stay away from you

MOD - No

PW - Why not

MOD - I told Robert to leave. And my mum told him to leave. If my dad knew he would have warned him too

PW - so your dad didn't know

MOD – No. I didn't tell him

PW - Why didn't you tell him? That's very strange most people would normally tell their fathers if they were frightened by people in their home

MOD - I didn't want any trouble and I thought it was over

PM – Was it that you didn't want him to know that your boyfriend was a protestant. He wouldn't like that, would he

MOD – that's not true

PW - But you still met Robert in the pub

MOD - I didn't know he was going to be there. I didn't invite him

PW - Who do you think told him you were there

MOD - I don't know

PW - Why didn't you tell your father when you got back

MOD - Sean told Robert to go away. To stop contacting me and not to tell lies. He did as Sean asked. He stopped doing those things.

PW - But your dad did find out, who told him

MOD - I don't know, Sean I think

PW - No it wasn't but we will come back to that.

PW - You say that Robert didn't contact you again? Did you contact him

MOD - No

PW - did you contact Mary?

MOD – No

PM – Was anyone else in contact with him

MOD – I don't think so

PM – We know there was. Do you know who that was?

MOD – No

I couldn't think who that could be. I was so tired now. Surely, they Couldn't go on for much longer. I wondered how long I'd been here. I looked at the broken clock and realised why they hadn't fixed it. They'd taken my watch with my bag. I couldn't check the time. I tuned back in to the question

PW – Molly. I asked whether you received a letter from Robert after he'd killed himself?

MOD - Yes

PW - Why do you think he killed himself

MOD - I think he was asking to many questions about IRA activities. He realised that people might notice that. This would've put himself and his sister at risk

PW - and you? That's what he said in that letter

MOD - Yes, he said that

PW - What about Sean, did he care about him

MOD - No I don't think he cared about him

PW - What about Saoirse, did he care about her

MOD - I don't think so

PW - Why because they are members of the IRA and were linked to his cousin witnessing a murder

MOD - No

PW - Molly, it's right in front of your face why can't you see it.

PW - What about Jack? Robert wouldn't care about your new boyfriend, would he?

MOD - Probably not

PW - and Maria?

MOD - He didn't know Maria

PW - Jacinta?

MOD - He didn't know Jacinta

PW - O yes, he did but we will come back to that

PW - Do you feel responsible for Robert's death

MOD - I feel sad that he killed himself. I feel sorry for his family. I disliked him. He scared me in my home and at the pub. I didn't feel responsible for his actions

PW - Was he protecting you because he thought you were an informer?

MOD - No

PW - Do you think he passed the information you gave him to anyone else

MOD - I didn't give him any information

PW - Do you really still believe that we don't know what's going on? We have been told that you and the people we have discussed are in an IRA cell. We know that you've passed information to a protestant. Which is punishable by death, by the IRA. So, you keep lying, even to the police. To prevent that. Is that correct?

He wanted to scare me. I was always scared. He was right. Just being here was putting me at risk. I knew there was desperation in my voice. Why couldn't he see I was telling the truth

MOD - No none of that is true

MOD – please, please can I have a solicitor

PW - He is on his way. Just a few more questions

PM - so to recap, you know that your father helped to find IRA members a place to stay, in Jacinta's safe house

MOD - No he found digs for family and friends from Ireland

PM - We have witnesses to say that you were present when Sean and Saoirse were making deliveries for the IRA

MOD – No! I don't know that any deliveries were made

PW - You know that your uncle Vincent is a convicted IRA bomber and that he was responsible the recent attacks?

MOD - No

PW - That you passed information that led to the death of a soldier

MOD – No no please no

PW - That you passed information to Robert about a planned bombing. To get him to forgive you for passing information to the IRA. Which had resulted in the death of a British soldier.

MOD - No that doesn't even make sense

PW - How did Jacinta fit into all this

MOD - I don't know

PW - Let's start from beginning. Did you know that her Mother was from the same place as your father?

MOD – Yes but I never saw her there

PW - Yes, she had stopped going to Ireland. She stopped going when she was ten after the death of her father. Can you think why? Was it lack of money?

MOD - It could be, Jacinta's mum didn't have a job. She relied on using her home

for digs, for other Irish people. She had a big house and only one child at home

PW - It was because her father died that they didn't have much money

MOD - No one had any money but that probably is true

   PW - So you started to go to Ireland when Jacinta stopped, yes?

MOD - It seems like that

PW - Were you still friends, when her dad died?

MOD - Not really, she was off school for a long time. Then she was in a different

class to me at secondary school. We still spoke to each other. She was always my

friend

   PW - What about when her Uncle died, was she unhappy?

MOD - very unhappy but she seemed better in college

PW - was that when she made friends with Maria?

MOD - and other people in her class, yes

PW - and later with Sean?

MOD - Yes, I suppose so

PW - and Saoirse?

MOD - I don't think so

   PW – Yes. Last year she went to Ireland on holiday for the first time. She

went to her mother's homeplace. She met Saoirse and Sean again. Did you know

that?

MOD - No

PW - They kept that from you, why do you think they did that?

MOD - I don't know

PW - The four of them, including Cillian, went all over Ireland, did you know that?

MOD - No

PW - Do you think that from what I've said, that they had something in common, a bond

MOD - No

PW - Molly they are in the IRA. They had that in common.

MOD – No, that can't be true

PW – We think that Jacinta had gone on holiday to be involved in the IRA. Do you know why?

MOD – No

PW – The death of her Uncle made her angry. Did you know that?

MOD – No

PW - She said that you suggested Brompton. You told her that she had a bomb maker in the house. Your Uncle Vincent. Is that true

MOD – No. This is all wrong

PW - She also had someone who was experienced in deliveries. Do you know who they were?

PW – You and Sean

MOD – No none of this was true.

Why would Jacinta say these things? There was a knock on the door the policeman rose and walked towards it. When it opened, it was only wide enough to know there was another person on the other side of the door. The policeman apologised to his colleague then left the room. I hoped it was to get my solicitor. The policewoman looked down at the file she leafed through it as if mulling the contents over.

She took out a note book from her jacket pocket. This was the first time they were going to write things down. They were going to make me give them a confession.

I was overtaken by exhaustion. I'd told the truth. They didn't believe me. I was going to prison. This was my own fault. This was my punishment. God blamed me too. I didn't do my penance. I couldn't persuade any one of my innocence to get forgiveness.

I lent down onto my elbows. The hands on my chin covering my mouth. My head dropped through my hands. Then my shoulders couldn't carry me anymore. My elbows parted until my forehead bounced on the table. My fingers were drawn to my head and they held my face off the desk. I wanted to go to sleep but thought they may write a statement in my absence from the interrogation.

The policewoman was watching me. I could feel the sweat dripping from my hair. It was still bright outside of the small dirty window. It must be a lovely warm evening to finish your exams. I licked my lips; they would be drinking beer. I just wanted water. I wiped my forehead with my fingertips to push the sweat from meeting the table.

I lifted my head off the table. My top was sticking to me. I needed air and I needed to change my clothes. I wondered when that would be. I sat up again and pulled at my clothes to release the material from my body. I shifted in the seat and then leaned onto my toes. It lifted my body from the seat only a few millimetres but enough.

My mouth was dry. I was so thirsty. I needed water now. I'd been trying to explain things but it hadn't worked. My voice was gone. I'd nothing left to say. I sat up straight then leaned my shoulders over the chair. The stretch didn't give me the strength that I needed to carry on. I knew I couldn't survive what came next. The policeman was gone so long. I knew that they would take me to a cell soon, if he didn't return. I didn't know what would be worse. Where was the solicitor.

The policeman re-entered the room. He had a jug of water and a stack of glasses. One on top of the other. He put them in the middle of the table. Under his shoulder he had a new file. Which he passed to the policewoman to read. He seemed more relaxed. Before he sat down, he went to the window and pushed it open. It needed some strength to do so. It seemed it hadn't been opened in a while. He took of his jacket and put it behind the chair.

The policeman let the policewoman read what was in the file. There were a number of batches stapled together. She skimmed the words and then looked at her colleague with her eyebrows raised.

PM – Molly it seems that you are the only person left providing us information on this matter. Your father, Sean, Cillian and your Uncle Vincent have declined to speak. Maria, Mary, Saoirse, Finola and Jacinta have all given statements now.

I leaned forward to see what they had said. The only person that would give a good account of me was my Dad. Would they believe that.

PM – We met with Jacinta yesterday and again today. We have her statement now. It was the basis of our further investigations. She told us that you were a member of the IRA. You have told us you are not. That's her word against yours, yes?

I nodded. Why would she say that?

PM – But all of the other parties mentioned have denied that. Now family and friends are not usually good alibis or evidence.

I nodded I'd heard that before.

PM – Given that you only speak to your father now, they are not your friends anymore. Is that correct.

It just reminded me of all the arguments that I'd caused. I nodded.

PM – That is quite strong evidence in your favour so we would consider that they would be believed by a jury.

PM – Jacinta has agreed that she was a sympathiser. It seems that your former friends think that aswell. She knows you far better than you know her.

I'd assumed that she was a republican just because of her family circumstances. I didn't think I knew anyone that didn't.

PM – We think that she maybe a volunteer too. Similarly, you said you didn't know that was true.

I confirmed that I'd said that with a nod

PM – Jacinta said you were the informer. That she had heard you tell someone about the Elliott's cousins. There is no evidence to suggest that this attack was planned in that way. Therefore, this allegation will not be followed up. Conspiracy to commit murder.

That was really serious. I was horrified. I didn't know it would be that crime. I shook my head and closed my eyes. I was relieved but then I knew other charges were the same or worse.

PM – Jacinta told us that Sean was recruited by your father last summer. That he arranged Sean's departure. Is that true

MOD – No my dad helped him move. He didn't recruit him.

PM - She also said that he was chosen after the successful deliveries of guns, money and drugs, on the occasions we have already discussed. We have not found any evidence to support her allegation. She said you told her about these drop offs yourself.

I shook my head vehemently and opened my mouth to speak but he continued.

PM – You said that you didn't tell her these events. Maria confirms that she told Jacinta when she became friends. She said they were funny stories. She knew Jacinta was your oldest friend. That there would be no harm to tell her. Maria is adamant that you would not have had the opportunity to tell her. You were in different classes at college. She didn't go to the club. You didn't go to the digs. When you saw each other at the Clifton it was always in a group.

PM – You have denied completing deliveries. Saoirse also denies her or your involvement. There is no proof of this yet. No charges to those offences, can be made at this time either.

I was breathing again now. I didn't know when I'd stopped, though the word yet didn't revive me fully

PM – Jacinta said that you passed details of four IRA events to Robert. Robert cannot as you know confirm or deny this. His sister Mary is adamant that you didn't pass on any information. Mary alleges that it was Jacinta. But you said that Jacinta was not friends with Robert

MOD – They never met.

PM – Jacinta says that too but Saoirse says that she saw Jacinta talking to Robert in a club. When they went there during Jacinta's holidays. Saoirse seemed to not care much for Jacinta. Maybe she suspected something did go on with Cillian. Anyway, Mary says that they met twice and communicated in letters. Yes, I can see you're surprised. The information has just come through to confirm this. Mary also suspects this is where the information of the IRA attacks came from. Robert refused to say but he said it was not you.

I was crying, why would she do this. She had a hand in Roberts death telling him this information. I couldn't speak my hand covered my mouth but the tears fell. The police woman passed me a tissue from a pack in her pocket. Then she poured the water into all three glasses. We all drank the small glass in one. She filled the glasses again but none of us drank anymore.

PW – Jacinta said she was unaware of Roberts visit to England. Mary believes it was at Jacinta's suggestion to confront Sean and protect you. Mary had begged him not to go. She knew even then he was being set up. That you were being set up and even Sean too. Were you aware of this?

MOD – No

PW – Did Jacinta know when Jack was coming to England?

MOD – I suppose so. He stayed at her house.

PW - Jacinta denies knowing about Jack's visit in advance. Maria said she had confirmed to Jacinta the date of Jack's arrival. Jacinta said to Maria she wanted to meet him at the Clifton, before he stayed at the digs. Maria had no reason not to say it was the Saturday of the reading week. Finola, Jacinta's Mother, also confirmed when Jack was staying as Jacinta had to clean the room. Can you think why that is important Molly?

MOD – Robert came on the Friday night.

PW – Yes. Mary had said her cousin would confirm that Robert was there as he stayed with him that week. It was a shame that your Dad wasn't there to protect you. Did he normally go out on a Friday night? Who knew that?

MOD – Yes. Everyone.

PW – Jacinta?

MOD - Possibly

PW - Jacinta says she couldn't go to the Broadway on the night of the arguments. Jacinta had said that she was going out with her cousin. Finola informed us that she stayed home that night. Finola was surprised that she didn't go because she really liked the band that were playing. Is that true?

MOD – Yes, she did

I hoped they were suggesting that Jacinta was the person responsible for the criminal elements but I knew I was still responsible for bringing the group together.

PW – After the arguments Jacinta said she didn't take a side but Maria said Jacinta had been odd about it. Jacinta had asked about it. Maria initially suspected Sean told Jacinta. Maria had confirmed what happened. Afterwards Jacinta had been telling Maria to keep away. Jacinta said you were fraternizing with the enemy. That's a strong statement?

I nodded

PM - Maria said that she was angry at you and agreed with Jacinta. Maria is angry at herself now. She encouraged the letter writing. She was scared. She thought if lots of people knew then nothing would come back on her. She didn't know at the time it was Jacinta who started the rumour but Maria agreed with the gossip being spread at your College. Did you know about the rumours?

MOD – Someone told me recently. I thought it had to be Sean or Maria as they were the only ones who knew, with access to my friends.

PW – When Robert returned home and discussed it with Mary. Mary told him what he had done had implicated you aswell as Sean. Mary said Robert became depressed and although he returned to university it didn't get better.

PW – Jacinta said she didn't know about Brompton. She said that the planning must have been done in advance. That your Dad, your uncle, Cillian and Sean would need an alibi on the day of attack. Did you arrange an alibi for your family?

MOD – No. And I definitely couldn't arrange one for Sean and Cillian to be there neither of them spoke to me.

PW – Maria said that Jacinta had been interested in your Uncle Emmett's wedding. Maria told her there was a family meeting planned on that day. She said it had been because you had been excited even before the reading week. You were going to discuss bridesmaid dresses on that day. Did you know Jacinta knew the date?

MOD – I don't know. It wasn't me. I didn't create an alibi

PW – Thank you for clarifying that

PW – You denied further contact with Robert. Mary said two letters came to their family home. Did you write them?

MOD – No I didn't want him to think I was interested in him. I was scared he'd come back to England

PW - Mary said she didn't think it was your writing on the envelope. Robert didn't tell her who they were from. Mary suspected they were from Jacinta. He had said he would be meeting her in London. Mary didn't like the effect she had on him. They had argued. Robert became even more upset. He said he knew too much and that he didn't know what to do. He was so distressed he dropped out of university. Did you write to him? Did you give him dates of future IRA attacks?

MOD – No I didn't know any dates.

PW – Robert denied to Mary that you were his informant. He still refused to say where the information had come from. Robert told Mary that he'd thought that the informant was warning him about Sean. But then he realised that it made you look like an IRA informer. Later he told Mary his fears about you but not who the informant was. Where you the informant, Molly?

MOD - It wasn't me.

PW – Thanks for clarifying that

PW – You were aware of the IRA's punishment for informing. How did that make you feel?

MOD – Terrified

PW – But if you weren't responsible, you needn't have been worried. What did you do wrong?

MOD – My letter writing to Mary led to Roberts death.

PW – You said that you didn't give him any information. Did you tell anyone about his information? About the attack planned in Brompton. About Deal.

MOD – My Mum and Jack knew

PW – Apart from them?

MOD – I didn't have anyone else to tell.

PW – No Mary, No Maria, No Saoirse, No Sean?

MOD – None of them would talk to me

PW – What about Jacinta. Could she talk to them?

I shrugged. It sounded like she could've. Even Mary if she had been in Ireland but I doubted that. I nodded

PW – Jacinta was very pleased about that. She was happy to tell us that the right punishment for you should be death. Both for being an informant and for lying to your family and friends for so long. Yes, that's quite a dramatic statement. No wonder you looked shocked.

PW – She also said your family deserve to be punished. She said if her father was alive, he would not have put hers in danger, by recruiting young IRA men. This is what she accuses your father of doing. There is no evidence that this was intentional. He did help IRA members and non-IRA members to find homes. No one else other than Jacinta has said that. Everyone else denies this. Finola has even said that without him she'd have had nothing, no income, no home. She couldn't be more grateful or effusive on this point.

PW – Jacinta alleges that your Uncle made the bomb for Deal. It is a similar incendiary device so we are investigating that. As we said he has chosen not to make a statement. She said you didn't deserve an Uncle when hers was dead.

PW – Jacinta alleges that Sean drove the car to Deal. Do you know if he drove the car at Deal?

MOD – No

PW – Maria said Jacinta was angry with Sean. He was very affected with the argument that he had with you. She didn't understand why he was conflicted after what you had done. Did you know Sean was conflicted?

MOD – No

I was surprised and pleased. Not that he was unhappy but that he had believed me. That he knew I was sorry.

PW – She said Cillian set the bomb. Cillian chose Saoirse so I don't think she has any loyalty to him.

PW – Jacinta said that you all deserve to be punished

PW – Finola disagrees with her Daughter. She says her home is not a safe house. She denies being a member of the IRA. She also denied knowledge of an IRA cell.

PW - None of the witnesses have confirmed that it is. The search of the property didn't provide any physical evidence. We will of course continue to investigate. If it is a cell it can no longer operate so it is a successful outcome whatever happens. Convictions of those responsible for the three IRA bombs will be sought. There will be ongoing investigations.

The policewoman was holding some papers from the file, she was reading from a statement now

PW – Jacinta denies all involvement in this London cell. She blames your family and friends entirely. She believes that you are now in the position that she is in. Like her, you will no longer have a father as he will be in prison. You will no longer have an Uncle as he will also be in prison. You have lost your friends in Ireland. Those that She'd have had, if her father hadn't died. Neither of you has Maria as a friend. So you are in exactly the same position.

PW – Molly, we have no evidence at this time that you have committed any criminal offences but we will of course talk to you again if we do.

PM - I advise you to choose the company that you keep, more wisely Know where you are going in the future and with whom.

PW - We will write your statement. We will ask that you sign it. To confirm if it is clear, concise and correct. You must believe it to be the whole truth as you may have to give evidence in court.

I was in shock. Jacinta had hated me. She blamed me. She lied. She caused this. I started this but she ended it. I was thankful that my Dad was not in trouble. Sad for my mum that the brother that she had searched for so long was in the IRA. I prayed that the boy who told good stories was not involved. I thought of Robert and Mary. The consequences were much worse for them. Jacinta's anger had damaged their lives so much. I knew I should be relieved by what the police were saying but it was only sorrow that I could feel.

#

Jack had been interviewed aswell but he said it was just to confirm my statement. He had no problems telling the truth.

Saoirse remained quiet. I apologised again in a letter. I knew too much had happened. I'd deceived her. I couldn't blame her decision, to no longer be my friend.

Maria still didn't want to talk to me. Such a lot had gone on for her too. The questions by the police must have been terrifying for her. Thankfully they would not have led to any charges against her. Like they were for me. She had told the truth. Which had protected me. Even though I knew I didn't deserve it.

Jacinta was in prison but obviously she was no friend of mine. I don't know what happened between her and Maria. My dad was not arrested nor any charges brought against him though I still had my dad but she didn't. I'm sure my mum had had alot to say to him about it all. It probably included the same advice that the police had given to me.

My mum told me everything about her life. Her behaviour and her beliefs around the Cause. She lost her brother, Vincent, again. Apart from Uncle Emmett there was no mention of her family in Ireland. She was sad and angry at herself. I knew how she was feeling. I felt just the same. Other than my family in England, I just had Jack.

This one lie. About me having a pen pal. It was the start of a devastating series of events. That led to this being able to happen. It might not be a criminal offence but I was still wrong. I compared it to be a venial sin instead to a mortal sin.

Other lies were told. Other actions had been taken. By people, sometimes in full knowledge of the consequences and some not.

I asked no one's advice. I wrote to Mary and told her everything. I gave her my sincere condolences. I acknowledged that her pain of losing her brother would never heal. Nor for her mum and dad losing their son. I did miss her and my letter writing days were over. Except her one response of *Thank you x.*

Jack would still write but it would not be the same. I wasn't a child anymore. Those confidences, hopes and dreams were finished. *"Tread softly as you tread on my dreams"* made me want to cry as it usually did. It would forever bring me back to this time of my life.

I needed to take the advice of the police. Which was the same as everyone else. To stop being so naïve. I prayed that I would change. I thought that it would always make me, me. My mum had said that I could go to university if I got the grades. She allowed me to visit Jack too. She said I needed it.

#

Jack had shown me the Molly Malone statue on Grafton street. We sang the song "*In Dublin's fair city ... Molly Malone.....*

When we walked past Trinity college Jack explained to me some architectural features. I thought it was nice too. We walked to the Liffey and passed by the Temple bar, for now. We sat on the bench near the quay to look at the view. It was not raining and the sun was shining. I still had a coat and jumper on.

We talked about Jacinta. She still denied everything and blamed me. The evidence against her was overwhelming. We tried to understand why She'd hate me. She felt no remorse about the death of Robert. Of course, she denied even meeting him. I would have to give evidence to refute her defence but that was another day.

Jack smiled at me tentatively. "I've got you a present. Don't laugh. I saw it when I was looking for a text book in a shop over the way." He gave me a book. I laughed. It was *Milly, Molly, Mandy stories.*

It transported me back to a different summer's day. The day we walked to the beach. When Saoirse, Sean, Jack and I'd still been friends. All those years ago. Which was also the time Jack and I started to plan my secret visits to see Mary. Then I was crying for everyone.

For Mary at the loss of her brother Robert. For the loss of my friendship with Saoirse. For Sean who was on remand but denying all charges. I hoped and prayed that was true.

Jack looked horrified. I explained the myriad of emotions. He nodded and expressed his guilt. About his involvement of keeping my friendship with Mary alive. He said we all had a part to play; some smaller or bigger than others.

I opened the book and I smiled. Jack had written the song of the same name, onto the front page of the old book. Which made me laugh;

Milly Molly Mandy sweet as sugar candy, ... I'm in love with you

I smiled as he had changed the eye colour. I looked through the book. I couldn't believe that it was published in 1928. It was such a long time ago but not in terms of the struggles in Ireland.

Jack looked at my face. Studying my mood. He seemed to be looking into my soul. Like the time when Sean and Robert had argued. He wanted to see how I was dealing with the effects of the truth. I knew it was my fault. I knew that was true. If

I'd not kept going back to Ireland. If I'd not written to Mary. If I'd not danced with Robert. I was so thankful to have Jack. I'd lost everyone else.

Jack was hesitant, "do you still want to do the Easter Rising walking tour?" But really, I thought the question was, "Do you still believe in the Cause...."

The End

Acknowledgements

The Cause is a fictional story set alongside the period of struggles between the Irish and English in the 20th Century but my research included many centuries before. I apologise for any errors; some are unintentional but in other parts helped me to move the story along. The characters are fictional too but some stray traits might have slipped in without me realising and may be recognisable.

I really appreciate memories shared by my Aunty Mary and Uncle Birklin. I'm so sorry that he will never be able to see it. They helped me with the chapters between the 1940's and 1970's without which it would have been impossible for me to write.

To my cousin Trisha for making my holidays in Ireland such fun and for taking me to similar places in the story.

To Barbara, for agreeing to read the 1st draft and struggled through the first few chapters which helped me realise the extensive amount of work that I needed to do to get my story told.

For Liz, whose advice on sentence construction was invaluable. She taught me what my English teacher, Mrs Woods, had tried to. She'd constantly asked if I knew what a full stop was. I hope I do now.

Also my patient friend Jo, who has not charged me for her counselling skills and for reading the 2nd draft which I sent to literary agents for my many rejections.

To Angela who read the 3rd draft and didn't complain that one character was based 'loosely' upon her.

For Shirley forever my sponsor and a reviewer of the final draft.

To 'the "Writers of City', particularly to Linda and Jonny for your honesty and criticism. It has helped The Cause become a book that I'm very proud of.

My niece, Catelin for designing the amazing website for me even when I asked for it to be purple! For also helping me with the book cover.

For my nephew, Manus who asked a million times, 'have you got it published yet? To the people who I've lost contact with who helped me along the way especially those from KCTMO and the "A Team." We are all "Still winning!"

For my sisters, Jackie and Tracey, who have supported me particularly since the death of our mum and dad with champagne and roast dinners, through all my other trials and tribulations, which are too many to mention. They gave me somewhere to stay when I was 'homeless. I'm so grateful for their support and happy that they are also my friends. I was very relieved when Tracey enjoyed the final draft and for her general 'guru' advice! This will be Jackie's first reading so I hope she enjoys it despite the number of words! Why use one when can use you ten!

To my Mum and Dad who took me to Ireland and sometimes allowed others too aswell! My dad, Manus Joseph O'Brien who'd vex anyone, always with a wink. My mum, Kathleen Redican, whose Irish welcome was renowned. Their upbringings aswell as mine helped to write my story. I wish they could see what I've achieved. And my daughter Erin, I hope this story will entice you into learning more about your own Irish heritage.

Thank you all